DON'T YOU KNOW
THE DANGERS OF

PLAYING WITH KNIVES

AJ MERLIN

Thank you Affinity Author services and Lunar Rose Editing.

eBook ISBN: 978-1-955540-01-8

Paperback ISBN: 978-1-955540-04-9

Created with Vellum

For everyone who loves the bad guys
A little too much.
(Just like I do.)

PLAYLIST

Bad Guy - Billie Eilish
Toxic – 2WEI
Can't Help Falling in Love – Tommee Profit
Bad Dream – Ruelle
Play with Fire – Sam Tinnesz
Blood // Water – Grandson
The Devil Within – Digital Daggers
All the Good Girls Go To hell – Billie Eilish
Cradles – Sub Urban
I Know What You Did – Henri Werner

CHAPTER ONE

AS THE DOOR swung open to reveal the police officer standing there with his hand resting on his utility belt and his lips pressed to a thin line, I could only think of one thing.

Oh God, he knows I broke into Ms. Clutterbucker's house while she was away on vacation and stole her remote batteries.

My heart fluttered in my chest, and my fingers tightened on the white, fake wood of the apartment door as our eyes met.

This was it. Out of all the things I'd stolen in my life—hell, all the things I'd stolen in the past *month*—I was going to go to jail…for batteries.

I blinked, mouth falling open in surprise and bafflement as the small, vertical scar that marked my left upper lip pulled just enough to be noticeable.

The officer just stood there, my eyes catching the way he rocked back on his heels to shift his sizable bulk in the doorway.

Nervously.

Like a child might rock back and forth when they'd been caught doing something bad.

But…if he was here to arrest me, why in the world was *he* nervous?

"Are you..." He took a notepad out of his pocket and flipped to a page and squinted at it, ducking his head enough so that the autumn sunlight caught the sweat shining on the sizable bald spot at the back of his head. "Willow Carlysle?" he grunted at last.

"Yeah?" I breathed, biting lightly down on my lower lip.

He was going to arrest me, and here I was in my Scooby-Doo t-shirt and matching pajama shorts.

What a classy mug shot I would take.

The officer cleared his throat and looked up at me from the notepad. "You live here with Miss Ashley Bellflower?"

"Yes...?" I didn't understand where this was going. Where were the cuffs? The perp walk? I'd seen enough true crime shows to know how this should be going.

"I'm Detective Granger. May I come in?" he asked quickly, like an afterthought, and looked around me to glance at the messy living room at my back.

"Oh uh-"

I shouldn't slam the door in his face and make a run for it, right? I couldn't help but ask myself silently.

"Sure. Yeah. Absolutely." With a flourish, I stepped back, bare feet making little noise on the fake hardwood floor as I pulled the door open wider to admit him.

"Thank you." The detective nodded and stepped inside, the handcuffs on his belt jingling and drawing my eye.

I did *not* want those going on my wrists.

But I also couldn't figure out why he was here if it wasn't to tell me that I was under arrest.

"Could we sit?" he went on, already making his way to the brown suede couch that lined the one wall.

"Sure?" I walked to the other side of it, perching on the end with my knees pressed tight and one leg shaking.

What in the *world* was going on here?

"Miss Carlysle..." He cleared his throat once, the sweat

still glistening even though it was cold outside *and* inside my apartment. "When was the last time you saw Miss Bellflower?"

"Ashley?" I blinked. My roommate was always in and out. She usually was either working her barista job or out with friends. The social butterfly to my *anti*social honey badger. It was rare we had the same schedule unless she'd managed to drag me out of my room with the promise of semi-good Italian food. I loved our weekly, questionable dinners. "Yesterday morning," I replied, remembering her face as she chucked a bagel in my direction when I stumbled out of my room at nearly eleven.

"Go to work, Will," she'd reminded me, as if I'd forgotten that I had a job at the local animal rescue. *"You gotta pay these bills somehow."*

Poor, naïve Ashley. Somehow she was still under the impression that saving puppies netted me enough to pay the bills, let alone order delivery almost every night of the week.

She really was a good roommate.

"I saw her before we both left for work," I replied with a shrug. "Why? Is everything okay?" A small sliver of worry edged its way into my brain, a shock of cold to the earlier fuzzy, sleep-deprived state I'd been in before answering the door.

Had she gotten hurt? Had *she* gotten in trouble? Sure, we were pretty close to best friend level, but I wasn't sure I was willing to bail her out of jail if she'd stolen a car or something. Still, I'd do what I could for my roommate, so long as the detectives didn't turn a questioning eye on *me.*

The detective cleared his throat again, playing with the notebook in his hands. "You didn't see her after that?"

"No...she goes out a lot at night. I figured I'd maybe missed her after I came in." I did *not* add from breaking into the Clutterbucker house to scavenge what I could from the nice lady's newest rich boy toy.

"I'm sorry to tell you this, but Miss Bellflower's body was found washed up on the shore of Hawk River."

I was sure I hadn't heard him right.

Ashley was *dead*?

I blinked once, brain taking that extra time to buffer and recompute what had been said to me.

"Excuse me?" I asked through numb lips. "Did you just say…?"

He nodded. "I was hoping to ask you a few questions about her recent activities. If you have the time?"

All of my relief at *not* being arrested, or suspected of stealing fled an instant after appearing.

Ashley was *dead*.

I'd only known her for the last eleven months, and all, but we were still very good friends. And we'd lived together long enough that I knew an embarrassing amount of her secrets.

But now she was…

"A few questions?" Detective Granger repeated. "I'd like to know if she'd been around any strangers recently or anyone who might have had a grudge against her."

Wait a minute.

My grey eyes narrowed as I found his gaze and held it. "A *grudge?*" I repeated. "Are you telling me she was murdered?"

Detective Granger hesitated, looking uncomfortable. "I can't give details of the case, Miss."

Of course, he couldn't. But I had a brain.

He was implying that Ashley had *not* died of natural causes.

"But," I licked my lips, frowning. "But there hasn't been a murder *here* in…" I looked at him, brows raised quizzically. "*Has* there ever been a murder here?"

The town of Scheffield, Michigan, population fourteen hundred and six, was certainly not known for violent crime.

I wasn't even sure if there had *been* a serious violent crime here in the whole twenty-five years I'd been alive and living in the cold, northern town that boasted one *whole* bar with an attached pizza shop.

Hawk River, he'd said. My mind did the necessary geography and mapping, though, without further details of exactly where she'd washed up on the river, all I knew was that she was on the other side of town, near the eastern outskirts—a favorite of kayakers and hikers, but not one of Ashley's regular haunts.

"The last murder in the county was back in the eighties," the officer admitted.

"I haven't seen her with any strangers. And I don't know of anyone who'd have a reason to hurt her," I said, sitting back and folding my arms over my chest as I thought. "She goes-*went*-out a lot, but I've never heard of any awful experiences. She never went out alone."

That was one thing Ashley had always preached. Buddy system safety, especially for adults, was mandatory in this day and age.

Apparently, the buddy system hadn't done it for Ashley.

"Have you talked to her friends?" I went on. "Does her mom know?" I'd met the wonderfully maternal woman, and while I had minimal experience with a non-judgmental, very attached mother, I could tell that they had an enviable relationship.

I was willing to bet her mother was inconsolable.

Would my mother feel the same if the situation was reversed? I'd gone low contact with my mom, who lived on the other side of the county. She'd never been the unquestionably supportive type, and I didn't mind not seeing her with the same frequency that Ashley and her mom got together.

"We've taken statements from her friends that say she was out with them two nights ago," Detective Granger assured me. "And her family has been informed."

"What did her friends say?" Hadn't they been with her?

Hadn't they been *watching*?

Anger curled in my stomach at the idea of them wandering off or letting her go home by herself. Had she been intoxicated? Had a stranger simply lured her off?

"They indicated that Miss Bellflower left after meeting up with a man she was familiar with," the detective replied. "That's why I was hoping that you might know more, Miss Carlysle. Her friends didn't seem to know much about the stranger."

Sighing, I frowned with a shake of my head. "No. I'm really sorry. If I knew, I'd tell you. But if they don't know him, I'm sure I don't either."

As far as I was aware, Ashley had still been dating her boyfriend of twenty-four days, Adam. I'd apparently been behind the times.

"All right then." The portly detective hauled himself to his feet, hands on his knees. "Thanks for your time, Miss Carlysle." He walked to the door, and I followed, the nervous klepto part of me itching for him to *leave* before he spotted some invisible speck of dust that would somehow tip him off about my less-than-legal hobbies.

On the other hand, I wished I could think of something-anything-to help point him in the direction of Ashley's killer.

"If I have any more questions, can I reach out?" he asked, drawing my attention back to his bald spot.

"Yeah, sure. No problem," I murmured. Without hesitation, I gave him my cell number, watching him write it in his little notebook with pudgy fingers and a less than reliable pen.

"And if you think of anything, don't hesitate to call the station," he added. "Miss Bellflower's death is our number one priority right now. Any information would help."

"No problem," I promised, hand on the door. "Thanks for stopping by, officer."

"Detective," he corrected automatically. "Have a nice rest of your day."

Nice rest of my day? Had he really said that?

He didn't wait for me to respond, rather just went to the end of the stone walkway that lined the outside of the apartment building and began his descent down the curving staircase at the corner.

I watched him go, eyes switching to observe the landlord's daughter spinning in the grass in the courtyard, a giggle bubbling on her lips.

Ashley was *dead*.

My fingers drummed against the wall as my stomach churned.

Had it been one of her friends? Was that why they'd told the cop some story about a guy she'd met?

Ashley was smart. I doubted she was the type of person to go home with a stranger or get in a car with someone she didn't know.

Right?

Closing the door, I sighed as my brain tried to process the tornado of information and feelings that I'd been bombarded with.

Until my phone vibrated off of the coffee table, anyway.

With a scowl, I grabbed it, eyes scanning the quick message from my boss.

Can you be here at five?

My shift at the local animal rescue league was supposed to start at six. If I had to be there at five…

Glancing at the clock on the wall, I found that I'd have to

leave within the next few minutes if I was going to grab a coffee on the way to what was probably going to be a night full of paperwork.

Sure, I replied, tossing the phone onto the arm of the sofa and striding through the small, two-bedroom apartment.

I studiously did not stop to look into Ashley's room. I couldn't deal with that uncertainty right now.

But I still felt so…strange about it. Sad, confused, and a bit angry, all rolled up into one ball that sat heavy in my stomach.

Trying to ignore it, I pulled on a pair of black, fleece-lined leggings, a loose sweatshirt, and a pair of mud-stained sneakers that had long since passed their prime.

But hey, if the puppies were going to chew a pair of my shoes to shreds, I'd prefer it be these than a new pair.

My shoulder-length chestnut hair went up into a ponytail that was nowhere close to the fashionable side of messy, and with a quick scan around the apartment, I hesitated.

Ashley really wasn't coming back.

When we'd first moved in together, I had never thought that she'd become one of my good friends. My *only* good friend, to be precise. But now, with her gone, I felt *strange.*

But it wasn't just a broken heart that tugged on my insides and gave me pause.

It was also *anger.*

Ashley was a good person. She'd been on her way to a nursing degree and had told me over and over how she wanted to be a psych nurse at our local hospital. Impassioned about the idea of improving things over there, I'd always found her idealistic in those pursuits.

But now, she'd never get the chance to prove me wrong.

She was *gone.*

Frustration caused my fingers to curl tightly around my phone, and I chewed my lip thoughtfully.

The cops would take care of it, right? This was a small town, after all. Surely there couldn't be that many suspects in her murder.

It wasn't my business. Nor my responsibility to catch a killer.

I was a *klepto,* not a scent hound.

Letting out the breath I hadn't known I was holding, I walked to the door and grabbed the keys off of the hook, remembering to lock up behind me, and strode out onto the landing proper to look down into the courtyard again.

The landlord's toddler was still there, hands ensconced in mittens as she gazed up at me from her spot in the grass.

I looked at her and waved once, a crooked smile on my lips.

I didn't like kids. I didn't want kids, either, which was always a sore spot for my mother.

Had Ashley wanted kids? She'd never spoken about them, but that didn't mean anything. I hadn't exactly asked.

"Don't do this to yourself, Will," I mumbled, walking to the far end of the building and descending my stairs. "There is literally no reason to do this to yourself. It's not your job. You have enough trouble without getting too involved in *that.*"

Though I was sure, the dogs I'd taken illegally from abusive households and relocated to rescues around the state didn't mind that I'd had to do some legal acrobatics to liberate them.

Still, it was *too* involved, I knew. I needed to take a step back sometimes, and if I tried to plunge myself into the middle of a murder investigation, that would be the exact opposite of stepping back.

My silver Sonata sat in its parking place, glittering after a cheap gas station drive-through wash. Normally it was just as muddy as my sneakers, but not today.

Not yet, anyway. The evening was still young.

It was only when I sat in the driver's seat with a sigh that I realized I'd forgotten my headphones in my apartment and plunked my head back against the headrest with a very long, very drawn-out groan.

CHAPTER TWO

WHILE COFFEE WOULD NOT SOOTHE the ache of not having my headphones with me for my abominably long shift at the rescue, I needed the caffeine all the same.

Somehow, hearing about Ashley's murder had me *tired*.

Even though I'd only been up since noon.

Our town was too small for a proper chain coffee shop, but *Monsoon Moon* was no disappointment. The small, rectangular building sat just off the main road, its light stone sides gleaming with taped, off-kilter signs in the windows, informing customers of their current specials.

Unlike a national chain, the owner, Marianne, could change the menu to fit her various whims, which happened often. Sure, some things remained the same. She never ran out of caramel macchiatos or French vanilla coffee, but other than that, I was taking a gamble on what kind of drinks she'd have.

Lychee milkshakes? Strong possibility.

It was more likely a fall flavor as we were heading into the spooky season, though it would never be something so simple as pumpkin or cinnamon.

No, no. Marianne liked to be unexpected. Last year she'd had maple-infused drinks, which hadn't been terrible.

Autumn spice, however, was awful. Whatever that concoction had been.

Pushing through the glass door and causing the small brass bell to ring against the heavy pane, I was surprised to see more people than usual for a late afternoon.

Her regular customers normally stopped by in the morning. And as she did *not* have Wi-Fi, no one stayed for too long unless it was some kind of social affair or they wanted to hear about the latest gossip.

The thought brought me up short.

Was *Ashley* that gossip today?

My grey eyes flitted over an older man sipping something that steamed as he read the newspaper, then to a lady gazing intently at her phone.

Did they already know?

Did anyone know other than me, the cops, and Ashley's family?

Something twisted unpleasantly in my chest as I chewed my lower lip.

There it was again—the anger and frustration at Ashley's murder.

But I didn't know what to *do* with it, and that made me feel helpless.

"Are you in line?" An unfamiliar voice drew me out of my thoughts, a sharp gaze sliding to the side as my mouth turned down in a slight frown.

"You can go ahead of me," I muttered, waving a hand towards the wide counter that ran parallel to one wall. Marianne was working, which was expected, and leaned on the wood surface to speak to a couple of men who stood, relaxed, on the other side.

The stranger smiled apologetically. "Sorry," he sighed. "I'm not usually in any kind of hurry, but they're waiting for me." He gestured at the two men by the counter.

Catching sight of his face, I was brought up short.

He was a *stranger*.

Which wasn't exactly a revelation, I supposed. But here, in the middle of nowhere, in a town with a population that barely exceeded four digits, a stranger was an *event*.

We weren't exactly a popular tourist destination. The only camping grounds we had were a small park used mainly by the locals who indulged in a staycation whenever they felt like doing something different.

Not to mention, I'd never before seen a man with such a pronounced scar on his face. It wound from his jaw up to his eyebrow, which had been sliced in half by where the scar parted it. It put my faint lip one to shame.

Somehow, it made him appear more attractive. Dark blonde hair lay tousled on his head, messy rather than stylish, which matched the stubble around a full, smiling mouth. With baby blue eyes set in a fair complexion that smiled, and lashes that had me swooning with envy. There was no way he could have been walking around the town of Scheffield for too long without having a stampede of eligible women, fighting to shove a ring on his finger.

At my inspection, his smile widened. "Are you okay?" he asked in a light, amused voice.

It occurred to me that my mouth was open slightly.

I slammed it shut, teeth clicking together.

I was *not* a teenager swooning over an out-of-towner, damn it!

"I'm fine," I sighed. "It's just that we don't get a lot of strangers around here. And you are most definitely *not* from around here, are you?"

His smile brightened. "No," he admitted, shoving his hands in his pockets and rocking back on his heels. "My pack and I live in Chicago, actually. We're just visiting."

I barely caught the rest of his sentence after *pack*.

"Pack?" I repeated, eyes narrowed and voice flat. "What are you, werewolves?"

The man looked away, bright eyes sliding in the direction of the counter.

I followed his gaze curiously, a jolt going up my spine when I saw that the two men at the counter were staring at us.

At *me*.

"It's just a stupid thing we made up when we were kids," the stranger chuckled. "We're more than friends, but we aren't related by blood, so..." He shrugged his shoulders. "And they're waiting for me. *Impatiently*, I might add," His voice raised, loud enough that when he spoke the ending the others could easily hear at the counter. "I'm Lysander," he added before I could speak.

The man—*Lysander*—stuck one hand out, reaching for mine in a greeting.

I stared at it as if it may bite me, then carefully rested my palm against his warm skin.

Compared to him, I almost seemed clammy.

"Will," I replied.

"It suits you." He closed his hand around mine, grasping it and pulling mine up and down. "See you later, Will." He brushed past me, my hand dropping and my fingers accidentally dipping into the pocket of his unzipped hoodie.

It was stupid. I was being stupid. Weren't we in a very public place?

Maybe Ashley's death had shaken me more than I had thought.

I dropped the wallet that had found its way into my palm, purposefully making it fall open on the cold tile floor below. "Oh, hey..." I bent down, making a show out of picking it up and letting my eye skim over the details of his ID.

Men were always so predictable when it came to what they kept in their wallets.

Lysander Ashford. Twenty-eight. Sure enough, it was an Illinois license.

Not that I had any reason *not* to believe him.

And what was I looking for, anyway?

His signature was almost as messy as mine, which was saying something, and with a last glance, I noticed his license was about to expire.

I couldn't read more, however. Nor could I go for the edges of the bills that stuck enticingly out of the top of the wallet. "You dropped this," I said, plastering a smile on my face and holding out the wallet to him.

Lysander's smile was genuine, though it showed more teeth than what I found to be *expected* in a person. "Thanks." He took the wallet from me and pocketed it once more. "Hey..." He glanced back at the two men of his 'pack', before looking into my face again. "Could I buy you a drink? Consider it my thanks for picking this up and also my apology for taking up your time and cutting in front of you."

A better, more sincere human would have told him that wasn't necessary and that it was the thought that counted.

I, however, was not above having anyone buy me a coffee so that I could forgo having to spend any of *my* money.

"Sure, if you really want to." I kept that fake smile on my face, the edges of it feeling like wires were pulling my mouth up.

Let him buy me coffee and go off with his *pack*, or whatever.

I figured they were just passing through, anyway—no reason for me to care when I already had too much to care about today.

He chuckled so softly I almost missed it before he asked me, "What would you like?"

"I'm pretty simple. Just a caramel macchiato," I shrugged.

As I watched, Lysander walked to the counter where the other two men stood. One of them—the man with darker olive skin and light hazel eyes—said something quietly enough that I could not hear.

Whatever it was, the other, lighter olive-skinned man grinned widely enough to show canines, and his dark eyes flashed.

I couldn't help but stare at the drastic difference between them and Lysander, with black hair and sharply handsome features.

"Are you in line?" The voice was bright, cheerful, and made me jump high enough that I was sure I nearly took flight.

When I turned, yet *another* stranger stood behind me, a shit-eating grin on his face and amusement dancing in his warm brown eyes.

"Are you with them?" I asked in reply, finding it harder and harder to wear the smile I did not feel.

The only reason they'd given me the time of day was because they didn't know me well enough to know to leave me alone. Marianne tolerated me, but I knew for a fact, she listened to my mother's woes about me. She definitely nodded along with her as my mom got teary-eyed, wishing for a daughter that came home more often.

All the while conveniently leaving out the things she'd said and done that had driven me away.

"How could you tell?" The laugh in his voice was sweet, not cruel, and I wondered if it was always there. He ran a hand through his messy brown hair, only disheveling it further, and looked me over quickly.

I had done the same and hadn't hidden it. Turnabout's fair play, I supposed.

"Because there are only so many strangers that show up in Scheffield every year," I shrugged and sidestepped pointedly so he could go to his friends.

Or did he also refer to them as a *pack*?

He started to go, then paused and beamed once more. "Oh, I saw what you did a minute ago. With Lysander's wallet."

My heart fell, fear clenching my insides tight, but my face remained carefully the same.

Had he *seen*?

My lips parted, though nothing came out. What was I supposed to say to that accusation?

I really was slipping up today. I usually was much more careful-

"It was really nice of you to pick it up for him and all."

When I glanced back up at his face, the man's grin was still firmly in place, and his eyes were watching my expression keenly.

"Oh....no, it's fine," I dismissed, feeling off-balance and strange around him. "Just trying to be nice and all."

"It's weird for us, is all," he went on with a shrug. "Not a lot of us in Chicago like to *be* nice."

Why did he keep staring at me?

Surely he had to look away at some point.

And what exactly was he watching *for*? To catch me in a lie? To catch me admitting that I'd done more than pick up Lysander's wallet from the ground?

"I'm Az," he said, still speaking as if this were a conversation, and not me contemplating my life choices. "Azriel Boone, but no one calls me all of that."

"Will," I replied through numb lips, happy he hadn't shaken my hand.

"That's gotta be short for something, right? Willemina or..." He raised his shoulders. "Help me out here. If you leave me hanging, I'll look like an idiot, and they'll laugh at me." He nodded at the other guys.

When I looked over, I found that the three of them now occupied the booth nearest the counter, and the only one of them even bothering to look over was the hazel-eyed, olive-skinned man with short black hair and a clean-shaven face.

I met his gaze briefly, a slight smirk curling over his thin lips before he looked away.

"Willow," I said, at last, not seeing any harm in telling him my actual name. "It's Willow. But I'm not really a fan."

If I was being honest, I'd never felt like much of a *Willow.* That was the name for a model or someone *else.*

Not for the five-foot-six, curvy brunette who lived in a newly half-vacated apartment and stole dogs and petty cash for a living.

Will just…seemed to fit.

A part of me wanted to ask if they were passing through and where they were going. We were a pretty long way from Chicago, after all.

And I wasn't sure what the four of them would be doing *here* for vacation.

Weighing my options and losing out to my curiosity, I finally did.

"You're just driving through?" I assumed, barely meaning to phrase it as a question.

"Hmm?" Azriel seemed surprised by the question.

Marianne called out a drink, and he went to the counter, plucking it up with a flourish and a wide grin at the owner-barista.

She set my macchiato down beside it, nodding to me, and I walked over to swipe it as well with a half-smile in her direction.

"No, we're staying here for a while. We rented out an Airbnb in town for a few weeks."

"*Why*?" I couldn't help the way my tone sounded dismissive, nor the harsh way the word had escaped my mouth.

I could only play nicely for so long, I supposed.

At the word, Marianne threw me an unfriendly glance, hearing the disbelief in my tone.

Azriel didn't seem bothered. His smile remained honey-sweet, and he maneuvered his grip on the cup of steaming caffeine that he held in a long-fingered hand.

Something glinted, drawing my attention, and when I peeked down, I saw that the man wore a large, ornate ring on the middle finger of his hand.

One that matched Lysander's, now that I thought about it. I hadn't been able to tell much about the blonde's ring, but now I could take the time to really *look.*

Too bad I couldn't find something like *that* just lying around. A golden snake curled around a black gem, and the ring itself was shiny rose-gold.

"Why?" Azriel repeated, seeming surprised by my question. "That's a bit of an odd question, don't you think?"

"No," I shrugged, throwing pleasantries to the wind. "No one comes here to *stay*. I'm not sure I even believe someone here has an Airbnb that they rent out. Who would even rent it?"

Whatever reaction I'd expected from him, it was not for the mahogany-eyed man with dark golden skin and messy black hair to chuckle. "Is this your way of asking for my address? You want to come over later to uh, *inspect* my accommodations, Will?"

The husky note in his voice set my heart racing, and my mouth fell open in surprise. "No!" I squeaked, aware that red coloring was more than likely rising in my cheeks to flaunt my embarrassment. "That's not what I-"

"Because I should probably inform you that we're *all* staying there."

I had no idea what I was supposed to say to that. Was he being serious?

More importantly, why did I *care* if he was? None of them were any of my business.

Even if they were sharing some Alaskan king-sized bed every night in some cottage in the woods.

"Well, whatever you're looking for in Scheffield, I hope it's worth our shitty hospitality, weather, and lack of good restaurants," I muttered, mock-toasting him with my macchiato and tucking a lock of brunette hair behind my ear.

I didn't need to look at him to see he was fighting back a laugh.

So I didn't. I turned on my heel, focused on the door and what was on the other side of it, my *car*.

After all, what *weirdos* vacationed here of all places?

Almost out the door, I couldn't miss the way his voice carried through the coffee shop. "I think it'll be more worth it than we were expecting, actually."

CHAPTER THREE

WHILE I'D EXPECT AZRIEL, Lysander, and the two other men to occupy my thoughts for a while longer, the sight that greeted me outside of the Scheffield humane society wiped them clear from my brain.

Two dogs were tied to the lone light post in the parking lot, lunging at the man who edged close to them with a catchpole clasped in shaking, white-knuckled hands.

I sighed, chugging the last of my coffee and shoving it into the cup holder before getting out with my phone and keys in my pockets. "Another drop-off?" I called, my voice dry.

I hated when people did this.

Sadly, my boss had informed me that we couldn't just track down their owners and break their noses.

Though, I was a big proponent of tying their humans up in a parking lot and leaving *them* out in the cold overnight.

A snarl and the pole dropping to the ground drew me from my dark thoughts, and my eyes went to the two dogs.

While I wasn't prejudiced towards any breed of dog, our normal surrenders tended to be exactly what one would expect.

Bully breeds. Those dogs with powerful statures that intimidated people and promised a very strong opposition.

But these were not mutts, nor the type of dogs I had been expecting.

Both of them appeared to be German Shepherds. And, as far as I could tell, purebred ones. With long fur and tails that nearly swept the ground, I could tell from here that they'd need to be shaved to get rid of their matts.

Poor things.

That was, of course, if we could even get them inside the building.

Joel, wielding the catchpole like a weapon, was doing a terrible job at getting the loop around either of them and whenever he tried, the dogs bit and nipped at the pole.

"I'll be right back," I called, walking to the building and entering through a side door that led into the large back office that doubled as storage for dog treats, food, and some other supplies.

My boss, Leah, looked up at me from her faux wood desk with a frown as she mumbled her agreement into the phone. "Yes, I *know* how microchips work," she snapped to whoever it was. "However, none of my staff have been able to get close enough to scan them yet."

At her words, I picked up the scanner from the shelf, a bag of treats already in my hand as I swerved for the door to head out again.

The dogs were still there, and seemingly just as personally offended at Joel's existence as they had been before.

"Take a break, Joel," I called, striding towards him and the dogs.

His shoulders sagged when I spoke, and he turned to hand off the catchpole to me, but I shook my head.

"After watching them trying to murder you for dangling it in front of them? No, *thanks*."

"Okay, but I don't see you capable of calming them with shitty dollar store *treats*," he pointed out, catching sight of them and the scanner. "And, Will, they'll chomp your arm off if you even try to scan them."

"*First* of all..." I dangled the plastic bag in front of him, showing him that I did not, in fact, have the cheap shit with me. I had the homemade treats Leah brought in, and I'd never met a dog that could deny their love for whatever magic she worked into these at her house. "I have Leah's good stuff. Second, I haven't lost an arm yet. I'll be fine."

One of the dogs-the darker and bigger one-snarled in disagreement.

I looked at it, taking in the pony-sized stature, large radar-like ears, and bared teeth. "Was that a challenge?" I asked, sitting down out of range of their lunges.

Joel sighed, the tip of the catchpole tapping the asphalt. "You need anything else?" he asked lamely, and I could hear the itch in his voice to get back *inside*.

"Nah," I replied, not bothering to look in his direction. *Go away*, I added silently, hoping he'd take the hint in my tone.

"If you're sure..." He so clearly wanted to be gone.

So fucking go, I wanted to say.

"I'm sure," I replied instead, my tone clipped. "I've got it." I hoped so, anyway. Not that I would get to try if he didn't *go* inside.

At last, the ginger-haired man left. His fast footsteps beat a hasty retreat into the building where more dogs barked for attention, and I was able to at last turn to the two large creatures in front of me who were intent on ripping my face off and using it as a tug-of-war rope.

"My name is Will," I knew they couldn't understand me, but I talked calmly and evenly anyway. "And I can't imagine you're here because you guys planned it." Were they guys? I had no way of telling unless I wanted to get in biting range.

Which, quite frankly, I did not.

"Here." I tossed a few of the pieces in their direction,

startling the dogs into taking a step back. The smaller, lighter shepherd stooped to sniff at the treats, but the bigger one stared at me with lips peeled back from long, curved canines.

"You'll like it," I encouraged the dog, crossing my legs under me.

The second dog was lipping at a treat, ears relaxing against its head slightly. Its fellow turned, nose to the ground, and spent a few seconds pushing one of the squishy treats around with its nose.

I sighed, broke up more treats, and tossed them to the dogs. "I'd really like to get you guys inside," I admitted, looking them over as best as I could from my spot. "You need a bath, for one. And a haircut. Plus, we have a super nice vet tech in there who wants to look at you."

Twenty minutes and half a bag of treats later, both of the dogs had finally become calm enough to be wrangled into the building.

As we were better funded and prepared than most shelters, it wasn't just luck that had a vet on standby, ready to look at the two of them.

As I'd half expected, the smaller of the two shepherds was a timid but sweet, male.

I had *not* expected the bigger, meaner one to be female, but that just showed me I supposed.

Work passed in a daze. After the excitement of the two dogs, I found myself wanting something else to focus on. However…that didn't seem to be the case.

Nothing, not paperwork nor dog walking, could keep my mind off of Ashley.

And why should it?

She had been *murdered.*

So far, no one else had said anything. I wasn't going to bring it up, either, but I'd expected *something*.

Finally, as I brought the last pair of dogs trotting in from the yard where they'd run circles around me, it happened.

As I put the last dog in its kennel, noise alerted me to the huffing and puffing of Joel as he came busting into the dog side of the kennels.

Immediately the dogs set up a clamor, protesting the younger man's presence.

Glancing at him, I saw him pale under his freckles and wondered yet again how a man so nervous around large canines had thought to find a job at the humane society of all places.

Didn't he understand that big and scary was what we found the most?

"Will!" His steps slowed as he approached, eyes going to a large mastiff mix that made its displeasure at his quick movements known from its kennel.

"Chill out, Myers," I sighed, pressing my hand to the front of his kennel and letting the dog sniff my skin. He licked my palm, bringing a smile to my lips before Joel began to speak again.

"Have you seen the news?" Joel demanded, finally stopping in front of me and wringing his hands together. "I guess not, since you've been outside and-"

"What was on the news?" I didn't have time for him to get to his point, and I didn't feel like standing here in the kennel with the noise reverberating in my ears. I strode past him without another word, leading the way out into the hallway and back up to the front office.

Immediately my eyes found the small tv that sat high on one wall.

Normally mute, the sound had been turned on as a voice spoke over a somewhat recent picture of my roommate.

Well, *my ex-roommate* now.

"The body of Ashley Bellflower, twenty-three, was found near the eastern bank of the Hawk River. Sources report that-"

I turned away, eyes closing as I tried to rein in the strange rush of emotion that threatened to overtake me.

We hadn't been *close*.

Not family, nor best friends.

I wasn't *sad*, exactly...

No. It was anger, once more, that bubbled up in my throat and promised to spill from my lips like something unpleasant.

Why did I feel so strongly about this?

"Did you know?" Joel asked, reaching out as if to shake me. He thought better of it when my grey eyes found his, dropping his arm as if that had been his intention all along.

He did not need a play-by-play of my earlier conversation with the detective.

It was none of Joel's business whatsoever.

"Yes," I said flatly, offering nothing else. When I turned my eyes up to the tv once more, it had gone to commercial.

Good. I didn't want to know what else was being said about her.

"Will?" Leah called out from her spot at the desk, where she'd also been watching the news on the small television in silence.

"Yeah?" I asked blankly, turning to face her.

I knew what I must look like—blank expression. Dead eyed, my mom would've said. Like I didn't give a shit about my surroundings or the people in them.

She called it selfishness.

If it were me being selfish to keep from being overwhelmed by my own feelings or the reactions of people around me, then I'd gladly take the label and run with it—something she'd never understood.

"Do you need to go home?" My boss asked kindly, an understanding look tugging on her features.

"Can I?" I asked, unsure of why I said it. Hadn't I told myself all day that I would be fine? That I was handling this just fine?

Leah nodded her head in acquiescence. "Absolutely. I'm sorry, Will. You should've called in and told me, and I would've said not to come in at all."

I just smiled, glad I hadn't done that.

If I hadn't been here, Joel would've never coaxed those shepherds in. They'd still be out in the parking lot, or worse.

"Thanks," I said lamely, barely managing to answer her question. She was the nicest person I knew and one of the few in town who thought I was an okay human being.

Not that I was so great at convincing people of that. My mother, someone well known around the county, had been loud for years about how selfish and ungrateful I was for not becoming just like her.

I wasn't so great at speaking of or making a case against her narcissism, and it had become easier just to *be* that person after a while.

"I'll be back on Thursday," I said, giving my boss a half-smile that I didn't really feel. Today was Tuesday, and I was always off on Wednesday.

I usually used that to work on my *other* job.

The one that I didn't list on any resumé.

Not that I was low on money this month. Thanks to a few well-thought-out heists a week or so back, I had been able to pay the bills in advance.

Which will now be double what they have been, the rational part of my brain reminded me as I pushed out of the building and strode to my car.

But that part of my brain was right.

With Ashley dead, I wasn't sure I *could* afford a two-bedroom apartment on my own unless I amped up the thievery and made myself more suspicious than I cared to.

But that was another problem for another day.

Still…my hands itched to paw through someone else's stuff. Call it a hobby or a calling, but I enjoyed breaking in and judging other people based on their homes and what they kept in their secret places where no one else ever thought to look.

Though, to be fair, those *secret places* typically tended to have dildos in them.

Or porn.

The number of times I'd found porn in someone's kitchen drawers was staggering and not an experience I ever looked forward to repeating.

It was a bad idea tonight, I reasoned with myself as I pulled out of the parking lot with a frown curving my lips downward and eyes fixed on some spot in the distance. While I found the art of relieving people of their things rather easy, I always made sure to be in the right frame of mind when I did so.

One mistake, after all, and I really *would* be standing up for my mug shot at the police station.

And no one cared enough about me to help me out of jail, should that happen, I was sure.

I should go home, I told myself firmly. Home, and nowhere else. I'd watch TV and figure out these feelings I kept having about Ashley's death instead of doing something stupid.

Yeah, that was a great idea. No stops, except maybe to the *only* fast food restaurant in town that served tacos, pizza, and vegan food.

I had never figured out exactly *why* the restaurant, *The Outlook,* couldn't find a lane and stick to it.

Its sister restaurant, *The Overlook,* was the only *fancy* restaurant in town.

Being our only civilized eatery, *The Overlook* usually

required a reservation for one to be served rare steak while they stared at the river.

Still, takeout from there would've been preferable over taco-pizza-soy-*something*.

"Maybe next time," I mumbled, swerving into the turn lane that would take me to town and *The Outlook*.

CHAPTER FOUR

WHILE I WASN'T a stalker-*not really*-it would've been impossible for me to miss the car that *screamed* tourist. Or at least, whoever owned it was not from around *here*.

Black tinted windows showed me a pale reflection and half-narrowed grey eyes, while the shine on the charcoal grey Camaro was so bright that it appeared as if it had just rolled off the production line.

No one in Scheffield owned a car like *this*. Or if they did, they'd stolen it. Sure, there were families north of the river who could probably afford it, but they'd still spend their money on big trucks or Escalades before getting anything so…sporty and unreasonable for Michigan's signature terrible winters.

With the drive-thru broken again, I was forced to park my hideously inferior Sonata next to the showpiece car and march inside with keys and debit card in hand, as I mentally sifted through the small restaurant's menu.

Honestly, a lot of people didn't bother to order from said menu. If I walked in and asked for a burger smothered in nacho cheese, they'd give it to me.

Not that I had any intentions of asking for something that greasy.

The inside of *The Outlook* could give any McDonalds a

run for their money, and I was pretty sure that's where they'd gotten their inspiration from. A glass door with silver framing and handle? Check. Dark brown tiled floor with a cream counter sitting against the far wall? Double check.

Air smelling of old grease and too many orders of fries?

Yeah, *The Outlook* was solid on that point too.

As I walked to the counter, I surreptitiously looked around the open room, wondering just who in the world had parked outside with their car that *begged* to be stolen.

Empty booths there…empty tables there…

When my eyes fell on the only likely culprits, my mouth tugged into a slight frown.

The four men from the coffee shop sat at a booth, trays of greasy fast food in front of them, while one of them spoke in a hushed, fervent whisper.

Unthinkingly, I drifted to a stop, eyes catching the face of the man I'd spoken to this afternoon. *Lysander.*

Only…he looked different, somehow.

He seemed *cold,* I realized, the thought going through my brain like a whisper. His eyes held no emotion whatsoever, save for annoyance, and his lips were pressed into a thin line. The boyish, shy hunch of his shoulders was gone, and he was utterly still.

It was creepy, in a way.

Though I couldn't figure out *why.*

Blinking, I dragged my gaze upward from his face, and my stomach clenched uncomfortably.

One of the other men, whose name I did not know, was staring right back at me. His hazel gaze was lazy as he *waited* for me to look at him.

And it was definitely not a friendly look. He had the same calm countenance, though without the annoyance, and looked me over as if to survey my worth.

I found myself feeling strangely humiliated at the dismissive flick of his gaze when he looked away.

As if I'd taken some kind of test…and failed.

What in the world was going on?

It wasn't my business. None of this was my business, and I was always *very good* at remaining out of things that had nothing to do with me.

Forcibly, I made my feet move to approach the counter where a blonde teenager sat, his weight resting on the edge closest to the register, and cleared my throat. Unless I was mistaken, I had gone to school with his older brother.

When the boy did not look up from his phone, I cleared my throat once more, feeling my own usual irritation swelling in my chest.

At last, he dragged his gaze up from whatever he was reading and sighed. "You know what you want?" he grumbled in a bored voice.

"Just a grilled cheese and an order of cheese fries," I replied, tossing my debit card onto the counter in front of me. "And a chocolate milkshake." Because damn, I deserved a milkshake after the shit show today had been. "A large one."

He grunted, one hand out so he could slide my card towards him across the counter and slide it once-twice, actually into the register. The old machine beeped, sounding *crusty*. Not that I was sure how exactly a beep could make such a sound.

But here we were.

"Thanks," I sighed, taking the card back and pocketing it.

"Yeah. Give me a few minutes." He walked away from the counter, ticket in hand, prompting me to wonder if he was the *only* one working tonight.

A few minutes here could mean five, seven, or fifteen. It was always impossible to tell, and it was a big reason their drive-thru was incredibly inefficient, even when it *did* work.

I'd just have to find a booth and wait.

Turning on my heel to look for a booth, spoiled for choice as I was in an empty restaurant. I froze when I saw that I was no longer alone.

Azriel was there, waiting and *silent* behind me.

How in the world had he snuck up on me?

I should've heard him, surely. He was only a few inches behind me, close enough that I *definitely* should've known he was there.

"Did I startle you?" he asked, even before my lips had parted in a gasp.

"No," I lied instantly, forcing myself to relax.

His smile brightened, and his chocolate eyes twinkled in amusement, silently calling me out on the lie. "Good. Want to come sit with us? You're the only person in town we know, and we'd love to hear more about this place."

"I ordered my food to go," I pointed out. "It'll be done in a couple of minutes or so."

Hopefully.

He shrugged his shoulders, not looking put out from my response. "You could stay and eat with us? Unless you're busy? I wouldn't want to inconvenience you."

I stared at him for longer than was polite, trying to puzzle out my feelings about this man.

Why did he make me *feel* so uneasy?

He was so *friendly*, like Lysander had been, and yet...

It was probably just me and the events of my day, but I simply did not want to stay here with them.

Besides, I had a shitty reputation around here for my social skills anyway.

Why tarnish it now?

"I'm not a good tour guide," I told him firmly. "And I have to go as soon as my food is ready." Throwing a look behind me, I mentally prayed that it would be ready *soon*.

"You scaring her off, Az?" Lysander drawled from their

table. I glanced up, not surprised to see his bright blue eyes on mine.

Still, the strange look in them made my stomach flip, though I couldn't for the life of me figure out why.

"Just for a few minutes," I said finally, hating the way Azriel smiled at the words. "But when my food is ready, I'm leaving."

It was only because my brain roared at me with so many different thoughts, and I would rather talk to them about something than keep dwelling on Ashley's death.

It wasn't until I stood at the side of their booth, nails digging crescents into my palms, that I remembered I didn't know the other two members of their group at all. Not even their names.

The dark-haired, dark-eyed man with olive skin stared up at me. His sharp face shrewd yet intrigued as he surveyed mine.

I stared back at him, unphased, before letting my gaze drift to his seating companion.

Only to find that the fourth of their group seemed as if he hadn't taken notice of my presence at all.

With one long arm draped over his friend's shoulders, the guy on the inner side of the booth sat back into the corner, posture open and comfortable as he scrolled through something on his phone without even a glance in my direction.

Startled, I didn't look away.

Did he *care* that I was here?

Or was I just that unimportant?

"Rhys is always rude," Lysander informed me, gesturing for me to sit down on the bench beside him. I looked at him, then at the cracked vinyl surface, and blatantly sat down in the chair that Azriel had dragged over instead, my actions receiving no protest.

"He isn't *rude*," tall, dark, and handsome drawled sweetly, watching me as I sat and turning to face me fully.

Like that wasn't creepy at all.

"Your name is Will, right? Lysander wouldn't stop talking about you after you so helpfully picked up his wallet for him earlier," the stranger continued, his voice sharply accented.

I hated the way he said it. With his head tilted just so and his eyes narrowing with his words, it was almost like he didn't believe me or wanted to catch me in a lie.

Had I really been so sloppy that these men suspected something more than goodwill from me?

"Yeah," I said, my reply slower than it should've been. Absently, I glanced at Lysander as Azriel sat next to him, not missing the intensity of those baby blues.

"I'm Nykos, or just Nyko," the man went on. "And this is Rhys." He gestured to the other guy, and *still* their fourth didn't bother to look up at me.

"Any marriage proposals yet?" I asked, plucking the first thing I could think of out of my mind.

Nyko's brows rose ever so slowly. "Excuse me?"

"Marriage. Proposals," I replied as if he had misheard me. "We don't get a lot of new faces around here, and it's kind of a local joke that eligible Scheffield ladies don't let handsome men escape them without a ring on their finger."

"We haven't spoken much to the locals," Lysander admitted in a chuckle. "After we got coffee, we went to our Airbnb and crashed."

"Sounds fulfilling." What did they *want* me to say? If they were so uninterested in interacting with anyone local, then why bother with me now?

Wasn't it obvious that I had no desire to play nice and make friends?

Didn't they care?

"Not much to do around here, is there?" Azriel hummed,

sliding his hands forward on the table until they crept dangerously close to mine. I glared at his fingers like the unwelcome promise they were, prepared to draw my hands back if need be.

"No," I agreed. "There's nothing to do, so no one really comes to visit. The only local activities are hiking or drinking."

"And which do you prefer?" Lysander cut in effortlessly.

"Neither," I sighed, sitting back and folding my arms over my chest. I glanced at the counter, biting my lip, when I caught the cashier just sitting on his phone as he'd been when I walked in.

"Then why stay?" Lysander asked as if it was the simplest question in the world. "Sounds like you don't enjoy it here much."

I didn't answer his question. Instead, I replied with one of my own. "Why visit?" I met his eyes. "You don't look like the hiking type, and I'm pretty sure Scheffield isn't the only place you can drink. Probably one of the worst alcohol selections in the country, too."

"Maybe there's more to do here than just those two things." The words came from Rhys, and they didn't disappoint. His voice was like richly accented satin, the sound threatening to draw me in and think about him in ways that definitely were not unpleasant.

"Yeah," I agreed with a sigh. "We also have *Jesus* on almost every street corner. Only you guys didn't strike me as the door-to-door religious speech types."

Azriel laughed, Lysander joining him with a snort.

The other two didn't even bother to smile. Nyko sat back, a sigh leaving him, and Rhys, again, went right back to his phone.

Why ask for my company if I was just going to be mostly ignored?

"So...do you guys want something from me?" I asked at

last, when an uncomfortable silence had fallen over their small table. "Directions to the nearest town limit? Pretty sure we're clear on me not being much of a hiker, so I'm not knowledgeable on any kind of nature stuff." Rubbing my hands against the fabric of my leggings, I was surprised to find my hands clammy with sweat.

Did they really bother me that much?

"Does anything interesting happen around here?" Azriel hummed as if my discomfort didn't bother him, or he simply didn't notice it at all. "Small towns keep the best secrets, right, Will?"

Ashley's face and my brain's picture of what her dead body had to look like thrown to the side of the river assaulted me, causing me to shudder and close my eyes hard.

That's not what they mean, Will, I reminded myself, blinking to clear my thoughts.

"No," I promised them dryly. "Nothing interesting ever happens in-"

"When was the last time you guys had some kind of violent crime?" Nyko seemed suddenly interested, one hand resting on his palm, as he gazed at me from under long, dark lashes.

"I don't know. A while?" Was I getting defensive? I sounded defensive.

"We're kind of....true crime junkies," Azriel supplied with a grin. "It's weird, but-"

"A while?" Rhys drawled in a voice accented similarly to Nyko's but thicker. Not English, like I suspected of Nyko's words, but maybe....Middle Eastern? Still, I couldn't place it.

"A while. I don't know-I'm *not* into watching our crime stats. Before today-"

I bit my lip, hating what I'd been about to say.

"How long has it been since someone was killed here,

before today?" Rhys hummed, eyes finally locking onto mine and his words causing my heart to sink.

My lips felt numb as I stared at him. "How did you-"

"Because you told me." The man shrugged, sitting back and looking away.

Looking around at the four of them, it occurred to me how much I did not want to be here.

The four of them were *wrong* somehow. Something about them was off.

Even Azriel, with his overt friendliness.

Even Lysander, who'd bought me coffee.

Something was wrong, and I knew, somehow, that these men knew something about Ashley's death.

Maybe they were even involved.

Slowly I stood, doing my best to gather my wits as I did. "Like I said," I murmured slowly, unwilling to meet their gazes. "I don't know what you're looking for, but nothing ever happens here. It's just a shitty town, full of shitty people. And I'm a terrible tour guide."

The cashier called out my order, giving me the excuse I barely needed. "Have a nice vacation," I mumbled and strode away from the four of them.

I took my bag, barely noticing that the cashier said something to me about having a nice night, and strode out the door with my eyes fixed firmly on the door.

They knew something about Ashley.

They *had* to, didn't they?

Didn't I have all the tools to find out exactly what that was as soon as they left wherever they were staying in the morning?

Trapped in my thoughts, I barely noticed starting my car or anything about the drive home.

CHAPTER FIVE

REQUESTING a few days off of work was much easier than I'd anticipated.

Though, I should've realized when the news broke and Ashley's face was all over the television that I wouldn't have to explain much about *why* I wanted to stay home instead of going to work.

Everyone in town knew, now.

Though, the news channel covering the story had been very sparse on the details of her death. According to them, the police were still unsure what had happened and had said it might have just been a tragic accident.

I knew better.

The police knew better, too.

So why not *say* something? As far as I knew, none of Ashley's friends had been called in for questioning, nor had the police come around to ask me more questions.

That bothered me.

Ashley had been *murdered,* and something needed to be done *now.*

Looking down at the hoodie in my arms, I tried to remember if I'd forgotten anything.

Inconspicuous but dark outfit? Check.

Once upon a time, I'd done the all-black thing when I

worked. But that was a dead giveaway that I was up to no good. People *noticed* when you wore all black and gloves, especially in the summer heat.

No, casual clothes without any trademark details on them were *much* better.

To that end, I wore a red t-shirt, dark grey leggings with artful slashes up and down the fronts, and scuffed red and white high-tops. The hoodie in my arms was black and bland, just like the rest of me.

Today, my hair was down, the medium-auburn strands like a curtain that I could use to conceal my discernible features.

After all, there were only so many pale girls with lip scars and blue-grey eyes running around bumfuck, Michigan.

Sure, people knew me in this town, but a person's memories were a *lot* more fallible than they liked to believe when all they had was a glimpse of a girl in a hoodie and leggings.

Jammed in my pocket was a soft case full of my well-used lock picks that I'd had for years and had sworn never to get rid of.

How could I, when they served me so well? By this point, I was sure the handles were molded into the shape of my grip, and that suited me just fine.

Not everything needed to be shiny and new to get the job done.

Finally, I pulled on my hoodie, phone sliding into my left pocket, and grabbed my keys to head out to my car.

Finding out where the four of them were staying had been *dreadfully* easy, frankly. And I wasn't that great of a detective.

Not that they were trying to hide. When I'd looked up Airbnbs in town, only three had popped up.

Which, admittedly, was three more than I'd been expecting.

From there I'd called them, asking about immediate reservations.

Two of them had been vacant, not shocking me at all, while the lady who owned the third house had proudly proclaimed she was booked up for at least two weeks, starting yesterday.

So really, my destination couldn't have been any clearer.

The annoying part was the *drive*. While I lived on the west side of town to be as far from my mother as possible, their place was on the *east* side.

Conspicuously close to the river where Ashley's body had turned up.

The twenty-six-minute drive gave me more than enough time to consider what I was doing and worry about it.

I didn't know anything about them, and here I was about to break into their place.

Whenever I stole from someone, I tracked them for *days,* if not *weeks,* to learn their schedule. I took things they wouldn't miss too much or just enough money that they might do a double-take later.

I was careful, and that was why I'd never gotten myself into trouble.

But this?

This was anything *but* careful.

Almost too soon, I had found their street, and before I could get much further along, I pulled my car into the parking lot of a small flower shop, thankful that it was closed.

Not only that, but nothing in town had any kind of high-tech security. That was definitely to my advantage and something I was always grateful for.

The wind ruffled my hair, sending the scent of smoke

and leaf mold through my nose as soon as I stood and closed my car door.

This late in September, I was surprised the leaves were just starting to turn. Typically our autumn was colder than this.

Not that I was particularly complaining, I supposed. While autumn was definitely my favorite season, I didn't relish the temperatures dropping enough that a hoodie and leggings were no longer comfortable outerwear. Which, of course, was inevitable due to living in northern Michigan.

Checking my phone, I let my eyes flick over the address I'd typed into my GPS.

1414 Chestnut Avenue.

The shop I'd parked in was 1001 Chestnut.

I wasn't too far.

My heart hammered in my chest as if this was the first time I'd ever approached a house I intended to steal from.

And well…

Sure, I'd broken into a lot of places in my life. It was practically my career at this point. But never had I done it to *spy* on someone.

I never did it because I suspected the people in the house were anything more than what they presented themselves to be.

As I walked along the street, my heartbeat sped up in my chest. It was getting dark, but I still pulled my hood up over my head and shoved my hands into the pockets of my hoodie.

I probably didn't know anyone here, but I couldn't be too careful.

There was always the chance this would go badly, and the fewer people who saw me walking up or down the street, the better.

There was also a *very* good chance that one or more of the guys were *at* the house. I'd picked this time specifically for the likelihood that they may have been out for dinner, but that didn't mean anything.

Maybe they were the kind of people who *cooked* on vacation?

Granted, I wasn't sure if this was a vacation at all.

My spirits rose against my will at the possibility of the lights being on and the men being in residence. If that were the case, I most certainly would not be breaking in.

Not that the idea should give me *relief*.

My scuffed footsteps took me too quickly along the sidewalk, brushing over fallen leaves and uneven cement as I passed wrought iron gates enclosing small but elegant houses.

All of them sat back from the road, and in many of them, I saw lights and movement. Food smells drifted to the road, blown to me by the soft breeze that chose once in a while to brush along my skin and remind me that, even though it wasn't warm, I still had sweat on my forehead and upper lip.

God, I was *nervous*.

At last, I stopped, eyes fixed on a red mailbox with the numbers *1414* cemented to the top of it.

Well. Here I was.

It was now or never.

Turning to look down the driveway, I found that there were no cars in the open that I could see.

Better yet, there were no lights on at all in the one-story house with its white stone finish and dark grey roof.

The *windows*, however, made my stomach twist and curl into knots. Even if there was no one home, the moment someone even looked inside, I would be noticed if I turned on any light at all.

Large bay windows decorated the front of the house, unblocked and giving everyone a clear view from the outside.

Why couldn't there be *curtains* drawn across the glass?

Anything to give me a bit of a buffer.

I faltered then, taking a few steps back from the mailbox and the house that seemed to loom behind the black fence.

This was a bad idea. I wasn't the police. I wasn't *anyone.* Finding Ashley's killer-or killers-wasn't my responsibility.

But...

I bit my lip, my brain flashing unhelpfully to one of the last conversations I'd had with her.

I think it's so great that you have your dream career, Will, Ashley had said, smiling at me from the counter where she ladled too many pancakes onto a dish.

That day she'd experimented with red velvet pancakes and had even made homemade cream cheese icing for them.

They'd been amazing.

Hey, when I finish college, I'll be doing the same. I want to work at County General in the ER, you know?

I know, I'd snorted, sitting down at the table and blinking sleep from my eyes. *You remind me all the time, Ash.*

I'm manifesting it. She'd dropped the stack of pancakes down and sat as well, forking two onto my plate. *Now try these so I can decide if I want to put them on my blog later.*

Blinking, I pushed the memory to the back of my mind where it belonged.

It wasn't *fair.*

All she'd wanted was to work in healthcare and make a difference. She hadn't wanted to be rich or famous or *anything.*

She hadn't been a thief like me, either.

Ashley had deserved more, and someone had taken that from her.

Yet again, the irritation boiled in my stomach, balling up like a bundle of thorns and causing a harsh sensation of discomfort to prickle through my body.

I *had* to know if these men were responsible for her death.

And if they were?

I'd find a way to alert the police as well.

Forcing myself to move, I made my way along the black driveway, letting my shoulders settle and setting my pace to casual.

I couldn't look hurried or suspicious on the off-chance that someone looked out their window at me. I needed to come across like I belonged.

Thankfully no one noticed. Or if they did, no one seemed to *care*. Perhaps it was normal for strangers to walk along this driveway if the owner had any kind of consistent business with out-of-towners.

Not that I believed *that* for a second.

The front door was locked, obviously, and I meandered along the porch, glancing sideways into the bay windows as I tried to hunt for any sign of life.

Nothing.

To my eyes and ears, there was no one home.

That meant it was time to get to work.

Picking the front door's lock would've been suicide, and I really didn't want to go to jail. Instead, I cast a look around, glad to see no one at either of the neighboring houses and thanked anything that could hear me that this house, in particular, had more than a few decorative trees blocking the view from most of the street.

That made my job easier.

Ambling around to the back of the house by way of the sidewalk, I noticed that the garden lights I'd barely looked at before were actually tiny lawn gnomes with glowing orbs, their faces merry and round-cheeked.

I couldn't help it. I curled my nose in disgust, absolutely judging whoever had decorated the garden with these little monstrosities.

It was the twenty-first century, after all. Who in the *world* still bought lawn gnomes for anything other than irony or as a joke decoration?

The smooth sidewalk continued around the house, taking me straight towards a screened-in porch with its own door that led into the fenced-in backyard.

Another lucky break. In my experience, flimsy doors like this one were the easiest to break into.

Reaching into my pocket, I knelt in front of the door, cocking my head to the side and shaking my hood back from my face as I did.

Was that....? I closed my eyes, trying to focus completely on the sounds around me instead of my sight.

Any noise that reached me seemed too far off to be coming from inside.

But just because it was empty *now* certainly did not mean I had time to sit around and wait for them to come home.

It also didn't necessarily mean that they were *all* gone. What if one or two of the men were still here? Sleeping off a hangover or doing something illegal?

What then?

I couldn't-wouldn't-consider that possibility right now. Not when so much rode on this house being empty so I could learn what I needed to about its temporary inhabitants.

My hands worked quickly, barely needing my brain to chime in as I gently worked the lock around in an attempt to get it open.

Another thought occurred to me, this one much less pleasant...

What if these men *were* the ones who had killed Ashley?

What if this door swung open, and there were bodies, or hostages, or *blood* on every surface?

What in the world would I do then if I had the evidence I had come here seeking?

Sure, 'taking it to the police' was a good idea and all…

But I wasn't sure how I'd even get from 'discovering evidence' to 'taking that evidence to the cops.'

Not for the first time, I found myself wishing I had a reason to chicken out.

Almost too quickly, the lock on the door popped open, and the door swung back, on its hinges, hitting the wall with a soft *thump* and rebounding.

The sound made me wince, my teeth grinding together at the noise that I was sure could be heard in California.

Get it together, Will, I chastised, getting to my feet and pushing the lock picks back into my pocket.

With the door open, and still no movement or lights in the house, I had lost any excuse to chicken out.

It was do or die, now.

Emphasis on the *die*.

As quietly as I could, I walked into the screened-in porch and gently closed the door behind me, keeping it unlocked. This would be my escape route, and I wanted to do as little as possible to impede it.

For a moment, I considered turning on the light. With my hand on the switch, I paused, shaking my head at my own stupidity.

No lights, Will, I reminded myself.

Especially tonight.

I pulled out my phone, tapping the flashlight icon and bringing it to medium brightness.

This would have to do.

Unsurprisingly, there was nothing that screamed suspicious on the screened-in porch. A hoodie lay over one of the chairs, and out of habit, I reached into the pockets to see what might be in them.

Nothing. Not even lint.

A large, locked door sat between me and the main house, but it was just as easy to pick as the screen door had been.

Not shocking. After all, the only thieving happening in Scheffield was probably me, and I was good about going to other neighboring counties to get shit done so that I wouldn't cause too much of a stir in my own backyard.

The last time I'd broken into someone's house in town had been my mother's. And that had just been to get some things of mine out of storage so that I didn't actually have to face her for them.

The door swung, admitting me into a spacious, wood-floored living room. A sectional took up most of the center of the room, a coffee table between it and a large television on a glass stand.

Here, at least, it appeared as if people were actually *staying*. A phone cord was draped over the coffee table, along with a small takeout bag.

Thankfully, there were no bloody knives or dead bodies.

Yet.

I crept through the house, flashlight still on, and carefully avoided the rooms that faced the windows and the streets. To my eyes, those rooms looked like a dining room and a small office, which I paused in the doorway of.

Could there be something important here? From a sweeping glance, the dining room had looked untouched, and frankly, the office did as well.

But that didn't mean there wasn't something in here, hidden, that I'd need to see.

Tapping my foot on the wooden floor, I bit my lip and considered it.

It would be my last stop. If I couldn't find *anything* else and I had the time, I would go into the office.

Otherwise, I'd avoid both of the rooms that would make me incredibly visible to anyone who might look inside from the street beyond.

The room at the corner of the house was a bedroom, and I immediately saw that someone was sleeping there. A duffle bag lay on the floor, clothes thrown around the rug that covered the hard floor.

The bed was unmade, navy blankets thrown back, and a phone charger on the bedside table.

There was nothing here that screamed 'murderer.'

However...

My eyes fell on the duffel bag at my feet, and my lips pursed together.

Had I really thought this would be so easy? That I'd walk in, grab a bloody knife and severed head, then skip on out?

If they were hiding something, it would probably be *hidden*...right?

Carefully I unzipped the small outer pockets of the bag, looking for anything that I could use against them.

Nothing.

Just clothes, socks, and an extra charging cable.

The next bedroom held the same, even down to the duffel that was a twin of the first.

Maybe there really wasn't anything to find.

The last bedroom proved to be the biggest, and *two* duffels sat against one wall, both of them unzipped.

That was unexpected. Especially since it appeared that the bed was unmade on both sides and heartily slept in.

Or...used, anyway.

Maybe the four guys were just *friends* like I'd expected.

More quickly than I had with the first two rooms, I reached into a black bag with the expectation of finding the same *nothing* as I had so far.

But as my fingers closed around something small and flexible, I found that to be false.

Gently I pulled my prize free, sitting on the edge of the bed to shine my phone down on the two booklets in my hand.

Passports.

Opening the first, I saw Rhys's face staring sourly up at me, eyes just as goading as they were in real life.

Rhys St. John.

According to the passport, he was twenty-nine, only four years older than me, and had been to fourteen different countries, including Norway and France.

The next passport was Nyko's.

Or, as this informed me, *Nykos Germaine.*

He, too, had been to the same fourteen countries as Rhys, and was also twenty-nine.

"Why passports?" I murmured, staring at them in my lap for a second longer. "We're in Michigan, and there's no border crossing anywhere *near* here."

Did they just carry them with them wherever they went?

Why hadn't I found passports in the others' luggage, if that were the case?

Bars of light crawled along the doorway, confusing me for a moment as they climbed the wall to the ceiling.

They brightened, causing my eyes to narrow a moment before my heart lurched into my throat and promptly tried to leave my body altogether at the sound of a car engine outside.

They were home, and here I was in their bedroom, with two of their passports in my hands.

If they caught me here, like this, I really *would* end up dead.

CHAPTER SIX

HOLY SHIT. I did not scream, somehow. I would *not* make any noise.

Not if I wanted to get out of here without being caught.

With hands that shook fiercely, I put both passports back where I'd found them. "Come on, Will," I hissed, my hands trembling so badly that I found it hard to zip the duffel bags.

Finally done, I booked it out of the room, looking around to ensure nothing was out of place.

I hadn't moved anything, right? And I hadn't taken anything.

On legs that ached to run, I strode quietly to the door of the screened porch, opening it as voices sounded near the front of the house.

With my heart hammering, I closed it gently behind me, hearing the front door open and listening to the conversation that drifted through the room.

"You're disgusting, man," Azriel chuckled, sounding like he was in the lead, and his footsteps sounded on the smooth wood as he crossed the entryway. "I didn't need to know *any* of that."

"Then don't listen at the door when we tell you to leave

us alone," the laugh came from Nykos, his sharp voice unmistakable.

"It's pathetic," added Rhys with a low scoff. "In fact-"

Footsteps in the grass made me freeze, my hand already on the door of the screened-in porch.

They were closer than they should've been.

And they sounded like they were getting closer to my side of the house.

Was Lysander coming in the back door?

Why?

My breathing picked up, sweat beading on my palms, unsure of what to do.

If he caught me here, the others would find me as well.

Should I make a run for it? With my hood up and hair around my face, surely they wouldn't know it was *me*.

Unless one of them chased after me and caught me.

Caught in my indecision, I flinched when the footsteps sounded on the cement stairs outside the door.

I had to hide. That was my only chance here. Hide and hope he didn't turn on the lights.

With the decision made, I scrambled to the side, ducking under a metal framed couch and squeezing myself under it as deftly as possible.

So long as no one turned on the light-

The handle turned, alerting me to my mistake.

I'd left the doors unlocked.

From my vantage point under the sofa, I watched Lysander step onto the porch, barely able to make out his face in the dark.

Why was my heart beating so loudly?

Surely he could hear it too. Hell, I was sure all of Michigan could hear that, along with the way I sucked in air too fast and too loudly.

God, I hoped I wasn't about to hyperventilate.

I expected him to say something. He'd call out to the

others, for certain, and let them know that the door was unlocked.

Then they'd know that someone had been here.

They'd start looking, and this hiding place really wasn't going to save me.

The door closed behind him, yet Lysander didn't move. His head turned in my direction, causing me to duck my face down against the cement floor.

Hopefully, if he couldn't see my pale skin, he would maybe only see the black of my clothes and not notice anything at all.

The great room door opened, making me kick myself again. I hadn't locked that one, either.

I was such an idiot. Leaving doors unlocked was such a rookie mistake. One I hadn't made in *years*. But of course, when my life was quite possibly in danger, this was the time I fucked up.

Damn it all.

It was probably time to start coming up with a better plan. Maybe I could play it off like the door was already unlocked and I was hiding because....

Because it was fun?

No, that definitely wouldn't work.

"Are you coming inside?" Nykos was the one to open the door, and as I peeked through my dark auburn hair, I saw that the olive-skinned man was leaning in the doorway, arms crossed over his chest.

"I am inside," Lysander chuckled, his voice cool and somehow *empty*. He shifted, head tilting in my direction again.

God, he had to know I was here.

Were they about to jump me?

Better they do it now, rather than waiting until my heart exploded in my chest and caused me to bleed all over their rented porch.

"Lys..." Nyko's voice was a warning. It seemed to me as if he was preaching caution to his friend.

Caution about *what*?

"I know." Warmth flooded Lysander's voice as he laughed softly under his breath, posture relaxing as he shoved his hands into his pockets. "I was just kicking myself for leaving these doors unlocked when we left. It could've been a real problem if someone had broken in."

The fist closed around my heart loosened just enough so that I didn't feel like I was about to have a heart attack.

He really thought that?

And neither of them knew I was here?

Really?

"I was thinking of spending some time out back tonight," Lysander went on, and the invisible fingers in my chest clamped down once again.

If he did that, what in the *world* would I do?

I couldn't hide from them all night.

Nyko shifted, leaning more of his weight on the door. Even from here, I could see in the dim light coming out of the great room that his attention was riveted on the other man.

"Why?" he asked, voice cold. "What would that achieve? You want us to end our trip earlier than intended because you got distracted?"

Lysander's shoulders hunched as if he'd been reprimanded.

I didn't understand.

Why did it matter if he wanted to be outside instead of in the house? He wasn't their pet dog who would keep the neighbors up all night or kill the local cats.

"Next time," Nyko went on, as another head appeared over his shoulder.

Azriel, my mind supplied when I saw the messy dark hair and bright smile.

"Dude, get off the porch," he laughed, his attention on Lysander. "You're being weird. And Rhys won't let us eat until you're inside, so come *on*."

Lysander shifted again, and I could *swear* his eyes found mine in the darkness.

But then he looked away as if he'd seen only shadows.

"Next time," he sighed, at last, dropping his shoulders and walking to the great room door. "This only works so many times a year, Nyko. You know I'm *itching* for-"

"The whole world knows you get itchy for it," Azriel cackled, throwing an arm over the blonde's shoulder. "Don't be so touchy."

They disappeared into the house, leaving Nyko in the doorway to stare at absolutely nothing.

So why was he still there?

The man shifted his weight with a sigh, and I saw him shake his head before he stepped back. "How reckless," he murmured and shut the great room door with a click.

I waited, counting to thirty under my breath before crawling out from underneath the sofa and to the door. Every noise had me flinching, and it seemed like an eternity before I made it to the door and slipped out, ready to disappear and never *ever* make such a stupid mistake again.

Monsoon Moon was just as empty as I'd thought it would be. The coffee shop would be closing soon at nearly nine p.m., and usually the regulars had filtered out by eight forty-five.

Tonight, however, there was absolutely no one. Not that shocking, since it was eight thirty-two, but…

I was just jumpy. Ever since leaving the house where the four guys were staying, I'd been looking over my shoulder like one of them would jump out and shout *boo*.

Or worse.

Stab me in the back.

As usual, Marianne stood leaning against the counter, writing something in a small notepad decorated with autumn leaves.

I watched her, standing back from the counter with one hand in my pocket and feeling entirely too exposed.

Calm down, Will, I told myself silently. *It was a close call, but you're fine.*

I…was fine, right?

Nyko's words whispered through my brain: *How reckless.*

But he couldn't have been speaking to *me*.

No way. If he'd known I was there, he would've done something. He would've helped Lysander tackle me and-

"You're here late, Willow."

The use of my full name snapped me out of my thoughts, and I opened my eyes to look at the owner of *Monsoon Moon*.

She didn't offer more than that, her hip pressed to the counter and her hand unmoving with its grip on the pink pen.

"You know, I bet you'd make a lot more money if you stayed open later," I told her dryly, a wry frown touching my lips.

Any concern in her face vanished, turning quickly to annoyance.

She didn't like me. Marianne didn't dislike me exactly either. Not to my knowledge, anyway, but that didn't mean much.

Opinions of me in Scheffield were never that high.

"If you just want some coffee, you can have it on the house," Marianne went on without answering my question. "I have too much left over, and it seems like you're my last customer tonight."

She looked me over, hesitated, then went on. "You all right? You look like you've seen a ghost."

"I'm fine," I dismissed, making my way to the counter.

"Yeah, coffee is fine. So long as you can dump enough cream in it to make me forget what I'm drinking."

"You got it." She turned away from me, swiping a plastic cup from the stack on the counter, and set it under the coffee machine. With a few taps of her fingers, the dark brown liquid began pouring from the machine into the cup, sloshing around and creating the only noise in the shop aside from the low *whoosh* of the fans overhead.

"Autumn is kind of late this year, huh?" I said conversationally, mind elsewhere. "Normally, it's colder than this by now."

"I was just telling Harold that earlier," Marianne agreed, naming her husband, who wanted nothing to do with the coffee shop and was thrilled to stay at home and parent their kids. "I hear it's supposed to storm most of next week, too."

Autumn storms weren't noteworthy, but the news made a smile touch my lips. I *loved* storms. Inclement weather was one of my favorite things about the season.

Until snow happened, anyway, since I wasn't a fan of snow.

The bell on the door chimed, making both Marianne and I turn.

"Welcome to *Monsoon Moon,*" the older woman said, her eyes crinkling in a smile at the two men who walked in.

My eyes narrowed, and I looked away almost immediately. While the two middle-aged men weren't *strangers,* they were a bit on the strange side.

Both of them owned a house near the river. According to my mother, they'd inherited it from their father even though neither of them had any interest in returning to the area as adults. Supposedly, a few people-Marianne included-had tried to buy the fifty-acre property from them more than once, but the men always turned it down.

A family heirloom, they always explained with apologetic

smiles and hands raised in surrender. *It's all we have left of Grandpa.*

Even still, they barely spent any time here. And never on any kind of schedule. A few times a year, the brothers would show up, hang out in town for a few weeks, then go back to....wherever they lived.

I'd never had any cause to get to know them, and the Deerling brothers had never spoken to me, either.

Until now, apparently.

The older man, David, looked at me and smiled. The look was unpleasant and only served to highlight his sweat-shiny face and thin lips. "You're Willow Carlysle, right?" he greeted, shoving his hands in his pockets.

The younger, taller brother ran a hand through greasy black hair, crossing immediately to the counter to lean on it and say something to Marianne.

"Yeah." I hadn't realized he knew my name, but I didn't bother to be polite in my answer.

And I certainly didn't *ask*.

"I know your mother. She and her church group helped us out a few years ago," David went on *as if I cared to know*.

"Cool," I replied, glancing back to see if my coffee was ready.

Marianne had apparently forgotten about it and laughed at something the younger brother-Donald-had said.

Was it just me, or did she look just as uncomfortable as I felt?

Her laugh didn't seem real, and the smile on her face had gone plastic.

"A real shame about that girl, Ashley." David's words caused me to stiffen, and I stared at him as if he'd grown a second head.

"What did you say?" I asked, my words a mumbled half-whisper.

"That was her name, right?" He walked past me to join

his brother at the counter, shrugging off my shock. "There hasn't been a reported murder here in..." He traded a look with Donald. "Thirty-something years."

Donald nodded his agreement. "Can't believe what happened. My friend at the police station said she'd been *stabbed.*" His eyes flicked to mine, then to Marianne's.

As if he wanted to see our reactions.

My eyes narrowed slightly.

No details of the murder had been released, save that she was killed, so this was news to me.

Stabbed?

"That's horrid!" Marianne put a hand to her mouth, drawing the attention of both brothers. "I just can't believe it. Poor Ashley. She was just about done with college. She wanted to be a nurse, you know. It just seems so unfair."

"An ER nurse," I corrected, not thinking about my words. "She wanted to work at the County Hospital to try and make things better for everyone."

"Tragic." David tossed a pained smile my way that didn't even come close to reaching his eyes. "I can't believe what happened. Poor girl." He stuffed a ten in the tip jar and took the hot coffee that Marianne held out for him.

"Thank you, Marianne," Donald put another ten in the jar, saluting her with his own cup. "We just got in a few days ago, so I expect we'll be back at least three more times." He chuckled. "No coffee in Chicago is anything like yours."

Chicago.

Weren't the men I'd met yesterday from Chicago as well?

That was a weird coincidence, for sure.

The two men left, going to their SUV with its tinted windows that screamed *bad guy*. My mom had told me once that they'd gotten countless tickets for that amount of tint on their windows, but the brothers always just laughed and paid the money without complaint.

They were *that* well off, apparently.

Must have been nice.

"How strange," Marianne murmured, setting my coffee on the counter.

"What? Them? They're always weird," I muttered, wrapping my fingers around the warm plastic.

"Yes, but…" She shook her head. "I've just never seen them here at this time of year, is all. My sister told me they've sworn off coming here in the fall since the storms are so frequent that the trip is never fun."

"They *drive* the whole way?" That seemed unnecessary. If they had so much money, why not just fly?

She nodded. "Donald doesn't do so good on planes, I hear."

"I don't like them." I didn't like anyone, but I *especially* didn't like them.

Especially with the mental images they'd given me tonight of Ashley being *stabbed*.

I really, really had not needed that in my brain.

"Have you heard from Ashley's mom?" Marianne asked when I was already halfway out the door.

Hesitating, I mulled over my thoughts. "No," I said finally, giving her the truth.

I'd been too afraid to call *her*, and she had not reached out to me.

Did she even want to?

Did she blame me, for some reason, for what had happened to Ashley?

"She's inconsolable," Marianne sighed, picking up her pen once more. "Rightfully so. No mother should have to bury her child. But I heard she had to be taken to the hospital when the detectives told her what happened."

I bit my lip, sawing on it almost painfully. "It's not fair," I murmured at last. "Ashley didn't deserve it. She was a really, *really* good person." She knew that, of course. Everyone knew how great Ashley was.

So what had she done to deserve *this*?

"I think I'll go on and close up." Marianne set the pen down on the counter. "I doubt I'll get any more customers tonight. Do you want anything to eat before you go?"

"No, that's okay," I promised, surprised at her sudden consideration for my well being. "I'm just going to go home and eat leftovers."

No matter my protests, somehow I still left *Monsoon Moon* with a bag full of this morning's donuts and fourteen cookies that smelled like the best things ever baked.

CHAPTER SEVEN

AS IF MARIANNE'S question had been an omen, knocking on my door in the morning had me stumbling out of bed to answer the door, still half-asleep.

When I opened the door to greet her, apologies and confusion on my lips, it occurred to me that I'd never seen a person look *worse* in my life. Even though it had only been four days since Ashley's death, this woman looked like she hadn't slept or eaten in *months*.

Puffy-eyed and tight-lipped, Ashley's mother, or Mrs. Bellflower as I'd always addressed her, looked as if she was fighting the battle not to cry and losing.

"Oh." I breathed, hand tightening on the door. "Mrs. Bellflower. I'm umm-"

"I didn't mean to wake you up." Her voice was hoarse like she'd spent the night crying.

If I had to guess, she'd spent more than the night doing so.

"No, it's okay. I wasn't really sleeping," I lied, stepping back to usher her into the apartment.

Not for the first time, I considered that all of Ashley's things were here, and at some point, I was sure her parents would want them *back*.

She chuckled unconvincingly, the sound like rocks

grating in her throat as Mrs. Bellflower walked inside and went to sit primly on the couch. She clasped her knees with her hands, fingers trembling with the effort of holding herself together.

"Can I…get you anything?" I whispered, finally remembering to close the door. I hovered around her, mentally cringing at the state of the apartment.

Not that it was any different than usual. She'd been here before and seen us at our worst after one of Ashley's parties, where she still had friends and clothes draped over the living room like decorations.

"No." She stared at her hands, not looking anywhere else. "Well…yes."

When she didn't continue, I sat down opposite her on the matching, if more worn, couch. "Something out of Ashley's room?" I prodded, wondering if she was here for my roommate's belongings.

Mrs. Bellflower lifted her head to look at me blankly. "When was the last time you saw her?" she asked as if she hadn't heard my question at all.

I blinked, taken aback, but recalled the memory. "About twenty-four hours before the cops found her," I admitted. "Can I ask, do they know or suspect-"

"They have no idea." Her voice turned sour, instantly. "They suspected her ex for a bit. But we all know he wouldn't do something like this."

Silence fell over us again, causing my stomach to churn in discomfort.

I wasn't good at this.

But then again-was *anyone* good at this?

"So now they have no idea. Any evidence was washed away by the river. And they have no idea what kind of weapons could have caused her injuries."

"I heard she was stabbed," I blurted out before I could stop myself.

Mrs. Bellflower laughed, though it came out as a sob instead. "Stabbed, cut, burned..." Her eyes swam with tears that wavered, then fell down her cheeks to carve already-visible tracks in her makeup. "I just don't understand it, Willow. Who would *do* this to her? Did she have any new friends or a new boyfriend-"

"I don't know," I admitted, the worry and sadness churning my gut, turning to something darker and *ugly*.

Bile rose in my throat, and I fought to swallow it down.

I wished I had the answers to give her.

"Of course not." Her voice dulled, eyes narrowing to pained slits. "I was hoping you'd let me in her room? I wanted to bring some things of hers home."

Already I was nodding, and I jumped to my feet. "Of course, Mrs. Bellflower. If there's anything I can help you find–"

She rose, and nearly collapsed. Concerned, I surged forward to catch her by the elbow, not letting go until I was reasonably sure she wouldn't keel over on my floor.

"Thank you, Willow." Without another look in my direction, she walked carefully down the hallway, her hand on the wall as if she needed it to brace her, and disappeared into Ashley's room.

What was I supposed to do *now*? It seemed incredibly rude to do something normal like turn on the TV or make breakfast. It was...disrespectful, in a way. Though, I wasn't sure why.

I should leave. That would be the best thing so that I could give Ashley's mother her space.

Quietly as I could and just as quickly, I changed out of my pjs and instead into a pair of sweatpants and a t-shirt, then snagged my hoodie off of the white door where it hung. I'd go to work. The unpaid, animal-centric side of it, anyway.

Surely walking the humane society's dogs would be better than staying *here.*

Anything would be better than staying here when it came down to it.

Once I was ready to leave, I stopped to hover in front of Ashley's door, unsure of what to say. "I'm...leaving," I said, at last, the words falling flat. "I'm going to-to work."

I could only see Mrs. Bellflower's shaking shoulders in the mirror, enough to know she was sitting on Ashley's bed.

I didn't need to see more than that.

"There's a spare key on the table," I went on, making a mental note to lay it there. "Just lock up...when you leave. But take your time, please." No way would I be rushing her out.

But I couldn't stay here either when the whole situation screamed at me to *get out.*

She didn't respond, but that was all right. Swiftly I put the spare key on the table and slipped on my sneakers, out the door, and to my car in record time.

With my mind on her and the way her face had looked from all the crying she'd been doing, I barely noticed the details of my drive to the humane society.

How could I? Guilt and frustration battled for space in my head, and all I wanted to do was simultaneously run away and grab the strangers to shake them until some piece of evidence fell out.

Finally pulling into the empty parking lot, I rested my head on my steering wheel with a sigh. "You've got to stop getting so in your head about this, Will," I told myself softly. "Stop it, or you're seriously going to drown in it."

My roommate had been *murdered.*

How in the world was I supposed to do more than the police could? Hadn't last night proved that I wasn't cut out for the private investigator title?

But then...

I hadn't been caught, *had I*? I'd gotten away just fine even though it had been a close call.

I'll do better next time.

The sudden thought sent a tremor of fear down my spine and had my eyes widening.

Next time?

Since when had I decided there would *be* a next time?

Harshly, I thrust my door open, wanting to get away from this train of thought as quickly as possible.

I was here to walk dogs. Not deal in existential crises.

To say that my coworkers were surprised to see me was an understatement. The front desk lady for today, Sarah, gazed at me with open-mouthed surprise and reminded me that I had the day off.

"I'm volunteering," I replied with a sigh, fixing her with a hard look from my blue-grey eyes. "Just here to walk a few of the dogs."

She studied me for a moment, then closed her mouth with an almost audible snap of her teeth before speaking again. "You can take the *monsters* you coaxed in for a stroll, then. If you're up to it," Sarah informed me. "Joel can't handle 'em. Says they act cagey around him."

According to Joel, *every* dog was cagey. I took that with a grain of salt.

"They passed their vet check okay?" I asked, going past her to where a sheet on the desk listed which dogs had been taken out and for how long.

She nodded. "Purebred German Shepherds. Both of them. Vet was surprised. She checked 'em for chips but couldn't find anything. Says they're in real good shape, and it's a surprise they were dropped off like that."

I shrugged my shoulders noncommittally. I'd been doing this job for two years now. Nothing surprised me about how people treated their animals.

"They in quarantine?" I assumed. Most dogs stayed there until we had a good idea of their do's and don'ts.

She nodded a few times, then went back to her phone.

I didn't blame her. Once I had the dogs a suitable distance away, I had every intention of pulling out my own phone and finding some amusing-if-trivial-article to take my mind off of everything else.

If the *cagey monsters* allowed it, anyway.

One look at the dogs in their quarantine kennel had me smiling, and some of the tension lessening in my shoulders and neck. "Well, don't you two look handsome?" I cooed, kneeling down outside their cage and holding my hands up for them to smell. It was a good thing they hadn't bitten anyone and had apparently calmed down for their exam.

Not that I'd worried about them. Most dogs were understandably upset when they got here. It was completely natural for two dogs tied to a pole, for who knows how long, to react out of instinct instead of trusting the strange humans who had come to see what was going on.

The female nosed my hand, teeth daintily grazing my skin in a way that made me think she would be the mouthier of the two. The male, smaller than her and timid, crept toward me with wary eyes and alert, radar-like ears that swiveled towards the sound of my voice.

"I'm in love," I told them, glancing at the paper on their kennel door to see what names the shelter had given them.

Frank and Angie?

Dreadful. The *worst* names I'd ever heard by a mile, that was certain.

"Well, I guess I should've stuck around if I wanted any input, huh, guys?" I sighed, deftly opening the kennel and slipping inside so that I could clip leashes to the collars they wore.

The scent of bleach tickled my nose unpleasantly. Silently, I was glad that I'd come when I had so that hopefully, the smell of *cleaner* could air out a little before these guys had to come back to their temporary home.

They'll get adopted, I told myself as the two dogs waited at the open gate. They'd been trained, obviously, to not pull me to hell and back as soon as the kennel gate was open.

And they were *gorgeous.*

Cleaner and no longer cowering against a lamp pole, I was able to appreciate the two dogs more closely.

Siblings, maybe? Both of them were more black than tan, with almost completely dark furred faces and the same large ears.

The only thing that might keep these two from getting a new home was their size. Not that it was their fault, but the shepherds were *huge.*

Sarah glanced up from her phone when I walked out, a look of surprise flitting over her face. "You're taking them *both* out?" she barked, surprised at my actions and sounding not at all approving of it.

"Don't see why it's an issue," I replied in a clipped tone.

"They're a lot to handle," she informed me. "What if they get the notion in their head to run off? You'll just be a flea at the end of that leash, if you can even hold on."

I shrugged one shoulder, not wanting to continue the conversation.

I wanted *out* of here. I wanted to be free of the oppressive sounds of the humane society that normally served as a kind of background noise that didn't bother me whatsoever.

Today, the din of barking and sharp voices was too much. It pounded against my ears, threatening to overwhelm me before I could get out the door.

Distantly, I wondered if Ashley's mom was still at the apartment.

That thought was unwelcome. I was *working.* Not for money, but still. These dogs deserved my full attention. They needed me to be present, not just off in my own head.

"Come on, kids," I sighed under my breath, shouldering the front door of the building open. "Let's go see what kind of trouble you both can find."

Hopefully, none, since I had a feeling Sarah's words about these dogs having the ability to drag me all over town with ease wasn't much of an exaggeration.

CHAPTER EIGHT

WAS it perhaps a reflection of my secret inner goth girl that I preferred to walk the humane society's dogs around the boundary of the cemetery?

I liked to think so. Like some part of the riverside area called to a part of my soul that had never gotten over raccoon-like eyeliner and handmade arm warmers that I'd worn so often in high school.

Certainly, my inner thirteen-year-old who'd tried to make edgy social media nicknames for herself loved the fact that I got to skirt the edge of gravestones and mausoleums on my walk with dogs that probably didn't give a damn *where* I took them, so long as I got them out of their smelly, chemical-laden kennels.

Today, however, my inner Wednesday Addams had betrayed me.

The usually empty cemetery was, to put it simply, *not* so empty. Though few people were buried on this side of town, a car sat parked on the long, winding drive, and two men stared down at a grave I didn't have any hope of reading from where I stood thirty yards away.

"Well, this was a bad idea," I told the German Shepherds, wishing that they had a speck of protection training in them so that I could set them loose on the two familiar strangers.

Only two, though, I thought slowly, eyes taking in the details of Rhys's and Nyko's backs.

What were they doing here? A lesser-known, small cemetery in a dead-end town seemed a strange place for anyone to go unless they had ties here.

Frankly, any cemetery seemed like a weird place to seek out unless a person sought out creepy haunted locations and local urban legends.

Of course, I was one of those people who paid exorbitant prices just to 'ooo' and 'ahhh' over tour guides trained to tell partly true legends with flourishes and hushed voices to make them more dramatic.

And I was damn proud of it.

Had I ever seen signs of the supernatural before?

Not a chance.

Did I expect my soul to leave my body as I wondered how I could get out of here without being seen?

Abso-fucking-lutely.

At the very least, they hadn't noticed me yet. And if it was just the two of them, I could probably go back the way I came with minimal issues.

Thank God for hoodies and the ability to use my hair like a curtain.

Transferring the leashes to one hand, I pulled my hood up over my head and turned, preparing to go right back out the stone gate from whence I came.

Well, until I saw who stood there.

Lysander leaned against one stone column, eyes fixed on the ground, scuffing his sneaker-clad foot along the grass. As if he just *happened* to stop at that spot, blocking my way out was simply a bonus.

Azriel leaned against the other column, completing the look of two non-stone gargoyles guarding my exit.

Would one of them growl at me that I could not pass, too?

Or would they just stand there silently until I got too close to get away from them?

They had no reason to think I was suspicious, *right*? It wasn't like they'd caught me the night before, and I hadn't given them any indication of suspicious intent.

"What kind of *normal* tourists go to a local cemetery?" The words were out before I could stop them, and I'd never in my life wanted to strangle myself so badly as I did at that moment.

Lysander glanced up as if noticing me for the first time, and his eyebrows rose by increments as he looked me over.

And then, because my mouth hadn't gotten me in enough trouble, I plowed on ahead. "Seriously-this is creepy. You guys aren't from here, and it isn't like this cemetery is on any kind of map."

Damn, I was on a winning streak today, apparently. Not only had I questioned their actions, but I'd also insinuated that they were creepy.

Which, to be fair, they totally were.

"Who walks *dogs* in a cemetery?" Lysander asked slowly in a measured, neutral voice. "Those yours?" He nodded at 'Frank' and 'Angie.'

"No." A bit of honesty probably wouldn't make much of a difference, especially since the dogs showed no indication of pouncing on the strangers for their transgressions. "I work at the humane society. I'm just walking them."

That was me—just a pitiful, law-abiding dog walker.

"I want them." Azriel's announcement was bold, and his voice was full of goodwill as he walked towards me and held his hands out for the dogs to sniff.

I watched, teeth in my lower lip, and couldn't decide if I wanted the dogs to play nice or bite off his fingers.

Instinctively, I looked over my shoulder towards the other two and found them in the same place as before.

"They don't care that you're here." Azriel hummed the words as if in answer to my question.

I was sure I hadn't asked one.

"They barely care that *we're* here. They're in the middle of an important conversation, and since Lys and I are just along for the ride...." He shrugged his shoulders and knelt down, hands still outstretched. "What are their names?"

"They don't really have names. Not good ones, anyway. Frank." I pointed at the male, who didn't respond to the alias. "And Angie. That's what the staff decided to call them."

"Those are dreadful," Azriel chuckled. "Honestly, some of the *worst* I've ever heard."

"I agree," I said, jumping on his statement. "Who names dogs some of the *worst* people names ever?"

He was silent, enraptured by the dogs, who, in turn, seemed smitten with him.

When I looked up, eyes stinging from the cold breeze that gusted around the clearing, I found Lysander's eyes still firmly fixed on me.

My heart raced in my chest, skipping a few beats before settling in a too-quick rhythm. "What?" I demanded, meeting his eyes. "Why are you staring at me?"

Unblinking, he raised one shoulder and let it fall. "Just thinking."

"About *what*?" What in the world could he be thinking of that required him to study me like....like a piece of a puzzle he couldn't understand.

"You."

His answer wasn't what I expected and it didn't at all make me feel better.

"Would you like to know why they dragged us here?" Lysander went on, and I didn't miss the questioning, warning glance that Azriel shot his way when he thought I wasn't looking.

I took my time in answering, not wanting to seem too eager. “Sure,” I agreed. “If you want to tell me.”

“Say please.” His voice remained calm and expectant.

I blinked. “Excuse me?”

“If you’re asking me for something…say please. Surely you’ve got *manners*, don’t you, Will?”

As I stared at him, I wondered where the sweet, good-humored man from the coffee shop had gone. Where had the blue-eyed, always smiling male who hadn’t even *noticed* when I’d picked his pockets run off to, and what was this creature that had replaced him?

“Manners are not my strong suit,” I stated, hands tightening on the leash loops that I still held.

If my nerves showed in the way my knuckles were white against the blue nylon of the leashes, none of us remarked on it.

"How, coincidental," Azriel commented from where he sat with the dogs, scratching both of their chests and causing Frank's tongue to loll in delight. "Manners aren't something that Lys is good at either."

I glanced between him and Lysander, who didn't react to the statement. Then I swallowed and went on. "If you don't want to tell me, that's fine. I probably don't need to know, and I doubt it's worth it if I have to curtsy and say, '*please,* milord. Won't you tell me-'"

"They're looking for someone they knew," Lysander interrupted, reaching up to comb blonde curls back from his face. "Someone that they…." He trailed off and shared a look with Azriel that I didn't bother to try to decipher.

I understood nothing about these men. That was obvious enough.

"So, how do I adopt these dogs?" Azriel went on, acting as if Lysander's weirdly cryptic statement hadn't just happened.

"Someone like a friend?" I asked, my curiosity getting the better of me.

The blonde snorted derisively and shook his head. "Not in the very least."

"So....like an enemy then?"

He blinked and knelt down to let Angie sniff his hand. "Something like that. But not quite in the way you'd think."

"And...what is 'the way I think' exactly, Lysander?" It was the first time I'd said his name out loud. The first time I'd allowed it to roll off of my tongue.

Lysander. Original. Strange. It seemed like a name from another time and place, rather than boring old Michigan.

In fact, all of their names were like that.

His gaze flickered, a strange light brightening those baby blues before they darkened once more. All that over the way I said his *name*?

Surely it was something else. Like the way, Azriel elbowed him in the side and nearly knocked his friend off balance.

The wind picked up around us, blowing my shoulder-length auburn hair into a whirlwind around my head. I closed my eyes against the stinging cold, hands still tight on the dog's leashes.

"An enemy implies...equal footing, I suppose," Azriel commented absently. "Someone who you hold respect for. The man whose grave they're spitting on? He was more like a parasite to them and our uncle."

"A pest," Lysander agreed. "Vermin, I would say."

"I get it," I told him flatly, drawing his gaze once more. "Really. I don't need twenty synonyms for a parasite to understand-"

"And I don't need that mouth of yours going off on me for no reason," Lysander cut in smoothly.

"No, but you kind of like it," his friend hissed teasingly.

I looked between them, utterly confused. "So...if it's someone they don't like, why are they visiting his grave?"

"Because I wasn't metaphorical about the *spitting*," answered the brunette sweetly. "And you never told me how I could adopt Frank and Angie."

I grimaced at the terrible names. "The humane society is a mile and a half *that way*." I pointed back behind me, gesturing with a flick of my fingers. "There's a big sign. You can't miss it, I promise."

"So, what's your *real* job?" That was Lysander again, reminding me of his presence in the worst way possible.

"That is my real job," I laughed briefly, tucking my hair behind my ear before another gust of wind could blow it into my mouth.

"No, that's called a hobby." His voice was mockingly patient, and I itched to punch the dismissive smirk off of his face. "What do you do for *money*?"

What the *hell*?

How was he going to sit here and rightfully assume that working at the humane society didn't net me enough money to live?

How would he even *know* something like that?

"It's...my real job," I mumbled, unsure of what to say and very aware of the fact that my face was probably starting to redden in confusion and embarrassment.

No one, not even my mother, had questioned my words when I'd said that I worked full time for the humane society.

So, where did Lysander get off in questioning me like this?

God, I was certain I'd never been so irritated with someone in my life.

And extremely intimidated at the same time.

"Is it?" He tilted his head to the side. "Because I had a friend who volunteered at a shelter in Chicago. He told me that the employees barely made enough to cover extra expenses, let alone rent a two-bedroom apartment and buy coffee all the time."

"Well, maybe Chicago's-" I broke off, the rest of his sentence sinking in. My heart pounded in my chest, making my panic known to me and, by how loudly it thundered in my ears, probably the rest of the county as well. "What did you...say?" I whispered, unable to properly voice the question.

Azriel had gone still. One of his hands lay against Frank's shoulder, but the man stared at me with rapt attention.

On the other hand, Lysander fixed me with the same dismissive look that I might give a child who I didn't particularly like. "I don't think I stuttered," he pointed out. "And I don't think you have a hearing problem."

A two-bedroom apartment.

Exactly the kind I lived in.

"How....how do you know what kind of apartment I live in?" I mumbled through suddenly dry lips.

"Maybe I broke in while you were working and went through your things." His words were just as soft as mine, but it wasn't fear that quieted his tone.

No. There was nothing *nervous* or *intimidated* about him—just cold certainty.

"No, you didn't."

What was going on? Had he *really* broken in at some point and gone through my shit?

Just like I'd done, or attempted to do, at their place?

Like whipping off a mask, his face changed. His eyes brightened, and a sweet, almost-meek smile curled over his lips. "I'm only playing, Will," Lysander chuckled in the same kind of voice I'd heard in the coffee shop. "Who does shit like that? Breaking and entering just to go through your bags or drawers?" he shook his head. "I was just trying to mess with you."

The fist around my heart loosened slightly, no longer trying to squeeze the life out of me. "Just messing with me?" I repeated dryly. "Who does *that*?"

"Him." The new voice startled me, and I dropped the leashes as I whirled around to see both Nykos and Rhys standing a few feet behind me, the former with his hands in his pockets and looking up at the cloudy sky. "You shouldn't let him get to you like that," Rhys advised mildly while Nykos's mouth curved into an unfriendly smirk towards the clouds. "You make it easy for him to toy with you however he likes. He'll get bored eventually."

He said it as if I should worry. As if Lysander getting bored with tormenting me would be some kind of *problem* for me.

I saw it as a win. I didn't want their attention, nor their interest.

"I won't get bored." Lysander's voice was warm and confident from behind me. When I peeked over my shoulder, remembering the dogs, I found that both Lys and Azriel held a leash, and neither looked displeased by it.

Neither did the dogs.

"You will," Nykos disagreed, clicking his tongue in disapproval at the other's words. "You always get bored."

"You always say you won't," added Azriel, causing Lys to scowl. "Hey, Rhys? We need dogs, right?"

"No," answered Rhys flatly. "We do not need-"

"Uncle thinks we need dogs," the smiling brunette went on, interrupting Rhys like he hadn't spoken.

I was grateful that their conversation had turned from me and moved to look at my charges again.

And caught Lysander's stare, which was fixed directly on my face.

My own eyes narrowed sharply, a challenge that I didn't want to voice. *I'm not afraid of you*, I wanted to say. But those words wouldn't be true.

Still, I wanted him to think that he couldn't shake me.

Even though it was pretty obvious I supposed that he *could.*

"I have to get going," I muttered, holding my hands out for the leashes. "If you really want to adopt them, I will tell you where the humane society is."

"We're not getting dogs," Rhys reminded me, his tone firm. "And if you really want dogs, you can get them back home."

"I don't know. Maybe you should lighten up," Nykos said, words slow and deliberate.

I didn't turn to see how Rhys responded, and I wiggled my fingers for the leashes that the men held. Azriel, the friendliest of the bunch, it seemed, placed the leash back on my hand with a kind smile and stood up to move towards the two men behind me.

Lysander stood, dusted off his knees, and held the blue nylon up in front of him.

Right in front of him.

It was apparent he was going to make me get the leash from him instead of holding it out so I could take it.

I hesitated, feeling a flash of fear that zipped up my spine like an unwelcome chill.

His smile warmed. "That's okay," he shrugged. "I can just come to you."

That was worse.

So much worse.

I watched with trepidation, my stomach in knots as Lysander crossed the grass between us to bring me Frank's leash.

Stop, I wanted to say, realizing again how much taller than me he was.

Then again, at five foot six inches, I didn't strike a very imposing figure.

"Here." He reached out for my hand, taking it in his, and

slipped the leash over my fingers and down to my wrist, where the other one rested. "Oh and, don't worry." He leaned down, lips close to my ear as I took a shuddering, fearful breath and willed my legs to *move.*

"I promise I left all of your things where I found them. And I didn't make much noise when I came to your apartment."

"What do you-"

"Otherwise, I might've woken you up."

My heart stopped in my chest. It had to have, with the way my ribs seemed to contract around it, and all of the air left in my lungs felt like it had been sucked out. "You were in my apartment."

"Your room could use a bit of tidying up," Lysander went on conversationally.

"You're just trying to get under my skin-"

"And I would not have taken you for a stuffed rabbit kind of girl."

Oh, God.

He had been in my room.

He'd broken inside, at some point, and gotten far enough that I hadn't even *known he was there.*

I didn't know what to do.

So I did the only thing I *could* do.

I power walked out of the cemetery, the dog leashes in my hand, and dragged both shepherds back towards the humane society before Lysander had the chance to say *anything* else.

And if I heard a chuckle behind me, or Azriel asking what my stuffed rabbit looked like?

Well, I pretended that I simply heard voices in the wind.

CHAPTER NINE

BY FAR, Mr. Ellison's house was one of the gaudiest I'd ever been in.

And as I'd stolen multiple times from Ms. Clutterbucker, that was saying something. She, at least, had a bit of taste when it came to how she decorated her lavish, luxurious house. Sure, it was jam-packed to the brim with weird cat statues made of jade and, in one room, a *giant* jade horse, but at least it was sort of fun to appreciate while I was there.

Ambiance, or whatever, was a powerful thing when I was pilfering enough petty cash and small items to make rent for the next few months.

And just how are we going to do that, Will? I asked myself silently, gazing at a painting of a *lawn gnome* on one wall.

A painting. For fuck's sake. More offensive still, the picture was a reproduction of the Delaware Crossing.

But with *lawn gnomes*.

Poor George Washington did not go to war so that some weirdo in the twenty-first century could reimagine him looking like a less blue papa smurf.

In retaliation, I dumped the batteries out of each and every one of his remotes and tossed them in my black backpack.

Having been here for a good twenty minutes, I had

already emptied his stash of half its cash, along with another few bills folded on the mantle.

It was amazing how loose rich people were with their money.

If I were ever rich, I'd have a safe. A *good* one.

While I couldn't speak for every other thief in the world, a safe definitely deterred me indefinitely. I had no desire to try breaking into one, only to leave my fingerprints everywhere and either fail or still be at it with a stethoscope and bobby pins when the homeowner returned.

No, thank you.

Which brought me back to my unexpected, insurmountable problem.

No matter how much I stole, within reason, I would not be able to cover the rest of the rent for my apartment.

Luckily, we'd paid up for the next two months. But even then, I would only be able to extend that by another month. Two, if I was fortunate.

So far this year, I was *not* incredibly lucky.

Mr. Ellison had been on my list for a while, truth be told. A county over from my own, his wealth that he'd inherited from his popcorn company made him a local legend.

So did his weird commercials where he called himself 'Cousin Eddy' and pandered his popcorn to the masses by promising it had that 'hometown taste, small-batch quality.'

Whatever that meant.

Personally, having tried his popcorn like everyone else in this town had at some point in their lives, I didn't see the big deal. It cost more, tasted sweeter than I preferred, and did *not* leave my fingers oily with butter.

I preferred movie theater style and wasn't satisfied if butter residue wasn't dripping out of the bag and into my microwave after heating it.

But more importantly.

Why *lawn gnomes*?

Dumping a jar of loose change and bills into my backpack, I sighed before setting it right back where I'd found it and shouldered my backpack.

It *jingled*. I jingled, thanks to the change, and I scowled at my own stupidity.

It was a damn good thing that Mr. Ellison would be gone for a few more days, and my car wasn't far. Otherwise, the jingling would've been a dead giveaway that I was carrying something weird.

And from there, a situation could very quickly devolve if someone found over two grand in cash in my backpack.

Thankfully the trip back to my car was uneventful, and I sighed with relief as I pulled away from the curb and out onto the highway. No one would remember a white sedan with a scuffed license plate-one I'd stolen from a junkyard car-when they were asked about the events of this night.

If Mr. Ellison even *noticed*. It was crazy to me how rich people threw their money around. More than once, the person I'd stolen from never made a police report or seemed to notice that they were hundreds of dollars less rich.

Didn't it matter to them?

It sure as hell mattered to me.

Unbidden, the idea of Lysander being in my apartment, pawing through my shit the same way I did to other people's houses, filled my brain. I shuddered, my hands tightening on the steering wheel as I passed the sign that marked the boundary between my town and Mr. Ellison's.

Lights illuminated my steering wheel and black interior, though I barely took any notice. With my mind too focused on Lysander, I found myself making the drive back without even turning on my radio or listening to an audiobook.

Had he really broken into my apartment?

At first, I'd assumed he had, and had gone home to tear apart the apartment to see if I could find *any* sign of his presence.

Surely I would have woken up to him, right?

There was no way I would've slept through his appearance.

....Right?

I shuddered, gloved fingers drumming out a rhythm on the steering wheel. I'd been so sure...but when I'd checked my Facebook later, I found that one of my profile pictures was one of Ashley and me from a few months ago, and I jokingly had my stuffed rabbit-the one I slept with and that Lysander had remarked upon-posed on my head for a laugh.

Had he broken in, or had it all been just a really good guess? He could've looked me up, and more than that, he could've easily just assumed my apartment had two bedrooms since they knew I'd lived with Ashley before she died.

The more I thought about it, the more I was willing to believe that I was just panicking over something that wasn't worth my fear.

Hadn't Rhys said Lysander *liked* to do shit like that? Hadn't he told me not to let it bother me?

But then again-why in the world would I take Rhys's word for *anything*. The silent, rude member of their little quartet barely seemed to know I was alive.

Though I supposed, better his silence than Nykos' dismissive sneers and taunting chuckles at my expense.

I wasn't sure what I'd done to them, but it was pretty evident that the two of them did *not* like me, nor did they have any desire to get to know me.

Which, at the end of the day, was absolutely fine with me.

As I passed the gas station and post office lights, I realized that I was rather hungry. It had been a while since I'd eaten. Breakfast, maybe? I scanned my brain and was embarrassed to discover that I hadn't eaten since the night before.

Whoops.

My stomach clenched, echoing that statement as it protested its emptiness.

Fine, fine, I thought to myself, making a split-second decision to go to *The Overlook* instead of stopping by *The Outlook.*

Sure, I couldn't get a table, but that didn't mean I couldn't just pick up a carry-out order.

Settling my car in the parking lot, I turned off the engine and thumped my head back against the headrest with a sigh.

I was *tired.* More than tired, really. I haven't gotten a good night's sleep since....

Since Ashley.

With that thought, I kicked the door to my car open, yanking my black gloves off as I did, and unzipped my hoodie to look more like a lazy millennial than a thief. With that done, I finger-combed my hair, threw my gloves on the floor in front of the passenger seat, and shut the door of my Sonata hard behind me.

As expected, *The Overlook* was packed. Most nights, it was like this.

But that was fine, since I rarely liked to eat *inside,* anyway.

Thankfully, the front entrance and benches that lined the walls were devoid of waiting people, though a wall of noise slammed into me the moment I pushed open the double glass doors.

Holy shit, was it always this loud? The noise pounded at my brain, laughter seeming to break through my eardrums to bitchslap my brain directly.

"Can I help you?" The hostess at the stand had seemingly appeared from nowhere and wore a very forced smile on her face. "You have a reservation, right?"

I shook my head, opening my mouth to speak, but she cut me off. "Then I really can't seat you. We're really busy-"

"No shit," I snapped, hating the harshness of my words. It wasn't *her* fault that situations like this made my ears bleed.

It wasn't her fault that I didn't like anyone enough to come here with a reservation.

Or vice-versa.

"I just...want to order carryout," I mumbled, looking away from her.

"What?" she nearly had to shout to be heard over the conversation.

"I'd just like to place an order for carryout!" I replied, speaking louder and stepping closer to the hostess stand.

"Oh!" The apprehension vanished from her face. "Yeah, we can do that. Just go to the bar." She gestured down a carpeted hallway. "And tell the bartender your order."

"Thanks!" I yelled again, but she was already turning away to face a customer that had come up to rudely touch her elbow to get her attention.

I didn't stand around. With long strides, I crossed the hard tile floor and moved onto the hallway's carpet, glad when a portion of the noise was muffled by the walls and no longer being in the big, open space of the main room.

The hallway itself was long, perfectly straight, and two open archways stood at attention on either wall. Through them, I knew, were private rooms for particular guests.

Not that I'd ever been in a group that had a private room. I wasn't even sure *how* one went about reserving one of the rooms. Did it cost extra?

As I walked, a semi-familiar laugh made me nearly trip. My stomach clenched as Lysander's husky laugh rolled through my brain, and I stopped walking.

Keep moving, I urged my body. *You really don't need to hear what they have to say.*

Or did I?

"I told him to calm down." Rhys's voice was sharp, but unmistakable. "This isn't Chicago. No one's going to clean up our *mess* except us."

"I think he was rather restrained, personally." I'd never heard such cruel humor in Azriel's voice, though I supposed I hadn't spoken to him enough to really *know* him.

Not like I wanted to know any of them. Especially after what had happened at the cemetery.

"Rather restrained for him is still more blood than I want to deal with right now," Nyko sounded humorous rather than dismissive.

But of course.

It was just *me* he didn't seem to like.

I couldn't help it. I stepped to one side of the hallway, glad for the little benches tucked into alcoves here for the first time. *The Overlook* had installed them a few years back as extra waiting areas, though they rarely used them unless the restaurant was full beyond capacity and needed the space.

I sat down now, curling my hands in my lap, and drew my legs up under me so I could tuck myself in the shadow of the hallway.

Hopefully, I could get away with it for a little while. Just long enough to hear what the four men were saying.

A waitress strode past, giving me a confused glance and shifting the tray on her arm. "Is everything okay?" she asked too loudly, causing me to wince.

I nodded vigorously and replied softly, "I just needed a few minutes away from my table."

Hopefully, they hadn't heard or at least didn't recognize the voice as *mine*.

This would be my best chance to learn more about why they were here.

Especially with them talking about a mess being *bloody*.

Could they be talking about Ashley?

She'd been stabbed repeatedly. That was *bloody*, and a mess. Had the four of them gone and tossed her body into the river?

This had to be my best chance to find out.

The waitress nodded, thankfully taking my words as the truth, and continued with her food-laden tray down the hallway. When I was sure she was gone, I focused my attention back on the room, leaning my head back against the wall behind me to try and hear them better.

"We can't stay much longer." That was Azriel again, though something in his voice made him sound like Lysander.

What a terrifying thought.

"No," Rhys mused, humming in agreement. "A few more days at the most. I worry about Uncle being alone back home."

"You know *they'll* be mad if we do this," Nyko pointed out.

"And you know we don't have any other choice." Rhys sounded weary as if this were an argument he'd had many times before. "We should've taken care of it before they left. But we didn't, and now look what washed up on the side of the river."

My heart sped up considerably in my chest, and I clenched the wooden bench below me.

So it was true.

They *had* to be involved in Ashley's murder.

Pulling away from the wall, I opened my eyes and immediately froze.

I wasn't alone on the bench any longer.

Lysander Ashford occupied the other side of it, sitting quietly with his hands clasped in front of him, thumbs twirling around one another.

"Strange, isn't it?" He asked, not bothering to glance up

at me. "All the things you can hear when you really shouldn't be listening."

Clenching the wooden bench under me, I fought not to waver under his attention.

"I don't know what you mean," I said, at last, unsure of *what* to do, exactly. "I'm just waiting for-"

"For your nose to get bitten right off for sticking it where it doesn't belong?" Lysander cut in. "Oh, I know. And haven't you heard, Will?" He suddenly slid closer to me on the bench and turned in a movement that was too fast for me to pull away from successfully.

Both of his hands slammed into the wall near my face, effectively caging me in and leaving me with nowhere to look except for his scarred yet handsome face. I flinched at the noise and his sudden closeness.

"Curiosity killed that cat." He leaned forward until I could feel his breath on my lips. Was he going to *kiss* me? "And I don't think any amount of satisfaction will bring this kitten back."

I stared at him, eyes wide, and couldn't help the shiver that ran up my spine and caused a visible tremor to run through me.

Visible, I knew, because when it happened, Lysander's blue eyes darkened, and a greedy, slow smile curled over his mouth. He leaned even closer, lips brushing mine in the smallest hint of a kiss. Where his mouth touched mine, my skin seemed to *burn*. What would it feel like, I wondered, if he pressed his lips to mine for real and kissed me like this, with me pinned against the wall and helpless?

"Get off of me," I whispered, reaching a hand up and pressing my shaking fingers cautiously to his shoulder as if even touching him there might burn me.

"Why?" He tilted his head to the side, not moving back even when I pushed at him. "You want to be near us *so badly*. Don't you?"

"No."

"No?" He parroted. "But you're here. *Here,* instead of where you should be. *Here,* listening to my pack discuss our business like it concerns *you."*

"But it does." The words were regrettably out of my mouth before I could stop to *think* and not say them at all.

"Oh?" He sounded incredulous and pulled away slightly. Was that unclenching of my stomach disappointment? No. Surely it was a relief that he was no longer so close. "Do go on, little cat."

I wasn't a cat, but I wasn't sure how much correcting I should be doing right now.

Not when he was here, like this. With the length of his warm body pressed nearly to mine and his arms caging me against the corner of the alcove.

"Ashley was my friend," I said in a voice that shook only slightly.

His eyebrows rose, inviting me to continue.

"I want-I *need* to know what happened to her." I forced some semblance of steel into my tone and prayed it worked. "It's not fair that she was killed. It isn't *right-"*

"Neither is breaking into our house."

My eyes widened.

So they knew.

His smile widened, amusement playing at his features. "Oh, Will," he chuckled softly. "Tell me you didn't *really* think we were unaware. Tell me you didn't think we didn't *know* you were on the porch. For how ineffective your hiding place was, you should've just come to the door, so I could hold it open for you."

I didn't want to answer that. But I couldn't help but ask, before I could think *not to.* "How did you know I was there?"

"Well." He drew back slightly, just enough to give me room to breathe. I was grateful and let out a sigh of partial relief. "Even if the house wasn't rigged with security cameras that connected to our phones..."

Damn. That was stupid of me not to have thought of *cameras.* Just because most people around here didn't use wifi security, that shouldn't have made me let my guard down.

"You switched the passports."

I blinked, confused. "What?"

"The passports in the bags you were pawing through." Oh, he was thoroughly amused now. It sang on his lips and in the way he tilted his head to the side. "You got scared and put them back in the wrong bags."

Damn.

That was undoubtedly a blow to my pride.

"Did you kill her?" I had no reason to dwell on my mistakes as a thief.

Lysander did not answer right away. He leaned away from me, gazing down the hallway towards another large room. "What if I did?" He asked at last. "What then? How do you think this would go if I *did*?"

"I..." I hadn't really thought of that. "You can't do anything to me in a crowded restaurant," I said in a bold rush. "Everyone can see-"

"No one is looking," he interrupted. I started to move-I just needed space away from this man who terrified me and...

And *exhilarated* me. There was something about him. Something more than his pretty face that had me wanting to ask him all kinds of things I shouldn't.

Don't you dare, I warned myself. *Not when he probably killed-*

"No," Lysander said, at last, interrupting my thoughts.

I blinked. "No?"

"No, darling Will. I did not kill your friend. My pack did not kill your friend."

"Then what–"

He slammed his hand against the wall again, causing me to flinch and the words to die in my throat. "I think it's time to go home. Don't you?" Lysander asked sweetly. "I've told you what you want to know. Now go *home*. And leave the police work to the people with guns and badges."

I considered not going. For a moment, I considered asking him again if he knew anything more about Ashley.

But then I looked at him.

His gaze held mine steadily. Bright blue, and…

Wrong.

There was something wrong behind those pretty eyes.

It terrified me.

It made every survival instinct inside my brain fire off all at once, and when he pulled away from me, I jumped to my feet without hesitation.

I didn't need to be told twice.

Without bothering to pick up anything for dinner, I *left*.

CHAPTER TEN

MY HEART DIDN'T CEASE POUNDING. NOT when I left the hallway and left Lysander behind me.

Not when I pushed out of the glass doors of *The Overlook,* ignoring the hostess when she asked me if I was all right.

It calmed down, finally, when I was sitting in my car with my hands on the steering wheel, trembling, and breathing in heavy pants of air to calm myself.

I did not kill your friend. My pack did not kill your friend.

Did I believe him?

I had no reason to.

And...no reason *not* to.

He's a stranger, Will, my rational brain reminded me. *And he isn't...right*.

Was he crazy? One of those unhinged psychopaths that my favorite late-night true-crime documentaries warned me about?

Or were all four of them something different altogether?

Pulling out of the restaurant parking lot, I was shocked when my stomach growled in discontent, reminding me that I had not eaten yet. And with no food in the car, plus an empty fridge back at the apartment, my prospects were starting to look a bit dismal.

There was always *Monsoon Moon.* It was only eight, and

if I looked pitiful enough, Marianne might fix me a sandwich.

It was better than nothing, wasn't it?

Sure, I would've preferred the lasagna that *The Overlook* was famous for, but that wasn't at all a possibility now.

Not when I was sure I couldn't step foot in there again until I knew Lysander's '*pack*' was back in Chicago.

Absently, I turned onto a side street, one that would take me in the proper direction of the coffee shop. Hunger was beginning to gnaw at my stomach and becoming a much more invasive sensation than it had a right to be when I was so freaked out.

With a frown still on my lips and my heart still beating too fast in my chest, I pulled into a parking spot with a sigh and rested my head on my steering wheel once the car was in park.

How in the world had my life gone from ordinary to...to *this* in just one morning.

I was no cop. Lysander was right about that.

Maybe I really should just-

My brain clamped down hard on that thought. If the police weren't going to find Ashley's killer, then I needed to. If only to give her memory some semblance of peace, and myself some quiet from these rolling, frustrating thoughts.

To my surprise, the coffee shop was empty again. A large, black truck sat in a parking spot at the end of the small building, but with its black tinted windows rolled almost all the way up, the only thing I could see was a curl of smoke from a lit cigarette that escaped the minuscule crack between painted glass and roof.

Marking it as strange, I shrugged the thought off and walked inside.

As per usual-especially for this late-Marianne was alone. She had been counting a stack of bills as I walked into the espresso-scented building. Her soft music was like background noise to my overworked brain.

When she glanced up, I smiled dully at her, glad for some semblance of familiarity even if I didn't particularly enjoy the company of most people in this town.

"Back again, Willow?" Marianne raised a brow. "You're not usually here this late so often."

She was right. I customarily came in before work or after a grand heist.

Well...that's how I liked to refer to them, anyway. Perhaps to other people, they weren't so grand in the long run.

"I'm having a rough week," I admitted, striding to the counter and dipping my head to look into the cold case. While it was mostly empty, a few danishes sat on their trays still. Worst case scenario, I could just take those home and go grocery shopping in the morning.

Marianne followed my gaze, her frown sympathetic. "Do you want something else?" she asked kindly. "I've actually got a few sandwiches leftover from about an hour ago. Some guy ordered them but never picked them up."

I perked up at the words, surprised and subtly delighted by them. "If it's not too much trouble?" I hinted. "What kind of sandwiches?"

"Ham and cheese on wheat. Standard for around here," she shrugged. "Here." She reached under the counter to where a mini-fridge sat, a place for her to keep to go orders whenever someone called them in.

When she reappeared, she held a wrapped sandwich in one hand and a water bottle in the other. "On the house," she added when I went to hand her my card.

I paused, befuddled at her actions. "Why?" I couldn't help but ask, wondering if my mother had anything to do with her sudden kindness towards me.

But...why would she? If anything, my mother was better

at convincing people that I was ungrateful, rude, and hostile towards her.

By all rights, I was sure half the town was under the impression I'd disowned my mom, judging by the way they acted towards me.

It sucked to be at odds with your mother when she worked *for* the town as the one and only city clerk and was known by almost everyone. Not to mention incredibly well-liked.

Marianne shrugged. "It'll go to waste anyhow. And you've been looking pretty miserable lately." She pushed the food towards me, and I took it, surprised but grateful. "I'm going to go on and close up," she added. "Do you want anything else?"

Hesitating, I tried to get a feel for my plans for the night. Did I *want* a big dinner?

No. Not when I still had seven cookies of Marianne's left at home.

I shook my head. "No. This is great, Marianne. I really appreciate it." I'd have to bring cash with me next time and slip a big tip into her gaudily decorated tip jar that perched on the counter.

"Go on and get home, Will," Marianne advised, leaning her hands on the counter and smiling wearily. Her grey-streaked blonde hair was falling from its ponytail, and I realized I'd never seen her look this tired.

"Have a good-" I began. Before I could finish my sentiment, however, rapping came from the drive-thru window.

She rolled her eyes. "I put a closed sign on that," she informed me. "They can just go-"

A louder *TAP TAP TAP* on the glass drowned out her words. Marianne groaned, throwing her head back with exasperation. "Fine!" she snapped irritably and waved a hand at me. "Scat," she ordered. "Before people see a car in the parking lot and I don't get to close up like I want."

Grinning despite myself, I dipped my head in a nod. "Good night," I called, turning and pushing out of the building as she stomped over to the drive-thru side of the shop.

Once in my car, I decided then and there that I was too hungry to eat at home. Sure, Marianne wanted me out of the parking lot, but I was sure that I could eat half of this sandwich in record time right now, then the rest of it when I got home.

She wouldn't mind. Probably.

As I ate, I glanced up towards the shop, hoping that Marianne hadn't had any trouble in getting her surprise drive-thru customers to leave. Sure, she was technically open until nine, but this was a small town. No one followed their own business hours here.

My eyes slid sideways, and on the last bite of the sandwich, I paused.

Wasn't...the black truck parked at the *end* of the building?

Well, it wasn't anymore. Now it was turned, and the truck had been backed up towards my car and the doors.

I could see the bed of the truck, visible because of the lowered tailgate, and my eyes refused to be drawn away from the interior.

Tools. Rope. A black bag that was barely visible in the shadow of the covered bed. Strange, but many things that people packed in the backs of their vehicles were of a questionable nature.

I myself had many questionable pieces of garbage and takeout containers in my own car that I was sure would cause most people to sneer and ponder my sanity.

But it wasn't the strange tools, the *rope,* or the bag that held my gaze and made the bite of my sandwich turn to ash in my mouth.

It was the sweater.

My roommate, Ashley Bellflower, had a very distinct taste in fashion. She'd loved things with insects on them and specifically had been head over heels for a honeybee cardigan she'd bought a few months ago. She'd waited and waited, moaning about how it wasn't cold enough yet for her to show it off.

But then, two weeks ago, she'd finally yanked it out of her closet and put it on, showing me first and posting it on her social media soon after. Anytime she'd gone out, she wore that cardigan over her outfit.

So why in God's name was it in the back of the black truck beside me?

My heart pounded in my chest, and I nearly dropped the corner of my sandwich before gulping water to clear my throat.

Could it have been a different piece of fabric?

Probably. *Maybe*. But.... I *knew* that print. It was so distinct, and not many people walked around wearing clothes with bees on them.

Maybe it was something else?

I couldn't help it. I couldn't just leave when that cardigan was taunting me as it was.

Please don't be hers, I begged, finding myself absolutely terrified.

Slowly I got out of my car, terrified that someone was about to jump out of the black truck and-

But no one did. As I walked closer, one foot in front of the other, I found that the engine was off, and there were no signs of anyone actually *in* the vehicle.

Which made no sense at all, but I pushed that to the back of my brain for the moment.

Curiosity killed the cat. And I don't think satisfaction will bring this kitten back.

Lysander's ominous words echoed loudly in my brain, causing my hands to shake.

What if he was here? What if he'd been lying to me, and they *had* killed Ashley?

Much too soon I was behind the truck, and only an arm's length separated me from the bag that the cardigan was spilling out of.

You don't know for sure, I reminded my terrified brain, even though this close, it was pretty damn certain.

That was Ashley's cardigan.

I reached forward with trembling fingers, unable to stop them from shaking, and pulled the piece of clothing gently from the black duffel bag that had half-obscured it from me.

Only when the whole thing lay in my hands, and the honeybees smiled up at me ridiculously from the cloth, I found my stomach turning with the desire to drop it.

Dried blood stained the fabric, soaking into the bees and making them dark, muddy red instead of bright yellow-orange.

"*Oh god,*" I whispered, eyes wide. I was paralyzed, unsure of what to do.

Until the lights in *Monsoon Moon* suddenly all flickered off.

I jumped at the sudden action, whirling in surprise to look at the darkened building.

There was no sign of Marianne. Had she closed that quickly?

But...no one had come around from the drive-thru, either.

I should leave, I reasoned, dropping the blood-stained fabric back on the truck bed. I could go to the police and tell them what I'd found. I just needed to take a picture of the license plate. I could do that, maybe take a quick snapshot of the sweater, and be *out of here.*

Scrabbling in my pocket, I nearly dropped my phone when I pulled it out. Cursing, I turned on the flashlight and turned back to the truck.

Only to find that I was no longer alone.

This time I *did* drop my phone with a gasp, the sharp crack against the pavement a not-so-great omen of what I might find when I picked it up again.

"*Shit!*" I gasped, surprised by a light that was illuminating my phone on the ground so I could pick it up.

"I'm so sorry." The familiar voice made me look up, phone in hand, and I shined the light at the person in front of me.

David Deerling stood there; eyes narrowed in confusion and sympathy. "I saw someone back here and thought..." He trailed off. "Are you all right?"

"I-I'm fine." Behind him, I saw his red car stopped in the middle of the parking lot, the light on and the door open. "What are you doing here?" I demanded.

His brows rose, then he sighed. "I can't find my brother," he admitted with a sound like resignation. "I saw his truck and I thought..." He gazed at the truck mournfully, eyes falling on the honeybee cardigan. "Oh, Donald," David breathed. "What did you *do*?"

"This..." I didn't know what I should say. Should I tell him that it was Ashley's?

Maybe...not. He looked mournful. Regret swam over his features, along with something darker. For all intents and purposes, he seemed truly shocked at what might have happened.

But I hadn't gotten this far by opening up to strangers and trusting their feelings.

Before I could speak, David straightened and looked towards the coffee shop. "Is Marianne in there?" he asked, eyes guarded.

Oh shit. I hadn't even thought about her when considering what I should do.

"I-I think she is," I stammered, my stomach clenching uncomfortably. "Shit. I'll call the police-"

"I already did," David interrupted. When I looked at him in surprise, the older man lowered his head. "My brother hasn't been okay lately," he said. "I called them when I pulled in. But I don't think he'd *hurt* her. He-*we*-like Marianne." He hesitated again, and looked at me. "Would you help me talk to him? I'm sure it's a misunderstanding, and I don't want Marianne getting the wrong idea *or* hurting him."

Hurting...*him*?

Something didn't seem right. Something in the older man's face.

As if his grief and fear were only skin deep.

If I went in there with him, would I come out still breathing?

Especially now that I all but *knew* his brother had done something awful to Ashley.

Don't do it, Will, my brain whispered in a voice that sounded suspiciously like Lysander's. *You'll regret it.*

Was Marianne worth my death?

No. Not when I found that I wasn't sure if I trusted that David had actually had called the police as he'd said.

"No," I said, shaking my head as my mind raced to come up with an excuse. "There are too many cars out here now. What if other people come here thinking the shop's open? You go, and let me turn people away until the cops get here."

Something flickered behind his dark eyes, turning my stomach even more.

But, to my astonishment, he nodded. "That's a good idea. Let me go in and talk to him, then. Tell the cops he's not a bad guy, okay? I don't want anyone getting hurt."

I did. If either of them had been the ones to hurt Ashley, I wanted them to hurt a lot.

But I nodded anyway and settled against the hood of my car. "Send Marianne out," I added as he walked to the glass doors and opened them.

I'd expected an argument, but he only nodded and walked into the dark coffee shop.

The moment he was gone, I was up and moving. I all but ran to my still-open car door, glad that I'd thought to leave it ajar.

I had to get out of here. Once seated, I didn't bother with my seatbelt. I threw my phone into the cup holder, forgetting all about the pictures I needed, and slammed the door closed.

Already three steps ahead in my plan, as I reached for the keys I'd left in the ignition and hit only empty air, my brain refused to register what was going on.

I reached for them again, and felt the empty space where they should have been.

Had they fallen?

I looked down, running my foot over the floorboard and feeling nothing.

Then, in the darkness of my car, I heard a telltale jingling from behind my driver's seat.

My eyes lifted slowly, dread slowing my actions, and the glint of metal caught my gaze in the mirror.

The keys were jingled again by the hand holding them, and I slid my eyes to the side to see Donald Deerling's unmistakable lopsided grin.

"Looking for these?" he asked, just as the car door opened and something sharp was plunged into my neck.

I screamed, or at least tried to, but the darkness rushed up to meet me quickly, and everything went black.

CHAPTER ELEVEN

VOICES WHISPERED FROM ABOVE ME, around me, and battered at my ears.

Curiosity killed the cat, Lysander whispered in my ear, though I knew that the echoing memory had to be just that.

And I don't think anything at all will bring you back, little cat.

His words rang in my head along with my own self-doubts and criticisms, chasing each other around in my brain until the words were all just slurred echoes that made no sense at all.

And then the cold crept in.

Little by little, the frigid chill found my fingers and wrapped around them, crawling like ivy up my arms and twining around my ankles. My back was freezing, and the cold seeped into me, trying to find my spine to turn it into the same ice I was sure coated my fingers.

Was I dead?

Slowly my eyes opened, the whispers finally filtering out through my ears and into the air beyond, leaving me solely with the oppressive silence in my head.

No. I was too cold to be dead.

Blinking, I stared up at the sky above me, watching the nearly full moon swell into focus high above my body.

I wasn't dead. But this wasn't right.

A breeze blew around me, sending soft murmurs through the air and ruffling my auburn hair. Finally, I curled my fingers, making sure they worked, and found cool, damp earth under my palms that fought to suck away as much of my warmth as it could.

I blinked again and sat up, shivering despite the hoodie I still wore and grimacing at the stiffness in my muscles.

How long had I been....?

The thought led me back into my memories, and I dragged the most recent ones to the surface.

I'd been at *Monsoon Moon.*

David's face as he looked back at me before stepping through the glass doors.

The smooth metal against my fingers as I'd brushed the place where my keys should've been in the ignition, ready for me to get the hell out of there.

The jingle of metal, accompanied by the sharp glint in the rearview mirror.

The sharp pain when-

I reached up slowly, feeling my neck for signs of a wound or mark that wasn't there.

It didn't take a genius to put the pieces together.

And it didn't take one to realize how much danger I was in, either.

Struggling to my feet, I looked around my surroundings, not recognizing the black trees with silver-lit trunks or the dark grass underfoot.

Where was I?

In front of me, a mostly torn-down building stood at angles with itself, two walls leaning against one another in support, and half of a floor still raised above the grass that had reclaimed most of it. It had been small. No more than a shed. Beyond it, in the distance, I could see another similar, decrepit shape.

Coldness sank into me once more, but this time it was *fear*, instead of the cold air of the night or the ground below.

I shivered, wrapping my arms around myself as I turned in a circle and fought not to cry.

The only sounds around me were the wind through leaf-bare branches and the ominous creaking of the partly gone buildings.

The only thing I knew for sure was that I was somewhere in the forest.

But so much of Scheffield was forest, that it didn't narrow down just where I might have been.

Not to mention, I had no way of knowing how long I'd been asleep. A few hours?

A few *days*?

Probably not the latter. I wasn't as hungry as I should've been, though my mouth was paper dry.

A day, perhaps, for the moon to be in the sky again?

Was anyone looking for me?

Biting my lip, I was unable to stop tears from cascading down and carving warm lines in the dirt on my cheeks.

Immediately I scrubbed them away, aware that my dirty hoodie sleeve was probably doing more harm than good at this point.

One thing was for certain, I couldn't stay here. Not when someone had obviously brought me to this spot and left me. I needed to go somewhere else, where I could at least hide, or maybe even find a way to get back to a place I recognized.

Still trembling, I turned away from the building and walked into the thicker trees, hoping that the further I went, the harder it would be for anyone to find me.

That plan, however, came to a very sudden halt.

Not even a hundred feet from the shambled shed, I found myself faced with a tall, chain link fence. Barbwire curled menacingly over the top of it, and the barrier was reinforced everywhere with smaller wire so that I could barely even get my fingers through without snagging my skin on rusty metal.

I walked along it, looking for a door, or a break or *something*.

The fence had to end somewhere, didn't it?

What was the point of a fence this tall in the middle of nowhere? What in the world could the owners be trying to keep out.

My steps slowed, my thoughts coming to a screeching standstill at the sudden realization that turned my blood cold.

With a fence this tall, I doubted very much that the person, or people who built it, were trying to keep something *out*.

No, it was much more likely that they were looking to keep people *in*.

My hand on the wire trembled as more tears threatened to run down my face, causing my sight to go blurry and watery.

Another old building was beside me, this one a bit more solid looking and standing straighter than the one I'd woken up in. Around this one, however, lay a few scattered pieces of what the building might have been. Stones. Wood. A few strips of metal, even.

Maybe I could-

Something inside rustled. A soft footstep sound caused my breath to stop again and my heart to jackrabbit wildly in my chest.

An animal, maybe?

Or perhaps just the wind.

But then the aging floor squeaked, announcing the presence of something that had to be bigger than an animal.

Were they waiting for me to walk by? Did they have

some kind of vantage point I hadn't seen, and they were just waiting for me to turn my back?

I bit my lip hard, tasting blood, and took a step forward so that I could lean down and pick up a slightly twisted rod of metal that had been thrown haphazardly into the tall grass.

Whoever it was, I wasn't going to let them get the jump on me.

Though every instinct told me to *run,* I tiptoed around the side of the old, damaged stone, eyes fixed on the place the wall ended and crumbled into a mass of debris on the ground.

There it was again. A shift and a sigh, like whoever it was couldn't get comfortable inside.

But I was at the end of the wall now. One more step would take me into view of the inside of the building and whatever lay within it.

You can do this, I told myself, finding that I didn't believe a word of it. *You can do it-you have a weapon. You have to.*

That part was true, at least. I *had* to do something before something happened to *me.*

Refusing to let myself wait any longer, I took a quick step around the wall of the building, stumbling into and over the pile of rubble and throwing myself off balance.

My heart lurched as I corrected myself, shifting my weight forward as I lifted the metal rod threateningly in my hands.

"Holy *shit!* Don't hit me with that!" The voice from inside was familiar, and for a moment, I felt terror race through me.

When I blinked, clearing tears from my eyes, I found that in front of me stood a person I hadn't expected to see at all.

In front of me, crouching in the stone and trash of the old building, was Azriel.

"Azriel?!" I shrieked, more confused than ever. He was

the last person I'd expected to see here, and by the look of shock on his normally friendly features, I could tell that he was just as surprised to see me.

"Please don't hit me with that!" The man raised his hands dramatically in surrender, a ring that matched Lysander's flashing in the dim light.

I looked down, realizing for the first time, that I still held the metal rod menacingly in my hands. "I'm sorry!" I dropped it with a clatter that made me wince, and curled my fingers into my palms so he couldn't see how hard they shook.

"What are you-" Azriel began, just as I demanded, "Why are you here?"

We stared at each other, a rueful, nervous smile appearing on the brunette's face. "Sorry," he said slowly, standing up and taking a step towards me.

Unsure, I found myself stepping back, and something dark flickered in his gaze. "Please don't tell me you think I'm the bad guy here."

"No...no, I..." I trailed off, considering his words.

I'd been wrong about them, hadn't I? I'd suspected the four of them of doing something, but with him here and looking just as ruffled and confused as me, that couldn't be the case.

The Deerling brothers had killed Ashley and taken me-us-hostage. Not Azriel and the others.

"I know it wasn't you," I breathed finally. "I'm sorry, I just-" Unbidden, tears ran down my face, and when I sank my teeth into my bottom lip once more, it only served to draw more blood from my mouth.

"Hey, hey, Will." Azriel stepped forward cautiously, his arms wrapping around my shoulders and pulling me close. "Don't cry, okay? I know you don't know me that well, but it'll be okay. We'll get out of this."

"I don't even know how long I've been here," I sniffed

against the soft fabric of his dark hoodie. "How long have *you* been here?"

He hesitated, prompting me to draw back. "Why don't you know?" he asked, eyes narrowed.

"They-the Deerling brothers knocked me out. In the parking lot of *Monsoon Moon*. I just woke up."

"Same," he answered quickly with a reassuring nod. "But I think I've only been out a few hours. If you've been missing since you and Lys talked, then you've been asleep for a day."

A *day*. Just like I'd estimated.

That didn't make it any better.

"I wonder if Marianne is okay," I mumbled, not pulling away immediately.

"Marianne?" Azriel prompted.

"At *Monsoon Moon*. The coffee shop in town. That's where...." I sighed and pulled back, wiping my eyes once more and only succeeding in rubbing dirt against my face.

Watching me, Azriel reached up with his own, cleaner sleeve and rubbed my cheekbones lightly to clean off some of the grime and wetness from my tears. "It's okay," he said. "It could be worse, you know. We're both alive."

"But...maybe not for long." My voice shook, and I felt like crumpling into a ball. "They killed my roommate, Azriel."

"Yeah..." he agreed absently, looking over my shoulder at something I couldn't see. When I turned as well, I found nothing except the darkness and the trees. "Hey, maybe you should wait here," he suggested, fixing me with his full attention once more. "I'll look around and see what I can do. Maybe there's a way out near here."

"No." My response was immediate and much firmer than I'd intended it to be. "No, I...I'll look with you. I don't want to be caught alone by them, and perhaps together, we'll have a better chance."

That was how the law of numbers worked or something, right?

Right.

He studied me once more. "Are you sure?" he asked at last.

I nodded fiercely, and he sighed.

"If there's no changing your mind, then. Come on." More confidently than I would've expected from him, the man led me out of the remains of the building to find cover in the trees nearby. I followed in his shadow, utterly silent as he strode along the metal fence.

"No holes, huh," Azriel murmured as if he were speaking to someone other than me. "No way out or in, except for the gate."

"The gate?" I asked in a tone just above a whisper. "Did you say *gate*?"

Azriel paused, glancing over his shoulder with his dark mahogany eyes. "Didn't you see it when they brought you in?"

"I was asleep, remember," I answered, confused. "I thought you were too."

"I was kind of starting to wake up," he admitted. "Anyway, there's a gate. I think it's down this way. Come on." He started walking once more, footsteps silent in the springy, lush grass.

As we walked, I watched for any sign of movement, and was bewildered when I saw none.

Where were the brothers? They had to be here. I was half-sure of that, anyway. But they hadn't popped out from behind a tree to stab Azriel, nor had they come lunging out of some secret hole in the ground to grab me.

But something else had started to catch my eye. There was a large building in the center of the forest, with warehouse doors opened and where light flooded onto the immediate ground beyond.

It was the only lit place out here, and the only building around that didn't show signs of disrepair.

But I found that the thought of going near it absolutely terrified me.

Without warning, Azriel stopped, whirling and grabbing me around the shoulders as I nearly walked into him. With a hand over my mouth, he dragged me behind a tree and to the ground. His body pressed to mine, and his arms were keeping me still and silent as he held me against him.

My heart thudded in my chest as my confusion had me writhing against him.

Something brushed against my lower back, where my body was pressed tightly against his, between the apex of his thighs.

Was he *really* getting–

"Sorry," Azriel chuckled in my ear, tightening his grip on me. "I can't exactly help it. But *shhhhh.*"

I stayed quiet, fear doing more than his words had to keep me perfectly still against him.

All of him.

I was confused for a moment, and the shriek of a faraway bird had me questioning what was going on in the world.

But then, I heard it.

Footsteps. Loud boots crunched through the undergrowth, and the static of a walkie-talkie met my ears.

A loud, irritated sigh drifted on the wind, and the walkie-talkie was silenced.

"Nah, haven't found her here either," Donald Deerling grunted. "Bet she headed to the warehouse."

Were they talking about me?

"*Maybe,*" the voice that might have been David's sounded skeptical. "*Keep looking. Check the gate. She might be looking for a way out over there.*"

Donald grunted his agreement, and the footsteps turned,

making as much racket in the dead leaves as they had when they came.

"I think they're looking for us," Azriel whispered against my temple, his arms loosening but still holding me against him.

I didn't reply, even when his hand slipped from my mouth and pulled away.

If they were looking for us...why had they just referred to a *her*?

Wouldn't they be looking for Azriel too?

Something didn't make sense, but I was much too afraid to open my mouth and speak my mind.

Things didn't quite add up, sure but...Azriel was at least trying to be helpful even if he did seem to be full of shit.

Was he a hostage here too, as he'd said?

There was no way in or out of this place, it seemed, especially based on what Donald had just said.

So if he was here, he had to have been taken against his will, just as I had.

Surely the rest was unimportant and not something I should be thinking about right now. Later, if I was still alive when the sun rose, I could question Azriel about the strangeness in his story.

If I even remembered to do so.

CHAPTER TWELVE

I STOOD, pulling away from Azriel so he could get to his feet and brush himself off. "Interesting," he breathed, not looking at me.

"What's interesting?" I huffed softly. "That we're just as stuck here as we were five minutes ago?"

He spared a glance at me like he'd forgotten I was there.

As if he hadn't been talking to me at all.

"I think we should head to the warehouse," Azriel said, at last, peering around the tree.

"*What*?" I approached him to look between the same trees, catching glimpses of the stone building in a small clearing. It was practically the size of a large barn and tall enough that I doubted it was only one floor.

"Well, that's clearly the only place we'll find anything," the man shrugged. "Otherwise, we'll be stuck wandering around until they find us." His eyes found mine, glinting in the dark. "Is that what you want?"

Of course, it wasn't.

But I also wasn't exactly a fan of facing my problems and fears head on.

Anxiety and dread curled my stomach into a ball, and I wondered if I might vomit.

"If...if you think that's best," I whispered finally, gazing at him with wide eyes.

He met my look with a calculating, curious one of his own. His lips parted, and he looked as if he might say something in return.

But then he only nodded, and beckoned me to follow him through the trees.

I did so hurriedly, hanging in his shadow as much as I could and glancing fearfully at every passing shadow or noise.

Every unnatural dark spot was a Deerling.

Every noise was one of them with a pitchfork or an ax, coming at me to slice my throat open.

Get a hold of yourself, Will. Keep thinking like that, and you'll never get out of here alive.

Much, *much* too soon, the two of us stood against the wall of the warehouse. I trembled, my legs nearly giving out as Azriel peeked into a windowsill.

When I slid down the wall to sit, he glanced at me as if bemused at my actions.

"Are you okay?" Azriel whispered softly.

I glared up at him, eyes sharp. "Of course not!" I hissed, letting my frustration and fear color my words. "Of course, I'm not *fucking okay-*"

A sound from the other side of the clearing made me shut up, and I watched, as a truck rolled across the grass towards one of the fences.

"Now's our chance," Azriel breathed, turning from me once more.

I sucked in a breath and pressed my hand against the ground to steady myself, drawing it back with a near-silent gasp as something sharp-edged cut into my hand.

It was glass.

Shards of a broken window pane lay scattered on the gravel under my shoes, and the one I'd pressed down upon looked long enough to do some real damage. At nearly eight inches in length, the jagged edges came together on one end in a sharp, deadly-looking point.

For a moment, I considered showing it to Azriel. I could give it to him and look for another since he seemed much more at ease with this situation than me. My mouth opened, the words on the tip of my tongue-

My throat closed, cutting them off.

Don't. The thought was clear in my brain as if someone had shouted it in my ear.

I shouldn't give it to him.

Why? I questioned, unsure of my own motives.

"Are you coming?" Azriel didn't look at me. He was already edging towards the open barn-style doors.

"....Yes," I whispered, picking up the glass and hiding it in the waistband of my leggings. The edges rode uncomfortably against my skin, and I grimaced at the discomfort, but made no other sign of having it.

Surely a bit of discomfort was better than being caught by one of the brothers without any kind of weapon at all.

When he disappeared into the warehouse, I hesitated for a moment longer.

Even this far, I could smell the sour stench of chemicals and the strong smell of metal.

And over that, the cloying scent of old blood.

Taking a breath, I took one step. Then another. Finally, I was in the warehouse proper, and *God*, I wished that I wasn't.

Had they brought Ashley here?

That was the only thought that went through my head when I saw the bloodsoaked table in the middle of the room, and the hooks that hung from beams in the ceiling that held ropes swaying in the gentle night air.

My entire body *begged* me not to go any farther. Everywhere I looked was some new horror.

Even the floor had swipes and stains of dried, dark blood.

"Azriel..." I began, but broke off immediately at a strange noise from the other man.

I looked up at the sound, thinking he was choking and found that he was covering his mouth with one hand while he surveyed a wicked-looking hunting knife.

Was he going to vomit?

Then he turned slightly, and the light from the warehouse made his face more visible.

He was...*laughing*.

Or trying very hard *not* to.

"Are you...?" I wasn't sure how to finish that statement. *'Okay'* certainly didn't work here any longer.

"I'm-I'm so sorry, Will." He lowered his hand to show the broad grin across his features that sent a chill down my spine. "I was really trying to keep it together here. But this." He brandished the knife before dropping it loudly to the table with a clatter. "Look at all this *shit*."

"I have been looking," I replied in a steady, even voice. "I'm not sure what I'm supposed to find *funny*."

Had he lost it?

Or was this never what it had seemed at all?

"I do." He gestured to the table full of bloody tools and rags. "This is a detective's wet *dream*. How pathetic is your town that they never found this?"

"What do you mean *never*?" I demanded. "We haven't had a murder here-"

"In over thirty years, right?" he asked teasingly, strolling towards me and petting my head like I was a child. "Over thirty years, yet there were never any bodies discovered here. Then all of a sudden, out of the blue, your roommate's body is found belly-up in the river with awful, dreadful wounds."

I didn't understand.

"Have you not looked around?" He spun in a circle, grinning broadly and showing off what had to be some kind of insanity. "You actually think this was all made *special* for your friend?"

At my gasp, he shot me a look. "Come on, Will," he sounded disappointed. "We both know she died here."

"Just like you're going to." The flat, unfriendly voice made me whirl, and my hand went to my hip where I'd stashed the shard of glass.

In the warehouse doorway stood both David and Donald, neither of them looking at all amused.

Azriel stopped his uncanny movements, turning instead to face them. "Well, look at you," he whistled. "I've seen pictures of your grandfather, you know. You're definitely related."

Their grandfather?

Donald's face was white with fury, and his hands shook. "How did you get in here?" he demanded, his attention all for Azriel. "There's no way in *or* out without us knowing about it."

My blood ran cold.

Azriel had lied to me.

No shit, Sherlock, that asshole part of my brain growled.

I stepped closer to him anyway, unsure of what to do. Better the devil I sort of knew than the ones who were apparently sadistic murderers, right?

The man at my side unexpectedly slung an arm over my shoulders. "You're just sloppy," he shrugged. "Or one of you has taken a nasty blow to the head recently. First, her roommate. Then the coffee shop owner *in her own business-"*

I couldn't help the whimper that escaped me, and I suddenly felt nauseous.

Marianne was *dead*?

"And then *her?*" He gestured to me with the hand that kept me at his side. "Right there, where her car would be found?" Azriel looked at them from beneath his lashes. "Who *raised* you boys to act like this?"

Donald started to move, reaching out to pick up the long ax that lay on the table, but David's hand snaked out to grab his sleeve before he could come any closer. "Wait," David demanded, eyes fixed on Azriel. "You know what he is. And where there's one, there's always three more."

"Three...more?" I breathed, risking a look up at Azriel.

And what exactly did David mean?

Who *was* Azriel?

With a question on my lips, I turned to look up at the brunette beside me. His grin had widened to the point of being macabre. Though, in my opinion, any look of pleasure in this place was cause for alarm.

"What are they talking about?" I whispered. "*What* are you?"

Donald Deerling straightened. "She doesn't know?" He spat messily to the side.

"Will doesn't need to know a damn thing. *No one* here does."

I hated being spoken of like I wasn't here.

Of course, I also hated being *here*.

"Then let *Will* go home," I mumbled, looking down at the concrete under my feet.

"Go home?" David's voice was full of false sympathy. "Sweetie-"

"Don't call me that." I didn't care what else he was going to say. I was not going to be called *sweetie* by a nasty, half bald, middle-aged *murderer*.

"It is pretty gross," agreed Azriel. "She's not your *grand-daughter*, Dave."

Donald thumped the ax menacingly on the table, making me jump. "So where are they?" he asked, lifting his arms and turning in a circle. "Where's your stupid *pack*, Azriel Boone?" He looked around theatrically, even peering under the table.

"You're in danger. You know it, and we know it. There's two of us, and one of you."

There were two of us as well, but I supposed it would have been rude to correct him.

Azriel didn't respond. He simply watched David like this was the most amusing thing he could possibly be doing.

"Come out, come out!" Donald twirled again, his words echoing off of the stone walls of the warehouse. "Come save your friend before I gut him like a pig."

"They aren't here." David's eyes were fixed on Azriel's, and his words were slow. Careful, even. "You got in by yourself...but they aren't here to back you up."

"I don't need any backup." Azriel pulled me closer to him and leaned against me, his head tilting to press against my temple. "I have Will."

David barely spared me a glance. He nudged his brother, who stopped looking around, and they both sneered towards the pair Azriel and I made.

"You have *Will*?" Donald remarked. "I think I'd rather have a barn cat. Look at her! She's too afraid even to move. If you let go of her shoulders, could she even hold herself up?"

I stared at him with my heart in my throat, not wanting to move or speak for fear that my words might betray me.

The glass shard I held on my hip felt heavy, and strange.

Would I use it if I had to?

Without a word, David took a step towards us. Then another one. Three steps in, and he was past the threshold and level with the table. From there, he grabbed a jagged knife, his eyes never leaving Azriel's as he twirled the hilt in his hands.

But Azriel didn't seem bothered.

Indeed, my companion only *grinned.*

And at last, I saw why.

The two brothers had been right in the beginning when

they'd accused Azriel of having backup other than whatever I was.

A dark shape strolled up the driveway, misshapen to my eyes because of the long weapon that he had rested on his shoulders.

Was that...*a bat?*

I blinked when he stepped into the light of the warehouse, deaf to whatever Donald was saying.

How could I look at them when Lysander Ashford had caught my eye and *winked* at me?

My lips parted, though I wasn't sure what I was going to do. Scream? Warn...*someone*?

It didn't matter. Lysander's arm moved, lifting the baseball bat off of his shoulders that seemed to glitter in the sharp light.

Barbed wire, I realized, a moment before the weapon collided with David's knee.

The older man went down with a roar, the knife still in his hand as he fell.

Donald shrieked, turning and chopping at Lysander with the ax. The blonde, in turn, blocked the strike with the bat, not minding the metal axehead digging deep into the wood.

"I knew you weren't alone!" bellowed David, fumbling around at the waistband of his jeans.

Confusion flitted across my brain a second before I saw the shine of smooth metal and the leather of a belt holster.

David had a *gun.*

"Lysander!" I screeched, drawing both men's attention to the older brother. Without hesitation, the blonde male lashed out at him with one boot, kicking his hand away from the gun.

"We mustn't touch toys that we don't know how to use," Azriel clucked his tongue sympathetically at David as he stalked forward.

Before David could try for the gun again, Azriel had put

a foot against his shoulder and *shoved* him back onto the cement.

"Do it," the brunette invited, when David's fingers inched towards the weapon. "Do you think you're faster than me?" He reached under his shirt and pulled a switchblade from his pocket that he flicked open in front of the man's wide, fearful eyes. "I'll cut something off if you try it," he added. "But, it's a surprise what I'll take-"

David didn't wait for him to finish speaking. He lunged for the gun, but true to his word, Azriel was faster.

It was a shame that I wasn't at a different angle. From where I stood, I was able to see Azriel's lunge and how the knife arced towards David's hand. And more than anything, I could hear David's ear-piercing scream when the blade *cut* into pale flesh.

As two fingers rolled across the floor, severed from his hand, I was sure I would definitely be vomiting.

"Holy *fuck*," I whispered, stumbling away from the fresh blood that had splattered onto the stone. "Oh, *shit-"* I reeled back, only to have a hand catch me by the shoulder to steady me.

Whirling around, I found myself face to face with Rhys.

He didn't look at all surprised or pleased. He barely had eyes for me, but rather found more interest in watching David as the man howled his agony.

"It's a shame your grandfather built this place so far from prying eyes," the quiet leader of their group remarked. "There's no one who might hear you scream and come to save you."

Only then did he turn, his eyes finding and holding mine in the bright light. "You should've taken Azriel's advice and gone to wait by the gate," he chastised in a quiet, almost disappointed tone. His eyes dipped to my waist, then found my gaze once more.

"I could go now," I croaked, my hands shaking. Should I

pull out the shard of glass? The only weapon I had against these men?

I had no way of knowing who, or if anyone, was on my side anymore.

Not after any of what had just happened.

Rhys's brows raised. "Now is too late," he told me. "Now, you get to stay and watch until I decide what to do with you."

"What to *do with me*?" I hissed, pulling away from him. "I-I didn't *do* anything to *you*."

"That's not how it works." Nyko appeared beside me like a shadow, pulling a frightened yelp from my throat. "Now, hush, and wait your turn, Willow."

"Will," I rebuked, voice a rasp in my throat. "You'll call me *Will*."

Nyko glanced at me in astonishment, and Lysander laughed. "Yeah, Nyko," he agreed. "You should've remembered that."

My own defiance surprised me, and I wasn't sure I'd have the heart for it again.

The black-haired, sharp-featured male shrugged. "My bad, I suppose." He walked forward lightly, arrogance and callousness in every step until he could rest his hip against the edge of the table. "We'll make this quick, yes? The police are out looking for *her*," He gestured at me over his shoulder. "And I'd rather not have any of you spend a night behind bars."

Lysander grinned, hoisting the bat over his shoulder once more, and rounded on David. "Lucky you," he hummed pleasantly. "That I don't get to take my time." In a fast movement, he struck downward with the bat, and I thought he was going to slam it into the ground beside David's head, just to scare him.

He didn't. The soft *thump* was one of wood meeting flesh, and David cried out in pain as Lysander drew the bat back with blood and something thicker splashing the ground behind him.

"I'll make sure to tell your cousins how you died," Nyko went on, not moving as Lysander lined up dramatically for another strike. "Screaming. Crying. *Begging* us to spare your life."

At least with him in front of me, I didn't have to see what was actually happening. I looked away, eyes finding Donald's, as a flurry of movement at the corner of my vision signified another blow from Lysander.

The younger Deerling's eyes shone fever bright, even in the yellow light of the warehouse, and I saw that the ax had been kicked to the floor between us.

Even when David cried out for him, Donald only looked at the ax...

And *me*.

"Then you can tell them this," the younger brother hissed, drawing himself up. "Tell my cousins that before you chose to outnumber us and attack us in our *own home*, we killed the girl that the four of you were going to take as your own."

He lunged forward, going for the ax that was mostly concealed by the table, and staggered towards me with the weapon raised and mouth open in a desperate roar.

Time seemed to slow. Distantly I heard Lysander's growl of warning, but that wouldn't do me any good.

Not when the only person even moderately close to me was Rhys, and he seemed to have no qualms about the younger Deerling murdering me in the warehouse.

I couldn't move. I barely seemed to be in control of my body as he lurched forward, the ax swinging wildly in a wide lunge.

And then, suddenly, he stopped.

Inches away from me, Donald's body came to a screeching halt, and he dropped the ax to the floor at his side with a clatter.

Mouth open and tears falling freely down my face, I couldn't help but *watch.* "I didn't mean to," I whispered, finally glancing between us at where I held the long, jagged shard of glass between my hands, the sharpest end impaling the man in front of me.

Blood was beginning to drip from his stomach, running along the glass and over my trembling hands. "I didn't-"

But I wasn't sorry, and I didn't know what to say.

He'd tried to *kill* me.

Without warning, arms folded around me in the semblance of a hug. When I turned to see Rhys behind me, body rested to mine, I had the strangest feeling that he was trying to *comfort* me for what I'd done.

That was until he forced my hands tighter around the glass, cutting it into my skin and driving the weapon deeper into Donald's gut.

I cried out as the older man did, trying to jerk away and finding every path blocked by Rhys's iron grip.

"Don't pull away," the quiet male murmured in my ear, not at all acting as if we were doing something so *wrong*. His matching ring flashed on his finger, the metal warm against my hand where he gripped me.

"Please," I breathed, trembling in his grip. "I don't want-"

"He would've killed you," Rhys went on, tucking his face against my throat so that his nose skimmed my shoulder lightly.

"I didn't want to kill him."

"Own it. There's no going back now." He used his grip on my hands to twist the glass by increments and watched Donald's face twist into an expression of agony. "No apologies to be made either. Look at where you stabbed him."

"I didn't-"

"Look at it." His voice was sharp. Commanding.

Demanding, really. Teeth grazed the side of my throat, over the point my pulse *jumped* under my skin.

I looked.

Blood spilled freely over my hands, wetting both mine and Rhys's skin.

"You've all but gutted him. See?" He drew the shining, bloodstained glass upward, cutting deeper into Donald's flesh.

"Stop!" I choked, fighting against his hold and jerking away from his mouth against my skin. "Please-*God*-"

"You're asking *God* to help you?" His tone was mocking, but not cruel. At once, he released me, and I staggered back, my ass hitting the cement hard.

But I couldn't look away from Donald. Without the glass held by both Rhys and myself, he couldn't hold himself up. His knees buckled, sending him crashing to the floor and finally to his side on the hard cement.

My body shook, and I looked down to see that my hands and sleeves were coated in blood.

Lysander walked over, pacing around Donald as the man heaved and retched his dying breaths. "Sloppy," he commented. "But still, Will's first kill should be celebrated like ours, right? Smile!"

I blinked up at him in confusion, just as the flash of a cell phone camera momentarily blinded me.

"Did you just..." I wet my lips, unaware of how dry they'd become. "Did you just *take a picture of me*?" My voice rose as I spoke, and I staggered to my feet to stare incredulously at the blonde.

He blinked, bemused. "Yeah, obviously. It's a milestone. Like a birthday, or learning to ride a bike-"

"This is nothing like riding a bike!" The venom in my words shocked me, but Lysander took no notice. He closed the distance between us and braced the bat against his leg,

reaching out a second later to take my hand in his and survey the shallow cuts in my palm.

"Your blood is going to be *all* over this place," the man pointed out sardonically. He sighed. "What do you want to do, Rhys?"

The black-haired man blinked, surprise coloring his features. "*Do*?" he repeated. "About what? *We* didn't leave any trace of being here."

"What about her, though?"

"I'd thought we'd just kill her and leave her here with them."

My ears roared, and I fought to pull my hand free from Lysander's iron grip. He didn't let me, no matter that I had tried to wrestle and stomp on the toe of his boot.

He barely seemed to *notice*.

"Oh, come *on*," Azriel whined. "You don't really want to kill her. Don't lie."

Rhys rolled his eyes at his friend, and huffed a sigh.

"He's right," Lysander agreed. "And even if you did–which you don't–I wouldn't let you."

My astonished grey gaze turned to find Lysander's.

He met my eyes levelly, a smirk in those baby blue depths.

"Oh?" Nyko picked his way over Donald's body to stand with Rhys. "Since when are *you* the reasonable one?"

"Since I like Will." He never looked away, his grin broadening. "And Will likes killing, don't you?"

"Of course not!" I hissed, trying to pull free again.

"The things you like never last long," Nyko went on, his tone turning dull. "You get bored. You get *frustrated*-"

"*Not* this time," Lysander snapped. "Besides, it's just this once." He looked away, as if trying to keep something from my eyes. "So what are we going to do, Rhys?"

I'd never seen a man roll his eyes so exhaustedly, nor so

loudly. How I didn't hear them rolling around in his skull, I wasn't sure.

Could he see his brain from how hard he'd done that?

"Just make it obvious we were here," Azriel shrugged, then looked at me with a broad grin. "You won't even have to lie. Say he charged you, and you stabbed him. Then you ran from us, and we left you for dead."

My heart sped up in my chest, my muscles tensing as if I were about to run.

"Don't you *dare* leave me here," I whispered. "Not with-with them, and this, and-"

"He's right," Rhys said finally. "The cops will find you before morning, and you'll tell them your brave, sad story. Only…" He waited until I looked his way. "When they ask, you'll tell them that you don't know us, nor where we're from." He said it so matter of factly, like he had no doubts in the world that I'd do just that.

"And you can say you were drugged most of the time," Azriel added, swiping a box from the bloody table and brandishing a syringe and bottle.

Dread pooled in my stomach, and I fought Lysander's hold again. "N-no!" I protested, trying to yank away from him.

In response, the blonde pulled me to him, wrapping me in his arms and pulling me back to him. "You're fine," the blonde murmured, shushing me when I screeched my protests. "He won't hurt you."

I was more worried about all of them as a unit, rather than Azriel himself.

"Don't!" I begged, turning to meet Lysander's eyes as my feet scrabbled against the cement in a bid for freedom. "I'll-I'll fake it! I won't tell them anything, I'll-"

"I doubt you're a good enough actress to fake being drugged," he chuckled like I'd made a particularly cute joke.

Azriel loomed in front of me with a syringe in hand, and a burning pain in my shoulder signified what he'd done, along with a raging coolness that brought a heaviness to my limbs.

"Too bad you're so far from home," Lysander murmured, lowering me to the floor as my struggles weakened and my eyelids dragged downwards. "But I suppose this is goodbye, Willow Carlysle."

Before I could respond, I was unconscious once again.

CHAPTER THIRTEEN

"I DON'T KNOW." My voice sounded hoarse. Brittle, even to my own ears.

The *same* detective that had shown up at my door a week ago, shifted on the too-small stool that he sat on. It squeaked under him, clearly not meant for a man of such largesse. "Are you *sure*?" he asked, not for the first time.

I didn't answer.

With my legs curled up under me in my hospital bed and the smell of antiseptic in my nose, I found it hard to do more than replay the events of two nights ago repeatedly in my head.

I peered down at my bandaged hands, running one finger over the edge of the gauze. Thankfully, none of the cuts had needed stitches.

I wasn't so great with needles, so that would've been a not-so fun time.

Sucking in a breath, I gathered my thoughts to speak again. "I don't know their names," I said at last. "I saw them once, at *Monsoon Moon*-" My throat closed around the words.

Marianne was *dead*. Donald and David had killed her when they'd taken me, and I felt partially to blame for that.

Maybe if I'd stayed behind instead of going to my car, things would've worked out differently.

"But I never caught their names. They said they were here on vacation, and they'd rented some Airbnb near the river."

The detective snorted, the chair wheels rolling backwards and then forwards with the action. "No one ever vacations in Scheffield," he muttered.

Frustrated, I turned a sharp glare on him, sore hands bunching in the white sheet. "Don't you think I know that?" I hissed in an unfriendly tone. "I didn't say I believed them, did I? I told you that's what they *said*."

He didn't look very impressed with my sudden attitude but jotted down a note on his small pad of paper. "Before I go..." He blinked small, watery eyes at me again. "There's one more thing I'd like to discuss."

"I don't know anything else about-"

"I believe you," the detective interrupted. "It's not about that. It's about your car."

My car? My thoughts were fuzzy, and I was confused at his words.

What could've been the problem with-

Uh-oh.

My backpack had been in my car. The one with the money and other shit from Mr. Ellison's house in the county next to ours.

Shit.

Why hadn't I thought about that before now?

Then again, what would I have done, even if I had remembered it?

"Okay?" I asked, in an effort to seem befuddled. "What about my car? It's okay, isn't it?"

The portly detective stared at me for a second before answering, "It's what we found *in* your car."

"Trash?" I assumed in a dry voice. "Old takeout? If I'd

known my car was going to be searched, I would've done you a favor and cleaned it out."

"Money," he interrupted. "In a backpack in the front seat."

Too bad Lysander and his friends couldn't have done me a favor and taken that with them.

Not that they had any idea it was there or what I did for a living.

Damn.

"Okay?" I tipped my head to the side. "I know my backpack was there and some cash." Would he believe that I carried around *thousands* in cash?

I doubted it.

"Well, a few hundred in bills just seems odd," the police officer went on. "As did the batteries in the backpack."

A few *hundred*?

I'd been robbed.

Grand theft backpack contents had occurred while I'd been asleep.

Too bad I couldn't exactly put a report out on my twice stolen money.

"Okay, I know it's weird. The battery thing," I snorted dismissively. "I have a *thing* about batteries. I have a lot, and I always have a *lot* with me." God, did that even sound believable? "And I just like having cash on hand for emergencies."

It wasn't quite untrue. I loved stealing things that would prove to be a minor inconvenience, and taking batteries accomplished that.

"It's just..." He frowned. "I'm sure it's nothing. I just had to ask. People have been reporting their homes broken into, and one of the things they have in common is the theft of *batteries*."

God damn it, Will.

I didn't know what to say. So I *laughed*. "What kind of thief steals *batteries*?"

A dumb one, obviously.

"I just would hate to see Ms. Sierra's daughter getting herself into any trouble," the cop sighed, naming my mother and making me want to barf. "I know she tried real hard for you, and it was difficult being a single mom for her and all."

Sure. *Sure* it had been. My mother was *not* mom of the year by any stretch, nor had she been hurting for money.

What had that meant for me?

A babysitter. All of the time, someone was there to watch me and keep me from doing anything stupid.

And that someone was rarely her. My mother had much better things to do than be overly caring or approachable to her own daughter.

She had a town to conquer, after all—one fundraiser at a time.

"Okay," I said, unsure of the answer he wanted.

Did he not believe me?

Hell, I wasn't sure if *I'd* believe my stupid excuse of 'I'm just like that.'

"Well." He got to his feet with a groan, the stool echoing his discomfort with a long squeak of its own. "I guess I'll leave you to it. You must be tired."

Frankly, I was the opposite of tired. I was wired, and felt like I needed to *do* something.

Like, burn my backpack and my battery collection.

Staring down at my hands, I frowned. "Sorry I couldn't help more," I said. "But that's really all I remember."

"That's fine. We've got a pretty good idea of where those boys are headed," the detective admitted.

I looked up, shocked. Had I said something wrong? Did they *know,* somehow, more about them than I did?

"Tampa," the man went on with a nod. "We're notifying

the branch down there later today that we think they have some killers in their midst."

"Just like we had?" I pointed out mildly, before I could stop myself.

The detective glanced at me sharply. "They weren't really *ours*. The Deerling brothers weren't born in Scheffield. Didn't spend that much time here, either. Should've been Chicago to do something about them, not us."

Chicago?

But...that was where the *pack* had said they were from.

A memory flickered at the edges of my brain, drawing up from the sleepy blackness that I hadn't been able to shake since waking up this morning in my own private room at County General.

I've seen pictures of your grandfather, you know. You're definitely related.

That's what Azriel had said at the warehouse.

They knew the Deerling brothers' grandfather, who had supposedly gifted the two men the property here in Scheffield.

Had they known more than I'd thought? Was their coming here *not* the coincidence I was starting to think it was?

Maybe I'd been wrong--again.

Perhaps they knew more about Ashley's death than I'd been led to believe. Or at least, *why* the brothers had killed her.

"Are you all right?" The detective stared at me, watching my clenched hands.

"I'm tired," I whispered. "My hands hurt." That was a lie. "I just...want to forget all of this."

And I wanted *him* to forget the stupid backpack in my front seat. Surely he had enough to worry about, with his 'Tampa killers' and all.

"I'm sure." He looked away. "Get better soon, Miss Carlysle. And tell your mother I said hi."

"Sure," I said, knowing my mother wouldn't show up here anytime soon. I wasn't in life-threatening danger, and I was fairly certain she had more important things to attend to.

In what was a terrible upset for my track record of knowing my mother's intentions, I'd been wrong.

Three hours later, she walked straight into my hospital room without knocking, and regarded me with a look of disappointed pity.

Or maybe just disappointment. I could've been projecting my wishes a little.

"I'm so sorry I couldn't come sooner, Willow," she apologized, sitting down heavily in the chair near the head of my hospital bed.

With my phone still in my bandaged hands, I only stared at her in surprise. "It's okay," I blurted out, unthinking. "I figured you were busy."

She crossed her legs, not wrinkling her expensive navy pantsuit in the least. Silver embroidered pinstripes gleamed in the fluorescent light, and she pushed her long ebony hair back over one shoulder.

It struck me, not for the first time, how different we looked. With her five-foot-ten height, long legs, shapely figure, and black hair, she could've stepped out of any women's magazine. My mother was *gorgeous.*

I, on the other hand, had taken after my dad. Auburn hair. A round face. A stockier build and legs that did *not* look miles long.

The only thing my mother and I shared was our storm grey eyes. Depending on our feelings or what we wore, they sometimes took on a blue tinge, as my mother's were now. Between that and our noticeably fuller mouths on the bottom, that was the only way to tell that we were related.

"Not too busy for my daughter when she's in the hospital." Her tone was sharp before she sighed and reached out for my hands. "Oh, sweetie..." She took my bandaged fingers in hers gently. "I'm so sorry. I should've been more supportive after Ashley's accident. I just didn't expect you to take her death so *hard*. I blame myself."

"For...getting kidnapped?" I clarified.

"I'm sure you were out doing something you shouldn't have when it happened. I know how you get when you're upset."

I didn't reply. What could I say, exactly? She made it sound like I was throwing a toddler tantrum, instead of trying to help my roommate.

"Okay," I said, at last, unsure of what else *to* reply with.

"Did you need stitches for anything? Are you hurt anywhere else? On the news, they said you were found with those brothers, and..." She shuddered. "In a *torture room*, no less."

Okay, so that word definitely hit me badly. My stomach flip-flopped, threatening me with nausea.

You're fine, Will, I told myself. *You're out of it. Everything's fine.*

Wasn't it?

"I guess...I'll have to look for a new roommate," I remarked softly, hating the words as they came out of my mouth. "We're paid up for this month and next, but I doubt I can make rent by myself. And you know I hate people..." I trailed off, looking up at her and her stricken expression.

Like I'd said something *stupid*.

"A new roommate?" she repeated. "Willow, you're coming *home*."

Excuse me?

I didn't reply, but she didn't need me to.

"This has been a real trauma for you! And you can't live in the apartment you shared with your *dead* roommate."

I flinched at her harsh tone and looked down at my hands.

"I've talked to my therapist about this. She agrees that you'll need a supportive environment for a while. I'll take care of moving your belongings back to our house, and your room is still *yours*." She kept speaking, kept *going on* as if I wanted any of this or had agreed to it.

"And I've already set you up with a doctor that my therapist recommended. Twice a week for now, and-"

"I'm not a child, mother," I mumbled, unable to look at her when I said it. My heart thudded in my chest, and my face suddenly felt hot.

"I didn't say you *were*." Her voice was a sharp warning that made me wince.

"I'm not going to run home," I went on. "I don't...I don't *need* to." I didn't want to, either. "I don't need therapy." That was probably debatable. "And I don't need you and *your* therapist deciding what I *do* need." My voice soured as I went on, and I drew my hand away from hers.

"I don't think you're in the position to know *what* you want, young lady." She was mad now. Irritated by my refusal to go along with her perfect, well-thought-out plan. "You've suffered a *trauma*. My therapist said that in these situations-"

"Your therapist doesn't know anything about me!" My voice was too loud for the hospital and echoed off of the white-washed walls. "Neither of you know what I *went* through. Or what happened. Or what I *need*!" My heart thudded in my chest, simultaneously warning me to stop and egging me onward. "I'm not moving back. I am an *adult*, and I can take care of *myself*."

"Oh?" My mom jumped on my words. "You just told me that you couldn't afford to make *rent*. And frankly, I'm not sure how you've been paying for yourself at all. Working at the humane society? Really? What kind of career is that?"

"I like my job!"

"If you'd finished college like you should have-"

"Mother, *stop!*" I all-but screeched, imploring her not to do this *here*. Didn't she understand that this was the reason I didn't want to be around her?

Didn't she care that I had no intention nor desire to fulfill the life plan she'd created for me when I'd been born?

My mother stared at me, arms crossed, as she rocked in her seat.

That always meant trouble. When she rocked, it meant she was gearing up to say something terrible in an attempt to win an argument or make sure I knew I'd fucked up.

"The police asked me about your *activities*. Did you know that?" she asked, her voice frigid. I was surprised I didn't see frost issuing from between her lips at this rate. "They found a *backpack* in your front seat with money and batteries. They asked me what that was about. What in the world are you doing that you have the cops thinking *you* might be a suspect in some crime?" She looked away with another shake of her head. "Do you know what the people in my office would say if they knew? Bad enough that I believe my assistant overheard."

Ah yes. There it was—the real crux of the issue.

What would her peers think of me? Already, I knew, the people in her life didn't think very highly of me at all. They'd made that obvious, and I hadn't done much to foster their affection for me.

It had led to a reputation of being rude, ungrateful, and unfriendly.

My eyes burned with unshed tears, surprising me. The feeling of humiliation had snuck up on me this time, and I fought not to let it show.

"I'm tired," I whispered, at last, not looking up from my hands. "I think I-I need to go back to sleep."

My mother rose wordlessly, her heels clicking on the hard floor as she went to the door.

Would she leave without saying goodbye?

"I'll send you the information for your therapist," she said flatly, once she'd reached the door. "They're expecting you on Thursday at four."

Stunned, I looked up at her, eyes wide. "But I'm not-"

"We'll have dinner after and revisit this conversation." She smiled, but it was forced and looked painted on her lips. "I hope you feel better soon, Willow. And I'm sorry about Ashley. She was such a nice girl. I was hoping she would have been a good influence on you."

"....Bye, Mom," I murmured, unable to say anything else.

Without another word, she left.

Finally, I allowed myself to cry, though I made no noise as tears tracked down my face. Not for the first time, I wished that Mrs. Bellflower was my mother.

Surely other people didn't expect this kind of thing from their child?

Surely *other* parents supported their kids in what they wanted to do....right?

I pushed my thoughts away from the behavior I should've expected, only to land on my other problem.

If the cops-and my mother-suspected me even a little of being a thief, then I wasn't sure how in the world I was going to go on doing what I did best.

And if I couldn't take people's shiny things like some kind of overgrown magpie with a battery fetish, how in the *world* would I even attempt to pay my rent or support myself?

CHAPTER FOURTEEN

IF I LEFT TOWN NOW, would the cops be suspicious?

Would that be worse, or better, in the long run?

Maybe if I just left for a few weeks...

I shook my head, agitated at my own stupid, farfetched ideas. Where the hell would I even *go*?

Wednesday already.

Tomorrow was *the day*. D-day, in my opinion. Or, in this case, *T-day.*

I was not going to my mother's therapist's *therapist* or whatever.

I didn't need therapy.

.....Well, I didn't need a therapist that would go behind my back and tell my mother *everything* I'd said, HIPAA be damned.

But if I didn't, and I tried to skip our 'dinner date' after, I'd better have a damned good excuse.

Absently I scrolled over to my internet browser, typing a few words into the search bar of my phone.

David Deerling.

Nothing much popped up. Not that surprising, really.

No one from Scheffield ever had any headlines written about them, except in the local papers.

But hadn't the detective said he'd been from Chicago?

"I looked him up too." My waitress appeared at the table and set my drink on the napkin she'd produced from a pocket in her apron.

Startled, I glanced up at the pretty brunette. "The Deerling brothers?" I clarified.

She nodded sagely. "I think *everyone* did. We were all trying to figure out what had made them snap like that and kill Ashley, then try to kill you."

"Well...I'm not finding anything." I scrolled through the results. "So I guess it's just-"

"That's because you need to look up their grandfather." Her voice had dropped to just above a whisper, and she leaned over the table to look down at my phone screen.

Invasion of space, much?

"Their grandfather?"

"Yeah. The guy who gave them all that property out here. His name was Declan Deerling." She nodded for me to type it in.

"Geez. They really like their *D's,* don't they," I muttered, doing as she'd indicated and typing in his name.

Sure enough, she was right.

Declan Deerling had more hits than I would've thought. Articles from across the country discussed the man's bravery in the line of duty, as well as his descent into 'dirty cop territory' soon after his supposed heroism.

"Where was he from?" I asked. "Surely, he didn't live *in* Scheffield. What dirty cop comes here?"

"Chicago," the waitress replied. "His lady friend came from around here. That's how he got all that property in the woods."

Chicago.

A coincidence?

No. No, I very much doubted Lysander and the others had come here *just* after the brothers murdered Ashley was anything close to coincidental.

"Wow," I murmured, aware of the brunette waitress's eyes still fixed on the search results as well. "That's just crazy. Can't believe something like that could be connected to *us*." I flicked upward, returning to my home screen with an air of boredom.

I didn't want her knowing just how much this gave me to ruminate on.

"But why Ashley, I wonder?" She went on as if I'd expressed a desire to talk to her more. "Do you think it was just random? Or..." She trailed off with a hum of bemusement. "I guess we'll never know."

She shrugged her shoulders, smiled, and left again.

"Yeah," I agreed softly. "Guess, we won't."

Unless Lysander or his friends knew.

It seemed likely, if I thought about it. If I went off the assumption that they'd come here *for* the purpose of hunting down the Deerling brothers, then maybe they'd know *why* they'd killed her in the first place.

Maybe I just needed to forget about it.

Only...that was proving a bit more challenging than it should've been. Even when I tried to put them out of my head, the memories of that night replayed over and over in my head.

And, much more concerning, so did the memory of when I'd come *here,* and Lysander had confronted me.

What he'd done had been terrifying. He'd threatened me, basically, and held me captive with his arms on either side of me in the alcove of the hallway.

It had been terrifying...

Or it should've been.

Yet, I was having some conflicting thoughts whenever I remembered it, and found myself remembering the feelings of his mouth so close to mine, and how his breath felt on my lips.

If I let myself examine my thoughts further, I was also

certain that I had been focusing too much on how it had felt in the woods when Azriel dragged me down to him, one hand over my mouth as he held me utterly still.

Okay, so there was clearly something wrong with me. Trauma had done a number on my brain. It wasn't *my* fault that my fear response had turned into....something else.

Not at all. Brains were weird like that.

It would go away on its own when the drama and adrenaline had gone away completely.

Right?

My phone dinged, prompting me to look down at the screen as two messages came in simultaneously.

Don't forget: appointment tomorrow.

My mother's text turned my stomach, and I didn't bother to open the message. Better to leave it unread, than to accept that I'd received it.

The other was from Joel.

You won't believe it. Frank and Angie got adopted yesterday.

I hope they love their new home. I typed back.

Really, I did. I also wished I could've taken them home myself, but that would've been impossible at my pet-free apartment.

That I couldn't even fucking pay for.

My mood sunk, excitement over Frank's and Angie's good fortune trickling out of me and onto the tile floor below.

What in the world was I going to do now, if I couldn't steal and I didn't have a roommate to make ends meet?

Would I actually have to move back in with my mother after all?

No. A visceral part of me rebelled against that possibility. *Not in a million years. Not on my life.*

God, I wouldn't *survive* living with her, I was sure.

I needed another idea, and I needed one fast. If I knew Mom, she was already lining up movers with the intention of getting me back under her roof as soon as possible so she could try to steamroll my life back onto *her* idea of the right track.

I could leave.

The thought danced around in my mind, and this time I didn't ignore it.

I could go to Chicago.

The thought struck me out of nowhere, surprising my brain into stuttering and repeating the idea over and over.

I could go to Chicago.

Not to live, of course.

But just to satiate my curiosity about the men I'd met and the Deerling brothers.

And learn, once and for all, why they had targeted Ashley.

What if you run into them, Will? That too-honest and always-worrying part of my brain pointed out. *They'll eat you alive.*

Would they? Lysander *liked* me. Or so he said. Surely that meant something?

Besides, Chicago was a prominent place. I very much doubted I'd run into them, especially if I was careful.

They couldn't be the only four people in the world who knew about David's and Donald's grandfather.

This is stupid, I argued, twisting the napkin between my fingers. Really, *really* a dumb idea. Spontaneous ideas were rarely good ones, right? That's what my mother had told me, anyway.

"Detectives aren't sure if the robberies are connected-"

The television on one wall caught my attention, sound just loud enough over the low music that I could hear it.

My head snapped up, eyes riveted on the screen where a woman stood in front of a house.

But not just any house.

Mr. Ellison's gaudy abode.

Shit.

"But are considering the idea that this robbery, along with others like it that fit the same pattern, are the work of one person located in a central location to where the burglaries took place."

I snorted under my breath. Pattern? What *pattern*? I was better than that.

.....Wasn't I?

Frankly, I wasn't sure how to take this news report. A sign from the God I didn't quite believe in, maybe?

If so, it was telling me to get out of town.

My phone vibrated on the cheap, green table, and I looked down in askance.

Did you get my message?

The text from my mother seemed magical, in a way.

It sealed the deal. I was leaving Scheffield, Michigan, and going to Chicago. At least for a little while, until I could figure out what I was doing with myself now that my life had been shattered like a baseball bat to glass.

I refused to consider the other possibility. The thought that sat at the edges of my brain, barely daring to form into something cohesive.

What if I left and found myself without a home to come back to?

CHAPTER FIFTEEN

I HADN'T BEEN EXPECTING the familiar car in the parking lot beside mine, and gritted my teeth as I threw a bag into the trunk of my Sonata.

Ashley's mother stepped out of her car, looking over me with concern. "Are you going somewhere?" she asked kindly.

"Ummm..." I looked at my half-packed trunk. "Yeah, I think so."

"Not to your mother's, I hope. I heard her telling Peter at lunch that you were moving back in so she could help you get through your trauma."

Of course, she'd said that.

And I was willing to bet she hadn't told anyone that she was *forcing* me to do it, either.

"No," I said with a sigh, heaving the bag on top of another one. "But...please don't tell her that."

Her weary eyes brightened, brows raising ever so slightly. "You're running away." It wasn't a question.

Looking away from her face that resembled Ashley's features and towards my newly cleaned car, I bit my lip. "I'm twenty-four," I said dryly. "I don't think it's running away when I'm a legal adult."

She chuckled without humor. "Call it what you want, but we both know why you're going."

Well. Not exactly. Ashley's mom didn't know *everything*.

"Where are you going?"

I hesitated, considering telling her the truth for a moment about my not-so-bright idea. "South," I settled on finally. "Not that you can really go *north* from here. But past that, I'm not sure. Indiana, somewhere? Kentucky?" Those were safe answers. I wouldn't say Illinois when that was the *truth*.

"All alone?"

"Well, I don't really have anyone else." A problem of my own making, I supposed.

But it left me here. With no couch to surf on and no one's guest bedroom to crash in.

The feeling hit me harder than it should've. Harder than it ever had before.

Without Ashley, I was *alone*.

She sighed, and visibly straightened her shoulders. "What can I do? Are all your things packed? I can help you repack your car, if you like." She cast a disdainful glance at my trunk. "Yes, I think that would be most efficient. If you bring your things down here, I'll make sure nothing gets jostled during the drive."

"Is it really that bad?" I craned my head to look in the trunk. Sure, everything was haphazard, but what could possibly happen during *a drive*.

"I'll spare you the truth." She shooed me with her hands. "Go. Get the rest of the stuff here, now."

Bemused by her offer of help and more grateful for it than I would've thought possible, I hustled back into the apartment, where the rest of the things I was bringing sat in duffel bags, canvas bags, and in one case, a garbage bag by the door.

And then I stopped.

My chest clenched tightly, ribs seeming to contract inside my body. Tears burned, unshed, in my eyes.

This was how she'd always spoken to me when she'd come to help her daughter with something. She'd offered help with whatever I'd been doing as well, and had always made an effort to take an interest in my day or what I had going on.

Why couldn't my mother be like her?

Why was it that *she'd* lost the daughter she'd *loved*, while my own mother acted like I was just a tool to get sympathy from her peers.

Had I ever, *ever* disliked my mother so much as I did in this moment?

I didn't think so.

Picking up as much as I could carry, including the backpack with my electronics, I towed my things down to the parking lot before coming back up for a second trip.

This time, I saw that Ashley's mother wasn't alone. Mrs. Bellflower was in conversation with Emma, our landlady, and the latter was nodding, a sympathetic expression on her face.

I approached cautiously, sneakers scuffing on the old pavement as I dropped my bags in the pile Mrs. Bellflower was sorting.

The two women turned, and I saw Ashley's mother surreptitiously wipe away a tear that had escaped her lashes.

"I'm so sorry about all this, Willow," Emma said, nodding her head in Mrs. Bellflower's direction. "Mrs. Bellflower has caught me up on everything. She says you're going on a little trip and that your mom will probably be here to pick up your stuff this week."

I nodded, a bit confused, and she went on.

"It's a bit late tonight, but tell you what. I'll deposit the rent you paid for the next couple of months back into your account. And your security deposit. That sound okay?"

"Ashley's too," Mrs. Bellflower put in.

My heart twisted. "You don't have to. I mean, I didn't expect-"

"I want to," Emma assured me. "It's the least I can do for an unprecedented situation, and I want you to have as much money as possible, so you don't get in a bad spot."

I opened my mouth, closed it, and opened it again. "Thank you," I said, trying for a smile. "You don't know how much I appreciate that."

"Don't mention it." Ashley's mother squared her shoulders again, and I wondered how difficult it was for her to keep herself from breaking down.

Would my own mother have been so inconsolable?

My dad might have, if he were alive. Between my two divorced parents, he'd always been the one to take an interest.

He'd *loved* me. And as a kid, I'd thought I'd live with him instead of her.

But then he died. The only good parent in my life had been swept away by the Big C.

My luck really fucking sucked.

"I guess that's everything." Mrs. Bellflower straightened, hands on her hips as she surveyed the ground around us. "You didn't forget anything? Do you want to check?"

I shook my head. I'd checked, double-checked, and triple-checked to make sure I had everything with me.

Well, everything I was taking. Some of my clothes and all of my furniture had stayed, of course.

"I guess I just need to give Emma the key?" I suggested, digging in my pocket for the bronze piece of metal that I'd already disconnected from my keyring.

"I'll take it from you!" Emma was back, her long silver

hair swinging in its braid as she power-walked over with a paper bag clutched in her fingers.

"Here." I held it out, the key at the edge of my fingers as I waited patiently for her.

"Thank ya, dear." She took it and stuffed it in one pocket of her tracksuit. "And this is for you." She thrust the bag towards me, making me blink in surprise.

"Me?" I asked, tilting my head to the side and taking the unmarked bag by the beige handles.

"I thought you might get hungry, and I made too much tonight."

When I peered inside, I saw a Tupperware container *full* of lasagna.

It was enough to feed a small army, in my opinion, but I smiled gratefully at my landlady. "Thank you," I whispered, shocked by her kind gesture.

It occurred to me that the only two people left in town that I could say that I *liked* were standing in the parking lot beside me.

What a sad fucking fact that was.

"I'm really sorry," I said to Mrs. Bellflower, unable to help myself. The words tumbled out of my mouth, but I couldn't stop myself. "If I could've-I should've known or-or something. I wish I could've done...*something*." It hadn't been fair.

She bit her lip. "I know," Mrs. Bellflower murmured. She stepped forward and wrapped her arms around my shoulders. Emma touched my arm, a frown on her lips. "Go before it gets too dark for you to drive, okay. I worry about you on an interstate with all those truckers in Indiana."

I laughed and pulled back. "Mrs. Bellflower, I'm twenty-four and I've never been in an accident. I drive okay."

"I'm sure you do," she nodded sagely. "It's those other idiots I worry about."

"Okay," I sighed, leaning into the driver's side of my car

and setting the paper bag on the floor. "Bye. And thank you so, *so* much. You don't know how much I appreciate it."

"You just stay safe, you hear." Emma's tone was a warning. "And it wouldn't hurt to check in once in a while. I'm sure Mrs. Bellflower would like to know you're doing okay just as much as I would."

I gave them both a crooked smile. "I will," I promised, hoping I meant every word of it. I wasn't that reliable at communication. I found it easier to forget or put it off for another day.

But I meant it. I'd *try*. That was the best I could do.

With one last round of goodbyes, I slid into my car, turning the keys as I did, and prepared to pull away from the curb.

And, ultimately, away from the only town I'd ever really known.

I'd definitely envisioned a more extended road trip than almost six hours.

Admittedly, I hadn't known precisely how far I was from Chicago until I'd plugged it into my phone, but....this was *it*?

Five hours and fifty-eight minutes?

Maybe this wasn't far enough. Was there a chance of the cops coming to knock on my door in the middle of the night if they suspected me of wrongdoing?

Driving through the night was easy. At some point in my life, I'd become a bit of a vampire, though I refused to attribute it to some stereotype of my thieving.

No. The dark was just...*nice*. Night, clouds, storms...I preferred stormy weather other than the bright-as-fuck sun that burned my impeccable probably-possessed-porcelain-doll complexion.

The hotel I found at two a.m., a well-known chain that

thankfully was *not* reputable by the numbers in its name, seemed okay. At the very least, the fast blinking girl behind the counter didn't act annoyed or weirded out that I asked for a room so late at night.

"Sure," she mumbled, typing something in on her computer and holding up a room key.

I looked out the window, standing on my toes to get a better view through the curved lobby window. "How far away are we from the city? How far of a drive, I mean?" I asked curiously.

"Maybe twenty minutes, if you beat the traffic. In rush hour, more like forty," the girl said, handing me the keys and my debit card. "First floor. You can park around the side and go in the door. It's the first room on the left, 109."

Well. That was incredibly convenient.

"Thanks. I appreciate it. Oh…" I stepped to the side of the counter, where a small niche in the wall was lined convenience-store style with shelves and a refrigerator case. Deftly I grabbed a few bags of chips and two bottles of water.

After a moment's hesitation, I went back for two chocolate bars. "Could I get these too?"

The lady nodded, taking my debit card once more and running it through.

I stared at my card, calculating and re-calculating the funds I had, doubting I could actually rent an *apartment* in Chicago.

How long was I even going to *stay*?

Absently, I took the card back from her with a smile. "Thanks," I said again, making my way back out to my car and, finally, to the room she'd given me.

I'd expected a very commercial-style hotel room, and that was what I walked into. A fake wood floor stopped beyond the bathroom, and a dark blue carpet covered the rest of the small room. With a desk in the corner, a tv on a stand in the middle of the room against one wall, and a king-sized bed against the other, I wasn't exactly caught off guard.

To me, the bed looked *wonderful*.

I fell onto it, bringing my own pillow, blanket, and stuffed rabbit with me. Groaning, I finally did drag my knees up and pulled my comforter over myself.

"God," I mumbled, my face on the black cover of my pillow instead of the sterile, pristine *white* of the ones the hotel had provided. "You've really made a weird choice here, Will."

Nothing-*no one*-answered.

Obviously. Who was I expecting? Ashley's ghost?

That thought made me wince, and I quickly pushed any kind of musing about that *way* out of my head.

And in their wake, I was left with the only two things I could even consider to let into my brain.

The four men who I'd come to spy on.

And my *mom*.

I really, *really* didn't want to fall asleep thinking of my mom. I scoured my brain, trying to bring up some detail of a conversation that stuck out in my brain with any of the men that had blown into my town like a storm.

Instead, all I could see as my mind started to get fuzzy at the edges was Lysander's smirk as he closed the distance between us. Azriel's grin, next, as he apologized in the woods. Finally, when I was sure that I was all but asleep, I felt the ghost of Rhys's mouth on my throat, urging me to stab *deeper* as blood flowed over my cut and bleeding hands.

You cannot be thinking like this, I managed to tell myself, drifting off to sleep to the feeling of blood on my hands that wouldn't come off.

CHAPTER SIXTEEN

MY PHONE RANG.

The funeral march music seemed to beat against my skull, and I burrowed my head deeper into the blankets instead of picking it up.

It would go to voicemail. Whoever it was could *wait*.

The noise stopped, blessedly allowing me to go back to silence.

Until it picked up again.

This time I could hear the sound of the phone vibrating on the nightstand, and I could feel the offensive strip of sunlight that cut through the break in the thick curtains to fall against my face in a blatant attack to my slumber.

Forcing myself to open my eyes, I groped with one hand and only successfully knocked the phone to the floor.

Oh well, I sighed to myself, dropping my arm to the mattress again. I *tried*.

From the floor, the terrible noise of the phone on the carpet sounded, the ringing seeming louder somehow in my poor, abused ears.

Finally awake, I reached over the bed and picked up the phone, not at all surprised to see that my *mother* was calling.

Fuck.

I'd hoped to have a few more hours until I dealt with this.

Hitting the button, I brought the phone to my ear with a sigh, not sitting up from my hotel pillow nest.

"Where are you?" My mother demanded, not bothering with any kind of greeting.

"Good morning to you too, oh honored matriarch of the Whitely clan," I yawned, my tone unhurried.

It had always bothered her that I'd kept my Dad's last name, and I saw that as a victory.

"Where are you?" Her voice was tight with anger, and it gave me pause.

What had I done to make her *this* upset?

"Why?" I said finally, not sure what I should say.

I sure as shit wouldn't be telling her I was in Chicago.

Or on the outskirts of it.

"The movers called me. Apparently, your landlord had to let them in, as you weren't there to do it. She told them you'd already moved out."

"Yeah. That's right. I moved out last night."

"What is that *supposed to mean?"*

Pinching the bridge of my nose, I rolled onto my back and out of the offending bar of light. "I. Moved. Out," I stated. "As you so eloquently reminded me, I don't have the money to keep making rent in a two-bedroom apartment with no roommate. So-"

"Where are you right now?"

I gazed around the interior of my hotel room, ears picking up the sound of cars rushing by on the highway in front of the building.

"I took a road trip," I said at last. "You were right. This uh, psychological trauma thing has really got me on edge. I needed-"

"You had better be joking."

"You've known me on a casual basis for twenty-four

years and eleven months. We both know I'm not much of a joker."

She didn't reply. The phone was silent long enough that I had to check to make sure we hadn't been disconnected, and an uncomfortableness settled over me. "Hello?" I asked, at last, hating that I was the one to break first.

My mother would see it as a victory for herself.

I'd never quite understood the competition or its rules.

"You'd better be at the therapist's office today," she said crisply, her voice holding no question. As if she thought I'd do it because she *told* me to.

Those days were long gone. Not that she was aware of that. Nor would she believe it.

But they *were*. I'd come too far this time to go back.

"No," I yawned. "I'll be back when I want to. Not because you tell me to. I'm independent. You haven't paid my bills in years."

Thank God for that. Otherwise, I was sure she would've had a GPS on my car or on my phone.

"I'm your *mother*!"

"Okay, and?"

The line went silent again.

Again, I broke first, and hated myself a little. "Why do you want me to come back?" As if a good answer would convince me to change my mind.

"Because this is your home. And because I told my therapist, you'd be at the office at four! I've told everyone *you're moving back in with me so I can help you with this. You're my daughter, Willow. What are they going to think if they find out you've just run off? I can only keep it quiet for so long."*

My chest felt as if my ribs were closing in. Like an invisible fist was squeezing my upper body and grinding my heart against my spine. "The same thing they thought when you told them I was ungrateful and rejected your help with college," I murmured, closing my eyes hard. "Or the same thing you told all of your friends when I refused to take your last name and wanted to keep Dad's. I'm not too worried, Mom. You're always so good at knowing just what to say to everyone else."

"Stop acting like this. You're just acting immature because you're upset. I won't ask you again, Willow. Where are you?"

"On. A. *Road trip!*" I shocked myself by almost shouting the last word, my voice echoing in the small room. "And I will be back when I feel like it! Have a good day, Mom. All my sympathy for telling your friends about how much of an *epic* disappointment I keep proving myself to be or whatever."

This time, before she could reply, I hung up the phone and tossed it to the nightstand, where it landed with a clatter.

She called again, and once more after that until finally, I put my phone on silent and stuffed it under one pillow.

You could block her, I thought to myself, but hesitated.

She was my *mom*? What if something happened and she needed me to help her, or-

Yeah, right. More likely, she'd cry wolf and be waiting for me with an intervention or worse.

But still…I didn't move to block her.

I *did,* however, pick up my phone a few minutes later with the idea that had hit me in the car last night on my way here.

It was apparent I'd never be able to afford an apartment here. At least not indefinitely. And who knew how long I'd actually stay? Probably not long enough to warrant signing a six or twelve-month lease.

So why not do what the 'pack' had done, and rent an Airbnb for myself?

It made the most sense, and *had* to be cheaper than furnishing and paying for an apartment and utilities.

One search later on my phone's browser, I found myself

scrolling through a rental site, looking closely at the listings for what I needed.

At last, I landed on a studio apartment that looked like what I was searching for.

A quick check showed me it was available, and the renter was willing to rent it out *today*.

With her text in hand to meet her at the property in an hour and bewilderment still clogging up my brain space, I leaned back on my pillow again, rabbit beside me on the bed. "Guess I'm really doing this," I muttered, and sighed loudly.

Chicago was nothing like the cities that dotted the edges of the region near Scheffield. I'd expected that, of course, but I hadn't considered the sheer magnitude of this place, or the way that the people seemed jam-packed into the city limits like clowns in a clown car.

How in the world would I find the guys when I could barely get to my potential new home in one piece?

You know their last names, Will, my brain reminded itself, and I thought back to the IDs I'd grabbed to look at.

Lysander Ashford.

Azriel Boone.

Nykos Germaine.

Rhys St. John.

With all four of their names, first and last, wouldn't it be rather easy for me to track them down? At least somewhat?

I'd spent my life tracking people down and following them around to learn their schedule so I could safely break into their homes and steal from them.

Which, now that I thought about it, was something else I'd have to do here. I wasn't looking to get a real nine-to-five job, and while I'd love to continue my 'hobby' of working for an animal rescue, that wasn't something that would ever help me pay rent in the long run.

Sticking with what worked seemed like the best option.

And being a klepto just *worked* for me.

I parked my car in the small driveway beside a dark blue SUV, glancing at its license plate absently before walking up the stairs of the townhouse and knocking politely on the door.

Even before my knuckles had left the wood, the door had been yanked open, and a woman who appeared to be in her early forties or so greeted me with a smile and a Tupperware container full of candy.

"Pretzel bars," she informed me, thrusting the plastic my way. "You sounded tired on the phone, and pretzel bars have always done the trick for me."

"I'm Tara," the lady went on, when I'd taken a bite and my teeth were nearly glued together by caramel. She stepped back, ushering me into the air-conditioned town-house. "I know the app says that, but I like to introduce myself anyway. This is it. I own the whole townhouse, but I've never needed to live here. It's just a studio, but I think you'll like it." She paused, thinking. "*I'd* like it if I didn't have two kids and a husband anyway."

Looking around while still chewing on the pretzel bar, I had to admit that she was absolutely right.

The apartment was long, and the area in front of me began with a kitchenette to my left with marble counters that doubled as a bar with two stools and appliances built into the wall that almost sparkled with how clean they were.

The entire floor looked to be white and cream swirled marble, and a cream rug had been thrown in the living room area, under the sofa and coffee table. The light, bright color scheme continued with a blue-grey sectional sofa, black coffee table, brown recliner, and a tv mounted against one wall.

Even from the entryway, I could see that the apartment was separated into two sections, and a wall ended at the edge of the sofa closest to me. Peeking around to the side, I saw a king-sized bed tucked into the back alcove that lay covered in neutral-colored pillows and a grey blanket.

Caught up in admiring the grandeur of the studio apartment, I hadn't even remembered to give her my name.

"Oh, sorry. I'm Willow Carlysle." I didn't want to shake her hand, so I didn't offer up my own.

Hopefully, she wouldn't-

Oh. There it was. Her arm lifted, hand making the motion of politeness I'd so wanted to avoid.

I reached up without hesitation, a pleasant smile on my face as I shook her hand. "This is *amazing*," I said, not holding back with the admiration in my voice. "Are you sure the price on the app is right?"

Tara nodded, releasing my hand and urging me into the studio. "It always makes me feel better when people rent for a month or more," she admitted. "Means I don't have to come check on the place. In fact, if you agree to two months, I'd drop the price even more for you." She turned to glance at me sidelong, her blonde hair curling around her face.

"How much are we talking?" I asked. Before I could even consider her offer, I had to think about how long I was even staying.

In the long run, though, would thirty days be enough to figure out everything I'd come here to learn? If I took off one night, it's not like this woman could really do anything if she had my money in hand for the sixty days.

She quoted a price that my miser's heart twisted for, and waved a hand towards the elegant, marble bathroom. "This is my favorite part," she said, showing me the room.

I whistled. While compact, the bathroom was large enough that a tub big enough for three filled the back wall.

"Bed's back there, of course. Not much privacy from the

rest of the apartment, but if it's just you, that won't be much of a problem?" Tara asked kindly.

I nodded in agreement, still considering the offer of a second month.

"I'll take the second month," I said finally, looking around again. "No reason not to."

She visibly relaxed, letting out a sigh of relief. "Thank *god,*" Tara stated, going back to the kitchenette with me on her heels and dropping the Tupperware onto the bar counter. Now that I was here, I saw that the rest of the counter space was under the cabinets against the walls, and everything looked as modern as possible.

"There's food in the fridge. Enough for a week or so?" She gestured to the black fridge and leaned on the bar herself. "And I'm so glad you aren't some weirdo. I get worried when I show this place. And anyway, what makes you in need of a place all of a sudden and for so long? Vacation? Retreat? A sabbatical from a stressful career?"

"From a stressful *mother,*" I told her, my brain searching for an acceptable story to give her that wouldn't be far enough from the truth to be completely unbelievable. "Some stuff happened back home. My uh. My roommate died."

Tara covered her mouth in surprise.

"Sorry. I know that's a bit of a downer, huh?" I lifted my mouth in a half-smile. "I just need a break. I just need some time away and to figure some things out."

"Oh honey, I'm sorry. I hope it wasn't anything *bad*. Well." She amended her words with a wince. "You know what I mean. I'd hate for it to have been out of the blue or unnatural."

It was. Ashley had been *murdered.*

But I didn't tell her that.

"It just hit me really hard," I said.

"Do you have friends in Chicago? Relatives, maybe?"

No.

But I *was* here looking for people. Did that count?

"I have some friends that live here," I lied. "I'm going to call them up and see about reconnecting with them."

"What part of the city do they live in? I could tell you a good way to get there to avoid the traffic."

Damn.

I had no idea where they lived.

"They moved here last year, and honestly, I have no idea *where* they live," I admitted with an apologetic chuckle. "I'll call them later and see if they'll come by, or at least meet them somewhere that won't be a hassle. Thanks again for the short notice rental."

Tara gently and awkwardly patted my arm. "No problem. I'm glad I can help you out, at least with a place to stay for a while. If you need anything, you have my number, yes?" She laid two keys on the bar. "Feel free to text me with anything. And if you're hungry, I really recommend Louie's down the street. Their subs are great and *huge* for the price." She paused, thoughtful. "Speaking of, I deserve one." With a nod of affirmation, she turned for the door. "Have a good day, Willow! I hope you enjoy the apartment. Oh-and keep the pretzel bars."

I watched her go silently, a hand raised in goodbye as she finally left the apartment.

Then I sighed, hand snagging the Tupperware of pretzel bars and glancing inside.

There had to be at least twelve in there.

And yeah-I was already a little addicted. Once I had my stuff inside, it was a strong possibility that I'd be calling the sandwich place she'd mentioned and buy myself too much food so I could hole myself up in the apartment with it and watch reality television.

I was sure there were at least six episodes of *There goes Sugar Boo* for me to catch up on.

CHAPTER SEVENTEEN

FOR THREE DAYS, I hung out at the apartment, ordered in sandwiches, and avoided the outside world like the plague.

This was my favorite thing to do. I didn't like people much and didn't have the urge to go out singing or trying to make friends.

The only useful thing I *did* do-unless one counted reading copious amounts of trashy literature-was look up the four names I had of the men I was seeking.

Somewhat predictably, their names did not appear in any national manhunt articles. It was a shame since that would have led me straight to them and told me most of what I needed to do.

The only thing that had come up was clearly a mistaken result unless Azriel Boone had at some point in his life gone by 'Catboy62' and posted embarrassing photos of his cat and himself in cat ears.

Though, judging by the fact that Catboy62 was blonde and fair-skinned, I doubted very much that it was my Azriel in the pictures.

Could I look him up by his name? Maybe I could find some record of any of them.

It took me a bit, but when I landed on a website that

looked promising, I typed in *Azriel Boone* and added *Chicago, Illinois,* where I was prompted.

And got absolutely nothing.

I tried again with Rhys.

No luck.

Nyko didn't give me anything either, and when I typed in *Lysander Ashford,* I expected much of the same.

The shock made me sit up straight when the website came back with a positive hit, and I surveyed the info provided by the site.

Lysander Ashford.

1313 Lampkin Drive.

Chicago, IL.

That was a start, wasn't it? Perhaps even up to date, seeing as it was a Chicago address.

Should I wait? Should I go at night, maybe, when I could sneak around without being seen by everyone so easily?

No, I decided at last. That would just make me look like a creeper. It would be better to go during the day, so that if anyone *was* there, I could pass myself off as just a person walking by. Maybe a new neighbor.

Whoever lived there might be able to give me information that I needed, and if I was going to put on my 'I'm a friendly, polite, well-adjusted person' face, I'd need a shower.

The moment I approached 1313 Lampkin Drive, I had a feeling that I wouldn't be getting any answers about the origin of Lysander Ashford or where he might live now.

The street was lined with houses that sat at the top of concrete stairs with iron rails, none of them with a yard or even strip of *grass* to call their own that I could see.

Did people really enjoy living like this?

Not only that, but this place seemed...not great. The

buildings weren't kept looking clean, and trash littered the sidewalk by the road. The smell of nicotine and weed wafted through the air, and I shoved my hands in the pockets of my hoodie and shivered in the cold afternoon breeze.

On the bright side, there was no chance of someone pegging me as *weird* when the few people I did see here looked every bit as unpleasant as they came.

Please don't be an arms deal, I pleaded silently, grey eyes falling on two men huddled with winter coats at the end of the street. One man held a crumpled paper bag that he passed to the other, and I looked away after seeing the flash of a toothy grin.

I hated it here. This was the Chicago I'd expected, instead of the sunny, well-lit place my new temporary home was. The Chicago I hadn't wanted to find, even though I'd known it probably existed *somewhere.*

Walking the sidewalk absently, I kept my eyes fixed on the mailboxes as I passed, hood drawn up and hiding most of my auburn hair.

1309.

1311.

1313.

I stopped in front of the mailbox, biting into my lower lip lightly. If ever there was a less lucky address, I'd never heard of it. I dragged my gaze across the sidewalk, up over the steps, and was surprised when I found that the steps were occupied.

An old man sat on them, eyes squinted and cane laid across his lap. He'd definitely seen better days, and the intensity of his blue eyes shocked me into standing still, mouth parted as I tried to come up with something to say that wasn't rude or outlandish.

"You want something?" the man snapped, taking care of my fear of being rude to *him.* "I don't know you. What did you stop for?"

"Umm..." His blatant rudeness had knocked me off-kilter, and all I could do was gape at him and the low growl of his voice.

"*Umm*?" the man went on. "That's all you can say to me?"

Yeah, frankly, it was at that moment.

I just needed to be subtle. I needed to ask him something that wouldn't tip him off to anything. *Just play it cool, Will.*

"Do you know Lysander Ashford?" I said, words in a rush as they poured out of my mouth.

Well shit.

That wasn't fucking *subtle.*

The man stared at me and finally snorted. He rolled his eyes derisively, not bothering to get up. "You came here for *that*? Well, I ain't got nothin' for ya, girl." His voice had hardened.

I didn't believe him.

"I looked him up," I blurted out, continuously amazed at how stupidly I was speaking. "The site said he lived here."

"Well, he *don't*."

I wouldn't correct his grammar. It wasn't good form. "Do you know him?" I asked, still trying to be polite.

The old man stared at me, looking me up and down with something like curiosity on his face. "Why?" he asked at last. "This some kind of *test*? I told your boss-" The guy broke off in a fit of coughs, hunching over to cover his mouth as he nearly coughed himself off the step.

My...*boss*?

What did he mean by that? And what kind of test could this be?

"I think you have me confused," I stated slowly, when his coughs had died down enough for the conversation to continue. I shifted my weight from foot to foot, and shivered as a cool breeze picked up. "I don't work for anyone. I met Lysander about a week ago. I'm looking to find him again."

The man shook his head fervently. "I'm not sure whether

you're the world's worst liar, or you're telling the truth. If you *are,* then you need to get lost. Now. No one just *looks* for the pack because they met 'em once or twice."

Now it was my turn to stare. My eyes widened slightly, hands clenched in my pockets. "What do you-"

"Bothering another jogger, Harrison?" The voice calling up the street sounded masculine and perhaps a touch overly friendly. For one fleeting, stupid moment, I thought it was one of the *pack* in question.

Which, now that I thought about that...

How did this old man know what they called themselves? Surely if it were just some kind of an inside joke between the four of them, the word wouldn't mean anything to anyone else.

Right?

Turning on my heel, I saw a man coming up the sidewalk, hands in the pockets of his long coat and a smile on his tan, ruddy face.

Something shone in the fading light on his chest, and when I dropped my eyes, I found myself looking at a badge.

Shit.

What was a cop doing here? Did they just patrol the streets in dress pants and tucked-in shirts?

I didn't want to think of the fact that maybe I'd stumbled into a situation that wasn't so casual.

"I was just-" I began, but the old man cut me off with another round of hacking.

When it cleared up, he answered with a wheezing rasp, "She's some damn tourist, Detective. I ain't botherin' no one. She came to ask me about Kenneth's old place."

Kenneth?

Had this man lost his mind? I most certainly had *not.*

Glancing his way in confusion, I saw that the old man had fixed me with a pointed stare, eyes glittering a warning.

Could he be any clearer?

"Oh?" The detective came to a halt beside the concrete stairs, leaning his arm on them and looking between us like we were old friends.

A chill went down my spine that had nothing to do with the weather.

"Where are you from?" he asked me. "It's not really vacation season, you know? Not with the cold settin' in like this."

"Michigan," I replied, wanting to give him some of the truth in case he asked more questions. Michigan had some prominent cities of its own, and it would be easy to say I'd come from one of those. Saying something completely false, like Florida, would've been too difficult. I would've tripped over my descriptions or answers to his questions, I was sure. "I'm just visiting some friends down here, but they're busy for the day, so I thought I'd walk around and see what I could find."

Even that wasn't entirely false.

"And I told her she's a bit far from where she'll want to be," Harrison, the old man, grunted. He pulled a pack of cigarettes from his coat with a hand that shook from age. "Don't know why you bothered to creep over here, expecting the worst from me."

But I saw how his manner had changed. I couldn't miss how he was clearly intimidated by the detective.

Perhaps he had a reason to be.

The dark-haired, dark-eyed detective found my eyes and smiled. "Sorry about ol' Harrison," he chuckled. "He's just about as old as these houses and not nearly so nice to look at, I know." He leaned down to clap the old man's shoulder, nearly sending him tumbling.

"It's fine," I shrugged dismissively, not needing to act the part of a politely interested party any longer. Not when it was evident that my time was up and I'd gotten no closer to what I sought. "I'll just go back the way I came. It's whatever to me."

It wasn't whatever, but I'd overstayed my welcome. Besides, I knew the layout of this street well enough, even though I'd only been here for a little while.

I'd just come back later.

Starting for my car, I mentally kicked myself a moment before the cop called out, "Have a good stay-what did you say your name was, again?"

I looked at him over my shoulder, grey eyes flat. I'd have to tell him something, and it would look suspicious if I lied. "Will," I answered, giving him my nickname instead of my full name. Willow was problematically unique, and I could only hope that my mother hadn't sent out some bulletin that I was missing.

She'd definitely do that, if she was so inclined.

"Have a good visit, Will," the detective nodded his head.

"Yeah, if the fumes don't *kill* me first," I griped, walking down the sidewalk and remembering my mistake.

I walked towards my *car*. Thankfully it faced me so that the cop couldn't see my license plate, but I still had to be careful.

I couldn't let him know it was mine.

Reaching the white Sonata, I didn't stop. I kept walking, feet scuffing on the ground as I strolled past the two men who still spoke in low whispers on the sidewalk, one of them clasping the paper bag to his chest and shooting furtive glances at the cop.

"Hey. *Psst*." My eyes closed hard when one of them called out to me, and I slowed my steps. "You be careful," the man grumbled under his breath. "Don't get on Yates' bad side. That detective who was talking to Harrison."

I blinked, collecting myself before I spoke. "I'm just a tourist," I shrugged, widening my eyes and shrugging my shoulders to give him my best naïve, country-girl act. "I don't know why he'd care about me at all, let alone enough for me to get on his bad side."

The other man chuckled, shaking his head as he drew in a drag off of his cigarette. "Sure, little girl," he agreed dryly. "If we don't believe that, neither does he. Just keep your head down and take care of your shit in the *dark*, like the rest of us."

What in the world did they take me for?

Without another word to them, I kept walking, intent on taking a trip around the block and leaving when the detective was no longer here to keep myself as unknown as possible here.

Though it had taken me an extra forty-five minutes to get my car and go home, I had been pleased to see that the detective was gone when I returned to my car from getting some pizza at a small place a block over.

Once back at my apartment, I'd decided a shower was in order, and took my time in killing the afternoon as easily as I knew how.

With a nap.

Stretched out on the king-sized bed in its alcove on the opposite side of the wall as the living room, I'd given in to my urge to lie down just on the inside of the large bay window that the bed sat under. In the afternoon, sunlight streamed through it, falling over my body in long rectangles and warming my skin.

While I preferred storms-something the weatherman was promising within the next few days-I absolutely loved feeling like a cat in the warmth given from direct sunlight, especially like this, where I could hide my face in a pillow and just let the heat seep into the skin of my back and hips.

One day, when I had miraculously stolen enough stupid,

petty things like loose cash, I would build myself a house and have this kind of window in my bedroom.

Too bad I couldn't stay here forever.

But this wasn't *home*. No matter how much I was starting to enjoy the rush of the city around me, the pizza, and the strangeness of somewhere I'd never been, it wasn't *home*.

It didn't have...

Well. I didn't have much in the way of friends or family at *home* either, so I supposed that wasn't a compelling argument against staying.

Still.

It wouldn't work.

I drifted off, incredibly comfortable in my patch of sunlight, and when I opened my eyes again, the sun had set. Only artificial light cut into my room harshly to cast a silvery shine across my floor and walls.

"Time to put my talents to use, I suppose," I murmured, wondering when I'd become less careful in my planning. Time was, I'd never *ever* go after a house until I'd staked it out for weeks and followed the homeowner for long enough that I knew their schedule well enough to be confident in their timing.

But here I was, planning on breaking into 1313 Lampkin Drive without even knowing who exactly lived there.

If it was Harrison, I was relatively sure that I could get around without him noticing me.

Hopefully, if it was, I'd find something in the house to point me in the direction of the pack.

It didn't take me long to change into black leggings, a dark green hoodie that fell to mid-thigh, and a pair of sneakers with no laces, only an elastic band over the tops of them. While they weren't my favorite, they'd work for tonight.

Last, I put my hair up into a bun, considering that I needed a haircut soon. I hadn't had hair longer than my chin in *years,* but here I was with auburn waves that now fell past my shoulders.

Surely I hadn't been *that* caught up for so long?

My phone vibrated, signifying a message. I glanced at it, only slightly surprised to see a message from my mother. She hadn't bothered to call or message me since our fight, and I'd half expected her to just write me off as dead to the rest of Scheffield.

Some might have said that would be an overreaction on her part, but to that I just said that they did not know my mother.

She, herself, was a pro at overreactions to just about everything if it would serve her in the long run.

A sigh left me, lips flattening as my eyes scanned the text that sat on the middle of my bright phone screen.

You should call me so we can discuss you coming home.

As if she hadn't heard me when I said I'd be back on *my terms.*

As if she did not *care.*

I knew it was definitely the second. She'd heard me and disregarded my intentions when I'd laid them out for her. Now she was going to pretend that I'd never told her my plan, and would go on with her own great idea for what I should be doing.

Not coming home. Rented an apartment. Talk to you soon.

I sent the message with no regrets, but waited a few minutes for her to reply. I didn't want her texting me while I was sneaking around. That would be irritating and troublesome.

Not to mention, it would throw me off my game if I couldn't take care of this right now.

I waited.

A minute passed, and when I glanced down at the screen I saw that my message had been read.

But she didn't reply.

At the three minute mark, I shook my head and ignored the twist of my stomach. It wasn't like her reaction was new. She'd probably ignore me for a few more days, then try again. Eventually, as always, she'd blow up again and then give up.

She was predictable, though I would never say that to her face.

Too bad she was predictable in all of the worst ways.

CHAPTER EIGHTEEN

WITH MY PHONE face down in the passenger seat, I drove back to Lampkin Drive easily, surprised at the still-heavy traffic of the city. Didn't people sleep?

Well, I didn't exactly sleep at night, so where did I get off wondering about anyone else's schedules?

This time I parked a street away, and as I walked down the street, I surreptitiously pulled the hood of my sweatshirt over my head, hiding my hair and casting my features into shadow.

This way, even if someone saw me walking down the street, I was featureless in the shadows and couldn't be identified later, if it became an issue.

God, I really hoped it wouldn't become that kind of issue. Police interference was the worst thing I could consider going wrong, and I didn't want to spend the rest of my days in *prison.*

Speaking of issues...

Glancing up from under my hood, I found more activity on Lampkin Drive *now* than there had been in the daytime. A few clusters of people stood on street corners, and I saw a couple of women glance my way, eyes like black marble in the night that glimmered with dark promise.

My stomach twisted, my heart sped up just a touch as if I needed reminding that this wasn't the best idea I'd ever had.

And I realized that if I wanted to get into the house, I'd have to go another way.

Thankfully, between 1313 and its neighbor, a very slim alley ran between the houses. I didn't enter it from this way-that would've been stupid, and kept walking down the block until I reached the end.

Even with my hands clenched in the pocket of my hoodie, however, I had a hard time not jumping at every little sound and every shadow that fell where I thought it shouldn't.

I didn't like being alone here.

At last, I rounded the corner and found this side street not so occupied. My steps sped up, my body wishing to be anywhere except here.

Just a bit longer, I told myself, feet making too much noise on the sidewalk under me as my strides lengthened of their own accord.

Just a little bit- My eyes fell on the opening of the alley on this side, and a relieved breath escaped my lungs in a *whoosh*.

Still keeping my casual pace, I swerved into it, my elbows almost brushing the walls of the houses on either side.

Now I just needed a way to get inside.

Stopping about halfway, I looked up at 1313 and searched the side for anything. *Anything* at all.

When I realized there was nothing at all on this side, I moved to the area behind the house that was only minimally bigger. Sure, it had grass and even a back porch, but it looked to me like a token effort.

Not to mention, I hated how out in the open this felt. Bracketed by other porches and windows, the back 'yard' was lit by two lamp posts that buzzed loudly in the night.

"Great," I muttered, gazing upward as I stood next to the porch.

But maybe, I wouldn't need to use the *yard* at all.

The columns, tiered and rough, were grown up with plants and lined with two drainage pipes. Though this wasn't my most ingenious idea, I reached up and found a handhold in the ivy and against the rough, chipped column.

I was so going to regret this.

And yet, I climbed anyway. One foot after the other, I hauled myself up the side of the porch column, thankful that there were so many other things to use as support on my way up.

And also very grateful that there was no one else to hear my heavy breathing and occasional cursing when my foot slipped, or the brick raked my skin.

At last, I was on the shingled roof, and my gaze landed on what I'd hoped I'd find here all along.

A window.

"Yes," I hissed under my breath, crawling quickly to the window and preparing to get out my lockpicks. It shouldn't be hard. I'd just need to jiggle-

The moment my fingers touched the glass it swung open, revealing that it had already been unlocked.

And greased not to make any noise.

Was this the work of someone like me?

Or was it that whoever lived here just wanted to make the thing easier to deal with.

I should go back. The thought punched me hard in the gut as I sat there, feet tucked under me and unsure of what to do in this situation. The logical answer would be to go back the way I'd come, jump in my car, and head to my adorable studio.

So why was I clambering silently into the window, hoping that no one was on the other side?

If I fell into some murderer's lair-the worst possible thing

I could think of-and found myself surrounded by bones and blood, it really would serve me right.

Instead, my feet landed lightly on the carpet, making no noise as I slid the rest of my body in and fell into a low crouch.

My initial thought had been right, I supposed. Whoever lived here had worked on the window recently, to my benefit.

I stayed still, listening for a few moments. While I heard the sound of voices, it was distant enough that I figured whoever it was stood outside, instead of in the house.

So, at last, I got to my feet, creeping through the attic and into the hallway beyond.

Maybe no one *did* live here. The thought occurred to me when I saw that most of the rooms sat empty, with only cobwebs and dust for residents, and a pang of disappointment went through my body.

Had I done all this for nothing?

At the top of the narrow stairs, I stopped to peer downward at the entryway of the house, where I could see the front door and the light coming in the small windows at its top.

A shadow passed in front of them, more muffled voices caught my ear, but I couldn't hear them well enough to hear what they said.

And I was too afraid to go down the stairs.

Something caught my eye in the bathroom to my left. I turned, at first seeing only broken tiles, exposed grout, and mold that made my nose wrinkle in disgust. Did I imagine things?

No. There were photos spread out here, and when I crept closer, I found that the pictures were all of the *pack*.

They looked candid, as well. As if the people in them-the four men I already had met-were unaware of their pictures being taken.

In one, Lysander leaned back against a wall, mouth open in a laugh as Azriel grinned.

In another, Nyko leaned on Rhys's shoulder as they sat at a park bench.

Three of the men appeared only as silhouettes against a street light, heads down and hoods up in the last.

Fingers trembling, I reached out to pick up the one of Azriel and Lysander laughing with each other and flipped it over.

Monday, August 3

Grill Fiesta

2:06 PM

The information was written in a messy pen, and when I found another, I saw that it also had an address, time, and date.

Was someone stalking them?

Well, someone other than me?

Is that what the man outside had said, when he spoke about my *boss*?

Perhaps it was the detective who was looking for them and had taken these on a stakeout or whatever police officers did in this situation.

But...if that were the case, why were they here?

Making a terrible, instant decision, I grabbed all of the scattered photos and folded them over, shoving them in my pocket as I stood. I could at least use them to figure out a good place to find the men, couldn't I?

That seemed like my best plan so far, anyway. And without anything better to go off of, I would just have to take it.

I walked, cat-quiet, back to the hallway's carpet, breathing in the scent of old wallpaper and mildew in the walls. I'd get to the window, get out, and get home before anyone knew I was here.

That was the plan, anyway.

The front door slammed open, shocking me into flinching and falling into a frozen, frightened crouch.

"I told you, I don't know where they are!" That was the old man, Harrison. It had to be. He sounded terrified, but I was much too scared for myself to turn and see who he spoke with.

A man growled, and when they spoke, I knew immediately it wasn't the police officer from this afternoon.

"They haven't just *fallen off* the face of the earth, you damned idiot!" the stranger spat. "Haven't you seen the news? David is *dead*, and we can't seem to catch that fucking pack out where we can get to them."

I had to move. I *had to move*. If I stayed here much longer, then I would be dead.

The window was close. So, *so* close.

I could make it.

Heart thudding like a battle drum against my ribs, I crept forward quickly, one foot in front of the other and my eyes fixed on the still-open glass.

Fixated as I was, I nearly missed the flurry of movement to my left.

My mouth opened, a gasp or a scream ready on my lips, but a hand sealed over my face as the other dragged me bodily into the empty old bedroom, my back hitting the floor just softly enough not to make a sound.

Through the bits of fragmented light from a slit of a window above me, I saw instantly that my captor was familiar.

It was Nyko.

"*Shhhh,*" he warned, tilting his head to the side and gazing at me with dark eyes. "Poor thing," he breathed, not moving his hand from my lips and sitting down to straddle my hips, weight keeping me from getting up. "Always looking the wrong way, aren't you? That's a shame."

Metal gleamed in the shifting light, and when I glanced to the side, I saw that his free hand held a switchblade.

Would he kill me for being here?

"Wait." He pulled it away, laying it on the floor beside us. "I'm not going to hurt you as long as you're quiet. Can you be quiet for me, Will?" His voice was cold and expectant, leaving no room at all for argument.

I nodded, wondering if I was going to throw up from fear or just pass out from how fast the blood pumped through my veins and begged me to *run*.

"One noise, and I slit your throat," Nyko warned, removing his hand from my mouth but not moving off of me.

I opened my mouth to ask him a question, then froze at the way his brow arched.

One noise, he'd said.

A question was, indeed, a noise.

Would he really kill me?

"Don't look at me like that." He picked up the switchblade again, running the blade over the tip of his thumb before pointing it at me. I flinched, prompting a smirk to curl over his lips. "Don't try me, Will. There's no Lysander or Azriel here tonight. I won't kill you when they ask me not to, but..." he rolled his shoulders in a shrug, voice deadly soft. "They aren't here, and I don't like you as they do."

What should I do?

The people downstairs were still speaking, though their voices had fallen to quiet snarls and withheld angry whispers. If I screamed, would they come to my rescue?

Or would Nyko have my throat open and gushing blood before they even made it to the bottom stair?

"They'll go away," Nyko went on, gazing towards the still-open door. "And Harrison won't come up here. He never does."

Well, *someone* did. Otherwise, the pictures wouldn't have been scattered on the bathroom floor.

Should I tell him about them?

Slowly I lifted my hand, drawing his gaze back down to mine instantly. As he watched, I reached into my pocket and pulled the photos free from it, unfolding them so he could see.

Nyko took them wordlessly, laying the blade down *on my stomach* to flip through them.

The metal felt heavy against me, even though it couldn't have weighed much at all. I froze again, still unable to move as my hands trembled.

"Where did you get these?" the black-haired male asked at last.

Was that a trick question?

He frowned, picked up the switchblade, and tapped my stomach with it, causing me to flinch and his eyes to darken like he'd enjoyed that a bit too much.

Maybe I'd enjoyed it a bit too much, too.

If I had to guess, Nyko enjoyed it all. He loved the way I seemed so afraid and appeared as if he drank it in.

In that way, he reminded me of Lysander.

Or perhaps, this was something they all shared.

"Bathroom," I whispered, swallowing before I spoke. "On the floor in the corner." They hadn't exactly been hidden, but I'd only caught sight of them by chance.

"And you just took them?" He folded them and shoved them in the pocket of his dark jeans. "Should I worry that *you* have some kind of business with my pack as well?"

"I..." Well, I was here, in Chicago, wasn't I? I sure as shit wasn't here to see the sights.

"*Oh*. I see." An unfriendly smirk made him look like a predator, and he drew the knife upward, between my breasts, and finally to the unprotected skin of my throat.

The metal was sharp and cold, and it seemed to burn

against my skin even though I knew he hadn't cut me yet. In the blade's trail, my skin burned, urging me to open my mouth and beg for more. Beg for him to tease that knife over *other* areas of my body, too.

God, maybe I was suffering from some kind of PTSD-related trauma that had scrambled my brain's proper reactions to this kind of thing.

"Did you come to Chicago to find *us*?"

I didn't answer that.

How could I?

He blinked, drawing the knife up to my cheek and tucking my hair back from my face. "I know we don't know each other very well, Willow, but I don't like to ask a question twice. However, I will this once, because I understand you might be going through a lot at the moment." The flat of the knife was laid against my cheek, and he tapped my skin with every word as he asked, "Did you come here seeking my pack?"

"Y-yes," I murmured, unsure of whether or not I feared answering him.

He blinked, brows raising in bemusement. "I wasn't expecting honesty," Nyko admitted.

I opened my mouth again, but before I could speak, he pressed the tip of the switchblade to my upper lip, tracing the scar there absently. My hands shook against the floor, feeling clammy as I continued staring at him.

"I don't need an explanation. Frankly, I don't care much about *why* you came here. And I won't even tell you to go home. I bet that place is a shit show for you right now, isn't it?" His blade didn't move, and I assumed the question was rhetorical.

So I only gave him my full attention and tried not to panic more than I already was.

"But this isn't your sweet little town in Michigan. This is *our* home. Not yours. And here, things work on a very different set of rules. If you come after my pack in any capacity, I don't care if you think it's to hurt us or not...you won't like the results. I stopped Lysander from doing something very regrettable once for you, and that's already one more than most people get." He pressed slightly harder against the scar, just enough that I could feel the sharpness of the blade following the threat of his words.

"I thought he liked me," I murmured when the knife left my mouth. Was it stupid to speak? Yeah. Absolutely.

Nyko's mouth quirked into a smirk I wasn't expecting, and his eyes narrowed in wicked amusement. "Do you think that's a *good* thing?" he asked incredulously. "Do you think him liking you means he'll bring you flowers and take you on dates? Darling, *Will...*" The knife descended again, every inch of its closeness making my body scream in anticipation and fear.

This time the touch didn't seem to burn. The blade at the base of my throat was still so sharp, but it sent shivers down my body that I couldn't ignore. The knifepoint pricked my flesh delicately, raising goosebumps on my arms.

As questionable as that reaction might have been, however, I was still petrified.

"If I were you, I'd be much more worried about the good impression you made on my pack than you seem to be. If you were smarter, you'd be on the other side of the country. Not in our backyard. So I'll say it again. Leave us alone. Not because I'm worried but because I know what *always* happens when those boys take an interest. Don't be stupid enough to stumble into them and give them a reason to think about you again."

The front door slammed, drawing his attention. He tilted his head to the side, listening. "I told you they wouldn't come up here," Nyko added and got to his feet.

I scrambled after him, my eyes on the blade in his hands as I backed towards the door. He watched me go, flipping the knife in his hand in a flourishing move before closing the blade and pocketing it. "And don't go around stealing shit from dangerous people," Nyko added, gesturing to the pocket that held the photos.

"Dangerous people?" I murmured.

"They're just as bad for you as we are, and won't give you this sweet warning when they catch you."

"Who..." I trailed off when he looked at me, his eyes hardening and the amusement falling from his sharp, elegant features.

"You can leave the way you came," he dismissed, stretching his arms over his head like a cat. "I'll give you a five-minute head start, and you'd better not be sneaking around outside when I get there."

I stared at him, watching as he proceeded to ignore me and look at his phone. At last, he looked up as if surprised I was still there.

"Time's already started," he said. "I don't know why you're still here, unless you're inviting me to *do something* about it."

I didn't know what that meant, and I didn't *want* to know what that meant.

I backtracked to the hallway and lunged for the window, not being nearly as quiet as I had been when I'd come in.

CHAPTER NINETEEN

GRILL FIESTA.

That was the only clue that I could remember, and I kicked myself for not looking at the backs of more of the photos.

Of course, I'd expected to be able to go back to the apartment and look for information about the addresses listed on them. I *had not* thought I'd be handing them over to Nyko before I'd scarcely had them for more than a few minutes.

That sucked.

For two days, I meandered around *Grill Fiesta* around lunch time. The second day, I went there at dinner time as well.

Calling it a restaurant, however, was being generous. *Grill Fiesta* sat at the edge of a block, tables both outside and inside. I'd gone in, played the pleasant customer, and scoped it out while eating one of the best tofu tacos of my life.

Of course, the bar wasn't exactly high, seeing as I made the only tofu tacos I'd ever had.

I wasn't an awful cook. Or, so I liked to tell myself. My food was edible at least.

But this place had me coming back to actually eat lunch there, and to even take dinner home.

The first two days had been a bust, save for the food, and

I wondered if I had the wrong *Grill Fiesta.* I didn't remember the picture well enough to know more than what I'd seen at a glance, and I'd looked this place up the morning after for its location.

Maybe they didn't eat here anymore? Or perhaps it was somewhere else all together?

Heavy storm clouds rolled overhead as I parked my car across the street, closing the door with my hip as I scanned the outside of the restaurant for any signs of familiar faces.

Sure, I was afraid of what Nyko had said—well, intimidated, at least. But I didn't quite take him as seriously as he might've intended. The four of them hadn't hurt me yet-

The memory of Rhys's hands around my own, his mouth against my neck, played treacherously through my mind until I shook my head.

They *hadn't* hurt me. Most likely, Nyko had been trying to scare me off.

Well, I didn't scare that easily. Azriel had been mostly friendly towards me. I had no reason to think he wouldn't speak to me if I asked.

Though, stalking them and waiting around to catch a glimpse of them *probably* wasn't my best plan ever. How in the world would I even explain it?

'Hey, guys. I didn't have your phone number, so I figured I'd just creep around and wait for you at the restaurant where someone took a picture of you! Hope that's not creepy!'

That was the only explanation my brain could come up with, but it sounded...not great. Even to my own ears, it didn't seem like something that would work in my favor.

If I could ever *find* them again.

Perhaps seeing Nyko had been a fluke. I'd considered going back to that house, but every time I started to plan that, I chickened out and turned my brain to something else.

Halfway across the street, I nearly stumbled and fell.

There they were.

Not all of them. I wasn't that lucky. But Rhys and Nyko stood outside the cafe talking to a waitress.

Of the two, Rhys looked to be doing most of the talking. He smiled, nodding as she spoke, while Nyko hung like a dark cloud at his side, hands shoved in the pockets of his suede coat.

And here I was, out in the open.

Shit.

As I reached the edge of the crosswalk, I kept going down the street, grateful that a small coffee shop was on the other side of the street and down just a little ways from *Grill Fiesta.*

There I hesitated, squinting back at the other restaurant. If they sat inside, I might not be able to watch them. That would be unlucky. But not unlikely. Only a few other people were sitting at an outside table, and I figured that any sensible person would go inside to escape the chill and the threat of eventual rain.

But they didn't. Much to my surprise, the two of them took an outside table which placed them in clear view of the small coffee shop I'd found.

I sat down as well at an outside table at the coffee shop, barely looking around except to nod at the waitress who looked my way to show her that, yeah, I really was sitting here and wanted something off the menu.

While I wasn't starving, I also knew I couldn't sit here and just stare at them.

Plus, caffeine was always a welcome addition to my body.

"Are you sure you wouldn't rather be inside?" the woman asked as I slipped on a pair of sunglasses and pulled my hair back into a ponytail.

"I'm sure," I told her. "I actually love the cold and the overcast weather." Nothing like the truth to back up suspicious behavior.

"Do you know what you might like?" She laid a small menu in front of me that I peeked at, but in the end, all coffee shops were similar enough that I could order without really *looking*.

"Caramel Macchiato?" I requested. "And umm." Was I hungry? I had been, coming here, but now I wasn't sure if my flip-flopping stomach could handle a meal. "And that's it," I said with a sigh. I'd get some food later, once I'd watched Nyko and Rhys in order to figure out....

Well, surely I'd figure out *something*.

I rested an elbow on my table, chin on my hand, and held my phone in my other hand. While I kept making the motions of scrolling as the waitress left, my eyes remained fixed on the two men.

Too bad I wasn't able to hear what they said. I'd have to track them for a while before knowing where to hide or how close I needed to get for that.

Or, I supposed, I could waltz up and ask them my questions.

Snorting to myself, I shook my head and let my gaze drift to my phone for a moment.

I had an unread message from my mother, but I had seen enough of it when it came through to know that I didn't want to deal with that headache today.

Or any day, frankly.

Reluctantly I dragged my gaze up from the dark wooden table under my hand and looked to Rhys and Nyko again.

They talked.

A waiter took their order.

They talked again.

This was *boring*.

At least they didn't know I was here, but that didn't mean much when there was no point in me actually being here. What was I accomplishing, other than acting like some strange voyeur?

My eyes fell to my phone again and I sighed heavily. They weren't even doing anything *interesting*.

I looked up again, and did a double-take.

They were holding hands. Even this far away, I could see the way Rhys had curled his fingers around Nyko's hand, stroking a thumb over the back of his palm.

Were they *boyfriends*?

Okay, yeah. They made an adorable couple. I had to admit that.

Now I really, *really* felt like a voyeur.

When I looked down at my table and the small empty plate, I narrowed my eyes.

What in the *world*...?

A small, wadded-up piece of straw paper lay on my plate.

Had that been there this whole time?

Of course, it had.

The waitress returned with my coffee and set it in front of me, asking me if I was sure I didn't want anything else.

I promised her I didn't.

"I'm just killing time," I admitted with a smile. "I'm meeting a friend later."

"Oh, I see!" She turned away. "Let me know if you want a refill." Then she walked away, approaching another table somewhere behind me and asking if she could take their order.

I didn't hear what they said. I didn't care. My attention snapped back to Nyko and Rhys, and I found that Nyko had his phone out and seemed to be showing Rhys something on it.

The latter grinned slightly, shaking his head in disapproval.

It really was a shame I couldn't hear them.

I picked up my cup, preparing to take a drink, when something small and white caught my eye.

A ball of straw paper *in my coffee* was soaking up liquid, losing its whiteness as it pulled in color.

"What the *fuck*?" I hissed, reaching into it and throwing the straw paper onto my plate. When I looked down, I discovered *more* evidence of someone playing a weird joke on me. Three more balls of straw paper were on the table and two more were on the sidewalk under my feet.

A giggle caught my attention from the table behind me that had sat a few minutes after I had.

"Can you tell your kid-"

I whirled in my chair, and the words died in my throat.

Lysander and Azriel sat at the table behind me, and when I looked, I saw that Azriel was covering his mouth to stifle the laughter that shook his shoulders.

Oh fuck.

"You-but-" My brain refused to put together words for a proper sentence as my hands tightened on the back of my chair. "How did you-"

On impulse, I spun around, looking at Rhys and Nyko again.

Only this time, they were looking right at me as well. Rhys raised a glass in a mock toast while Nyko watched me, unimpressed.

"I tried to make him stop," Lysander informed me, voice as level as he could manage with Azriel devolving into another fit of snickering. "I mean-you're taking this rather seriously and all. Hair up, sunglasses on. You look like a professional."

Turning to look at them again, I saw Azriel nodding his agreement from behind his hand.

"But how did you know?" I demanded. "I haven't been close, and I've been extremely careful! This is what I do at home, and it works *just fine.*"

"Let's break this down into simple steps, shall we?" Lysander got to his feet, swiping his coffee as he strolled over and sat down at my table. I watched him lean back, his foot pressed against mine absently.

I didn't move. I *wouldn't* move, as if this was some kind of power-play between us. I wouldn't give up so easily.

Azriel followed him, but didn't take the seat that would've mostly blocked my view of Rhys and Nyko.

When I looked between him and them suspiciously, he shook his head. "I won't block your view," he said in a mock-solemn tone. "You worked *so hard* to find the perfect spot to watch them. I already feel bad for interrupting you. But don't worry, they aren't coming over here."

"I'm not worried," I spat in irritation, slamming the cup down on the wooden table and splashing liquid on my hand.

Surreptitiously, Lysander reached forward with a napkin, but I snatched my own up and dropped it onto the slight mess. "I can clean it myself!" I hissed, feeling like a pissed-off cat.

Lysander lifted his hands in surrender, eyes gleaming with dark amusement. "Whatever you say. Would you like to hear where you went wrong in this little stakeout of yours, detective?"

I scowled at him, not as afraid of the two of them as I was of Nyko or Rhys.

Especially Nyko.

"No," I snapped.

"The sunglasses are a terrible idea," Lysander went on as if I'd agreed. "It's overcast. Even if I didn't know you personally, I'd know you were up to something. And where's your chill, Willow?" He shook his head. "You looking at your phone wasn't believable in the slightest. Try watching them again, but look less obvious."

"No!" I said again, voice louder than I'd intended. I clenched the edge of the table between clammy fingers. "I'm not going to-to mess up for your amusement! That's messed up."

"I can have them do something interesting?" Azriel lifted a hand that held his phone.

"Have...have you been *texting them* since you realized I was over here?"

I hated this. I hated them.

They traded a look. Azriel sighed and laid it down. "Yes," he said at last. "Absolutely."

"Oh, don't lie to her," Lysander snorted. "We saw you here yesterday, actually. And since we have the photos you found, it was pretty obvious why you were here."

"But you didn't eat here yesterday-" I broke off, aware of the self-implication of my words.

Well, there was no denying it now.

Lysander rested his head on his hand and gazed sweetly at me. "We got takeout," he informed me. "And then they volunteered to eat out here and see what you'd do. I thought you'd run away."

"Honestly, none of us thought you were *stalking* us, Will," Azriel agreed. "It's kind of cute. In a creepy way. Like, you even watched them *hold hands*."

"*I'm* creepy?" I gasped, drawing up indignantly. "*Me*? Have you seen yourselves?"

They traded a look. Lysander shrugged.

"So, what are you doing here?" Azriel sat back in his chair, ignoring what I'd said, I supposed. "Like, *actually* doing here. I hope you didn't come all the way to Chicago just to spy on us or watch them hold hands."

"How was I supposed to know they would *do that*?"

"You have a message," Lysander observed, giving me whiplash by the sudden turn of the conversation. Before I could stop him, the man picked up my phone and swiped it to open my messages.

"Wait-" I began, but he didn't.

Lysander whistled, and my heart sank. "These are from your *mom*? This is pretty vitriolic, you know?"

"Let me see?" Azriel requested, leaning over the table.

I considered taking the phone back, but instead just buried my face in my hands.

What in the world was going on? Was it possible that I was still dreaming?

After all, none of this seemed...*real*. Talking with them was strange. Draining.

Unnatural.

"She really wants you to come home, huh?" Azriel laid my phone back beside my plate.

"Want me to reply?" Lysander picked it up again. "I can get her to leave you alone."

I shook my head fervently, one hand out in a silent request for the phone. "Can I have it back?"

"What's the magic word?

He waited.

I stayed quiet.

At last, I gave in first with a sigh, and a muttered, "Please."

The cold surface of my phone found my hand, and I put it in my pocket without a second glance.

"Look. I hate to be the bad guy, but if I don't do it, then Lysander will," Azriel said after a moment. "But you can't follow us around like this. It gives us the wrong idea."

"The wrong *idea*?" I snapped. "Is there a right idea?"

"Well, I suppose you could be in love with us," Lysander commented. "If so, say it now. I quite like that possibility."

"I'm not in love with you."

"Then we're back to the wrong idea."

Azriel faced me fully. "I'm sorry if Nyko scared you the other night, but he was being nice," the dark-haired man stated. "You can't follow us around like this. We've been really, *really* nice to you. And that's not like us either. It's only going to last for so long."

"So if you have a question, *ask,*" Lysander intoned.

"Umm..." I hadn't thought about this conversation. I'd thought about finding them and demanding what they knew, but that didn't seem to work well here. "Okay. Uh." I sucked in a breath. "Why did the Deerling brothers kill my roommate?"

They looked between one another, a confounded look evident on Azriel's features while Lysander just read...bored.

"That's what you wanted to ask us?" Lysander assured.

"Yeah. *Yes.* You knew their grandfather, didn't you? And you followed them from here after they did it. So you *must* know why they killed her!" I hadn't meant to make it sound like a demand, but here I was. *Demanding* an answer from them. "I need to know *why*. She didn't deserve it. *Any* of it!"

Azriel frowned, but didn't speak.

I glanced at Lysander, but still, he just appeared incredibly *bored*.

"Well?!" I snapped.

"You're not going to like the answer," Azriel said finally. "I think maybe this is a case where you should just go home and try to move on. Seriously. Coming here...It's not going to give you the answers you're hoping for."

"I don't know what you-"

"They killed her because she was their *type*. Just like you were," Lysander interrupted, voice quiet but firm. "Not because she did something or because she owed the mafia some kind of *debt*. The world doesn't work that way, Will. Sometimes bad things happen to good people, and your roommate is a perfect example of that. She caught their eye, and they went after her like predators to prey." He shrugged his lean shoulders, letting them fall. "I don't know what else you want to hear. And if that's why you came, then I'm sorry to disappoint you."

That was *it*? An invisible fist closed around my heart. Because she was *their type*? I shook my head, unsure of what to say or do, or even *think*. "But that's...not fair," I murmured. "It's not *right*."

"Could've just as easily been you," Azriel pointed out. "They'd done it many times before. The way I heard it, they dragged girls back to that little forest building they had, and you know..." He waved his hands dramatically. "Their *type* was pretty broad. They went for all kinds of pretty girls. Your roommate just seemed unlucky."

"Then why did you come after them?" I asked, barely thinking of what I was saying. "If they'd done it before, why did you care this time?"

Neither of them answered for a moment.

At last, Lysander sighed. "Don't do this again," he advised. "There's no profound truth for you here. Only danger and problems. This is your last warning, Will. If you stick around, we'll have to be *interested*. You might not like us interested in you."

Interested?

I wanted to ask what that meant, but I couldn't find the words to do so.

"Seriously," agreed Azriel. "We're not going to tell you to leave Chicago or something. That would be stupid. But don't come looking for us again."

"Next time, you won't like who you find." Lysander's voice was cold, and when I met his blue eyes, all I could see were chips of ice that showed nothing but stony coldness.

For the first time, I saw something other than the strange, questionable men I hadn't known that long at all.

I saw monsters.

CHAPTER TWENTY

WHILE GOING HOME FELT like the best option for two hours or so after I crept back to my temporary home, that feeling ebbed away rather quickly when I remembered my mother had texted me during my meeting with Lysander and Azriel.

My eyes raking over her message only served to cement that fact, and I felt my mouth turn down into a frown of its own accord.

Hope you're on your way home soon. I rescheduled your appointment.

I didn't respond. What could I say that I hadn't said a thousand times before?

She would either respect my decisions, or she wouldn't.

My odds were on *not*.

That night I ordered *Grill Fiesta* and had it dropped off at my door as my own personal *fuck you* to the pack who thought they could just order me around.

Later that night, when I *finally* slept, I dreamed of Lysander sitting in my window, humming softly, and Nyko's knife running lightly over the scar on my lip while he whispered half-threats that sounded more like promises in my ear.

Maybe a therapist wasn't such a bad idea after all.

The next day dawned with rain-or so I assumed. By the time the sun rose, I was fast asleep and only knew that when I *did* rejoin the land of the living around noon, the rain pelted my window and slid down it in fat, heavy rivulets.

I *loved* the rain. It took everything in me not to just open the window and drape myself out it.

But perhaps the still-fraying memory of my dream stopped me. It had been so real that I found myself checking for signs of a break-in, and had to do so twice before my brain was convinced nothing had happened and no one had gotten inside.

I had to doubt that they even knew where I was staying.

My doorbell sounded, or at least, I assumed it was my doorbell. The sound was low and sonorous, but made its way through the studio apartment and to my ears with ease.

Who in the world would be visiting me here?

Throwing on a long t-shirt over my tank top and shorts, I padded on bare feet to the kitchen. I pulled open the front door with the expectation of seeing Tara and, hopefully, another Tupperware container full of her pretzel bars which I would gladly trade a kidney for.

For a moment, my brain rebelled, warning me that it might be someone dangerous, like Lysander or Detective Yates.

But the former didn't know where I was, while the latter didn't even know my *name.*

To my great pleasure, the person on the other side of the door turned out to be Tara Blueford, the woman who'd rented me this apartment.

She beamed at my appearance, and lifted a hand that held a paper bag of...something. "Apartment warming gift," she said, hovering at the door like an excited hummingbird. "Can I come in?"

"Oh-sure. Absolutely." I blinked in surprise and stepped

back. "It's totally still your place, I mean." And god damn, I was glad that I hadn't messed it up yet.

Not too badly, at least.

Tara barely seemed to notice the dirty clothes in a pile by the bed, and didn't remark on the pillows of my own I'd piled onto it.

She set the bag down on the bar counter and shed her jacket, which went to a hanger on the back of the door. "So...I hope you don't mind me dropping in. I just had to ask...how are you liking Chicago?" Tara asked, taking a seat at the bar and unloading the contents of the bag.

One box, a purple and pink affair wrapped in a bow, she pushed towards me and gestured for me to open it.

"It's been good," I lied. "Though my friends don't have as much time for me as I thought, so I've had to entertain myself quite a bit. How are you doing?" I wanted to be polite. Tara reminded me, in a way, of Marianne from *Monsoon Moon*.

The thought sent a pang of regret through my chest that I fought hard to ignore. Swallowing, I focused on the box in front of me and pulled off the lid.

Inside was a spa gift set, full of bath bombs, a bottle of lavender-infused shower gel, and a cream that promised relaxation and urged the body to rest.

"You just looked really tired the last time I was here," Tara admitted. "I was worried about your stress and if something was going on. Of course, I won't pry, but I know for me, a bath and a book do *wonders* to help me at the end of the day. I thought maybe it would be the same for you."

"Thank you," I whispered, surprised at the gift. I felt warm, and urged myself not to blush and give away just how unfamiliar I was with this kind of thing.

"I also brought lunch," Tara went on. "I picked up some extra. Do you like sub sandwiches?" She laid out two different half sandwiches. "I got a meatball sub and a chicken salad. Figured I'd give you whichever you wanted, and I'd take the other."

"You seriously didn't have to do this," I told her, dragging a bar stool to my side of the counter and sitting down. "It's really *really* nice of you, though."

"Oh, I like the company." Tara slid a bottle of water my way. "And I'm sure I'll talk your ear off about my husband, so think of this as a bribe if you'd like."

Great. I couldn't think of anything I wanted to do *less*.

But...

Tara seemed so sincere. Even as she chatted away about her husband, daughter, and *cat* of all things. All I wanted to do was tell her I was tired so I could do something else with my day.

But every time I tried, I got another pang of sadness of how much she reminded me of Marianne and couldn't bring myself to say the words to make her leave.

Was this survivor's guilt over what had happened? If so, I wondered where I could hit the return to sender button.

It sucked.

With my mind in a place it shouldn't have been, and my thoughts in a whirlpool of negativity, I slipped back into things that comforted me.

Such as the pursuit of shiny things that their owners wouldn't miss.

As a teenager, I'd started swiping things that didn't belong to me from stores. Little items, like keychains or pens that I could practice on but wouldn't be missed.

I did it now, just for the cheap thrill that it used to give me.

This time, I only felt a twinge of amusement from the activity and found myself with pens and magnets all but falling out of my pockets.

With a sigh, I found myself wishing I'd brought my car to dump my 'haul' into instead of leaving it in the driveway of my new home.

I moved on, leaving the pile of things I'd grabbed at the front of the store rather than taking them with me. No one noticed. I knew they wouldn't; stealing from a store was one of the easiest things I'd taught myself.

Stealing from people themselves was the challenge I needed today. Not so I could keep anything, no. I had no problem putting everything I'd taken back on the shelves after the glow of serotonin had faded from my body.

Absently, I realized that I wasn't far from *Grill Fiesta* and wrinkled my nose at the notion that I'd come here on purpose.

Was it worse if my choice of direction hadn't been a conscious decision at all, and my body was secretly trying to punish me for what I'd done?

Whatever.

A group of young-ish men stood outside the restaurant, whispering to one another without a care in the world. Something about them gave me pause, and I leaned against a wall to glance at my phone as if I'd meant to stop there.

What was it?

The men were strangers: Twenty-five, thirty at the very most. There was nothing off about them that I could see, save for a few bad choices of tattoos.

I was *pretty* sure, after all, that 'regrets' was not spelled with an 'a' anywhere in the world.

Something flashed in their eyes as they looked at a woman with her hands full and a phone tucked to her ear, but I couldn't place it.

Until I *could*.

I'd seen that look before. In Donald Deerling's eyes when he'd looked at me in the mirror of my car.

In Lysander's eyes, when he'd hit David Deerling from behind with his bat.

It wasn't a friendly look.

Quit projecting, Will! I chastised myself with a shake of my head. It was raining, the drizzle steady as it cut through the air around me.

These *boys* were nothing like any of them, I was sure.

I was jumpy, and that was an issue if I wanted to do this right.

When one of them broke off from the group and turned away, I followed him at a distance. Casually, as if we just happened to be going in the same direction.

He was an easy target. With a wallet attached to one of those stupid chains in his back pocket, he was just *begging* for his shit to be stolen.

I'd teach him a lesson and take a teacher's fee for doing my civic duty in this world.

He walked on, leading me past *Grill Fiesta* and down a quieter street. I barely noticed. I wanted him to be a little further before I struck, and he was doing me a favor by going so far from his buddies.

At last, I sped up, catching up to the man but not stopping, even as my hand drifted out and slipped into the pocket that held his wallet.

I'd been doing this long enough that I could tell what I was looking for in a split second, and found a solitary bill as the man looked the other way.

I didn't even need to slow down.

With his money crumpled in my hand, I kept walking. One foot in front of the other, and only the *rush* of adrenaline sending me to the high I wanted as my heart thudded faster in my chest.

This was the feeling I loved. Half of the reason I stole was because of it, and I couldn't imagine a day when I *didn't* love this.

Not to mention it was pretty profitable. This time, however, I'd only managed to steal a twenty from the guy. That was fine. In this day and age, not many people carried around a lot of cash.

"Excuse me."

The voice was too close for comfort, making me jump. I glanced over my shoulder and was shocked to see the man I'd pickpocketed had my phone in his hand.

What the hell?

"I think you dropped this," he told me sweetly, the smile on his thin face and the sparkle in his eyes telling me I hadn't done any such thing.

Fuck.

"What a funny coincidence," I told him flatly, a wry grin on my face. "As it turns out, I'm not the only one who dropped something." I held the bill up between my fingers. "Want to trade?"

He looked around, prompting me to do so as well.

We were alone. I'd followed him to a side street devoid of people without meaning to do so, and now my heart sank to my stomach.

"Sure," he chuckled, reaching out with my phone. "Just watch whose pockets you reach into around here, okay?"

Was I honestly being taught pickpocket lessons from someone my own age?

Well. If I'd lost my phone to him without noticing-*and* he'd known what I was doing-I probably deserved it.

Giving him a rueful grin, I dipped my head in a yawn, taking my phone and handing him the twenty. "Yeah. Okay. That's fair-"

In a move too fast for me to follow, he reached up with his other hand, and something flashed, a shine of metal catching my gaze.

Was that a-

Hot, searing pain made me cry out and yank my arm

back, but the damage had already been done. I stumbled backward, slamming into the wall behind me and sliding to the ground.

He'd *cut* me.

Hot blood poured down my body, soaking my shirt from a long, deep gash just above my collarbone. I reached up with both hands, covering the wound even as blood seeped between my fingers.

It *hurt*. My brain could only scream in panic, refusing to do more than tell me that I *was very hurt* and needed to *do something* about it.

But that wasn't very helpful. Especially with the man approaching me, a small knife still in his hand.

"I really hate that I have to do this," he told me with a grin that betrayed the lie in his words. "But a job's a job, you know? And it's your bad decision-making in hanging out with the pack. Don't you know any better?"

"The-pack?!" I gasped, confused and only able to think about the pain in my shoulder. Tears coursed down my face, mixing with the rain on my skin.

"Don't play dumb." He brandished the knife at me. "I've seen the pictures of you with them. Was it worth it? Are they really *that* good or something that you just had to risk your neck by being with them?"

"I don't know what you're talking about!" I sobbed, drawing my knees up protectively to my chest as he swaggered forward.

"No point in lying-"

"She's not." The voice was cold, devoid of any emotion whatsoever, and had come from around the corner at my left. Suddenly, someone moved to stand in front of me.

From around dark-jean-clad legs, I saw the boy who'd stabbed me go pale. "Oh *shit*," he breathed, hands up in the air and the knife clattering to the ground. "They said you'd be-"

"On the other side of town dealing with your friend?" Lysander asked sweetly. I couldn't see his face, but I could hear the sudden humor in his tone and wondered if he was smiling. "Bad luck for you that I'm here then, isn't it?"

The man opened his mouth to speak, but without warning, a loud *pop* rang through the air.

He fell to the ground, a bullet in his head and his eyes still open wide with fear.

Lysander had *killed him*.

I yelped, one hand going to my mouth as nausea climbed my insides. The bullet wound bled sluggishly, but it was his *eyes* that bothered me most of all.

Somehow, he still looked to me just that least bit alive, even though I knew that no one survived a wound like *that*.

Holy *shit*.

Lysander was a fucking murderer.

Which, okay, I'd *known* that.

He stood in front of me like it didn't bother him at all, and didn't act like he'd even known this person.

I'd really gotten myself into it this time.

Immediately the blonde whirled and knelt in front of me, gaze cool and curious as he surveyed me. "Where did he get you, Will?" Lysander murmured in a soft voice.

I trembled, eyes squeezed shut against the pain. "The shoulder," I whispered at last. "I think, Lysander, I need to go to a hospital." I wanted my phone, and I was intent on gathering my wits enough to call a damn ambulance.

God, it hurt so badly. I'd never in my wildest dreams *imagined* being stabbed, and the pain burned hot and bright.

I closed my hand around empty air before realizing that Lysander had taken my phone from my grasp and slid it into his pocket.

"Let me see," he urged.

"I'm gonna throw up," I declared instead, leaning back and whacking my head against the stone wall behind me.

The pain of that didn't even *register* with how much my shoulder burned.

"Don't throw up," he advised, pushing my arm down from where I had pressed it to the bleeding wound. "You'll live," he announced.

"Yeah, *at a hospital*.....right?"

Something was wrong. Something was...*off* with him.

He cocked his head to the side, staring at my face. "You should've left well enough alone," he said slowly, at last. "I warned you. Even *Nyko* warned you."

"I wasn't looking for you!" I snapped, pain making my anger flare even though my whole body trembled.

He shrugged off the words and continued. "I can't just leave you here. That'd be really, *really* bad of me."

"Well, of course not." I knew fear showed in my voice. "Just-just call an ambulance for me. Then you can go if you want."

He shook his head and rocked back on his heels. "I'm going to help you," he announced, at last, the words causing his blue eyes to brighten. "You need help. You *really* really..." He trailed off and put a hand to my chest, just under the bleeding wound.

When he pressed down slightly, I yelped, tears blurring my vision. "Stop-*please*. That hurts."

"Oh," he murmured. Like that wasn't *obvious*. "Don't worry, okay?" he said again, rolling his eyes up to meet mine.

"I'm worried. What can I say to convince you to call an *ambulance?!*" I nearly shrieked. Didn't he see I was probably going to bleed out?

"You don't need an ambulance. Do you know how much a ride to the ER costs? Even with good insurance?" He shook his head. "Besides..." He trailed off, not finishing the thought. At last, he shook his head again, eyes finding and holding mine. "If you're going to pass out from blood loss, now would be the time," he said, somehow knowing that my head was beginning to spin.

Was it from pain? Adrenaline? Blood loss?

I couldn't be sure.

"I'd better wake up in a hospital," I whispered, hating that I could feel his arms around me as darkness fluttered at the edges of my vision. I was scared, and I knew he could see it. Not that I could hide it very well. I couldn't stop myself from shaking, just like I couldn't stop the soft sob that escaped my lips unbidden.

"Don't worry, Will," he said, blocking my view and pulling me to him. "I'll do you one better."

Whatever I wanted to say would have to wait, as I slowly faded into unconsciousness in Lysander's arms and wondered if I'd ever wake up.

CHAPTER TWENTY-ONE

WITHOUT THE SERENADE of beeping machines and hushed voices in my ears or the scent of medicine and chemicals burning my nostrils, I could only deduce one thing as I swam into wakefulness.

Lysander Ashford had not, in fact, taken me to the hospital.

Damn it.

Had I expected to wake up in the ER with stitches in my shoulder and a monstrous bill that I'd have to steal a car to pay for?

Kind of.

Part of me had been sure that I wouldn't wake up at all.

My eyes opened slowly while I silently begged to wake up in my bedroom. Almost like the whole thing had been just a bad dream.

The first sight of a dark ceiling and a lazily spinning ceiling fan put that hope to rest.

Damn it.

Shakily I sat up, barely noticing the dragging feeling against my right hand. It was connected to my right arm and shoulder, giving me the feeling that it was also part of the injury there.

Two problems presented themselves to me.

Was I okay? That seemed pretty important.

But so too did the other question screaming at me.

Where the fuck was I?

"Hello?" I murmured, curling my legs up under me in the large bed. I still wore my leggings and t-shirt I'd been in when I'd been stabbed, but where was my hoodie?

And my shoes.

And my fucking *phone.*

"Shit," I breathed, reaching up with my left hand to press lightly over my shoulder. My t-shirt was dried with blood, and I had expected it to be sticking uncomfortably to my skin.

Instead, the area of the shoulder had been cut, causing the material to hang from my shoulder and barely touch what felt like a bandage underneath.

I needed to see it. For my own peace of mind, if anything.

Unfolding my legs, I stood up from the bed and looked around more closely at the room I'd awoken in. The bed was covered in a dark blue comforter, and a matching rug lay under it on the floor. The ceiling fan was the only noise in the room, and against the wall over the bed was a triplicate of a snowy forest photograph.

Two doors sat against one wall, another on the wall opposite them.

I went for the one, thinking it had to be an exit.

That was when I noticed the dragging again and the sound of metal on the wood of the floor.

What in the world?

My eyes dropped, finding a long coil of metal.

Of *chain.*

My heart thudded in my chest, singing our own funeral dirge.

A *chain?!*

My eyes followed the metal, but I already knew where it would lead.

The dragging on my wrist wasn't a remnant from the pain in my shoulder.

It was a handcuff.

"Oh fuck," I whispered, and nearly fainted on the spot.

Instead, I grabbed at it wildly, trying to pull my hand free from the metal loop. While it was loose enough not to bother me, it wasn't at all in a position to come off.

This couldn't be happening.

The chain was long and light, but when I yanked at the links, I found them to be solid and unbreakable. A pile of chains lay on the floor by the bed, and it looked to me as if I had a reasonable distance I could go before it was pulled tight.

I trembled where I stood, barefoot on the plush carpet, as my body begged me to do the one thing I absolutely couldn't.

Run.

Belatedly I heard the door swing open, and whirled around with my chained hand pressed to my chest as if to hide it.

Nykos stood in the doorframe, leaning against it as he looked me over with dark, glittering eyes.

"Look who's finally awake. I thought you'd sleep forever, princess," he greeted mockingly. "Thought maybe Lysander would have to come in here and kiss you like Prince Charming-"

"Where am I?!" I demanded, cutting him off as my thoughts raced.

He stared at me, unimpressed. The dismissiveness of his attitude was so easily seen on his sharp-featured face that it couldn't have been more clear if he'd *said* how little he thought of me.

"Our house," he said finally, gaze wandering to look over

the room. "More specifically, the second guest bedroom. Lysander punched a hole in the one we usually give to our guests. And he thought that might bother you."

"Oh, *right,*" I sneered, unable to think straight, and fear driving my words. "A hole in the wall would've frightened me, but I shouldn't be at all terrified that you have me *chained to a wall?!*"

Nykos surveyed his fingernails studiously. "Are you finished?" he asked at last.

"Why? Am I keeping you? Do you have other guests chained to walls in this place to see to?" I would not cry. I *refused* to show them how afraid I was.

"I'm the only one home, actually. And *you're* the only guest here. Chained to a wall or otherwise."

He was the only one here?

Perhaps that could work in my favor.

Well, it couldn't hurt to try *something* here, right?

"You don't like me." It wasn't a question, and he didn't answer me. "That's obvious. And-and you can't possibly want me here for long. Just let me go. *Please*."

"I already did," Nykos pointed out. "The other night, remember? If I let you go again, you might get the wrong idea about me." He blinked slowly, eyeing me up and down.

"But..." I trailed off, thoughts warring in my head as I tried to think of a way to convince him. "I don't *want* to be here!" I shrieked at last.

"Okay, *and*?"

I hadn't expected that to convince him, but my heart sank anyway.

I felt like crying.

"Are..." I swallowed the question, and tried again. I was afraid of the words on my lips, and even more afraid of his answer.

"Are you going to kill me?" I whispered, wishing I had the guts to say it louder.

Nyko sighed and pushed off of the doorframe, dropping his arms as he drew towards me like a panther sizing up its prey.

And with this chain attached to my wrist, what *could* I be but prey for any predator that came along?

But if it came to that, I wouldn't go down without drawing a little blood.

"I tried to help you," he reminded me, stepping forward until we were nearly pressed together. I stepped back, and he did it again. Then once more.

Before I knew it, my back had found the wall beside one of the doors, and Nyko leaned forward to rest the length of his forearms on the wall on either side of my face.

I felt caged. Trapped and unable to do anything other than stare up into his cold brown eyes that glimmered with an amusement I didn't understand.

As with all of them, something swam beneath the surface of his gaze. A coldness, I supposed.

Danger.

Something that they tried to hide but couldn't entirely push away.

Why couldn't I have just stayed away from Chicago?

"I told you what would happen. *Well.*" He looked around airily. "Not this in particular, I suppose. Even I didn't expect Lysander to carry you home all bloody and..." He blinked and trailed off thoughtfully.

"And what?" I breathed.

He leaned down towards me, not taking his eyes off of mine. "*Helpless.*"

"I'm not-"

"You are *helpless.* Tell me...what can you even do right now? I could kiss you, or slit your throat. I could do whatever I want to you, and all you could possibly hope to do is *beg* for me to stop or *keep going.*"

"Are you going to?" I breathed, the words barely leaving

my mouth. My clammy palms pressed against the wall behind me. I was too scared to even consider pushing him away.

Unbidden and unwelcome, I remembered how his knife had felt tracing along the scar on my lip.

Did he have his knife with him now?

No. Bad thoughts, Will, I chastised myself. *Get back on track. Save your own life and worry about your new kinks later.*

Later, if I had one when I was back at my apartment with my stuffed rabbit and all of the doors locked.

"Am I going to...what?" His brows rose slightly, and this close, I could see the slight grin that played over his full lips. "Am I going to slit your throat?" He reached down with one hand and wrapped long fingers around the base of my throat. His skin was warm, his hand a heavy but almost gentle weight where it rested.

"No," I breathed, a sharp, bitter edge finding my words and tinging them with my own frustration. "I'm clearly falling over myself because I want you to *kiss* me."

What kind of stupid question was that? Why in the world would I *ever* want him to?

"Oh, I suppose. But only because afraid and bratty is a good look on you."

Wait, what?

"Nyko-" He cut me off with a kiss...or whatever *this* was.

His teeth found my lip and bit down, not *asking* or requesting entrance into my mouth. No. He took what he wanted, his tongue pressing to mine as his thigh slid between both of mine.

Holy shit.

This wasn't a kiss. That was poor advertising on his part.

This was a whole crisis for my body to try to figure out.

The fingers around my neck tightened ever so slightly, and he was careful not to touch the edges of the bandage that I still hadn't gotten to inspect.

I didn't know where to focus. How could I concentrate on *anything* other than his teeth that were so sharp and bit at my lip hard enough, I wondered if I would bleed.

Or, so I thought, until he began to move his leg against the apex of my thighs, sending waves of heat surging up my body. I couldn't help but whine into his mouth from the feeling.

It was better than getting stabbed, right?

So much better.

When he pulled away, I didn't know what to think or say. I panted, staring into his face as he met my gaze with absolute calm.

As if what we'd just done hadn't affected him at all.

"You know..." His thumb stroked over the base of my throat as he eyed me thoughtfully. "Lysander's brought home toys before. They've lasted a few days or so at most until he gets bored or they irritate him. Once in a while, it's Azriel who decides our guests are overdue to leave the only way they ever possibly can from our house."

I knew what he meant. I wasn't an idiot.

I closed my eyes and leaned back against the wall to get his face out of my mind. "I don't care about Lysander's *toys* or your weird obsession with scaring me," I hissed with more confidence than I felt.

I was truly proud that I could string together words other than *please fucking let me go, you psychopath.*

"You don't?"

"No. Because they aren't me. If you don't let me go, then I'll..." Do what? Escape?

"You'll...free yourself? Maybe you'll go to the cops? Oh! I know." I felt him lean in, though I didn't open my eyes to see it. My heart raced in my chest, and I fought to keep myself from pulling away as his lips brushed my ear.

"Maybe you'll get a piece of glass and try to pull that same trick on my *pack* as you did with Donald Deerling?"

Steeling myself, I opened my eyes and looked at him, still petrified. "Maybe I will," I breathed back.

Whatever I was expecting. It wasn't the smile that spread across his lips, lighting up his entire face like I had turned on a switch in Nyko's brain.

"Well, well, princess, maybe there's hope for you yet."

CHAPTER TWENTY-TWO

THE STORM that I'd heard about broke a few hours later, thunder shaking the windows of my new room that I'd already tried to unlock.

I sat on the bed, doors open beside me that led into a bathroom and closet, respectively.

What could I do?

Nyko had left me with too many questions, and now I found myself biting my lip and wishing I had *some* kind of activity to entertain myself with.

The bedroom didn't even have a television. For rich serial killers, they sure were inhospitable to their guests.

The thought made me snort, and I drew my legs up under my chest. Guest. What a joke. I wasn't a guest here.

I was a prisoner.

The handcuff on my wrist was proof of that, wasn't it?

The door to my room opened, making me jump, and when two furry shapes barreled into the room, I was sure that I was going to die. Were these attack dogs that Nyko had let in to eat me?

Seemed like something he'd do.

Hands halfway up to my face, I paused.

I knew those faces.

"*Frank*?" I whispered as the first dog nosed at my leg from beside the bed. The female, Angie, hopped up onto the blankets and licked my face affectionately.

Holy *shit*.

"What-how did you-"

"Az, I told you not to let them run in here!" Lysander's voice was loud enough to make me wince, and I paused with my fingers buried in Frank's scruff to look up as the blonde entered my room with two duffel bags over his arms and another almost dragging the floor at his side.

"Why do you have them? Did you steal them?" I demanded, suspicion in my voice.

Frank wandered over to Lysander and nosed his pocket, his tail wagging. If he had stolen them, they weren't exactly upset about it.

"How are you feeling?" Lysander let the bags fall and pushed them against the wall. I briefly looked at them, but immediately my gaze was back on Lysander as thunder sounded once more.

"*Did you*?" I snapped, the harshness of my voice not holding up well while the German Shepherd that bathed my hand with her tongue.

Lysander rolled his eyes. "We adopted them from your shelter on our way out, darling," he told me slowly, explaining it as if I were a child.

I scowled at him to hide my fear.

"I take it you're feeling okay? Uncle gave you a pain shot when he was here, and he said it should keep the worst of it away for a day or so."

Uncle?

No. That was too much. I couldn't focus on another question when I had too many to worry about already.

"Yeah, I'm...I'm fine," I said, absently scratching Angie's ears.

"Great. Catch." He'd unzipped one of the bags and produced something from it about the length of my forearm.

I caught it as the dusky brown thing sailed across the room, and when I did, I stared down at the stuffed animal in my lap, nonplussed.

It was my rabbit.

"You...broke into my apartment?" I asked through numb lips, unsure of why I was so shocked when they'd proven that this was part of their *modus operandi* back in Scheffield.

"I wanted to bring you all of your stuff," Lysander shrugged. "Didn't think you'd want to wear my clothes the whole time you're here."

"Yeah, see. About that." I licked my lips nervously and bit down, sinking teeth into my bottom lip. "Maybe I could, uh, leave?"

Why was it *him* I was so afraid of? Nyko had made it evident he didn't like me, and Rhys had helped me *stab a guy*. But it was this blonde-haired, blue-eyed man with a gorgeous face and lean body that had me wanting to simultaneously crawl into a corner and ask for more who made my pulse race.

With fear, clearly.

"Why?" he asked, sitting down on the bed in front of me. He picked up the hand with the cuff around it and traced the metal along with my skin beside it.

Why?

"Because...." I didn't know how to answer that. "Because I want to?"

His smile was sly when he turned his face up to mine again. "I kind of don't think you *do*," Lysander admitted shrewdly. "If you didn't want my attention-*our* attention fixed on you...why would you come here?"

"I told you, that was to figure out why-"

"Why did you keep looking for us after Nyko warned you off? Really, Will..." He leaned forward as if we were sharing secrets.

"What kind of upstanding girl follows four serial killers after *watching them commit a murder*?"

"I..."

I didn't have an answer for that, and I hated myself for it.

"Besides, I'm helping you out."

That brought me out of my reveries, and I lifted my chin to glare at him. "Come again?"

He didn't speak. In answer, he reached a hand up to trace his fingers around the edge of the bandage. "You could've died. You would've if I hadn't been there to save you."

And to *kill a man*.

But I didn't say anything about that.

Or about the questionable nature of him showing up right when I needed him, as if he'd been following me all along.

Frankly, I had a feeling it hadn't been much of a coincidence that he'd been there.

"I don't need this much help," I breathed, feeling like a terrified deer as he continued to trace the bandage. "I'm incredibly grateful, but-"

"But I want to help." He shifted to shoo Angie off the bed and pushed me back onto the mattress, shifting to *loom* over me.

Maybe that was what had drawn the four of them together—their fetish of playing the predator to someone else's prey.

The hunter to the hunted.

Or maybe they just liked to practice their *looms*.

The ridiculous thought almost made me grin. *Almost*.

Too bad I was busy with my stomach twisting itself into knots as he braced himself on both arms over me, face twelve inches or so from mine.

"You wouldn't take care of it properly if I wasn't here to help. Do you know how fast a wound like this could get infected?" Lysander breathed, watching my face as he spoke for any reaction I might give away.

"I had stitches after my gallbladder was removed last year," I murmured. "It's probably the same thing."

A grin broke over his features just as lightning flashed in the window, illuminating his face and turning the grin into a leer. "It's not," he promised. "Let me take care of you, okay? It's my fault you were stabbed anyway."

"No, really I-" The rest of his sentence clicked. "What did you say?"

"That man who stabbed you? He doesn't like me much." Lysander rolled onto the bed beside me with a sigh, leaving me with no fucking idea *what* to do.

Could I strangle him into submission with the chain that held me captive?

His jacket fell back, exposing the gun at his waist that I hadn't thought about since he'd shot the man who'd hurt me. My insides lurched, then twisted.

Should I make a grab for it?

I wouldn't have to shoot him-or any of them. I just needed them to let me go.

I was too slow. Lysander followed my gaze, his hand brushing lightly on the gun. He chuckled. "Not for you," he told me. "So don't even think about it."

Oh, but I was definitely thinking about it.

He moved his hand to the bed between us and watched me, amusement causing his blue eyes to twinkle.

Did he know I was going to do it?

Was I really not being that subtle?

I lunged forward, the wound in my shoulder searing with pain as I reached for the gun.

But instantly he was there, hands on my wrists and rolling back onto me. This time he rested his weight against my body, straddling my hips and holding my wrists in one hand as I fought him.

"Let go!" I snapped, fear causing my voice to shake. "Just-let me *go!*"

"No."

"*Let me go!*" I couldn't help it. I *screamed* the words in his face, fighting him like a wild animal caught in a trap.

But he simply held me, my struggles neither moving him physically nor emotionally. "No," he said, at last, reaching out and tapping my nose with one finger. "I'm sure you've heard it a *thousand* times by now, so I won't repeat it after this, but you could've left a long time ago if you didn't want this."

"Well, I didn't know you were going to kidnap me!" I shrieked. "You think I would've stuck around if you'd told me *that* part of this!?"

Lysander shrugged. "Kind of seems like it. You did manage to find a member of an opposing family who most certainly does not like my pack and me. And even *they* thought you were our friend. Or something else."

We were *not* friends. Wasn't that pretty clear?

"Friends don't kidnap friends," I muttered mutinously.

"Ah, but friends *do* save friends from big medical bills! And that's precisely what I did for you. Why go to a hospital when my uncle can stitch up just about anything?"

"Because-because I *asked* you to call an ambulance! If you were my friend, you would've done it!"

"Didn't you just say we weren't friends?"

I snarled in irritation up at him, only to see that he was grinning.

"You *like* doing this!" I accused.

"Which part?"

"This-upsetting me and-and..." I couldn't speak past the seething fear and frustration that had turned into some kind of monster made up of both in my chest. "*All of it!*"

"Guilty as charged, I suppose." He sat up straighter. "The door is open now and will be until I go to sleep," he informed me sweetly. "You can come out of your room, *princess*." He said the word mockingly, though I was unsure why.

It wasn't like I'd asked for Nykos to give me some stupid nickname either.

"Oh, right, and get shanked when I go around a corner?"

He chuckled and smoothed his hands down my sides. I shivered under the touch, and it only prompted him to do it again.

"Stop," I hissed, though a big part of me hoped he ignored my words and kept going. The warmth of his hands seemed to seep into my skin, sending bolts of electricity through me that I couldn't ignore.

God, maybe he *really* wouldn't stop.

He didn't. Instead, his thumbs traced lightly over my hip bones, taking advantage of the way my shirt had ridden up.

"No one's going to shank you in the hall. Or anywhere else, for that matter. You can't leave this floor, but as long as you're careful, you can go pretty far with that."

"If we were friends, you'd take it off."

"If we were *friends,* I could trust you enough to do so."

I was pretty sure that was *not* how that worked at all, but I didn't argue. I couldn't, with the distracting feeling of his touch on my skin.

"Nyko might shank me," I added, just to be disagreeable. "He doesn't like me."

"If Nyko truly didn't like you, he would've killed you while I was gone and made it look like an accident. I was half expecting it, truth be told."

Startled, I looked at him as my heart tried to escape through my throat. "*What?!*"

Lysander shrugged like it wasn't that big of a deal. "You should get some sleep," he advised. "It's supposed to storm on and off for the next few days. Do you like storms?"

"I...like storms," I found myself admitting. "A lot."

"Never would've guessed it, with how much you jump."

I sighed and averted my gaze, not liking how conflicted I felt over his teasing and the way his touch made me squirm with something other than fear. "Can I at least have my phone back?" I asked unthinkingly.

Lysander snorted and stood. "Not a chance. If you're bored, stop pretending you're a princess stuck in a tower waiting for Prince Charming to come along."

Yeah, right. I'd stay in here until I could develop a better plan, or died of old age trying.

CHAPTER TWENTY-THREE

FOR TWENTY-FOUR HOURS, I made good on my word of not leaving. No one came to bother me, except when Nyko *graciously* let me off the chain for an hour or so and I took the time to change my clothes. The door stayed only a little cracked, except when I opened it and found food from *Grill Fiesta* sitting outside.

I wasn't at all surprised to see that it was my *exact* takeout order from the last time I was there and I ate it while glaring out the window.

Were they really going to leave me alone? It seemed like it, though I'd heard people walk by the room at least four times during the day.

At last, I found that I couldn't do it anymore. I *needed* to get out of this room and see where in the world I was, and what had been going on outside.

I had to if I wanted to get free from here.

And we want that, I told my body firmly, pressing the door open slowly. The storms had picked back up around nightfall, and from where my room was situated in the house–a very *big* house, it seemed to me–I could see the clouds that blanketed the sky with no end in sight.

Were they out? Gone, perhaps, to murder someone *else*?

That was a dark thought, and I focused instead on the

floor and decor around me rather than what the *pack* might be doing.

And how was it, I wondered, that they could afford all of this? Even without seeing the whole house, it was apparent that it was enormous and very pricey. With white-washed walls, ornate crown molding, and wooden floors scrubbed until they polished, I had to wonder if they were also keeping a maid prisoner here as well.

Noise drifted down the hallway, catching my ears and drawing my attention. A television, maybe? The voices were too distorted to be real, and a sound like the lower beats of a movie soundtrack could be heard every few seconds.

So someone was here, after all.

Please be Azriel, I begged silently, following the noise as the ridiculous chain dragged behind me, making it so that I wouldn't be sneaking up on anyone until I could get it off.

Speaking of...

Why *couldn't* I get it off? Sure, I no longer had my pack of lockpicks—that was evident when I'd woken up in this terrifying place— but, I was resourceful. I would make more out of things I could find around their house.

My steps carried me to an open room, the walls around me disappearing and leaving me more exposed than I'd expected.

If anyone was here-

"I was wondering when you'd finally come out." The lazy, accented voice belonged to Rhys, and my eyes fell to where he sat on the sofa opposite a mounted television.

I didn't answer. Instead, I took my time in examining the ample, luxurious space. This room was covered in a plush dark grey rug, and a huge sectional took up a good portion of the room. Two recliners flanked it, and a coffee table strewn with books and an empty bowl lay low to the floor in front of the sofa.

From my spot at the edge of the room, I could barely see the man sprawled out on the sofa.

"How did you know it was me?" I asked stupidly, and immediately regretted my question when he chuckled.

"You jingle like a kitten with a bell. It's quite adorable, actually."

I wasn't sure how I felt about being called *adorable* by this man.

"Where are the others?" I asked, standing braced in the opening of the hallway and looking around as if I expected them to pop out of the woodwork.

And in a way, maybe I did.

"Your *favorites* aren't here, I'm afraid. It's just you, me, and Nyko. Wherever he's lurking."

That caught me off guard. "You don't know where he is?"

I was still unable to see his face. Horizontal on the couch, all I could see of Rhys was the ruffled black hair that stuck out over the pillow he was resting his cheek on.

"I am not his nanny, am I?"

"But...you're *together,* aren't you? I *saw* you at *Grill Fiesta.*"

"As I said before. I am not his *nanny.* Just because I share his bed does not mean I know where Nyko is every moment of the day."

Share his bed? Right-that was obvious. But still. It was another inappropriate train of thought that had to be shoved into the locked box at the back of my brain that was starting to be overfull.

How long until all of the things I *shouldn't* think or feel around these men overflowed my lockbox completely, and I could no longer ignore them?

"Why are you keeping me here?" I asked finally, not trusting myself with any other line of conversation.

Rhys sighed, but didn't answer. As I watched, he lifted a hand and pointedly beckoned me over, one finger curling to signal the command.

I hesitated, yet approached him anyway, the chain still slack on the ground as I went to stand in front of the older man.

In the light from the television, he looked...eerie. Thunder rumbled outside, signifying another storm, but I simply studied Rhys's face as he did the same to me.

"Sit," he told me, face unreadable.

"Where?" I asked stupidly, not thinking about the question.

"There. *Right* there, on your knees."

Again I hesitated, my eyes narrowing. "*Why*?"

He shrugged, the movement awkward with him lying down. "Then don't. I care very little either way."

Would he give me answers if I did as he requested?

Or was it just a terrible prank that I'd regret as soon as Nyko loomed out of the shadows from wherever he was apparently hiding?

My skin prickled, and I looked around for him, trying to spot any shadows that weren't natural or movement that was caused by something *human*.

"He isn't here," Rhys said patiently. "And you do not have to sit on the floor, little girl."

"I'm an adult."

As I stared, Rhys lifted a hand and twisted it in the 'somewhat' motion. Like he didn't believe the *obvious* fact I'd laid in front of him.

"I am!"

"Then sit down, and don't stomp your foot at me like a child."

Startled, I sat down hard on the edge of a recliner, wondering if I'd done as he'd implied and *stomped*.

I hadn't, had I?

Blinking to push away that thought, I looked up to see that Rhys was *watching* me. Or rather, *studying* me for my reactions.

"What?" I demanded with no venom in my tone. It seemed that tonight, I just couldn't muster it.

"You," he replied tersely. "What do you *want,* little girl? You're interrupting me."

"You're not doing anything."

He rolled his eyes and shifted his gaze back to the television.

What did I want? What a stupid question. Fiddling with my hands in my lap, I twisted the chain around my wrist once, then dropped it to the floor again. "I want to leave," I murmured at last.

Rhys, honest to God, *snorted.*

The sound made me scowl, and I wished for a chance to smack him with this stupid chain, or possibly threaten to wrap it around his throat and choke some sense into him. "I don't know what that's for, but you're an idiot if you think I want to be here."

"Are you calling me an idiot in my own house, Will?"

"Yeah, if this is your house, then I indeed am. I *don't want to be here*. No matter what you, or Nyko, or-"

Rhys sat up suddenly and got to his feet in a smooth movement. I swallowed my words and scrambled to my feet as well, however, Rhys didn't stalk towards me.

He picked up the chain from the floor, and my heart sank to my stomach.

Well *fuck.*

"I don't think you understand." With a *yank* on the metal, my arm snapped out in front of me, forcing me to stagger forward. Before he could do it again, I braced myself better, but that only made him snort.

He did it again, looping the chain around his hand as my heart thundered a warning. I reached for the chain as well, as if my grabbing it would do anything to lessen the issue.

"What has *ever* made you think that you get a say in this?" He pulled again, dragging me across the wooden floor. I nearly stumbled, the action only drawing me closer to him.

"L-let go!" I hissed.

"No."

"I said-"

"*I know* what you said. I'm not hurting you, am I?"

I looked at him in askance, confused by the question. Of course, he wasn't hurting me. But that wasn't the *point.*

He yanked on the chain reproachfully. "Am I?" Rhys asked again.

"No...?"

"Have you stopped to think? Perhaps utilize that brain of yours more since somehow it seems to stop working when you're around any of us. Which..." His mouth curved into a wicked smirk. "Is probably another thing for you to ponder, isn't it?"

How in the *world* did he know any of that?

"I don't understand what you mean." And I would *not* comment on the rest of his statement.

"Come here," Rhys ordered coolly.

I stood my ground. "Why?"

"Because I asked nicely, and I am not like Lysander. I don't like the *fight* or the arguments."

What would he do if I didn't move?

Was I brave enough to find out?

I stared at him as he watched me, my bound wrist in my grip and the pain in my shoulder becoming more and more noticeable. I supposed, at this point, the pain shot that Lysander had mentioned was wearing off.

Which quite frankly *sucked.*

What did I have to lose by going to him? If Rhys wanted to kill me, he could achieve that in a myriad of ways. My agreement to his order wouldn't change the outcome, I was sure.

And what other choice did I really have, when a small

part of me was almost anxiously wondering what he'd do if I *did*?

Fuck, Will, *you've really got to figure your shit out,* I told myself, and took one small step towards him.

He didn't move. I took another. Then another still, until at last, I was right in front of the dark-haired, olive-skinned man.

It was too bad that there were no proper lights on. This was the first chance I'd been given to study his features appropriately, and I had a feeling I wouldn't get another.

Rhys murmured something, the words too soft for me to hear.

And if some part of my brain was sure he'd said '*good girl,*' then I would just disregard that completely before it went to some part of me it most definitely should not.

"Does this hurt?" he asked, moving the strap of the tank top I'd changed into and surveying the bandage on my shoulder.

I hesitated, and Rhys sighed, eyes flicking upward to meet mine once more.

Before he could speak, I answered his question. "Y-yeah. It's fine-I can handle it-"

"I thought the pain would've made you come find one of us sooner," He moved to grab something off of the end table.

As I observed him carefully, Rhys picked up a bottle of pills and shook it in front of me. "Pain pills," he informed me almost sweetly. "The really good kind."

"Aren't those, like, addictive?"

"Don't you *trust me* not to let you get addicted?"

Why in the world would I trust him?

Like a parent measuring out pills for their child, Rhys shook two out onto his palm and presented them to me. I took them and tossed them into my mouth, the throbbing ache of the stab in my shoulder driving me to my impulsive, probably regrettable decision.

What if they were poison?

But again,what use did he have to *poison* me when he could kill me however he wanted?

"When will the others be back?" I found myself asking, if only to make conversation.

"Morning, probably, when they're done working. Those pills will have to hold you over until Uncle returns. Unless you'd like Lysander to clean that for you." He hesitated, then went on with a smirk. "I would wait for Uncle, if I were you."

"Who is *Uncle*?"

"He's our *uncle*. Was that not clear?"

"Are you all related, then?"

"Not at all."

I didn't understand, and I was confident that it showed on my face.

Rhys snickered and flapped a hand at me. "Go back to bed before those pills knock you off your feet, little girl. I don't have the energy for you tonight."

"I am not a toddler," I found myself saying, one hand going to my hip. The other-the chained one- rested at my side.

"Then stop making me think that I would do well to throw you over my lap and *spank* you."

I was so glad for the darkness. At least this way, Rhys couldn't see my blush. I averted my stare, eyes wide, and tried to formulate a response. Unfortunately, all I found were my own confused thoughts to the picture of Rhys doing just that.

"Didn't you hear me?" Rhys tugged lightly on the chain. "Not tonight. If you're so set on pushing my buttons, you may do so when I'm not so tired. Perhaps you'll even get what you so clearly want out of it."

My eyes widened, startled. "You'll let me go?" I asked, almost breathless.

Rhys scoffed. "No. That is not what I was referring to, and we *both* know it." He wound the chain tighter around his hand, drawing me towards him much as Nyko had done.

I *hated* this chain and how easy it was for the men of this house to pull me around like a pet.

Much too soon, I was in front of Rhys, watching as he lifted his free hand to run his thumb over my bottom lip.

As he did, my stomach tied itself into a pretzel, and I couldn't suppress the shudder that undoubtedly *had* to be from fear.

I wouldn't accept anything else.

"We both know you enjoy this more than you let on."

If I knew anything, I wouldn't say it. Not now, not ever.

There was no way I wanted *that* from any of them.

Especially when *that* included things I'd never even considered myself into, and I was starting to wonder if I was undergoing an identity crisis over kinks that I shouldn't be interested in.

CHAPTER TWENTY-FOUR

THE PAIN PILLS kicked in quickly, granting me a reprieve from the burn in my shoulder and causing my thoughts to blur together just a touch.

Not enough to impair me, really, but enough to be noticeable.

That just meant I'd have to be a little more careful in my actions.

Leaving Rhys behind with sure steps as I pretended that he hadn't knocked me completely off balance mentally, I found my way to a half-open door that led to an old-fashioned, fancy office.

I flipped the light on, eyes surveying the high-backed chair and mahogany desk that probably cost more than my car.

"Wow," I muttered, walking further inside. I was at the end of my not-so-proverbial chain now, but I could *just* reach the drawers of the desk if I laid on the wooden surface and leaned over it.

Everyone and their *mother* had paperclips, even if they didn't use them. I very much doubted that this was the one household in America that did not.

Sure enough, in a box in the middle drawer, I located an unopened box of paperclips that would suit my needs. Three of those I held between my teeth, then continued to dig through the drawer to see what else I might find.

My hand brushed something cold and sharp. A point met my fingertip, and I paused.

Was that what I thought it was?

Slowly I extracted a fancy, decorative letter opener that had a snake wrapped around the handle, its jeweled eyes glinting in the light.

How gaudy.

Not that I was complaining. A weapon was a weapon, and if I needed to get out of a bad situation, I'd rather have a letter opener than nothing at all.

"There's a lighter in the bottom drawer if you're trying to set us all on fire," a voice drawled from behind me, causing me to freeze.

It hit me with how ridiculous I must look at this moment. Ass up on this huge desk, leaning off of the far side, and dressed in shorts and a tank top that had ridden halfway up my stomach from the rummaging I'd done.

I sighed around the paperclips and pushed myself up, my hand with the letter opener still obscured by the desk.

Peeking over my shoulder, I saw that Nyko stood behind me, standing to the side of the doorway where the chain attached to my wrist was pulled taut.

"What are you doing?" I mumbled around my mouthful of soon-to-be lockpicks.

"It's my house."

I hated his non-answers.

Looking him over, I was surprised to see him dressed casually as well. I'd never seen him out of his dark, fitted jeans and v-necks. So sweatpants and a t-shirt were a new, foreign look for him.

It was hotter than it had a right to be, and I hated the way a part of me wanted to waltz over and do something that was *not* stabbing him with a letter opener.

Rationally, though, I figured this was my chance. If I could get him in a bad position, I wouldn't need my lock-picks. I could *force* Rhys to unchain my arm, and I'd be out of here before they had a chance to do something about it.

Sure, there were probably a few more steps before the *escape*, but I could handle them. If all these men were going to do was posture at me, then that would give me somewhat of a chance to put a plan into action.

Especially as it seemed they didn't want to do anything other than *talk*.

And chain me to a wall.

"Fair," I shrugged, dropping the paperclips into my chained hand. I leaned on the desk, ankles crossed and met his gaze.

He dropped his eyes to my hand. "What are you doing with those?"

I hesitated, then decided that honesty would be the best policy here. "Turning them into lockpicks."

"Seriously?"

"Absolutely."

Nyko blinked and looked away, confusion flitting through his dark eyes before fading away. "You're going to turn a bunch of paperclips into lockpicks? This isn't a movie, you know."

"I'm aware."

"So then, what? You'll break free, creep through the house, unlock a window or something, and end up in our driveway. Then I suppose you'll climb the gate?"

"Yeah, that sounds pretty solid."

"It's a *bitch* to climb. I'd bring gloves if I were you."

"You're very calm about the whole thing."

Nyko shrugged, a half-frown of dismissal crossing his face. "I don't know, I just don't see it happening. But no one's here other than Rhys and me, so I figure this is probably your best chance without Lysander *fawning* all over you."

He turned to leave, dismissal in every line of his body.

This was my chance, and I wouldn't have another. I dropped the paperclips into my pocket.

Don't do it, that rational part of my brain warned. *You'll piss him off if you mess it up.* My heart sped up in my chest as I considered my plan and everything that could go wrong.

Unfortunately, that part of my brain was right. Better to have the letter opener in a bad situation than *create* a bad situation with the pathetic weapon. I sighed and slipped the letter opener into the waistband of my shorts, walking hastily past him instead of leaping onto his back with a warcry and a shitty, spontaneous plan.

If I were hasty, I'd regret it. They were *criminals*, and-

The sudden tug of the chain attached to my wrist brought me up short. I turned, expecting to see it caught on something, and narrowed my eyes when I saw that *something* was Nyko. His hand on the chain sported the same ring as the others, and when he twisted his fingers it glittered in the soft light.

"*What*?" I snapped, my insides clenching.

He stared at me strangely, as if he wasn't quite sure *what* he was looking at.

"*Really*?" he asked finally, a hint of disbelief in his voice.

I blinked, gaze shifting to look at the crown molding to my left, then back at him. "Really, *what*?"

"You're just going to *boldly* walk down the hallway with that? Not even try to hide it?"

My heart sank, but I refused to let it show on my face. Did he know about the letter opener?

"What are you talking about?" I asked again, my eyebrows knitting together in confusion that I only just had to force.

"Give it to me."

He totally meant the letter opener.

But instead of acquiescing, I widened my eyes in a show

of absolute confusion. "You already knew about the paperclips. But if you want them-"

He wrapped the chain around his hand, forcing me towards him a step.

I *hated* this leash that was starting to present more of a problem than just keeping me here, in their house.

"I was going to go find Rhys and make him pay attention to me," Nyko commented offhandedly, "but if you're going to beg for *my* attention like this, I could probably adjust my plans."

Thunder rumbled outside, permeating the silence as he stared at me.

Was that a *threat*?

My brain seemed to think so, but the thrill that went through my body said otherwise.

"So....you want the paperclips?" I tried again, reaching into my pocket and digging out two of the five. I'd only *really* need two, but I liked to be prepared for any mistakes I made.

He leveled a baleful stare at me. "Are you *bored*? Is that what this is?"

"Well, now that you mention it, I could do with a bit of entertainment," I sneered with more confidence than I felt.

"Ah, entertainment." He nodded, looking thoughtful. "You can keep the paperclips. That seems like it'd be entertaining for all of us. I won't even tell Lys."

"That's very thoughtful of you. I'm quite thankful actually-"

"*But*, you don't get to keep the letter opener."

I didn't reply immediately.

What was there to say?

At last, I blinked up at him, trying my best to look completely taken aback and in shock. "Letter opener?"

"Yeah. From the office? Has a snake around the hilt and a pretty dull blade?"

Ouch.

"Never heard of it."

"You don't have something like that on your person right now?"

Blithely, I shook my head.

He wrapped another length of the chain around his hand, pulling me another step forward.

Still, I met his eyes, trying to hide the way my hands trembled or how my heart sped up in my chest.

So much for my grand plan of having a weapon for emergencies.

"We're running out of *chain* here, Will."

"Well, I don't have what you're talking about!"

Without another word, he *jerked* hard on the chain, pulling me forward so that I stumbled the rest of the way and fell into him.

He caught me easily, one hand going to my lower back and yanking the letter opener away from my skin.

Shit.

"Oh, look. There's the mysterious blade. Thought you'd said you'd never seen it before," Nykos sneered, holding it between us as he gripped both my wrists in one hand.

I stared at it, the metal reflecting my face just enough that I could see the startled look in my wide, blue-grey eyes.

"Oops," I murmured, looking away from the blade and to him. "How did that get there?"

"How indeed?" He turned me until he could push me into the wall, the letter opener finding its way to the hollow of my throat. "As I said, *Will*. This is very dull. I'd have to push hard to cut you with it." He pushed the blade harder against my throat with every word, tightly enough to burn but not enough to cut.

My breathing picked up, my mouth falling open as I closed my eyes and tried to ignore the way that *fear* wasn't my first response to Nyko having a knife at my throat.

Or, in this case, a fucking letter opener.

"Since we're *here*," the dark-haired male drawled, dragging the blade up my throat and over my chin. "Let's discuss *you* for a moment."

"Pretty sure you don't need a letter opener for that-" I broke off when he laid the flat of the blade against my lips, and I felt a tremble go through my body.

"Seems like I do. Is that why you took it? And you hid it so poorly...it's like you *wanted* me to catch you." He tapped my bottom lip with it. "There were a lot of easier ways to end up like this. You didn't have to try so hard."

"Try so-*what*?" I hissed when he pulled the blade away slightly. "You think I wanted-"

"I think you have a lot of intriguing reactions for someone who should be scared of me with or *without* a sharp object in my hand."

"Then maybe it's the *knife* and not *you*," I snapped, trying to wiggle out of his hold.

In a blur, Nyko released my hands and instead used his free hand to tangle his fingers in my hair as he leaned forward, one knee going between my thighs *again*.

This time, however, he didn't remain unmoving. His leg rubbed against me, teasing me through the fabric of my shorts and panties.

I gasped before I could stop myself, and Nyko took the unintended invitation.

Our second kiss was just as rough as the first, mouth hot and urging as he nipped at my mouth.

Without a thought, I found myself kissing him back, and with a *shock* I found that I was moving, rolling my hips against his thigh that created a delicious friction exactly where I wanted it.

The letter opener was gone, and his other free hand found my waist and kept me pressed to the wall while he devoured my mouth like he owned it.

If *all* of them kissed like Nyko, they really could do this whenever they wanted, and I doubted I'd mind.

I panted into his mouth, drawing back for air as my chest burned. His hand at my hip vanished, only to come back with the letter opener, the metal of it flickering in the dim light of the hallway and sending butterflies into action in my stomach.

Wait-

I did a double-take, realizing instantly that he no longer held the letter opener.

That was his *knife*.

The blade flicked open, and he twisted the switchblade in his fingers while his eyes drank in my expression.

"You trusted me with the letter opener, princess," Nyko purred, lips skimming my cheek as he turned to glance at the hand that held the blade. "Don't you trust me with this?"

"I..." I wasn't so sure about that. He released my hair, only to wrap long fingers around my throat to hold me still.

I had nowhere to go, honestly. Behind me, the solid wall kept me in place, and in front of me...

Well, the hand around my throat and the thigh between mine might as well have been a cage, with how well they kept me in place.

If I'd thought he was looking for me to grant him permission, I was sorely mistaken. He moved the knife, letting the light catch the edge of the sharp blade before drawing it up the side of my face.

I shuddered, my heart pounding in unreserved fear. At the same time, his leg between my thighs rubbed against me once more, sending pleasure rippling up my body.

It was very, *very* confusing.

"Nyko-" I ended his name with a soft yelp when he leaned back enough to catch the hem of my tank top with the knife.

"I hope you're not attached to this," he remarked, his

voice rough with enjoyment and arousal. He shifted his grip, tilting my chin down, so I was forced to watch as the blade parted the thin fabric of the tank top I'd planned to sleep in.

"Wait a minute-"

"No." With a quick, practiced movement, he'd cut through it, leaving the black fabric hanging open like a vest and leaving my upper body fully bare to his eyes.

I could feel the blush creeping up my face as he looked at me, and I found myself watching raptly, as his lips parted and he finished his inspection, gaze meeting mine once more.

I shivered under that look, and heard him chuckle in response.

Nyko leaned in close, his lips brushing my ear, and murmured, "You'd look so good with a bit of blood on your skin."

"Please don't-"

"I don't mean your own...necessarily," he went on, sliding the flat of the blade up my hip and eliciting a flinch from me.

"I don't kill people."

"So you *say...*" He drew away in order to bring the blade up my throat and traced the scar on my lip as he did the first time he'd caught me in Chicago. "But I just can't help but remember the look on your face when Rhys helped you stab the Deerling brother."

"I wasn't-"

"I think you liked it. Just a little." His knee came back to rest on the wall between my thighs, tight enough to me that when he moved against me, I inhaled sharply at the sudden, sharp pleasure.

"I didn't *want* to."

"So? I doubt you wanted my knife against your throat tonight, either...but look at you now." The knife vanished, the hand holding it replacing his knee as deft fingers pushed my panties and pajama shorts aside. "I bet you'd get off if I took my time with the knife, wouldn't you? I wouldn't even need to touch you like this." He brushed his finger over my clit, lightly at first and then more insistently until my hips arched off the wall.

"I don't think you could-"

"You don't? Not even if I tied you down, cut off your clothes, and drew it out?"

I shook my head.

"I disagree. I think you'd be begging me for my cock before I was even halfway through. Just like now." As he spoke, he pressed a finger into me.

Going up on my tiptoes, I reached up and grabbed for Nyko, twining my arms around his shoulders and digging the fingers of one hand into his short hair.

"You need to hold on already?" he teased. "But I'm just having fun. I don't even *mean* it yet, princess."

I opened my eyes and found his face close to mine. Another finger joined the first, and when I opened my mouth to speak, whether to encourage him or to protest, I wasn't sure as he caught my mouth in a bruising kiss.

When I tried to pull away to speak, he denied me. His mouth chased mine, catching me again as he fucked me with his fingers, thumb on my clit sending little shocks of electricity through my body.

"You know..." he drawled, pulling away and leaving me a panting mess with his fingers still inside me. "You're really into this for someone who swears she isn't."

"Maybe I'm imagining you naked, and that's what got me like this," I growled in reply, my arms still around his neck.

"You want me out of these?" He blinked innocently at me as if only now thinking about it. "Oh, I'm so sorry, princess. How about you ask me nicely to strip for you, hmm?" He spoke so casually for someone with three fingers inside me.

"*Please* take your fucking clothes off, Nyko." When in the *world* had I decided that was what I wanted?

"No." His smile grew, and I figured this was the happiest I'd ever seen him. "What in the *world* have you done to deserve that from me?"

"But-"

He kissed me again. Hard. His teeth clashed with mine, and when he moved to nip at my jaw, I was stunned to see the flash of the switchblade in his hand again. "What are you doing?" I panted, moving my hand to grip his wrist between my thighs.

"I'm thinking of cutting off the *rest* of your clothes, actually."

"*Why?*"

He fixed me with a flat look that I couldn't read. A second later, both of his hands were on the waistband of my shorts, and before I could stop him, he'd pulled both them and my panties off, sending them to the floor and, a second later, the remains of my tank top.

"Nyko!" I felt incredibly exposed, and pressed my thighs together as humiliation burned my face. "What if someone *sees me-*"

"Who?" Nyko hummed, the knife still in his hand. He leaned away from me just enough to look me over, and the knife followed the path of his eyes up my arm, to my throat, and *down*. "Rhys? Do you want him to watch?"

I shook my head, unable to look away as he traced the point of the knife over my breast, drawing the blade closer and closer to my nipple. I couldn't breathe when he touched it. I could barely even *watch*.

But I couldn't *not* watch. He teased my nipples with the blade until I trembled, and only then drew the knife down further until he could trace circles over my hip bones, and...

"Spread your legs," Nyko murmured, his voice soft.

I shook my head.

"I won't ask you again." The knifepoint dug in slightly, no longer a sharp-edged promise but an acute pain.

I didn't speak. My lips parted at the heat that radiated from that one point, and I was embarrassed to realize it wasn't *just* fear that made my hands go clammy against the wall.

"Will..." His voice had a warning that I couldn't ignore.

"But..."

"Promise you won't hurt me," I demanded breathily.

"No."

"But-"

"Do as I say, Will."

Could I?

He hadn't hurt me yet. That was true. And hadn't I said all along that if any of them had *wanted* to kill me, they have had ample opportunity?

I looked up at him, catching the darkened look in his eyes, and wondered if that applied here too.

Holy shit, was I really about to do this?

His knee pressed against my thighs, urging them open, and this time I let him. He purred his approval, the sound deep and barely there. The knife dipped over my belly, down my thigh, and I shivered as my stomach clenched. He teased me with it, drinking in every shiver and soft gasp as the blade trailed closer and closer to where I feared it going the most.

But some part of me wanted it. A small, soft piece of my brain begged for him to go closer. That part of me *needed* to feel the metal of his switchblade on the insides of my thighs.

"Shit, Will," Nyko whispered, his mouth close to my ear again. "I thought you might like it, but..." He took a breath that didn't sound as steady as it should've.

Yeah. I hadn't thought I'd react this way, either.

"I was kind of teasing when I said I could make you come apart with just this but..." He moved to stand closer to me again, the knife coming back up my body so he could draw it again over my breasts, teasing my nipples once more.

I couldn't help it. I moaned at the sensation, my head thumping against the wall behind me and my hips arching.

It was very apparent then, just how into this he was as well. At the brush of my body against his, Nyko groaned against my mouth as if shocked at his own body's reaction.

"*Fuck,*" he growled, the knife clattering to the floor beside us as he reached down to free himself from his sweatpants. Before I could process what was happening, Nykos had one hand under my knee and had drawn my hip up over his waist.

"Lysander is going to *kill me,*" he growled in my ear, and I felt his length brush my thigh that he held in a bruising grip.

A muted rush of uncertainty, followed by a thrill of *want,* ran through me. "What?" I asked, surprised at his words.

"He wanted you first." His grin was savage, and as Nykos kept eye contact, he slid into me. I started to reach up to grip his shoulders, but the dark-haired male was faster. He grabbed both of my wrists and shoved them into the wall above me, not caring that the wound in my shoulder protested the action.

It was a damn good thing Rhys had given me pain killers earlier.

"He wanted to have you screaming for him before any of us even *considered* it. But how could I not?" He rolled his hips into me, and I cried out in surprise and pleasure, surprised at how close I was already from all his teasing. Unconsciously my knee hooked around his thigh, pulling him closer even as I fought at his grip that kept my hands above me.

"How could I not when you look like *that*?" He fucked me hard, punishing, almost, as if I'd been the one teasing him, and he was taking revenge. "Have you always had a thing for knives, princess?"

"No-no I-"

"So it's just me, then?" He leaned forward to kiss me hard, and I was unable to do anything except kiss him back and meet his hips as he fucked me against the wall. "You just love the way I tease you with my blade?" He let go of my leg to run his hand up my body, roughly kneading my breast. "Especially here, right?"

I nodded, mouth open to pant for air.

"When Lys comes in and wants my head, we're going to tell him it was your fault," he growled, face against my neck as his thrusts started to lose their rhythm.

"But I didn't-"

"We're going to tell him that you're just too fuckable to allow to walk around like this and *not* expect for this to happen. I'll warn him, too. That unless he keeps you in his room, I'll do this exact same thing *whenever* I want."

That should not have turned me on as much as it did. I should *not* have been considering that perhaps it wouldn't be so bad for Nykos to drag me off somewhere in this house with his knives and whatever else he wanted to use on me.

When I came, it was in a toe-curling rush that had me throwing my head back against the wall, nails digging into the only part of his hand that I could find.

He didn't last much longer. Nykos lunged forward to bite at the junction of my throat and shoulder. Biting a mark into my skin as he sank into me one last time. Riding out my own orgasm, I was grateful for his grip that kept me in one place and almost missed Nyko's words in my ear.

"Don't wear anything around here that you don't want to be cut to pieces. I can't promise that I *won't*, if the mood hits me."

CHAPTER TWENTY-FIVE

AS MY BRAIN clawed its way out of sleep, I realized there was something in my hands.

My fingers ran over cool metal, rough decoration, and a smooth, dull blade.

Before I opened my eyes, I knew *precisely* what I held, and the sight of the object only solidified the fact.

The letter opener.

I ran the pads of my fingers up and down the blade, feeling a twinge in my lower body at the memory of *Nyko.*

Self-doubt doused any arousal I felt a second later, and I sighed and closed my eyes once more. *Shit.* Had I really done that?

Wasn't I supposed to be focused on getting out of here?

I drifted off again, hands clenched around the all-but useless weapon, and kicked the heavy comforter off of me as one last act of defiance.

It wasn't morning yet, anyway.

"He wasn't supposed to get you first, Will." The words came slowly into my brain, and the brush of lips against my jaw barely served to draw me from sleep any faster.

At last, I opened my eyes, my hand still around the letter opener, but...

I wasn't alone.

I turned my head, only half-surprised to see that *Lysander* was stretched out on the bed behind me, the length of his body pressed to mine.

"*Lysander!*" I gasped, eyes widening at the spray of dried blood that decorated his face. "*Holy shit! Your face...*"

"It's not my blood, pretty girl," he purred against my ear. "And you're dodging the issue."

"The...issue?" I murmured, brain not working quite at full capacity.

He 'tsked' softly, one hand moving up to sweep my hair back from my throat. "You allowed Nyko to have you first. *Bad,* Will." Lysander tapped my nose as if to admonish me.

"Let Nyko-*what*? You can't just-just claim me or take turns or-"

"That's *precisely* what we can do." He leaned forward to kiss my jaw, his mouth working up towards my ear. "Are you going to stab me with your pretty new toy?"

My fingers tightened on the letter opener. "Maybe. Whose blood is that on your face?"

"No one you know. So don't think about it."

How in the world was I supposed to *not think about it*? The more I looked, the more signs of violence I saw. The blood had sprayed over his long-sleeved shirt, and I had a feeling if I skimmed lower, I'd see it on his jeans as well. "It's on your shirt-"

Before I could finish, Lysander pulled his shirt off and sent it sailing off of the bed.

Well, okay then.

I stared at him, surprised at the long scar that ran up his chest, carving a path that twined towards his throat.

"You can touch it," Lysander murmured, eyes fixed on my face.

"I don't-"

He grabbed my hand anyway, pulling it up until my

fingers skimmed over the scar tissue. "I almost died," he told me, not sounding at all put out about it. "But they died instead. So..." He looked towards the letter opener. "Are you going to try to stab me with that?"

Unthinkingly, I snapped, "You keep asking. Do you *want* me to?"

"Maybe. I like a little *fight* when I know my partner does too."

"Then maybe I'll just lay here and flutter my lashes at you, just for spite."

Lysander shrugged, pulling the blade from my hand and tossing it to the bedside table. "Up to you. I'm fucking you until you can't walk, either way."

The words nearly made my brain short circuit, and a flush of arousal had a blush creeping up my neck.

That should *not* have sounded as hot as it did.

Fuck, I really had it bad for at *least* two of these men, didn't I?

"You like that." Lysander hadn't missed the look on my face, and when I met his eyes, I found he'd never looked away. "Don't you, Will?"

"Maybe I like the idea of stabbing you."

"We can skip the stabbing since I don't think that's the part that's going to get you off."

My heart pounded in my chest, and I sucked in a breath to calm myself. "And what is the part that you think will do that?"

"The part where I don't let you off this bed until I'm *thoroughly* satisfied with how well you've been fucked."

Well, that was incredibly direct.

"You have blood on you," I reminded him delicately, moving to roll away from him.

He caught me, his hand on my arm like iron.

"Did I say you could go anywhere?"

Dragging me back to him, I felt anticipation war with doubt in my stomach once more.

I was supposed to be trying to get out of here.

"You have *blood* on you!" I repeated, reveling in the feel of his warm skin pressed against me, separated only by the thin material of the t-shirt I'd slept in.

"Yeah? Do I?" He looped an arm over my thigh and paused, searching my gaze with bright eyes.

I stared at him, aware of the question that lay in his bright blue eyes.

Are you okay with this? He seemed to be asking without words.

I narrowed my eyes at him and sniffed. "Seems kind of *dirty* if you ask me."

He growled in my ear. "*You* seem like the kind of girl who'd like it," he accused, his fingers pushing my panties to the side.

It was embarrassing how easily his two fingers slid into me. And at the sudden intrusion, I gasped, thighs tightening around him.

"What did I say?" he chuckled. "You're already *wet*. What was it, hmm? The blood?" He pressed his thumb to my clit, and I yelped.

"No...it's not. Like I said, you just want to get to the good part, I know." He fingered me roughly as if impatient himself.

"Lysander, if you don't slow the fuck down-"

He bit my shoulder, right beside the place where Nyko had bitten me the night before. "You'll what?" he snickered. "You'll cum all over my fingers? *Good*." He added a third finger, curling them and rubbing my clit more roughly still. "Let's see how fast we can make that happen, shall we?"

It was so hard to focus with his fingers inside me, and harder still when he pushed my t-shirt up to tease and pinch at my nipples which still felt on edge from the night before.

"Don't worry, Will. I'm not mad at you," Lysander murmured in my ear, and for a second, I worried that I'd done something for him to be mad at me *for*. "I totally understand. Nyko told me how much you *love* a knife on your skin. I wonder what else gets you going, hmm? I've never been much into blades, but I have a feeling there's *so much* more to you to discover. And I have all the time in the world."

The words sounded like a threat and a promise. My thighs clenched even tighter around his hand, and he laughed softly. "You like the sound of that? I'll *make* the time for it. I can't think of anything I'd love more than to have you begging for me to give you what you want."

"Lysander-" The feel of his fingers was sharp, bordering on too much too fast, and I snaked a hand down to grip his wrist. My nails bit into his skin and I felt the way they dug into his tender flesh, yet Lysander didn't seem to care.

But he slowed anyway, teeth grazing my neck again. "I'm being inconsiderate, aren't I?" he breathed against my cheek. "It's so obvious that you want to cum with my cock inside you, instead of my fingers."

The words barely had time to register before Lysander had pushed me onto my stomach, one hand on my back as he moved to sit between my thighs.

"Are you-" When I tried to get to my knees, he pushed me down again, shoving my face half into a pillow.

Lysander grabbed my panties and tugged, the fabric tightening around my waist before I heard a *ripping* noise, and suddenly, they were gone.

"You did *not* just-"

"Maybe it's bad for your wardrobe if you wear those when I'm here, hmm?" Lysander chuckled, urging my hips upward.

Before I could respond, I felt him at my entrance, his

length brushing along my slit and making my intake of breath turn into a huff of surprise.

"You look perfect like this," Lysander informed me, his hands on both of my thighs. "So wet from my fingers and *all* mine."

I rocked back against him, the doubt at postponing my *get the fuck out of here* plan turning instead to *need* for his cock inside me.

"I hope you didn't have any plans for today," Lysander remarked almost airily like we *weren't* in the middle of him about to fuck me.

"Well, I'd planned on going for a stroll in the park," I muttered mutinously.

He smoothed a hand up my spine, nails sharp as he brought it back down. "Postpone it," he advised and entered me roughly, his hand on my lower back holding me in place.

It occurred to me instantly that he was bigger than Nyko. His length took a bit of getting used to, though the burn was insanely pleasurable in the best of ways.

If I'd thought he'd let me up so I could turn the tables, however, I was mistaken. He held me in place, fucking me just how he wanted. My sounds of approval seemed to encourage him, and when I let out a particularly loud cry from his cock brushing a sensitive place inside me, Lysander rewarded me by hitting that spot on every rough thrust.

"I've been thinking about this for so long," the killer growled, leaning over me and bracing himself on the bed with a hand beside my shoulder. "Ever since you broke into our house in Michigan. I wanted to take you right there. Nyko stopped me, but do you know how *hard* it was to let you go?" He delivered a rough, deep thrust into me that had me seeing stars. "Then you showed up *here* of all places, and I figured that was it."

"What do you mean?" I asked, trying to focus on his words even though my body wanted to do anything else.

He was quiet for a few moments. The only noises from him were his quick pants and softer, whispered hisses of pleasure.

At last, he pulled out, leaving me feeling empty and *so close,* before Lysander rolled me over, using his grip on my hips to keep me spread for him as he re-entered me and leaned over so he could meet my eyes.

"What do I mean?" he repeated as if the question had never occurred to him. His eyes glinted, dancing in the dim light of morning as his long fingers reached up to wrap around my throat in a hold that didn't hurt but kept me where I was. "Why don't you cum for me, and I'll tell you?"

"Why don't you tell me now?" I panted, my hips finally able to move to meet his thrusts.

"No." His grin turned wicked. Something not-so-nice lurked behind his eyes like it did whenever he didn't care to mask it. "Let me see you come apart for me, Will."

I couldn't exactly say *no.* Not with the way he managed to drag pleasured moans out of me with every thrust, or the way his fingers tightening ever so slightly on my throat made everything that much better.

He wasn't choking me. And it wasn't that aspect that got me going. No. It was the fact that I was *here,* where he wanted me, with no chance of getting away. The feeling of being held, of being *helpless*...kind of did it for me.

My brain took that moment to remind me of just how fucked I really was, in the proverbial way along *with* the physical.

Not that I could dwell on it. I came at his urging, falling apart at his harsh movements and the way he growled filthy half-compliments in my ear, telling me how *good* I felt as he followed right after me.

As I panted, my muscles slack and trembling, Lysander kissed the side of my throat, still trapping me under him. "I'll tell you what I meant, pretty girl," he breathed sweetly, his tone at odds from his delicious roughness. "I mean that once you stepped foot into *our* city, you were going to be ours no matter what I had to do to get you."

Unable to formulate a response, I looked away from him and closed my eyes, wondering why that didn't bother me nearly as much as it would have a few days ago.

CHAPTER TWENTY-SIX

"WILL IT SCAR?" I asked as the older man, '*Uncle* Liam,' as he'd been introduced, looked over the well-stitched wound on my shoulder.

"Probably," Liam admitted, his grey eyes sharp. While I'd been told he wasn't actually related to any of the boys, I would've believed him to be a distant relative of Lysander's. His hair was auburn, a few shades lighter than mine, and he had the same glittering eyes and boyish features as my blonde-haired psycho.

Who, currently, was sitting beside me on the bed with his head resting on my opposite shoulder.

"Does that bother you?" Liam went on, bandaging it again.

"It doesn't bother me," Lysander commented, one arm encircling my waist. "I think it's hot."

Liam rolled his eyes. "No one asked you, Lys," he pointed out dryly. I liked this man, if only because he had no problem firing off backtalk to the boys.

Of course, Lysander only shrugged and didn't look the least bit bothered by the man's tone.

Could I get away with that?

Maybe with Lysander. Possibly Azriel. But I wouldn't *dare* with Rhys or Nykos.

"It doesn't really bother me," I stated.

"How bad is the pain? Do you want another shot?"

I hated needles.

"What was in that, anyway? I'd like to know before I say yes."

Liam blinked at me, surprised at the question. "Morphine," he said like it was the obvious answer.

"Ah. Of course." A dry edge colored my voice. "Stupid of me to be surprised that you have *hospital-grade drugs* on hand."

He traded a look with Lysander, who sighed. "She's new to this."

"I gathered." Liam gave me a sweet, if not forced, smile. "Do you want it or not?"

"I'd rather not. I like being conscious, thank you."

He shrugged and stood up, stretching his arms over his head and rolling his neck. To loosen his muscles. "I've already told Rhys, but I'll tell you too. The meeting tomorrow is *not* optional. You're expected there."

Meeting?

The blonde huffed, his chin finding my shoulder again. "I'd rather not."

"I'm sure you wouldn't. But you're an adult. And adults have responsibilities. Especially when they have such high stakes careers."

"I didn't think being a serial killer was a career," I muttered.

My words were met with stunned silence.

At last, Liam laughed, the sound full-throated and full of amusement. "You *must* be joking," he said, at last, looking down at me incredulously. "You *really think* that's what we are?"

I was confused.

Weren't they? What else *could* they be?

"Are you okay?" The not-at-all worried question came

from Azriel, who stood at the door with Frank at his side. The dog stared up at him with a devotion I hadn't expected, his tail wagging slowly and ears pricked.

"Did you know that your new *obsession* thinks you're all serial killers?"

Lysander's hold tightened around my waist. "She isn't an obsession, Uncle," he stated icily.

"*Oh*?" Liam whirled to look at us with wide eyes. "Then I can't help but be more and more *curious*. What is she, if not your toy? Your *girlfriend*?"

"Their in-house klepto," I sneered, finding myself the epitome of uncomfortable.

"I didn't know you all needed a thief." He looked at me again. "Are you any good?"

"That's enough." Azriel stepped into the room, mirth dancing in his dark gaze and his lips upturned in a smile. "Don't tease. You can see Lys isn't in the mood."

He was right. I could tell that Lysander wasn't thrilled by Liam's words, and found myself being pulled further back onto the blonde's lap.

Not that I minded, exactly.

Lysander's lap was not such a terrible place to be.

I'd miss it when I escaped this place and ran for the Michigan hills.

Will you truly run? A small, nagging voice whispered inside my head. *Are you sure you want to?*

I...well, of course, I was.

Wasn't I?

"Fine." Liam held his hands up in surrender. He cast me one quick look of something I couldn't quite read. "Just remember that three of you have to be present for the meeting. Understand?"

Lysander mumbled his agreement. Azriel's smile grew. "I'm so glad you guys are the ones in trouble and not me."

Liam left, touching Frank affectionately on the head as he went.

Azriel stayed, and Lysander didn't move.

"So...you aren't serial killers?" I asked when it was obvious they weren't going to offer up an explanation of their own.

"I guess we could be, to some," Azriel shrugged. "But overall, probably not."

"But you killed those brothers. And the man who stabbed me."

"And many, *many* more people," Lysander agreed. "But that doesn't make us serial killers."

"Uh, actually, I think it does," I informed him.

"Well then, we're a club of serial killers," Azriel explained. "One branch of a club, anyway."

"A *club*?" I asked disbelievingly.

"Yeah. A really, *really* exclusive club."

"More like a family," Lysander added.

"Yes. A *family*."

This was getting me nowhere, and giving me a headache.

"They're trying to tell you, in a roundabout way, that we're a bit like the mafia." Rhys's voice that drifted in from the open doorway was a welcome straight answer. "Only we are not so mysterious and not nearly as forgiving. We may not be a large family of crime bosses, Will, but we don't need that." His cold eyes found mine from where he leaned on the frame. "Not when the people that pay us owe us many, *many* debts and a lifetime of goodwill."

"So you're *literally* the mafia," I said, my voice tight.

Rhys shrugged and disappeared into the hallway.

Azriel snorted as he dropped onto the bed beside me. "I don't really like to use that word," he explained, holding up my t-shirt so I could put it on now that Liam had finished looking at the injury and bandaging it up. "It's really Hollywood, and people get the wrong idea."

"So if I ask you what this meeting is about...?" I trailed off, my curiosity piqued.

"It's because we killed the Deerling brothers," Lysander answered, shifting once more like he couldn't quite get comfortable. "Their grandfather was the founder of....another family somewhat like ours in Chicago."

"But less talented and not so efficient," Azriel reassured me.

Was that supposed to comfort me?

"We killed the prodigal sons to make a point. They're upset about it, even though they don't really have a right to be," Lysander went on. "They're mad at me, specifically. So they'll try to demand something from Rhys with me present."

"Like what?"

"Blood, maybe? The chance to beat the shit out of poor Lys?" Azriel patted the blonde's head teasingly.

I couldn't help but draw back, finding Lysander's gaze and meeting it with wide eyes. "Holy *shit*! That's insane, Lysander! You won't *actually* let them, will you?"

He shook his head, unruffled. "It's just what we expect. We'll say no, and they'll demand *some* kind of token from us for it."

"Will you give them something?"

"Nah," Azriel said. "No reason to. The brothers deserved every inch of what they got, for what they did."

"What they...did?" I asked, not quite understanding.

"Killing in our territory is one thing when it's warranted," Lysander explained. "The cops here will cover it up, and no one will be the wiser. But everyone's known for *years* what they were doing with girls from Chicago when they'd take them to Michigan."

Horror gnawed at my insides. How could they talk so casually about this? Like it barely even mattered to them? "You *knew*?" I repeated.

"Everyone knew. It was embarrassing, quite frankly."

Everyone knew?

I sat there in shocked horror, unsure of what to even say.

"If you'd done something sooner, then maybe Ashley would still be alive," I said, at last, pulling away from Lysander ever so slightly.

From the corner of my eye, I saw them trade a quick, confused glance. Azriel shrugged one shoulder. Lysander heaved a sigh and buried his face against my hair.

"Look..." Azriel laid a hand on my bare thigh like he was trying to comfort me. "I like you a lot. Lysander likes you a *lot*. Even Nyko and Rhys are into you. It's weird, but I don't question it. *Anyway*, none of us are going to hurt you, unless you do something terrible like stab Frank or Angie or, I don't know, break the wifi."

I couldn't help myself. I snorted despite myself.

"But you can't be so naïve, okay? You can't think of us as some kind of *revenge* takers or whatever. We're bad people. Maybe not to *you* explicitly."

"Well..." Lysander broke in thoughtfully. "I did kidnap you."

"I'm so glad you're admitting it."

"But either you look at us and see us for *exactly* what we are and decide that maybe, just maybe, there's a reason all of us let Lysander bring you home, or you go back to making lockpicks and stealing letter openers for your escape plan."

I met his eyes, confused. "I know what you are. And, I know the reason you let Lysander bring me here."

"Then tell me what that reason is."

"It's..." I looked between them, suddenly a bit embarrassed. "Well-I figured you were just into me in a sexy or murderous way." Thankfully not murderous, as I was starting to understand.

"Well, yeah." Lysander chuckled, kissing my shoulder.

"But if it was just because I was into you sexually, I could've just broken into your apartment or taken you out on a date."

What a novel idea.

Serial killers on *dates*.

"So then, why go to the trouble of kidnapping me?"

They traded another look, but this one I couldn't even begin to read.

At last, Azriel snorted and got to his feet. "Because you ask the *cutest* questions," he told me in a teasing, mocking tone. "And it's fun watching you puzzle out stuff."

I glared at him as he left, but it didn't seem to dampen his mood in the slightest.

With a deeper frown, I turned to look at Lysander, who had busied himself in kissing my shoulder, one hand splayed on my stomach. "Can you *please* tell me what he meant?" I asked as he drew me back to him and his kisses became more intentional rather than teasing.

"Not today," he informed me, delivering a quick nip to my throat. "Ask me again tomorrow."

CHAPTER TWENTY-SEVEN

LOCKPICKS WERE EASY TO MAKE. A twist here, a touch there with the pliers I'd stolen out of a drawer, and I had the tension wrench of my dreams in my hands.

Well, okay. Not the wrench of my *dreams*, exactly. But it would do to get the job done of releasing the handcuff around my wrist, if I was careful not to bend it out of shape by applying too much pressure to the lock.

Frank lounged at my side on the sofa, half asleep with his head on my knee, and Angie was lying at the edge of the sectional with her ears alert as she stared towards the staircase leading to the upper floor of the castle I was currently trapped in.

Like a princess, I commented silently, rolling my eyes at the absurdity of it.

Now that they were gone, doing whatever it took to prepare for a 'meeting' with a family they'd pissed off, cold reality had crept back in.

They were *murderers*.

Career murderers, in fact. Obviously, killing didn't bother them, nor did the deaths of anyone they didn't care for.

I couldn't stay here, since I couldn't trust that one day they might turn on *me*.

Besides, I wasn't like that.

....Right?

Stop being an idiot, I chastised myself with a quick shake of my head. Clearly, I was going stir crazy to be conjuring up daydreams of staying here because I *wanted* to.

They kept me on a chain, for fuck's sake.

I could never love them for that.

Who said they're even interested in your love? A small part of my brain whispered cruelly.

It would be better to get out now before they got bored of me than to stick around and wait for them to want me gone.

Absently I moved the lockpicks to my wrist, finding that it was harder to do this one-handed than I would've anticipated.

But I was out of options.

I sucked in a breath and exhaled slowly, counting to ten as I moved the ends of the paperclip around in the simple lock. I bent it purposefully, glad it wasn't one of the flimsy, cheap ones, and twisted it once more until I could depress the ridge that I knew was there.

Success.

The handcuff clicked open, allowing me to slide right out of it and massage my barely-sore wrist. They'd been nice. The handcuffs were loose and smooth, but a shackle was still a shackle.

It was time for me to leave.

With a sigh of regret, I stroked a hand over Frank's head, drawing my fingers back along the black markings as he stared at me fondly. "I'll miss you," I told the sweet shepherd, meaning every word.

Too bad he and his sister couldn't live with me.

But they *loved* the pack. I saw it in the way they followed Azriel everywhere, and in the way Rhys fed him scraps out of his hand when he thought no one was paying attention.

I couldn't think of a better home for them, unless something unforeseen happened.

Already dressed in a dark red hoodie over a black t-shirt and black leggings, I grabbed my backpack from the floor that I'd packed a little while ago, assuming everything had gone to plan. Perhaps I'd have to say goodbye to most of my clothes and things that Lysander had brought here when he'd kidnapped me, but as long as I had my stuffed rabbit, I'd be fine.

It was a shame I hadn't found my phone. It wasn't life or death, but it was still *important* to me.

Had my mother messaged me in the time that I'd been here?

Was she worried about me?

Doubtful. I frowned and tried to push away the thought, knowing it wouldn't benefit me to dwell on her reaction to me moving or whatever else I'd done to irritate her.

And no way would I be telling her about any of this.

With my backpack on my shoulders, I walked quickly toward the stairs, lamenting once more about the loss of my phone as I went down them swiftly.

The first floor looked just as gorgeous as the second, and I gave myself a few seconds to glance around the foyer before striding to the giant front door.

This had been easy. Easier than it had a right to be, honestly. Did they know how lax their security was?

Did they even *have* security?

Reaching out, I froze when a familiar voice cut through the silence.

"What are you going to do with *her*?" It was Nykos, sounding just as dismissive as usual.

"She could come?" Azriel's response was optimistic. "I think she'd like it."

"And why in the world should we bring her?" They'd stopped on the other side of the door, and I couldn't help but *listen* instead of doing anything productive.

Like hiding.

"Because maybe she'd find it interesting. I think she'd like it, anyway. Maybe not as much as us..." Lysander's words trailed off hopefully.

"No one likes these meetings as much as you do," Azriel chuckled. "Our glares aren't nearly so effective as the scar and your eyes."

Having met all of them, I could confirm that Lysander's glare game was strong.

"Stop." Rhys's voice was admonishing, and harsher than I'd expected. "Doing that, Lysander."

The men quieted, until Lysander finally asked again, "Stop doing *what,* Rhys?"

"She'll never love you," Rhys said evenly. "And you shouldn't try to love her. *Everyone* knows you can never really love what you keep on a chain. Given the chance, she'd run from us and never look back."

He was right.

Wasn't he?

These men couldn't love me. Not *really.* Not only had I only known them for a short time, but they were...

Well. They were what they were, I supposed.

But what did that make me?

The men were quiet, and all too late, I realized the lock was turning, and the knob followed after.

The door swung wide to admit the pack, and their eyes fell on me as the fading light hit my face.

Fuck.

"....Hi," I greeted, lifting a hand to wave it lamely. "Great weather we're having, huh?"

Rhys tilted his head, surveying me with a curious expression. Nyko brushed past as if he had no time for me at all, and couldn't care *less* that I'd picked the lock and was on my way out the door.

Lysander, however...

It wasn't *hurt* on his face.

It couldn't have been. He was a monster. He wasn't upset that I was leaving because he cared about my feelings.

Right?

Azriel snorted, the noise breaking the tension as he elbowed the blonde in the side. "Pay up," he ordered, hand palm up in front of his face. "You thought it would take her another day at least to get out."

My mouth fell open as their words registered in my foggy brain. "Wait-you were *betting* on me getting out?!"

"Which pliers did you get?" Azriel asked, his twinkling gaze turned to me. "The ones from the office or the dining room?"

"....dining room?" I replied, at a loss.

Lysander blinked and glanced sidelong at his friend. "I don't owe you *shit*," he replied. "You said she'd get the ones from the office."

They walked inside, following Rhys, and closed the door firmly behind them.

Well...*fuck*.

What was I supposed to do now?

I stared at it, then down at my sneakers at a loss. "I was about to use that," I quipped at last, voice dry.

No point in playing nice, was there? Not when they knew my intentions.

"Oh, *right*. I'm *so* rude," Azriel hissed in apology, opening the door wide. "Go on, then."

Looking at him incredulously, I didn't move. "You're *letting* me go?"

Azriel beamed.

"No." Rhys's voice was an admonishment all on its own, and Azriel had the good sense to look ashamed. "He wants to see what you do when you see the gates around the house. Not even a monkey could climb them."

My shoulders fell, stomach twisting into a knot.

"Do you *want* to leave?" Lysander asked, a strange note in his voice.

"You kidnapped me," I pointed out. "*Non* consensually."

"So if it had been consensual-"

"Shut up, Az," Lysander snarled.

"Are *you* going to let me go?" I went on. "Or are you going to keep me here, fenced in like Frank and Angie?"

Rhys didn't speak. He didn't even *look* at me. His eyes were, instead, on Lysander's face. He looked interested rather than judgmental. Over his shoulder, I saw that even Nyko had stopped to glance back at the blonde.

"I could keep you here," Lysander pointed out. "Besides. I brought you here to *help* you."

"I know." I blinked at the admission, my own words surprising me. "I'm not...mad. I know what you said."

"Is it really such a bad place to be?"

“It's not my home."

"I could convince you it is." He stepped forward and I fought not to flinch back, my heart beating wildly, like a rabbit who was cornered by a wolf.

But Lysander was so much more terrifying than a wolf.

His hand came up, knuckles brushing my cheek as he stepped close enough that I had to tip my head back to look at him. "I could *make you* want to stay. I've done it before."

I didn't want to think of the implications of that.

"No," I told him levelly, refusing to let myself be afraid of him. "You could make me tell you what you wanted to hear, maybe. But I'm not like...whoever was here before. You can't *make me* want to stay." I reached up with trembling fingers and wrapped them around his wrist. "Rhys is right." I glanced at the other man, who now stood with Nyko draped over his shoulder. "You can't love me, if you keep me on a chain."

If I thought I saw a smile of approval in Rhys's face, it

was gone too fast for me to make sure I wasn't hallucinating.

"All right." If I'd expected anger or disapproval, I didn't find it.

Instead, Lysander was...

Amused? Intrigued, perhaps? His blue eyes were wide and fixed on my face, and his lips parted slightly as he leaned down so that they brushed just over mine.

"Then consider this your *liberation* from any chain I could put on your wrist. But don't you dare for one *second* think that makes us less *interested*."

"Obsessed, in some of our cases," Nyko murmured, hiding a grin against Rhys's throat.

"Are you saying that you'll let me go?" I couldn't believe it. This *had* to be a joke.

"If that's what you want. Though why you'd prefer that little apartment to *our* house, I'll never know." He shrugged one shoulder as he pulled back. "But if you want a ride home, it'll have to wait until after our meeting."

"*Well...*" Azriel threw an arm over my shoulders and drew me close, mischief dancing in his dark gaze. "There's always the other option. You could come with us, Will. And I'll take you home after."

"Go with you to your 'meeting?'" I assumed, letting him draw me against him until he could wrap his arms around my upper body and rest his jaw against my shoulder.

"It'll be *fun*," Azriel promised. "Not as fun for us. We aren't like Lysander. Unless you get off on making people afraid of you?"

"I thought that was kind of an *all of you* thing, actually."

"Nah, mostly just *him*."

Lysander didn't argue.

"Won't it be dangerous?"

"Not really," Rhys replied, looking from Azriel's face to

mine. "But it might be boring for you and Azriel since you won't really be in it."

I hesitated, tapping my sneaker on the marble floor. "Will anyone *die*?"

"Hopefully," Azriel snickered.

Nyko threw him a disapproving look. "Not unless someone in the other party does something unfortunate," he assured me.

I couldn't go. No *fucking* way. I wasn't a killer, or a mafia member, or a-

"I'll go." I didn't know where in the world the words came from, but it was worth it to see the glow of approval on Lysander's face.

Fuck. I should not have liked it when he looked at me like that.

I shouldn't have been wanting to see just how far his approval went, or how much happier I could make him with me.

Another time, Will.

Another time, I'd have to wonder why all of my inhibitions tried to march right out of my brain whenever I was around them, and why on some deep, barely-there instinct in my soul I didn't want to leave at all.

Somewhere, deep down where I was sure it was mostly imaginary, a strange, unseen part of me felt like I *belonged* here with the four of them, instead of my little apartment, or back in my town of Scheffield, Michigan, where I'd never connected to anyone half as well as I had done so with this *pack*.

CHAPTER TWENTY-EIGHT

"SO...WE aren't actually going to be at the *meeting*?" I asked as Azriel opened the door of the red mustang and gestured for me to get out.

"Correct. I've convinced everyone that it's a terrible idea for me to attend. So you and I are going to eat dinner and enjoy looking at their shitty expressions in lieu of actually participating."

"That sounds irresponsible."

Az threw me a quick, measured glance and shrugged his shoulders. Unlike the others, who wore v-neck shirts and nice jeans, he wore a graphic tee, unzipped black hoodie, and relaxed jeans. I'd changed as well, and instead of my leggings, I now wore snug-fitting dark jeans tucked into knee-high boots and a grey hoodie that fell to mid-thigh.

When I'd come out of the guest room dressed in this and without my backpack, Lysander had immediately grabbed me and pulled me into a kiss, his mouth so fierce against mine I had wondered if he was trying to suck out my soul. Rhys had to remind him that they had an appointment, and had assured Lys that he could fuck me later, to his heart's content.

I *should* have argued. I should've reminded them that I

was the one who decided who'd be fucking me and how much.

Yet I couldn't find it in me to argue with him, not with Lysander looking at me like he wanted to take me back into the guest room and keep me there all night.

You're going home after this, Will, I reminded myself.

The excitement and relief that should've hit me at that thought...didn't come. Not when I reminded myself that I *wanted* to go home. Not when I tried to remember that Lysander had *kidnapped* me.

It *was* a relief. I knew that it had to be, and that perhaps my wires were just crossed.

Besides, no one in their right mind could get attached to someone-or four someones in my case-this fast. That was crazy.

It had to be.

The restaurant they'd picked was incredibly different from *The Overlook* back home. The carpets were fancier, for one. And *actually* clean, not just vacuumed once in a while.

"Are we dressed well enough?" I hissed as Az led me in, his fingers wrapped around mine.

"They don't care how we dress," Az chuckled, leaning back to murmur, "Uncle owns this place."

Oh.

I blinked, wide-eyed as I tried to take in the decor of the place. It was small, cozy, and art pieces decorated the walls. Soft music played, not oppressive, and just barely loud enough to register.

A large, round table sat against one floor-to-ceiling wall of windows, the lights in the outdoor park twinkling on the other side of the tinted glass.

"This is *nice,*" I commented. "I know you said it's fine, but I really do feel underdressed."

"Next time, I'll buy you a dress, then." Nyko's voice in my ear was a surprise. So was the way he tugged me by my throat into an alcove by the door. I tilted my head to the side, glad that my shoulder-length hair was in a haphazard bun to grant him with as much access as he might like. "Don't let Azriel convince you to do something *stupid*," he advised.

"Okay...how will I know if it's stupid?"

"Because it comes out of his mouth."

I couldn't help my snort.

Rhys entered the restaurant, eyes flicking over the room before landing on us. "I thought they'd be early," he admitted, walking straight into the alcove until he stood mere inches in front of me.

I hadn't expected it. I'd been fully prepared to move, but Nyko hadn't released me, and now here I was, basically trapped between the two darker-skinned men of the pack.

It was intimidating, frankly. Anxiety warred with the butterflies in my stomach, and I couldn't help but measure the distance between Rhys's body and mine.

The unofficial pack leader rested a hand on my head, gaze flicking down to mine. "Settle," he told me as if I were a *dog*.

I hadn't acted *unsettled*.

But I just frowned up at him insolently as he reached over my shoulder to cup Nyko's jaw. "If you think Lysander is going to break, tell me," he said seriously.

"You have Az watching him."

"Az is distracted." He didn't look down at me. I didn't need him to.

"I can leave if you want," I whispered, just loud enough for the two of them to hear.

Now they looked down at me, and I found that in a different situation I would not have minded at all being the sole fixation of both men.

They're killers, Will, I reminded myself. *Murderers. Psychopaths.*

This time the reminder barely turned my stomach at all.

I cared. I *had* to remind myself that I cared, that what they were wasn't okay with me.

"No need for that." Rhys cupped my jaw as he had Nyko's, his thumb stroking over my lip. "You're not the sole cause of his distraction. But they'll throw you in our face, I'm sure."

"*Why*?"

"Because you're still alive," Nyko shrugged. "They aren't aware you killed one of the brothers. Don't advertise it, all right?"

"Because they'll do something to me?"

"Because then people will start to think you're one of *us*. And according to you, that's not what you want."

"But I didn't..." I trailed off, unwilling to say more, and closed off that line of thought. "All right," I murmured instead, nipping treacherously at Rhys' thumb.

He pulled away with one eyebrow quirked. "One day, you're going to do that at the *right* time," he informed me. "And I'll have time, energy, and a place to show you that *my* attention is very different than that of my boys."

Oh.

I wasn't sure exactly what *his attention* entailed, but...

Fuck, I really wanted to find out.

Lysander walked in the door and glanced towards us, eyes only resting on me for a moment before he jerked his head at the others in a gesture towards the parking lot.

"Let's get this over with," Nyko sighed, releasing me and following Rhys away from the alcove.

Azriel caught my hand again, prompting me to follow him across the restaurant to a booth. "You get this seat," he said, and instead of sitting across from me, the dark-haired male sat down on the bench beside me, scooting the menu in my direction. "Their spaghetti is *amazing*," he said. "But I kind of prefer the ribeye."

I blinked, surprised by his words, and my attention

dropped to the menu at my fingertips. "We're allowed to *eat*?"

"Of course. They have to, as well. Not eating would come off as rude. They'll have their little dinner party over there, and we'll sit here, *judge,* and have a much better time than them."

"You don't seem worried."

"Oh, I'm not. I'm preparing to be bored. Just as you will be."

I didn't believe him in the least. How in the world could a meeting between killers and gangsters be *boring*?

Correction: boring had been an understatement.

The family that the Deerling brothers belonged to arrived without much ceremony. Their patriarch was grinning like a snake at Rhys, then giving both Nyko and Lysander snub-nosed glances before sitting down with his entourage of both a man and a woman.

We watched.

And watched...

And *watched...*

Whatever was happening, Azriel seemed better informed than I was, which made sense. He explained things to me once in a while, or who they were, but apart from learning that the oldest man was an uncle of the Deerlings and the woman was David's wife-which I had a lot of questions about-all I got out of the interaction was that no one here liked one another.

At last, it was over, and by the time they got to their feet, I'd checked my phone again for the eighth time. Lysander had returned it to me and it had shown there were *no* messages from my mother in all the time he had kept it in his possession.

"*Finally,*" I breathed, and Azriel nodded his vehement agreement. "So we can go home now?"

"Pretty much," Azriel said.

I didn't even know what the meeting had been *about*. I'd expected yelling or at least something apart from a polite conversation that barely strayed from the realm of normal topics *once*.

I walked with Azriel to the front of the restaurant and out into the parking lot, tailing the family as the oldest man spoke to Rhys, his hand moving in a dismissive signal to the woman.

I followed the gesture and saw her readjust her jacket.

Was that-

Whatever was rolled up and creased in her back pocket had the distinct look of a photo.

I doubted she was carrying around pictures of her children to a place like this.

Stepping forward, I stumbled, arms flailing to catch myself. Both the man and woman spun, their arms out to help me. I let the man do so, but I intentionally missed the woman's helping hand as apologies bubbled from my lips. "I-I'm sorry." I let the embarrassment flood my face with a blush and gave the woman a guilty, humiliated look. Letting my eyes unfocus slightly, I tried to appear as if I was tipsy.

Even though I hadn't had a *single* drink tonight.

I doubted she noticed that, of course.

"It's all right, hun," the lady said, petting the elbow that she'd tried to use to steady me with. "You have a good night, all right?" With a less friendly look at Azriel, she followed the older man to the car, getting in before her younger companion.

Rhys closed the door for them politely, smiling as the car pulled smoothly away from the curb.

I stayed still as Azriel wandered away from me, looking at the rest of his group. "Everything okay?" I heard him ask, but I didn't wait for an answer as the cold breeze brushed against my face.

The papers in my hand were indeed photos. At least partially. The first two were both of Liam, the pack's *uncle*. The last was a copy of a contract.

How sloppy, I couldn't help but think.

"Will?" The question came from Azriel, and I barely looked up at him as I stared at the scrawled, signed document. "What's that?"

"Oh." I blinked, realizing that I might've done something not-so-good. Would they be mad at me? "So...my hand slipped," I admitted and held up the papers. "A few times."

Rhys reached out, not coming any closer. I walked to him, my sneakers loud on the pavement as I laid the documents in his hand.

"You say you...slipped?" he asked, a smirk twitching at his lips.

"Multiple times. My hand just...found those. In that lady's back pocket."

The other three looked at me, half-startled and appraising. "You *stole* these from her? Just now?" Azriel asked incredulously.

"Depends on if you're mad about it."

"They aren't." Rhys folded up the papers and stuffed them into his pocket. "I think they're just working up to ask why you aren't on the payroll."

"Oh..." I didn't know what to say to that, and I scuffed my foot against the pavement. "It's not a big deal or anything. I just like to take shit."

"Like a magpie," Nyko commented thoughtfully.

"An *adorable* magpie," added Lysander.

"Well, either way, the magpie is going *home*," Rhys reminded them. "So say goodnight, you two. I suppose I'll see you soon, Will?"

I realized that I could tell him *no*. They were giving me that choice by having Azriel take me home.

I could say *no,* and they would respect that.

Maybe.

If I so wanted, these men could be out of my life, and their crazy wouldn't have any more chances to dig its claws into me and drag me to their side.

"Yeah," I said at last. "I'll see you soon."

That was noncommittal, I explained to my inner, rational side. *It's not a hard yes, or a no*. I'd go home, and I'd take it from there.

CHAPTER TWENTY-NINE

"WELL, it's certainly a place to stay, I guess," Azriel commented, the mustang stopping on the curb in front of my tiny studio apartment.

"Have you seen the inside?" I asked, half-thinking that he had. After all, he'd been one of the people who'd brought my things to their house, hadn't he?

"Yeah. It's cute," the male replied without hesitation. "It's uh... *Small*, though."

"Well, it is just me staying there."

"What if we want to spend the night? Nyko and Rhys wouldn't, obviously. But Lysander and me?" He wasn't *asking* for permission, I realized.

In fact, it just seemed like he was letting me know to be polite.

I sucked in a breath, indecision and nerves warring for a place in my stomach again.

It was so *easy* to forget what the four of them were. Easy to think they were just strangely eccentric and unique.

It was like a part of me wanted to brush aside the most significant fact about them.

The pack were a bunch of *serial killers*.

And, if I were honest with myself, I knew that being their current fixation probably wasn't conducive to my health.

"You okay?" Azriel unbuckled his seatbelt as the car turned off.

"I'm fine," I told him, giving him a half-smile. "You don't have to help me drag my stuff in. It's okay."

"Uh, no, *Miss Independent*. I'm not going to just sit out here and *not* help you. What would the neighbors think?"

"Nothing? I doubt any of them actually care."

"You sure?"

I blinked, confused until Azriel gestured upward.

Following his hand, I saw that the balcony on the second floor of the townhouse was indeed occupied.

That was a surprise. I'd never seen anyone up there. Though, I'd heard the sounds of the roommates that shared it a few times before.

Perhaps they were nocturnal.

"I wonder what they're doing," I murmured, watching the two of them converse. The woman, a petite blonde with a thin, lithe figure, waved an arm at the large bear-like man, and in the light from their lamps, I saw him scowl.

"Fighting?" Azriel offered. "Definitely kind of seems like they're pissed at each other."

I supposed that had to be the case.

He followed me into the apartment, prompting my stomach to twist nervously, as I peered back at Azriel, surveying my fridge as if he'd never seen it. "Where do you want these?" he asked offhandedly, gesturing to the duffel bags he held that he'd recently *removed* from here.

"Back where you found them?" I asked, trying to keep the dryness from my tone.

He nodded, still unbothered, and went to the small bedroom area of the apartment to drop them beside my bed.

Well, that wasn't precisely where my stuff went. I would've preferred for my clothes to go back in the drawers where they belonged, but....

A shadow passed in front of the curtained window,

making me jump and drop my backpack. Azriel turned, looking simply interested, and waltzed towards the couch, one knee dropping to hold his weight on the cushions before he lifted the windowpane to admit the sound from outside.

"*Seriously?!*" The girl sounded a bit drunk, and when she walked by again, I saw her throw her hands into the air. "With my *sister*, you dick?"

Oh. Well, that sounded rather serious. Setting my armload of things down by the table, I made sure the door was locked and tiptoed to the living room, wishing the curtains were a bit thicker as I sat down next to Azriel.

"Why are we eavesdropping?" I whispered, my eyes fixed on the shapes moving back and forth. Apparently, they'd taken their disagreement from the balcony to behind the house instead. Maybe they'd fight it out in Tara's back garden?

"It's *fun*," Azriel breathed in my ear. "You really don't want to know what they're talking about?" He sounded doubtful and shifted on the plush sofa cushion to drape his arms over the side.

Thankfully all of the lights in my apartment were still out, and the only illumination came from the light that always filtered in through this window. Hopefully, that meant no one could see us.

And he was right. Eavesdropping was a filthy, terrible habit of mine, and I loved sticking my nose in other people's business.

Perhaps it came with judging people when I broke into their homes. Had my love for casting my opinion on other people finally gone too far?

....No. Not at all.

"It's not my fault she looks at me like I mean something!" The male voice was nasally and whiny like he'd been smacked in the nose with a baseball bat and now had to talk around the injury. I wondered if that was his normal voice or she'd decked him.

Azriel's leg brushed mine, surprising me and prompting me to peek in his direction.

He wasn't looking at the window.

He was looking at *me*.

I frowned at him with absolutely no actual irritation and wondered what in the world he was up to. Wasn't *he* the one who'd come up with the idea of listening in on their conversation in the first place? Hell, he'd been the one to open the damn window.

Watching him for any clue of what he might want, I gave up with a shrug when nothing was forthcoming from the male.

Admittedly, it wasn't like I needed to watch the window. I couldn't see much except for the blur of shapes through the curtains, and that wasn't very fun unless they started actually fighting with each other. Still, I couldn't help how my eyes drifted back to watch the couple walk close to the window.

Footsteps thundered down the back stairs, and another girl walked across the yard. Her shadow was smaller than the other two by a few inches.

"You're such an asshole," she hissed to the man, and I saw a flurry of movement that might have been her stabbing him.

Oh *shit*. If I hadn't been trying *not* to be noticed behind the half-sheer curtain of the living room, I would've whistled.

It took me a moment to realize Azriel had moved again. His hand on my leg surprised me, and when I looked at him in confusion, I found his face much closer than I'd anticipated.

"You look so *into this*," he breathed against my lips,

leaning forward just a bit more. "Seriously, you'd think that eavesdropping was your kink or some shit."

"I don't think it's that at all," I breathed, bewildered at his reaction. "I just like being nosy."

"Clearly, it's done wonders in keeping you out of trouble, huh?" His tone was teasing, but the dark look in his eyes was anything but.

He was right.

"Well, let's hope the three of them aren't *killers* or gangsters or in the Chicago mafia, shall we?" I intoned dryly, fixing my level gaze on his dark brown eyes.

Out of the four men, Azriel was the one who'd always struck me as *cute*. He had a more boyish face than the others, though I knew from their passports they were all around the same age and a few years older than me. However, Azriel had always seemed playful. Especially now, while he sat beside me on the sofa and listened to my upstairs neighbors get into it with me.

A soft voice in my head whispered that his 'playfulness' might not have been as benign as I'd always thought.

"I heard about you and Nyko," the dark-haired male said suddenly, surprising me with the words. "From him, actually. He doesn't seem like it, but he likes to brag. *Especially* when he can get under Lysander's skin."

"Should I worry that you're about to pull a knife on me?" I asked, turning to give Azriel my full attention and folding my legs under me.

He shook his head with a snort. "Blades and sharp objects are Nyk's thing. Not mine."

"And what's yours, exactly?" I couldn't help but notice the way my heart fluttered in my throat, warring between anxiety and excitement.

"You mean you haven't figured it out yet?" He looked away from me, towards the window again, and draped his body over the back of my couch as the voices outside picked up.

"I..." *Had* I? Looking back on our interactions, I couldn't pinpoint something other than his amusement and playfulness that had really stood out.

But perhaps that in itself was it.

"You like to play."

The smirk that curved his lips upward was approving and amused. "Yeah," he agreed. "I like to play with my food too much. Rhys and Nyk aren't so fond of it. But thankfully, Lys gives them enough shit to worry about, that I get to play how I want most of the time."

"What do you mean?"

"You don't see it?" He didn't look at me this time, and I mirrored him in looking towards the obscured shapes of now *four* people in the backyard yelling about someone cheating on someone else.

"He's just *so* aggressive. I heard what he wanted to do to you back in Michigan when you broke in. I wouldn't have stopped him, you know."

"From *killing* me?"

From the corner of my eye, I saw his gaze flicker to mine briefly. "*Oh,* Will. He hasn't wanted to kill you in a long time. Not even when Rhys wanted him to."

That wasn't so comforting to hear about their little pack leader, and I couldn't help but shiver.

"Who do you think's going to apologize first?" Azriel nodded towards the window.

"The guy, obviously. You hear him? He sounds like he's about to *cry*."

Azriel snickered at that. "I'm surprised he hasn't. Maybe his friend out there won't let him, huh?"

"I still think he will."

The man beside me shrugged one shoulder. I went back to listening, suddenly intent on their conversation. Now that

Azriel had said something, I was *invested* in the argument. Would the girl leave him? It had sounded like it in the beginning, but now I wasn't so sure-

Azriel moving hadn't meant anything to me at first. I'd thought he was going to just get up and maybe walk around. Or get ready to leave.

I hadn't expected him to sit down on my other side, the one closest to the wall, and reach out to run his fingers up my leggings-covered thigh.

Throwing a glare in his direction, I gestured towards the window. "I thought you wanted to *listen*."

"I do," he assured me. "I'm also very good at multitasking."

"Well maybe I'm *not*." Didn't it matter to him that, at any loud noise, the people outside would know we were listening? They were only a few feet from the window after all, and even though they hadn't noticed that my window was now open to admit their voices, they'd realize real quick if they heard us making *that* kind of noise.

"Yeah, you are. Oh, you aren't worried about them hearing you, are you, Will?"

"Of course not." I mean, I was. I absolutely was.

"Then I don't see the issue." He fell silent again as we listened, though his touches became more insistent as the argument progressed.

As one of the girls started to yell, Azriel shifted closer, causing my heart rate to speed up in my chest. He urged me back onto the sofa, my back hitting the cushion with a soft *thump*.

"What are you doing?" I breathed, thankful for the darkness hiding my face for the most part.

"*Shhh*," he reminded me, hooking his hands in my leggings and *jerking* them downward, along with my panties.

I couldn't let him. Not when we could be heard at the slightest misstep.

"Azriel-" I broke off when he tossed the clothing to the floor, leaving me bare from the waist down.

It hit me how *cold* it was in my apartment.

Shit. I wasn't really going to let him do this, was I?

Outside, the people arguing shifted closer to the window, so close that a woman's fingertips grazed the glass as she threw her arm out in a dismissive gesture.

"Chill *out*!" one of the men snapped. "What if other people are home? They'll hear you if you go knocking on their fucking windows."

"We haven't seen that girl in almost a week. She's not home," the woman dismissed, barely taking a breath before she dove back into her argument with him.

"See?" Azriel breathed, smoothing his hands up my pale thighs as he sat between my knees and gazed down at me appreciatively. "You haven't been home in almost a *week*. Besides..." He tilted his head to the side, his eyes glinting mischievously in the dark. "I won't even do anything. Not really. I just want to touch you, okay?"

No. *Not* okay. That had a lot of implications, and I glared my disagreement at him. "Another time!" I hissed from between clenched teeth. "Touch me all you want another time when there aren't people right outside the window!"

"Why?" He kept his own voice just as quiet as mine. "Are you worried that you won't be able to stay quiet?" He ran his warm hands up over my knees, up my thighs, and lifted my shirt up over my stomach. "They can't see you," he added. "Not unless they really, *really* look."

God, that was something terrifying to think about. If they saw me-

A shudder went through my body, one that I was sure he felt.

"Don't tell me you *like* the idea of that," Azriel purred, jumping on my reaction.

"No! Of course not-"

"*Shhh.*" He put a finger to his smiling lips, his other hand still on my hip. "Don't be so loud."

As if he had to tell *me* that, when he was the one starting shit.

"I know the nice thing to do would be to gag you, right?" he hummed, looking down at me again and tugging my t-shirt up until it was around my shoulders and he could see my black, lacy bra. "I'm not really nice, though."

Yeah, that was pretty obvious.

"You can at least wait until they're done," I complained, reaching my hands up to grab onto his wrists so the male would listen to me.

"I could," he agreed, shaking me off with little effort and reaching for my bra again. "But it's pretty hot to see you all flushed and worried they're going to look in here." He unhooked it much too easily, the lace falling open around my chest. "I kind of think you're into it."

"I am not!"

"Are you sure? You did just let me get you *naked* on your sofa about four feet away from your upstairs neighbors. You know..." He reached out and moved the curtains ever so slightly, just enough that a tiny sliver of light shone across my body. "If they looked in here right now, they'd see you."

"Holy *shit,* Az!" I tried to sit up, hand going to yank the curtain closed.

But Azriel didn't let me. With an honest to god *growl,* the man pushed me back down, face pressed against my throat and one hand grabbing my wrists in his.

"Don't you dare," he breathed against my ear. "If you touch that curtain, I'll make sure they get to *watch* as I fuck you."

"But you just said-"

"I'm a filthy liar, Will. Didn't you know?" He pulled away just enough that I could see his eyes dance with glee. "Now, be a good girl and be *quiet*." He dropped my wrists, and shot me a warning look before cupping my jaw in his hands, thumb teasing my lower lip before dipping inside to press against my tongue.

I stayed there, completely still under him as he explored my body with light, quick touches. Thankfully, he avoided the places where I *ached* for him to touch me.

I'd never tried to be quiet during sex before. I wasn't sure this would be a very successful trial run.

But it had to be if he kept going.

"They're probably almost done!" I snapped, stomach twisting nervously. "If you can just *wait*-"

"Then I should stop teasing you, shouldn't I?" He reached up to knead my breast roughly, while his other hand deftly caught my wrists when I attempted to stop him. His teasing touches were rough, but that didn't mean I didn't enjoy it.

Quite the opposite, actually. I swallowed a gasp as he pinched my nipple, teasing the hardening bud with his fingers before moving to the other and repeating the process.

"Azriel..." I breathed, my nails digging into my palms as he held me in an iron grip.

"You like it when I play a little rough, don't you? I bet compared to the others, this is practically *tender*, huh?" He splayed his hand over my stomach, keeping me pressed to the sofa as his eyes raked over me, settling on my face at last. "You're so cute like this."

"Like *what*?"

"All flustered and embarrassed. You're just so nervous they'll catch you, and it shows all over your face, Will."

"Of course I am!" I forced myself not to yell, but my hands trembled as the voices of my neighbors drifted closer to the window.

I saw a shape pass by, and stiffened.

"*Shhh.* They won't look if you're quiet. It's really dark, and they'd have to work hard to see you. Although..." His hand trailed lower and lower until finally, it rested just under my navel. "Keep making noises, and I'm sure they *will* look."

He moved his hand away, and I relaxed, only to stiffen a moment later as his finger ran up my slit, circled my clit, and traced along my folds once again. My hips arched slightly off the sofa as I trembled, though I wasn't sure if it was to get him to do more or pull away entirely.

It had to be the latter.

Nothing else was even an *option* here.

"It'll take more than that to pull away from me," he chuckled, following my movements with his hand. "And you can't tell me you don't like it, even just a little."

"I'm pretty sure that I absolutely *do not*-"

"Then you shouldn't be wet for me, should you?"

Of course not. Of *course* I wasn't, when I was horrified of being seen by my neighbors.

One of which had just shrieked a stream of obscenities that had *me* almost blushing. How creative of her.

"Did you hear me, Will?"

"Yeah. I'm-of course I'm not," I replied, voice faltering at my own uncertainty.

Fuck.

He heard it. I saw it in his eyes when my voice cracked, and he jumped on the opportunity. "So if I slide my fingers into you...just like this..." He made good on his word, two fingers sliding into me effortlessly and causing my body to clench around the welcome intrusion. "Then...you shouldn't already be *begging* me for more...right?"

"...Right," I mumbled lamely, looking away from him.

His hand that held my hands tightened, fingers digging

in just slightly as he removed his fingers and brought them up to the light.

It was impossible to miss the way his fingers didn't look at all dry in the sliver of light.

Well, *fuck.*

"I can explain," I mumbled. "There's a really, really good explanation as to why-"

"As to why you're apparently really turned on by this?" He couldn't keep the glee out of words, and didn't even try. "Maybe you're an exhibitionist."

"Maybe I'm not."

"Seems like it." He lowered his hand, both fingers sliding into me again. His thumb pressed to my clit, rubbing light circles around it. "If I let go of your hands, are you going to move?" he asked suddenly.

"I..."

"Because if you do, there are going to be consequences, you know?"

That should not have been as hot as it was. As he waited for my answer, he fingered me lazily, the action taking valuable attention away from the decision at hand.

"I won't if you close the curtain like it was earlier."

"No. But if you move, I'll tear it off the window," Azriel replied cheerfully.

"....I've reconsidered my position and decided that, perhaps, I'll stay here instead of getting up for a glass of water." My sarcastic, dry smile was nothing in the face of his beaming.

"*Thank* you," he replied like I'd really had a choice in the matter. "Why don't you go on and put your arms over your head for me. Cross your wrists?" I did so, moving them until he was happy. "Just don't move, all right, Will?"

"Why?"

"Because I told you to."

Ugh. That definitely wasn't a good enough reason.

I swallowed the fear that rose in my chest. What *if someone truly did look in here*? What would they see?

That answer was easy. They'd see me, spread out on my couch with my body out on display for *anyone* to just look at.

I wasn't okay with that.

So why in the world did my breath quicken slightly when the people outside moved closer? Why did I look up, wide-eyed, and feel my thighs tremble, just a little, around Azriel's body?

He drew my attention with his hand on my thigh, holding me in place as three fingers replaced two, and his thumb found my clit once more.

I fought not to moan. This time he was insistent, his fingers delving deep into my body as he worked me open, and his thumb on my clit rubbed circles until I could *hear* the slick sounds of his fingers inside of me telling me just how into this I was.

"Shhh, Will!" His admonishment was soft and full of enjoyment. "Stop making noises like that. You don't want them to see you, do you?"

I shook my head and moved to cover my mouth, but Azriel stopped and pressed a hand to my hip in a warning. "What did I *just* say?"

"I'm not going to touch the curtain. I'm just going to cover my mouth, so I don't-"

"I told you not to move, didn't I? Pretty sure I didn't say you could cover your mouth."

"But that's-"

"Awful of me, isn't it? Just dreadful." Every word was punctuated by a thrust of his fingers deep into my folds. "Tell me all about it. But maybe do so quietly."

I shook my head, teeth clamped together. I couldn't tell him, not when I wasn't sure of my own voice.

"I hope you aren't loud when you cum," Azriel added casually, like an afterthought. His hand on my hip had become a grip that held me in place. "That'd be *so awkward,* right? If they looked in just to see you come apart from my fingers in you?"

Was I loud?

Well, I hadn't precisely measured it on a decibel scale before, but if I had to guess, I wasn't quiet enough to keep from being heard.

My fingers twisted in the blanket that lay on the sofa, wanting so badly to cover my mouth and grab his hand to keep him from doing what he was doing.

"Oh man...sounds like they're almost done, doesn't it?" Azriel murmured, his ministrations becoming less hurried.

I listened, realizing the argument outside was, in fact, coming to a close, and nodded quickly.

Thank God.

"Huh. Guess I need to hurry you along then. What a *shame.*"

Wait. "*What?!*" I hissed, my voice just a smidge louder than I'd intended it to be.

"What's the fun in this if I don't have you falling apart while they're right outside?" He held my hip in a vice-like grip when I tried to pull away, with his fingers moving inside me starting to become hurried again.

"Azriel-please-"

"I know, I know. You'd rather it was my cock, right?" He flashed me that boyish smile that I was absolutely starting to distrust. "But we can't have everything. So you'll just have to settle for my fingers. But I think you like them, don't you?" He changed the direction of his movement, his fingers rubbing over a new spot inside of me, and I saw stars. "That's what I thought. Look at that *face.* A little louder, Will, and they're going to see-"

"Please, Azriel-"

"Is that what you want? You want your neighbors to look in here and see you shaking, about to come apart for me?"

"No-"

"I think you do. You got wet just thinking about it, and here you are like an exhibitionist, all but fucking yourself on my fingers. You *let* me do this, even though they're right there. You like it, don't you?"

I was dying. Absolutely dying. My body was on fire, and I wasn't sure how much longer I could hold out.

Truthfully, I was terrified and exhilarated, at the thought of the people just on the other side of my window.

Fuck, Will, you have it bad, I couldn't help but laugh silently.

My orgasm hit me fast, my mouth opening so I could probably *wail* at the intense release that had my toes curling and my hands twisting tighter into the blanket, as my body clamped down around Az's fingers that had brought me here so effortlessly.

Thankfully, the killer took pity on me.

Azriel lunged forward, his hand that had been on my hip tangling in my hair as he crushed his lips to mine and drank up the sounds I was trying so hard not to make.

He didn't stop when I came, instead finger-fucking me through it to draw it out for as long as possible.

Finally, as I came down trembling, my eyes watering, I realized something important.

My neighbors had left.

Thank *God*.

Azriel saw my sigh of relief and grinned, his teeth grazing my jaw. "Close one, Will," he hummed sweetly. "I saved you there at the end, don't you think? Next time you *owe* me for that."

"I'm pretty sure I *don't,*" I grumped. "You're the reason they could've caught us in the first place."

"I'm the reason you got off so hard. Don't lie to yourself," he purred and nipped my neck to chastise me for the lie.

CHAPTER THIRTY

"I SAID I'd see you *soon!*" I growled, rolling over in my bed and pulling the blanket higher to cover my face.

Or perhaps this was what they meant by letting me go. That all four *pack* members would be at my apartment, rain or shine, until I gave up or ran away.

"I'll call you *later!*" I yelled, not bothering to get up. "It's like nine in the morning, and-"

"Miss Carlysle?" The voice that cut into my irritated rant was most definitely not the one I'd been expecting.

I wasn't sure I'd even heard it before.

My eyes flew open, and I got to my shirt, unsure of what to do. Was it my neighbor from upstairs? Had they actually seen what Azriel and I had done before I'd managed to chase him out of my apartment and send him home?

What in the world was I going to say that wouldn't make things ten times more embarrassing?

"It's Detective Yates," the man went on patiently, lightly tapping on the wood of the door once more. "I was hoping we could have a chat."

Have a chat?

But...I raked my mind for the memory of crimes I'd committed in Chicago and came up with very few. Why in the world was a detective at my door this time?

Was someone else from back home dead?

That didn't make sense either.

However, I wasn't going to learn anything by just standing around. With a sigh of disbelief, I grabbed a hoodie and jeans, pulling them on and slipping my feet into high tops before answering the door and pulling it open.

Dark hair, a dark complexion, and a face with lines told me the man standing in front of me had to be in his fifties or so.

Wait a minute.

I knew this man.

He'd been the one on Lampkin, just outside Lysander's address.

My hand tightened on the doorknob where he couldn't see it, and I froze. No way was this going to go well. Not when I'd seen him there. If he had cared enough to track me down, I definitely had to worry about what he wanted.

In the face of my hesitation, the detective smiled. "Good morning," he greeted. "I take it I'm not who you were expecting. My apologies. I was just wondering if we could chat a little, Miss Carlysle?"

How had he learned my name?

Had my mother put out some nationwide alert for me? Could she *do* that as a city clerk?

"Yeah...okay," I mumbled and stepped back. "Do you want to come in?"

"Oh, no. Actually, I thought we could go down to the station if that's okay with you?" He kept that affable smile glued to his face, but I heard his words for what they truly were.

And they were not a request.

"Can I ask why?" What should I do? I couldn't just run from the cops, could I? And while Azriel had made sure I had his number before leaving my apartment, I could *not* just call in the pack like my own personal hit squad to take out this detective.

Could I?

No, Will, I chastised silently. *You most certainly cannot.* You aren't that type of person.

Of course, I wasn't.

"I'm actually looking for some guys that call Chicago home," the detective explained, spreading his hands in front of him. "Some real *bad* guys. I was looking for them when we met last week. Do you remember?"

"Yeah," I breathed, afraid to say more.

"Well, I was surprised to see someone like you show up there. That side of town is full of people *not* like us."

Like...*us*?

I wasn't like him, though.

"Okay..." I motioned for him to go on, afraid to draw any conclusions.

"So could we continue this at the station?" he asked, stepping back to show me he'd driven an old, black sedan that was now parked at the end of my driveway. " I can take better notes there."

What a lie.

But, as I'd previously assumed, it didn't seem like much of a request. If I refused, would he be suspicious?

Absolutely.

"I don't think I can help you," I admitted, rolling my shoulders in a shrug. "I don't know much about anything here, but-" I saw him open his mouth and hurried to finish. "If you'd like me to come down, of course, I will."

He smiled, mouth closing. "Great. I appreciate your cooperation, Miss Carlysle. I'll try to have you back before noon, okay?"

"Yeah, okay. No problem." I kept as much friendliness in my tone as I could, but as I stepped off of the porch and locked my door behind me, all I could consider was how fucked I was and how much I did not want to be going down to the police station with this man.

Checking my phone, I saw that noon had come and gone while I'd been asked to wait in the interview room. While I hadn't checked to see if the door had been locked, I very much doubted I'd be allowed by the station swarming with police officers to just *leave*.

Irritation rose in my chest, battling the apprehension there. Twice I'd considered texting Azriel, but both times I'd deleted the message and pocketed my phone.

What would they even do? Break-in and take me out at gunpoint.

Compared to sitting here with an empty stomach for the rest of the day, the idea seemed more promising than it should have.

The door opened, at last, admitting Detective Yates and his smiling demeanor. He didn't speak but sat down across from me with files that he arranged side by side as I watched.

Four files.

It didn't take a genius to know what they were.

"Sorry about the wait," he apologized, resting his elbows on the table and meeting my eyes at last. "Took me a while to find these. Seems they got thrown to the bottom of the pile for some reason."

"Weird," I replied airily, not sure what I was supposed to say. I picked at the metal of the table under my fingers, hating the hum from the fluorescent bulb that hung above me.

Was this the nicest interview room they had, or the worst? I still couldn't tell what the detective suspected me of. Maybe he just thought I knew more than I was letting on?

Or perhaps he thought I was part of the *pack*.

Which, obviously, I was not.

Aren't you? A small, treacherous part of my brain whispered.

No. Fucking someone-or three out of four someones-was not the same as being part of the group.

Not even when my first thought had been to call them to bail me out of this situation.

"I'll get right to it." He opened the folders in front of him, flipping the covers with a flourish to reveal the top paper of the four files.

I'd been right. Each cover held the face of one of the men of the pack. All of them were mugshots, and the pack members looked significantly younger than they did now.

Reaching out, I slid the mugshot of Rhys towards me, surprised by the gleam of malicious enjoyment in his eyes and the smear of blood on his face. *All* of them were bloody, but only his look surprised me.

He seemed so...indifferent. Aloof, mostly. It was hard to imagine that he had the same dark side as the others.

But, I supposed, he was their leader for a reason.

Carefully, I placed the photo back on the file and met the detective's gaze.

"You know him?" he asked, gaze fixed on mine as if he could will the answers from me.

I knew that I couldn't play completely innocent here. Most of the country knew about Scheffield, and that these men were suspected of the Deerling murder case.

Hadn't I already blamed all my problems on them once?

"I remember meeting them," I shrugged. "I'm sure you know that too. Back in my hometown." If he knew my name, I was sure he knew about what had happened. "Did you read the report of what happened there?"

"I spoke to the local officers, actually." He tapped Lysander's photo. "They were surprised to learn that you'd gone all the way to Chicago. The detective I talked to said he'd been questioning you for some local burglaries."

"Is that what this is about?" I sighed, keeping the fear off my face. "Yeah, he asked me about a backpack he found in my front seat after I was kidnapped."

Yates waved his hand as he spoke. "Not at all, Willow--is it all right if I call you that?"

I nodded, wishing I could tell him *no*. I hated the way he said my name.

"I don't give a damn about some petty, local burglaries. Whether you did them or not isn't my concern, and I won't pretend to give it any consideration. I care about *these men*." He jabbed a finger at the folders in front of them. "You met them in Scheffield, right? The night the Deerling brothers were killed? Then, for some reason, you showed up *here* in my backyard, looking for them at the only address connected to any of them."

I wondered if Lysander knew that his name was connected to that address. Next time I saw him, I'd advise him to get a new one or change the one he had.

But that wasn't my current problem. How could I lie when the detective had caught me looking into the pack?

I couldn't. Not entirely, at least.

"I was having a lot of trouble adjusting back home," I said, at last, sitting back hard in my chair and causing it to squeak. "After that night. I felt guilty, I guess, for what happened to Ashley." Grief over her death swept through me for the first time in days, nearly knocking me to the floor.

God, I missed her.

Yet again, I wanted to howl that it hadn't been *fair*. That Ashley hadn't done anything wrong.

"Ashley was your roommate, right? The one killed by the brothers?"

I nodded. "So after it all happened...I guess I couldn't just sit still if that makes any sense. I wanted to know why, and one of the news reports said that the brothers were from Chicago. I came here to see if I could learn anything about *why* Ashley had been killed."

"That doesn't explain what you were doing at that address."

"Oh, that was kind of a hail Mary, to be honest." I gave him a half-smile full of wide-eyed sincerity. "When they were in Scheffield, he dropped his wallet in a coffee shop. I picked it up and saw his ID in it." Hopefully that wasn't too much of a stretch. "I remembered it and looked it up. But then, when I went to see *what* was there, that's when I met you." I shrugged my shoulders once more. "I guess you know the rest."

"*Do* I?" He fiddled with his pen and looked down, the smile ebbing from his face. "Where have you been the past week, Willow?"

"Here? I guess?" I tipped my head to the side as my stomach twisted into knots. Had he been watching me. "In Chicago."

"You haven't been back to your apartment in a week," he said slowly. "Why is that?"

'Why is that,' he'd asked. Fuck if I had a good answer.

"I met a guy," I blurted out at last, deciding on the fly to go with it. "We had dinner, and it went really, *really* well. Like..." I leaned forward. "Gone for a week well, okay?"

"Can you give me his name?" Did Detective Yates look a little less friendly, maybe? Or just disappointed?

"No," I replied, sitting back in my seat and folding my arms in my lap. "Look, I'm sorry but I'm not going to drag some innocent guy I'll never see again into this. I'm not going to disrupt someone's life like that." I tried to sound earnest, even as my brain worked at about fifty miles an hour to try to figure out how in the world I'd keep going with this.

What if he *demanded* the guy's name? Could he keep me here if I refused to answer?

The black-haired detective shifted in his own chair, which I noticed did *not* creak.

So, I was in the shitty interrogation room, then. In a chair meant to make someone uncomfortable.

That also explained why it wobbled a bit. Wonderful.

"Miss Carlysle..." He trailed off, using my last name in a much less friendly tone. "I think you're not being honest with me."

No shit, Sherlock.

"These men are really *bad* men," he emphasized, laying his hands on the files. "Do you know what they've done?"

I shook my head. "I guess they killed the Deerling brothers? But they were kind of awful too, so I wasn't exactly crying about it-"

"Arson," the detective began, looking down to Azriel's folder. "Kidnapping. They cut off a man's hand before giving him back. Murder in the third degree, not just a few times, but many times over. Do you know what men like this do to girls like you?"

Fuck us, apparently.

Again I shook my head, eyes widening at his words.

"They *take* you, and you don't resurface. What is it about them, huh? Is it their looks? Their charm? They're *dangerous,* Miss Carlysle. I don't know where you've been or if you've been with them this week, but if you have and you've somehow escaped, you need to understand that escaping won't happen a second time. They probably *let* you go."

They had, in fact. He was absolutely right about that.

What great detective work.

"But they only did it as a game to entertain themselves. They'll find you again, and next time you'll turn up dead, or not at all." His face was beginning to redden, and his friendliness had vanished. "So I'm begging you. If you know *anything* at all about them, I need to know. I want to find these guys and make them face the consequences of all the terrible things they've done over the years."

Unsure of what to say, other than another denial, I fiddled with the phone in my lap and stared at the Detective.

"I don't know anything about them," I said slowly. "Like I *told* you-"

The door opened quickly. An older man, with a mustache that looked like it absorbed his mouth, stepping in to stare at Detective Yates with narrowed eyes.

"*What did I tell you*?" he thundered from under that glorious facial hair. Voice loud enough to shake the room.

I flinched, surprised at his anger.

Detective Yates only swiveled in his chair to look at the suit-wearing man. "Sergeant, I know what you said, but-"

"Then I'm unsure what's going on. Your partner tells me you brought some girl in for questioning and dug out the files on the Ashford group from the back." His words were loud, but I found his appearance much, much more intriguing.

Sweat rolled down his face, beading on his forehead as though it was hot in the station. But that wasn't the case at all. In fact, the whole place had made me shiver, even in my hoodie.

His hand shook on the knob, causing the glass to rattle in its frame.

The sergeant was terrified.

Of what?

It clicked as Detective Yates eased himself to his feet, flipping the folders shut with hands that shook from rage rather than fear.

"I'm so sorry, Miss," the sergeant said, turning to look at me. "Detective Yates is new here and doesn't understand how we do things. He should never have brought you in."

I looked at him, wondering if I could learn anything more than what his words suggested. "That's all right." I smiled, widening my eyes to look sincere. "If I can help you catch this group of killers, then I will."

He jerked at the words and looked out the door, then back to me. "No, Miss. Really. It's not a matter that we should be bothering you with. Detective Yates should really know better."

"Not like any of you are doing anything about them," Yates muttered under his breath indignantly. He gathered the folders and swept out of the room, not bothering to look back at me.

The sergeant stayed, his shoulder slumping as Yates disappeared.

Was he worried about Yates saying something he shouldn't have in front of me?

"I'm so sorry," he repeated, his voice unsure. "Really. Will you let one of my officers drive you home? I promise the detective won't bother you about this again."

"Is there anyone else that needs to talk to me?" I wanted to push him further, to see what else he could tell me without meaning to. "If I need to answer anything-"

"No!" His reply was sharp. "No, that's quite alright. That's not an open case, anyway. Please." He ushered me out of the room and I followed, taking my time.

"Don't worry about a ride," I said. "I'm not far from my apartment. I'll walk back."

Walking would give me a chance to think about this. And a chance for my nerves to calm down.

"Are you sure?" he asked, confusion coloring his tone. "I don't mind. I'll take you home myself, if you like."

"No," I said firmly, amazed at the fact he'd offer to do so. "Really. It's okay. I'm sorry I couldn't help more."

There it was again. The drawn tension in his body that screamed about how little he wanted to discuss the subject.

"If you're sure," he shrugged, at last, leading me to the front doors of the station. "My apologies again, Miss. I'll see to it that Detective Yates is properly reprimanded."

I considered needling him further, but I only nodded and said at the look on his face. "Have a good day, Sir."

More questions could wait for me to decide if I wanted the answers to them or not.

CHAPTER THIRTY-ONE

ROUNDING the corner of the police station, I stopped dead in the middle of the sidewalk, eyes narrowed.

A man leaned against the wall of the building, sunglasses obscuring his eyes and posture arrogant.

It wasn't a member of the *pack*, but I knew him anyway.

At my pointed stare, Uncle Liam looked over with a reckless grin and sarcastic, tiny wave. "How's the shoulder doing, Will?" he drawled. "Healing okay?"

"Yeah," I replied softly, stepping out of the flow of foot traffic to stand beside him.

For a few minutes, he didn't speak, and I wondered if he wanted me to leave instead of hanging around.

As the silence grew heavier, I spoke instead. "What are you doing here?"

"Looking out for my boys," he answered inscrutably.

"What does that mean?"

Liam hummed quietly, shrugging his shoulders like it was obvious. "Their little pack is, well, *little*. Only the four of them. A while back, I tried to get them to accept some outside help, but they're not like the rest of us."

"Because you're so upstanding?" I asked blithely, leaning against the wall at his side and watching the people walking on either side of the busy street.

A bus went by, blaring its horn and sending up a small breeze that buffeted my loose auburn hair.

"No, not that. I know the value of allies, is all."

"But...aren't you *their* ally?" I didn't quite understand what he was getting at or what he was trying to say.

"Their *only* ally, in the grand scheme of things. Sure, they work for the families here, and once in a while, someone pays them to go to New York and do something awful and horrifying to keep someone in line..." He trailed off, side-eyeing me from behind his aviators to see my reaction. "They helped me out of a bad situation a few years ago, and we've been kind of close ever since. I've made it my business to keep them out of jail or the ground. Still, shit like this?" He flicked his fingers towards the station behind us. "Before I was in the picture with them, that would've gotten messy. That detective would've locked you up, for one."

"How did you know I was here?"

"*Allies,* Willow. Or at least-" He broke off, considering. "People that will tell me when I need to know something, for fear that I might *do* something if they don't."

His words made it clear. "The sergeant. He was terrified when he told the detective to leave me alone. It's because you told him to, didn't you?"

"Not directly," Liam flashed a smile at a woman who looked over at him, and she turned away to speak in hushed, giggling whispers to her friend.

I studied his profile. He was quite attractive, though he was probably twice my age and reminded me of a snake-oil salesman.

Only, he wasn't selling harmless, fake products.

"No police officer or detective in this town will go near those boys. They've tried. I've made a few examples out of them, their families, their kids."

"Their pets?" I assumed.

"What? No. I'm not a monster, Will."

I cocked a brow, and he shrugged. "Not that kind of monster, anyway. So, yeah. When the new guy in town shows up and wants to talk about my boys and drags you in for questioning, I know about it. Which leads us to the not-so-fun part."

He turned to face me, standing so close that I saw my face mirrored in his aviators clearly. Before I could step back, however, he reached out with one hand and gripped my wrist in his firm grip.

"What did you tell him?"

"Nothing," I snapped, my heart suddenly racing. When he only looked at me, I went on. "Seriously. He asked me where I'd been for the week, and I told Yates I'd been with some guy I went on a date with. I didn't tell him anything."

"Not anything you shouldn't have? Not even a little detail-"

"I've been stealing for years," I informed Liam, twisting my arm to break out of his grip. "And I've had to keep my story straight before when someone has asked me where I was." Not often, but it was true enough. "I can assure you that I *did not* tell him anything about your boys. Though, for a moment, I wasn't sure the last one was *Rhys*. He looked...different."

"Different how?"

"Like Azriel does sometimes. Gleeful and scary-happy."

Liam released me with a snort and stepped back, thankfully leaving my personal space. "He's not always so in control, but he rarely lets loose. Trust me when I say you don't want it happening with you."

I believed him.

"So what now?" I asked, at last, looking anywhere except at him. "Do the others know about this? About..." I didn't know how to finish the question.

"About you being dragged in for questioning? I don't think so. Well, I doubt *all* of them know. But I wouldn't put it past Rhys to have guessed that something like this might happen."

"Why's that?"

"Because you aren't good at being the quiet, unobtrusive thief *all* of the time, and he sees that too."

Was that an insult? It definitely felt like one.

I sighed heavily and squinted in the bright light, wishing for the storms from a few days before or at least a pair of sunglasses to shield me from the unpleasant rays of the sun.

"I think you need a break," Liam observed, his eyes still presumably studying my face.

"From what? I don't have a real job."

"From *them*. It's hard, isn't it? Being swept up in their tornado. They move so *fast*, right?"

I wasn't sure how he knew that or could so aptly put it into words that made perfect sense.

My brow knit in confusion, and I looked down at the sidewalk to escape his scrutiny. "They act like...we're *something*," I muttered at last. "But that's not realistic. I've only known them a few weeks, and I'm not sure that being kidnapped counts as getting to know them. I get *interest* from them as an excuse. But they act like it's more than that. It's like..."

"Obsession?" Liam tilted his head to the side.

I hated that he put *that* so well into words too.

Reluctantly, I nodded, trying to look nonchalant by leaning on the wall at our side. "It'll fade. I guess when it does, I can see where we actually stand."

The choked, amused noise that Liam made caused me to startle, as did his sudden bark of laughter. "You think it'll *fade*?" He snorted. "If you wanted it to do that, you should've never come to Chicago."

My eyes widened as my stomach twisted into anxious pretzels. "It'll *fade*," I snapped. "No one can be so...so *much* all the time."

"They can. They are with each other. You're their new, shiny puppy, sure. But you think Rhys and Nyko have ever cooled off from one another? I can guarantee you that I know what they're doing, and what they'll be doing at least twice more today."

Oh. Well, that was...

Unsettling?

No. That wasn't right. Though my brain screamed that it *had* to be unsettling to me, I couldn't quite push myself to believe it.

It was *exciting*. Would they be like this forever with me? Spontaneous and pushy and willing to do anything to get me in situations that shocked, confused, and ultimately turned me on?

"I'm not like them," I mumbled offhandedly, looking for something to reply with that wouldn't betray my confusion.

"*Aren't* you? Looks to me like you're drowning in them, though you say you aren't." I opened my mouth to argue, but Liam continued, "Take a *break*, Will. Two days." He held up two fingers as if I couldn't hear. "Don't text them. Don't invite them over. See how you feel at the end of those two days."

"Probably the same as I feel now."

His brows rose above the rims of his sunglasses. "And how is that, exactly? Do you miss them? Were you thinking of calling them when you were in there?"

"I don't *miss* them," I snapped, looking away and shifting in discomfort.

I *had* thought about calling them in there.

But that was normal. Who wouldn't fantasize about a quick rescue out of an uncomfortable situation?

He was making more of this than was necessary, clearly.

It was ridiculous to think that the pack's crazy was contagious.

"I'll take a break since you think it'll make some kind of difference," I sighed in resignation, not looking at him.

"Oh, *no,* sweetie." Liam stepped back, a hand on his chest. "*I* don't think it's going to make any damn difference at all. I think in two days, you'll still be pining over them, and they'll be just as obsessed." I hated when he used that word. It sounded *wrong*. If I was in a relationship-

My train of thought slammed to a halt.

This was not a relationship.

If I started thinking that way, then I might as well hop right on that crazy train *with* the pack.

No one could decide they had strong feelings about any person this quickly.

Love didn't work that way.

Unless it's a different kind of love.

I clamped down, not letting that thought go any further. "Sure," I said, my words flat. "Though I'm not *pining* over them now."

"Whatever you say, Will." His smile was blinding. "Get your phone out so I can give you my number."

At my surprised face, he explained, "For if this happens again, I won't need to wait to be told by someone else. I'd rather take care of a situation quickly and quietly."

He gave me his number, my fingers moving without thinking over the information. "What will you do if the detective doesn't leave me alone?" I asked, wondering if I'd regret the question."

Liam shrugged. "Whatever I have to. I told you, I care a lot about that little pack, and I'd do whatever I have to in order to keep them safe."

I didn't ask him anything else.

Not when I wasn't sure I'd like the answers to any of my questions very much.

CHAPTER THIRTY-TWO

WHILE I WASN'T sure what I would do if Azriel texted me and wanted something, I made good on my promise to Liam and took two days *off* from them.

Which was frankly easy when I slept most of the day away after being dragged down to the station by the too-friendly detective. In the end, I only woke up to eat bad Tex-Mex food and watch questionable reality television.

All in all, it was a great day.

Waking up on the second day, I found I had that familiar itch in my throat for my favorite hobby.

Doing illegal shit for profit.

It wasn't like I was super low on money, but one couldn't exactly have too much of it, could they? Especially when I was living in one of the more expensive cities in the country.

Besides, a big part of the reason I was a thief was because of the joy of it. Or rather, the way that it made me feel. Stealing was a *rush* that I'd come to love, and even when I didn't need money, I found myself grabbing things just to grab them.

I supposed a therapist would call it a bad response to a mother wanting me to be perfect and me looking for a way to act out.

I called it a hobby.

Putting on my typical, nondescript clothing, I barely registered my actions as I went through them robotically.

Instead, I found my mind wandering to dangerous lines of thought.

What did the pack think of my thieving? Sure, I'd fucked it up when I broke into their rental back in Michigan, but in my defense, I had been *terrified* that they'd find me.

Even now, I wondered what they would've done if Lysander had grabbed me. Would they have let me go? Would they have killed me, or...

I couldn't help the way my brain conjured up the idea of Lysander throwing me over his shoulder, taking me into the house, and tossing me onto his bed to have his way with me.

The fact that, back then, I hadn't been smitten with them—something I was learning to admit in my own brain—didn't play into my daydream.

By the time I was walking down the sidewalk in a random direction to see what I could find while out and about, I had finally snapped back into the present instead of considering all the ways they could've done *bad things* to me that night.

And none of my fantasies ended with something so mundane as my death.

I should *not* have been imagining the four of them taking turns with me, using me for their own pleasure while another member of the pack held me down, as my steps took me past the shops and stores that I'd thought about going to.

And I *certainly* needed to rein myself in when my brain took things even further and perused the possibilities of them 'catching' me again. Especially when I wasn't so afraid of not waking up and having the reassurance that they wouldn't do terrible things to me.

Well. Terrible things I didn't want, at least.

Fuck. I was starting to lose plausible deniability that their attention was apparently affecting me in some way that made me think in ways that weren't...*me.*

I'd never been this kind of person before, and people didn't just change overnight.

Not like this.

Barking drew my attention down a side street, the sounds increasing as I finally found myself in front of an okay-ish house that sat back from a large, dirty yard which needed to be mowed *very* badly.

As it was, the yard looked more like a little jungle full of weeds and garbage.

And a cat.

The creature lay on the walkway, looking thinner than was ever healthy and barely noticing the flies that buzzed around its head.

I bit my lip, looking around to see if anyone was around to notice me.

They were not.

Turning back to the cat, I gritted my teeth in frustration at the fence that separated me from it.

That, and the wound on its leg that looked to be days old.

I really hated people sometimes.

Don't do it, Will, I chastised myself. *Seriously, don't do this.*

It would be incredibly stupid of me to go in now and steal that cat away from this place.

Even though there was no food in sight, I could see the white and orange feline's *ribs* and *hip bones* sticking up like markers of abuse.

God, I definitely wasn't going to be able to leave here without doing something.

Was it wrong in the eyes of the law to steal someone's cat?

Yeah. Absolutely.

Did I give a fuck when *said* cat looked like it hadn't eaten in a week?

Nope.

"God damn it, Will," I mumbled, looking around again. Still, no one. Would I be lucky enough that whoever lived here was at work, or at least somewhere *not here*?

Kneeling on the other side of the gate, I *tsked* at the cat, trying to draw its attention.

The creature barely flicked an ear and certainly didn't *move*.

"Oh, come on," I begged quietly. "Make this easy for me, please?" My heartbeat sped up slightly in my chest, reminding me of the consequences of being caught stealing some asshole's cat.

I didn't even know where a *vet* was.

Well, that wasn't a problem for right now. Getting the cat was my current conundrum.

If I was truly going to do this, I needed to get over my fear and get to it.

Standing, I clambered over the fence awkwardly, glad I wore a loose hoodie that I could use to conceal the cat.

Once my feet touched the other side, and I silently gave thanks that the gate was only four feet or so high, I walked quickly to the creature that lay on the sidewalk, gritting my teeth as I prepared for the door to open at any moment and for someone to come out shrieking for me to get off their property.

Somehow, that didn't happen. I was able to gather up the creature in my arms, all the more concerned when it barely opened one green eye to gaze at me pitifully.

Close up, I saw that the other looked infected and not at all okay.

"Please don't die," I breathed, going back to the gate and trying not to panic over the bad shape this cat was in. It hadn't fought me at all. It barely seemed to care that I'd come by and swooped in to catnap it.

That really wasn't a good sign.

If this cat died in my arms, I would without a doubt cry myself to sleep for at least a month.

Once I had gotten back onto the sidewalk, I power walked back the way I'd come, heart now hammering in my throat.

I needed a vet. A good vet, and hopefully one that wouldn't care where I'd gotten the cat.

Then again, I could always just say I'd found it on the sidewalk, or something. That was believable...probably.

Pulling out my phone to look up the nearest vet, I hesitated as a better idea occurred to me.

The pack had Frank and Angie now. Surely they cared enough about them to have gotten them a vet.

Maybe I could find out which vet it was and take this poor cat there.

Or you could call Tara, instead, a more sensible part of my brain reminded me.

That would probably be the correct option. I was still taking a 'break' from the pack until tomorrow, and Tara would definitely be able to point me in the right direction.

But when my finger tapped the call button, it wasn't over Tara's number.

As the phone rang twice, then three times, I wondered if Azriel would even pick up. They were probably busy grocery shopping or killing off a branch of the local government or *something*.

"Hello?" Azriel's voice was tinged with surprise. *"Wasn't expecting a call from you today, Will."*

"Do you have a vet?" I blurted out, causing all my plans of a quick explanation to fly out the window.

He was quiet for a moment, then laughed, *"Is this an*

animal welfare check on Frank and Angie? Should I be worried you'll show up to take them back?"

"What? *No,* of course not. Look, do you have a vet you like?" I looked again at the small shape that I carried against my chest, happy to be back on a familiar street with my car not far away.

"Are you okay?"

"Not if I don't find a vet."

"You know, those movies about vets patching up mob members to stay out of the way of the law are all lies. That isn't even remotely real."

"I stole a cat!" I snapped, getting in my car and slamming the door. Removing my hoodie, I used it as a cushion for the cat in my front passenger seat.

"Come again?"

"*I stole a cat,* and I need a *vet.*"

"Oh. Okay. That's....not what I was expecting." I could hear the genuine surprise in his voice. *"Yeah, of course, I have a vet. I'll hang up and send you the info. Is the cat okay?"*

I looked at it, teeth digging into my lower lip. The cat looked asleep again. "No," I whispered, furious tears burning in my eyes.

Without hesitation, I reached out to run my hand over the cat's filthy fur, hoping that if it did die, it would know that someone had at least cared about it in the end.

God, I really hoped this cat didn't die.

"Address is going to your phone. I'll see you later."

"Thanks, Az," I whispered, trying to keep the fear out of my words and failing.

Did he know I was on the verge of tears?

If he knew and made fun of me for it, then this would undoubtedly be the end of my association with them.

"No problem." He hung up without another word, and I barely stopped to think about his quick dismissal. My phone pinged with his text, and I deftly loaded the address into my

GPS app before peeling out of the driveway and nearly nailing another car.

Because *that* was all I needed today.

I should've expected a very well-to-do clinic. And this one didn't disappoint. The large, neat building was made of light-colored stone, and glass windows enclosed the front of the waiting room where a tall, marble counter separated the front desk and waiting area from the exam rooms in the back.

After parking as close as I could to the entrance, I bundled the cat into my arms, hoodie and all, and walked into the office—praying that they had enough time to help me.

Why hadn't I called on the way here? That would've been the smart thing to do, but I had been so busy pleading with the cat in my front seat not to die to even think about it.

A lady from the other side of the counter looked up and adjusted her glasses. "Hi," she greeted before I could speak. "You must be the woman Mr. Boone told me would be here."

"O-oh." I stopped in front of her, shock hitting me square in the face. *Azriel* had called her?

That was...thoughtful.

And incredibly helpful.

"Yes. He said you'd found a cat in bad condition." Her eyes were on the bundle in my arms, and she walked around the counter to look at him, one hand going to his head to stroke over his ears. "That seems to be an understatement, huh?"

I nodded my head, terrified she was about to tell me it was too late for the little thing.

"Come on back. Let's see what we can do for him."

I followed her, still holding onto the small animal as I looked around the clean, pleasant-looking office. Pictures of animals hung on the walls, and the whole place just seemed cheery, from its white tile floor to its light blue walls.

Even the vet tech was a picture of good cheer in her scrubs that had smiling puppies in stethoscopes on them.

After ushering me into a small, white room with an adjustable table in the middle, she walked around to the counter and laid down the folder she'd been carrying. "Can you put him there so I can take a look?"

I was afraid to. Afraid that when I put him down, I'd find that he'd died or was incredibly close to it.

In my anxiety, I held the cat tighter to me, knowing it was an irrational reaction.

The tech glanced at me with a sympathetic smile, tucking her greying blonde hair over her ear. "I know," she said. "I just want to take a look."

Forcing myself to nod, I released the hoodie bundle from my chest and laid it down, hating that I was still so emotional over a situation that I'd become familiar with.

Though I hadn't had many animals I'd brought to the shelter *die*. Only once before, and it had been years since that happened.

I wasn't sure I was ready for that to happen again.

In fact, I doubted I'd handle it gracefully if it was the case.

The cat barely moved as I laid it down, and I saw the tech's mouth twitch into a frown when she saw it. "Poor little man," she sighed, running a hand over his ears and tipping his head back to get a better look at his face. "I doubt you'll get to keep that eye," she went on, causing my heart to sink into my chest.

Be rational, Will, I told myself over and over again. *Distance yourself. You did as much as you could.*

She felt around on him, before finally finding the wound on his back leg. "This one isn't so bad, at least. If we can get it cleaned up all right."

"Will he be okay?" I asked quietly, even though I knew that the tech couldn't give me an answer on that.

"I can't answer that," she said truthfully. "He's very dehydrated and emaciated. I don't think we can save his eye, and his leg is infected. He's in...really bad shape."

Like I hadn't known that.

Biting my lip again to keep myself in check, I nodded jerkily. "Yeah, no, I get that. Sorry."

"No reason to be. Let me go get Dr. Adams."

I sat down on the bench as she left, my eyes fixed on the cat. "Please be okay," I mumbled. "Because otherwise, I'll have to assume this is some kind of...of *metaphor* for how my life is going right now and I'll take all of this a lot more personally than I should."

The cat's ears flicked, and I noticed that one of them had a small 'v' nicked out of it like the cat had been in a fight.

Tears burned my eyes again, prompting me to scrub my palms over my eyes and shut them hard. I was *not* going to cry right now.

The door opened, admitting an older, grey-haired doctor with dark eyes and a friendly, if a bit tired, smile.

"Well, who's this?" he murmured, going straight to the table and picking up the cat's head gently in his hand. "Jessica?" The tech reappeared at his side. "I'm going to need an antibiotic flush for his leg. And get the surgery table ready for him? He's..." He turned the cat's head back and forth. "No, I don't see him keeping that eye."

I closed my eyes again, willing myself not to cry.

Not only that, but I couldn't help but wonder how in the world I was going to pay for this. Would they charge me, even though it wasn't my cat? *Obviously*, right? I'd brought it in, after all.

"Where did you say you found him?" the vet asked, examining the cat all over and pulling his leg out so he could get a better look at the wound there.

"I...." *Crap.* What was the story again? "At-at the side of the road. On a residential street."

"I'll check him for a chip, then, too."

"Why?" I asked, my tone bewildered. "If someone let him get like this, you can't really want to give him *back.*" *If he survives,* my brain added unhelpfully.

"Because he could be lost." The vet picked the cat up, my hoodie included, and handed him off to the tech. "I'm going to take him back to operate on that eye and close up his leg wound. With him being in this shape, I *doubt* I'll find a chip. So..." I glanced up and saw he was looking at me. "Do you want to give him a name? So long as I don't find one, I'm going to go on and neuter him."

"Yeah, okay," I mumbled. That was definitely the best thing to do, I knew.

But a name?

"Let's call him. Umm." I ran through lists in my head, trying to conjure up something that might fit.

Well, it was almost Halloween, right?

Not to mention my birthday. If the cat lived, I'd count it as a birthday present to myself.

"How about October?" It was the best I could come up with right now.

"Is that your new name?" the vet tech cooed to the cat, taking him back with her. "You definitely look like a Toby with your orange patches."

The vet gave me a warm, assuring smile. "I'll take care of him. You go back to the front and get the details settled, all right?" He closed the door behind him, leaving me in the white waiting room with the quiet *whoosh* of the fan overhead.

Details.

He meant payment.

I really should've stolen some money this morning. With

what I was sure that surgery would cost, I'd be eating ramen for the next two months that I stayed here.

The same tech, Jessica, was waiting for me at the counter when I made my way out, smiling as I strolled on by like it was my own funeral, and awaited to hear how much money I was going to lose.

"Okay, so I just have a few questions," the woman said. "We won't know everything until after the surgery, and Mr. October wakes up." That was very optimistic of her. "But a few things now. Do you plan on keeping him?"

"I..." *Did I?* The thought honestly hadn't crossed my mind.

But I'd lost a hoodie to the cat, damn it. And I hadn't driven him here for nothing.

Would Tara be okay with it?

An idea struck me, and I pulled up the page I'd saved with my Airbnb info on it. I could get the answer without even asking, actually.

Scrolling through, the hand around my heart loosened when I saw the two words I was looking for.

Pets welcome.

That settled that issue.

"Yeah," I said at last. "I'm going to keep him." If he lived.

"Okay, that's an easy one then." She typed in something on her keyboard, face illuminated by the computer screen as she squinted at it. "You live in Chicago?"

"Yeah," I said, cringing a bit at the lie.

"And do you want your receipt with you, or just emailed like usual?"

Like *usual*?

I was utterly confused.

Blinking at the woman, I narrowed my eyes. "What do you mean, emailed? And I need to give you my card, right? To pay the bill?"

"Oh...no." She glanced up at me, confusion on *her* face now, too. "It's been paid for."

"By-" I didn't say *who*. Of course, I knew. There was only one answer.

Had he really done that for me?

"Just...email it, I guess," I mumbled. I wondered if Azriel had figured that I'd put a cat's emergency surgery on his credit card.

Would he be mad when he saw the bill?

As if reading my mind, my phone rang in my pocket, vibrating against my hip. Taking it out, I found that it was *precisely* who I'd expected it to be.

Azriel.

"One moment?" I requested, giving my sweetest smile to the tech, who nodded. I walked away, going over instead to sit on the booth against one wall with my finger on the accept call button.

"Hello?" I answered, with a bit of uncertainty as I put the phone to my ear.

"How's your cat?" Azriel inquired.

"Oh. Umm..." I shut my eyes. "They took him into surgery. They umm... Put it on your card. But I can pay you back. I didn't know that-"

"*Why?*" he sounded bewildered.

"Because they thought it was going to your account, and-"

"No, I get that. I told them to. Why are you paying me back?"

Now it was my turn to be bewildered. "Because...it's not your responsibility? I'm the one who stole-" I swallowed the word. "*Found* the cat."

"You stole *it."*

I ignored the correction. "They emailed you the receipt." It occurred to me that I *should've* asked for a copy. "Can you tell me how much it is, and I really will pay for it?"

"No."

"....What?" I picked at the frayed edges of the pillow, needing something to do with my hands that didn't involve finding stray threads in my own clothes to yank on.

"Absolutely, not. I told them to put it on my account, and I'd take care of it."

"Yeah, but..." I lowered my voice to a whisper. "It's probably thousands of dollars, Az."

"*And*?"

"And that's a lot for you to be paying!"

"Correction. That's a lot for you to be paying."

He let that sink in, and I felt my brows raise in surprise.

That was certainly a statement about his own wealth.

"I'll uh, consider this the pack's birthday present to me, then," I muttered off-handedly.

"Today's your birthday?"

"No, it's tomorrow."

"Oh. Good. What are you going to do?"

My eyes strayed back to the counter, where the tech was still tapping away at whatever she was working on.

Should I be leaving? I doubted I'd be able to take October home tonight.

If he lived.

"Trying not to cry over a cat that may or may not survive," I said flatly.

"That sounds...morbid," Azriel admitted. *"But seriously. Don't worry about the money, all right? Whatever the vet says it needs, do it. Are you taking it home?"*

"I'm taking him home if he lives." I hated saying the last part out loud.

"Then get the food they sell there. It's supposed to be really good for animals. Vet recommended and all that shit. Put that and whatever else on my account as well, okay?"

"That's....really too much," I hesitated, knowing that was way too good to be true. "I can't do that."

"Please, do it. Otherwise, I'll have to sneak money into your bank account or something. Okay?"

"Yeah. Thanks. I really owe you for this, Az." I couldn't help the touch of relief that wove through my tone.

"It's fine, Will. Don't mention it. I'll see you tomorrow?"

"Yeah, sure–*wait*. Tomorrow? Since when–"

"You said you weren't doing anything." The teasing lilt to his voice was back. *"And it's your birthday. I'm not letting you sulk through it. So, we'll see you tomorrow. Got it?"* His words didn't exactly leave room for argument.

I liked that about his statement.

"Okay. But when-" He hung up, right in the middle of my question.

Was he just going to *come over*?

Yeah, yeah, that definitely sounded like him.

And he'd said *we*.

Would Lysander come too?

So much for my break from these boys. What had Liam said? To see if I felt the same after not seeing them for a bit?

Yeah, that had gone well.

CHAPTER THIRTY-THREE

CURIOSITY KILLED THE CAT.

I remembered those words. And the person that voice belonged to. Now the words sent shivers through me, even as my brain tried to sort through the blankets of sleep that still had me wrapped in a very warm snuggly cocoon.

My eyes cracked open, vision blurry as shapes swam in front of my dry eyes. Why was I so *tired*?

Then it all came back to me. The animal theft. *October*. His surgery.

When I'd left the night before, the tech had told me the vet was very optimistic, and no news would be good news. If their estimations were correct, the orange and white cat that I'd dubbed October out of a lack of creativity would be ready to go home in a week or so.

Unless he died, of course, or took a turn for the worse.

Lost in my sobering thoughts, it took me longer than it should have to realize I was staring at someone in my window.

In my window. Sitting on the sill with their legs curled up under their body, feet resting on the edge of my bed. Behind them, the glass had been lifted up to show the cloudy sky beyond.

"Lysander?" I breathed, unsure of what I was really looking at. "Are you real?"

"He's real," another, sweeter voice assured me as the arm wrapped around my waist pulled me tighter to the body behind me. "We thought you were ignoring us when you didn't answer our messages, Will."

"Who would've thought you'd sleep the day away," teased Lysander, a smile curving his gorgeous face.

"Especially, your birthday."

Oh. *Right.*

I closed my eyes and rolled onto my stomach, only succeeding in bringing Azriel with me so that he laid against my back. The black-haired male moved my hair to the side, kissing my jaw just under my ear.

"Do you not like your birthday?" Lysander asked curiously, not moving.

"How did you get in here? I locked the doors *and* the windows." Including the one, Lysander's ass was currently occupying.

"We broke in, obviously," the blonde replied. "So, what's wrong with it being your birthday?"

Of course, he couldn't just leave it alone, could he? With a sigh, I shifted so I could look at him from under my hair. "It's just never been great," I shrugged. "My mom always takes the chance to remind me that I keep missing out on opportunities to better myself. How at twenty-five, I should have a lot more work experience and an education." God. I was twenty-five now. Another year closer to thirty.

Not that thirty was a bad thing. But I wasn't looking forward to the fit my mom would throw when I hit the big three-o.

"Twenty-five?" Azriel sounded surprised. "I thought you were a little older than that. Lysander's age, for sure."

"How old are you two, again?" I'd read it in their passports, but that was a long time ago, and I was still sixty percent asleep.

"I'm twenty-eight," Lysander said smoothly. "He's twenty-seven. Nyko and Rhys are both twenty-nine, though Nyko is a few months older."

That didn't surprise me. They definitely seemed like the oldest of the group.

My phone vibrated, and I knew it wasn't these two trying to get a hold of me, and it wasn't the vet, so it could only be one person. As if summoned from the depths of hell just by speaking of her and her title.

My lovely mother.

Sure enough, when I dragged the phone towards me, I saw the word MOM flash on the screen. Sighing, I buried my face in the pillow again. "You should've let me sleep through the day," I grumbled, my words muffled in the sheets. "Now, good manners say I have to answer her."

"Why? If she makes your life miserable..." Azriel trailed off with a shrug. "Ignore her. *Block* her, for fuck's sake."

"You must have never had a helicopter, tiger parent."

"No, actually. I grew up in foster care with Lysander."

Well, that made me feel shitty. I frowned apologetically over my shoulder, my finger on the accept button.

"Put it on speaker," Lysander requested quickly. "I want to see if she's as bad as you say."

I froze. "*Promise* you won't say anything?" This was an awful idea, I knew. But maybe if they understood how shitty she was, they'd let me mope in peace.

The phone stopped ringing, then promptly began again.

He crossed his heart dramatically. I rolled my eyes, yet hit the accept button, then the speaker icon.

"Happy birthday, Willow." Even the tinny quality of the connection wasn't enough to mask the displeasure in my mother's voice. *"Though I'd hoped to spend it with you here, instead of you off being a child somewhere else."*

"You're in a sentimental mood," I sighed, hyper-aware of both men in the room with me.

"I'm frustrated with you. I don't know what I did to deserve you acting like this, but I wish you'd just tell me."

There she went again, making this about her.

Azriel snorted softly into my shoulder, kissing it a second later.

"Okay, well, none of this has anything to do with you, Mom," I said patiently, though I wasn't sure why I had to in the first place. There was nothing to further explain. I was an independent adult who made her own decisions.

Not that anyone had bothered to inform my mom of that.

"You missed Ashley's funeral. For someone who claims to be torn up over her death, you sure aren't acting like a very good friend."

Her words were unexpected, and struck like a razor blade in my chest. I opened my mouth, staring at the screen, but didn't reply.

I hadn't even considered *going*.

She was right.

I truly was an *awful* friend. An awful daughter, too, if she was right about that as well.

"I..." Without knowing what to say, I didn't have something innovative to reply with.

She knew it and capitalized on the weakness she could hear in my words.

"You know, I was talking to Mrs. Flowers today. You remember her, right? Your fourth-grade teacher? The one you said you hated?"

Lysander shifted uncomfortably on the window, and when I looked up at him, I saw the look on his face was one of disgust. His eyes were stormy blue-grey, instead of their usual cornflower color, and his hands were white-knuckled as they clenched the windowsill.

What was he so angry about?

Surely it wasn't over my mother's words to *me.*

"I remember," I muttered, searching my brain for what she could use to hurt me with concerning my teachers.

"Why do you let her talk to you like this?" Azriel whispered, his words just above a breath and only for my ears. "You're an adult, Will. She's upsetting you. Tell her to stop."

I glanced at him with wide eyes. "I can't. Not...really. She is still my mother."

"*What did you say?*" my mother snapped.

I flinched, even though she couldn't hear me. "N–nothing. Sorry. The TV is on in the background."

"*Just like you to not even give me your full attention.*"

Yeah. Just like *me* to do something so rude.

"Mom..." I'd just woken up, and she'd already managed to ruin my day. "Can you just tell me happy birthday and mean it? Please?"

"*What makes you think I don't mean it?!*" she asked, taken aback by my words. "*I've always meant it, Willow. Is it wrong of me to want you to understand how I feel? To express my worry over your current predicament and actions*?" Something cracked on the other side of the line as if she'd dropped something hard.

"But you're not-"

"*I'm sorry I won't say what you want me to. Maybe I shouldn't have called since you don't want to listen to what I have to say. Will that make you happy? If I just zip my lips and nod at your words? That way you can't misconstrue them?*"

I hadn't meant to get her worked up for a rant.

God, now I wasn't sure what to do except let her keep going, and with every word it caused a flush of humiliation to creep higher up my cheeks.

"Well, I know what I was taught." Lysander's voice came out as a pleasant, charming drawl. "If you don't have nothin' nice to say, don't say *nothin'* at all."

I looked up at him in surprise, eyes wide. "Lysander-"

"*Am I on speaker?*" My mother's tone was indignant. "*Where are you, exactly*?"

"Mom, I–"

"Don't worry, Willow's mother." Azriel's voice, a counterpoint to Lysander's drawl, was chipper and overly polite. "We're going to take your daughter out for her birthday. But, she's looking pretty sad, so I'm going to have her hang up on you before you ruin it for her."

Mom gasped. "*What do you think–*"

"Hang up, Will," Lysander ordered. The request wasn't a polite one.

"She's my *mom*," I hissed between clenched teeth. "I can't just–"

Lysander leaned forward smoothly and yanked the phone out of my hands, causing me to yelp and reach for it. "Hey!"

Azriel pulled me back, his grip like iron around my shoulders.

"Sorry," Lysander apologized into the phone with a savage grin, his eyes on mine. "But Will can't come to the phone right now. Or for the rest of today. Or tomorrow. Hell, how about you let her call *you*."

"When she wants to," chipped in Azriel.

"*If* she wants to," finished Lysander. "You have a good day now." Before my mother or I could get a word in, he hung up.

Mouth open, I gaped at him. "You did *not* just do that."

"I did." He pocketed the phone with a flourish.

"Hey, *no*. What if the vet calls?"

"Then I'll give you the phone. Until then, it's mine. No arguments."

Though his tone exuded finality, I struggled out of Azriel's grip and got to my knees in front of him, bracing my hands on his thighs. "You can't steal my phone from me," I argued, my heart speeding up in my chest at the allure of being so close to him.

You're mad, Will, I reminded myself. *Angry with him.*

I needed to stop looking at his lips and the way his eyes sparkled with amusement. "Are you going to take it back from me?" he asked in a voice like velvet.

"You're sitting on the window sill. I could push you out," I threatened.

"Try." The word was an invitation. "*Try,* so I have a perfect excuse to retaliate."

I wanted to. I wanted to see how far I'd get, and what his idea of retaliation would be.

Lysander must've seen it in my face. He reached up with both hands to cup my jaw, cradling my face in his grip. "You're so fucking adorable," he informed me. "Like a little cat that thinks she can hurt me with her kitten claws. Would you like to scratch me, Will? You can do it. Dig your claws in and mark me up, so everyone on the street knows I belong to you?"

"Yes," I murmured, before I could stop myself. Surprise flickered in his eyes, approval instantly replacing the shock.

Wait a minute.

This wasn't *me.*

Belong to me? We weren't even dating!

He wasn't *mine,* like that.

And I wasn't *his* or *theirs,* or anything else.

That sudden thought made my gut wrench like I'd delivered an unpleasant possibility to my system.

Like my body and most of my brain already considered that not to be the case.

"I–that's not right." I covered up the reaction with my rambling explanation. "I just got excited-I barely know you!"

"I know you enough," Lysander interrupted. "Or...are you under the impression you're *not* mine?"

Holy shit. That should not have done the things it did to my body.

"You let me go when you kidnapped me," I pointed out, unsure of where I was going with my statement.

Azriel's arms twined around my shoulders, holding me between them.

I was caught like a bird, with my wings to the sides and nowhere to go.

I couldn't even look away. I was forced to watch the slow, arrogant grin that made its leisurely way up Lysander's face, leaving him to look like a satisfied cat himself.

Not a cat, rather.

But a *predator*.

"Oh, Will," he chuckled. "I let you leave my house and didn't bother with chains, but I don't really need to, do I?"

When I didn't answer, he tapped my lip with his thumb. "That wasn't a rhetorical question, kitten. Do I need a chain or collar to keep you close to me? Close to *us*?"

It wasn't rhetorical, sure.

But it was an impossible question all the same.

Utterly impossible to answer when I couldn't bring myself to say *yes* or *no*.

Especially when I knew what the truth was.

And so did they.

"Hey, come on." Azriel nipped at my shoulder, sparing me the impossible decision. "It's her *birthday*. And we're supposed to be doing something fun. We were going to take you to lunch, Will. *Well*." He looked dramatically at the watch he wore, showing off the same snake ring that matched the one that all of the pack wore on different fingers. "You're making it a bit of a *late* lunch now. You really sleep forever, you know that?"

"Yeah," I laughed softly, unable to take my eyes from Lysander's. "I'm the worst sometimes, huh?"

• • •

I had expected *Grill Fiesta,* so when the two of them took me to the restaurant that Liam owned instead, I was pleasantly surprised. More so when the waitress brought out an actual ice cream birthday cake for me.

"You guys are...really nice," I admitted, finishing my glass of wine once the last bite of cake was gone and I had a reprieve from them telling stupid stories about things they'd done when they were younger. "Hey, can I ask you something that might not be my business?"

It occurred to me that I couldn't remember exactly how many glasses of sweet white wine I'd had, but it was indeed enough to make me looser with my words with these two members of my pack.

Wait, no.

The pack.

Not...necessarily *mine.*

"Nothing is *your* business when it comes to us, Will," Azriel reminded me with a grin. "But would you like it to be?"

I hated that the two of them seemed full of questions with hidden meanings that I worried would contract me into a life of being *in with the pack.*

"*Anyway.*" I ignored the question. "The papers I stole the other night." I lowered my voice as I spoke. "What was it?"

"Oh, that?" Lysander swiped his spoon around his bowl, gathering up the last bit of ice cream and sucking it clean. "It was a contract on Liam's life."

"*What?!*" I yelped in surprise, feeling my pulse skyrocket. "Oh my *god!*"

"It's really not that big of a deal. They happen. He's fine, and it's not going to be a thing," Azriel assured me. "He should've led with that." The dark-haired male threw a narrow-eyed look at Lysander, which the latter just shrugged off.

"What did you do? Does he know? Did you guys, like,

pay off a hitman or something to forget about it?" I wasn't entirely sure how getting a hitman off your trail worked, but I could only assume money was involved.

"Murder," Lysander replied simply. "Last night during your cat theft, I think."

Did *all* of them know I'd stolen October?

And why wasn't I more worried about the murder?

"Who'd you kill?" I asked, directing the question to Lysander.

"Everyone."

At that, I wasn't sure what to say. My mouth fell open as I tried to form a sentence, but at last, I only nodded. "Okay. Everyone, then."

"The hitman, his partner..." Lysander ticked off the people on his fingers. "Two of the people from that meeting. The younger man and woman. They'd gone behind their boss's back to put the hit out, so he would've killed them anyway."

"It's a thing," Azriel explained at my obvious confusion. "They betrayed him, and they knew what would happen once we found out. Real *oopsie* on their part, huh?"

"That's...certainly one way to put it." I rested my elbow on the table, trying to sort through my own feelings on the matter. “Won't they be seeking some kind of revenge?”

They didn't answer. The silence was long enough that I peered up, eyes slightly wide as I took in their expressions.

They gazed at each other, having some kind of quiet conversation that I wasn't privy to.

“Yes,” Lysander said, just as Azriel replied with, “No.”

They looked at each other again, and Lysander snorted.

“Don't lie to her. They'll absolutely come for revenge. Andy-that's their *guy* that they flock to-he'll try something sooner or later.”

“Sooner,” Azriel bargained. “That would work best for me, and then we'd know who wants so *badly* to exit their mortal coil and help them along.” He beamed.

Somehow I couldn't find it in me to be upset, exactly. However, I worried that my friends would get on the wrong side of things.

I hadn't known them long and they were bad people. What was the point in letting them take up space in my brain, rent-free?

I wasn't a bad person. Just practical.

"Okay, next unwise question." This one undoubtedly *was* unwise, but it had been lurking in my brain since they'd shown up in my bed with me this morning.

I had to ask, even though I was sure it would crush my inner fantasies that I would be filing away for a later, frequent use.

"Ask," invited Azriel comfortably. He had piled up his own dishes, and a moment later, had done the same with both Lysander's and mine before setting them at the edge of the table.

I waited on the passing server to pick them up, flashing her a smile that she returned brightly.

"I'm going to regret this," I admitted. "But umm. Back in Michigan. When I was trying to learn more about you by going to your Airbnb."

"When you broke in," Lysander amended absently.

"Yeah. *Sure*. We'll put it that way."

He snorted, and side-eyed me from his chair, both elbows on the table and hands clasped in front of him. "How else is there to put it? You. Broke. In."

I met his gaze, one brow raised. "Do you want to hear the question, or not?"

Because I thought about it so much now that I *had* to know.

Even if the answer was a terrifying one.

"If Nyko hadn't stopped you, what would you have done?"

Lysander blinked, again caught by surprise and allowing

it to show on his face. "With you?" he clarified. "Why are you so certain I wouldn't have called the friendly neighborhood police to take the thief out of my home?"

"Would you have?"

"Fuck no. But I wondered if you'd thought I might. What *were* you afraid of that night when you were lying on the porch praying I didn't see you?"

My body seemed to prickle with fear at the memory, my hands clenching involuntarily at the rush of adrenaline that had my heart beating rabbit-fast.

"I thought you might kill me," I admitted. "If you knew I'd broken in."

"You took us for murderers, even back then?"

I drew back, eyebrows shooting upward. "Of course, I did. I *always* suspected you of bad things, even when it was clear you didn't murder Ashley."

"It's because you're a bad actor," Azriel explained sweetly, patting Lysander's elbow. "Rhys has been telling you that for years-"

"Shut up, Az," the blonde growled, shoving at his comrade. "I want to hear the rest of this." He gestured for me to continue, but I shrugged.

"I just had a feeling. You were nice at the coffee shop, but then at *The Outlook,* you were..." I trailed off, remembering the cold, savageness in Lysander's eyes. "You were so *cold*. Your eyes were different, and you looked at me like..."

I didn't want to finish, so I shrugged.

Thankfully, he didn't ask for more of an answer. Lysander rolled his shoulders back, looking thoughtful. "You want to know what I would've done? Why? Do you think about it still? Are you *afraid* of what I could've done to you that night?" His voice had gone soft with promise, and I snuck a look at him at his guess.

Whatever he saw in my eyes, Lysander's own gaze

narrowed. "No," he guessed correctly. "You're not *afraid*. That's not why you want to know."

I hated how easy it was for him to read me.

"Just tell me?"

"Only if you promise to tell *me* what you think about when you imagine I *had* pulled you out of your horrendous hiding place."

I thought about it and realized that it probably couldn't hurt anything to admit to him my fantasy. "Okay," I agreed. "But you first."

"You didn't catch me on a good night back then," Lysander admitted. "I *wanted* an excuse for blood. And I had wanted you the moment I saw you in that coffee shop, then every moment *after* you stole my wallet out of my pocket."

Ouch. That hurt my pride.

"We aren't exactly nice people," Lysander went on. "I would've done not-so nice things to you that night."

Holy shit.

Did he mean he would've *killed* me?

"Like...illegal things?" I asked stupidly.

His flat look morphed instantly into a grin. "Everything I do is illegal," he reminded me. "So, yeah."

I realized he wasn't going to tell me anything else.

Was he worried it would scare me off?

A better question-he *cared* about my impression of him?

"Okay, your turn," Azriel prompted, flicking his hand at me.

"What?" I asked, caught off guard from my inner thoughts.

"He told you, in his way, that he would've done *bloody and violent* things with you, Will. So how about *you* tell *us* what you imagine we would've done."

Fuck.

It was worse now that they'd admitted that to me. Now I felt *wrong*.

I imagined my own brush with death as something sexy.

There was probably something wrong with that.

Scratch that...definitely something wrong.

"*Well,*" I began, shuffling in my seat and pleating my napkin between my fingers. The actions caused shreds of paper to fall to the green-topped tables.

Neither of them stopped me.

"So before I knew you were going to chop me up into mincemeat and probably feed me to the local wildlife, I kind of thought...maybe..." God, was I actually admitting this?

I was *not* about to do this.

But I'd given them my *word*.

"Maybe you'd...do the same thing you did when you...kidnapped me."

Neither of them spoke.

At last, Azriel batted his eyelashes and asked, "I'm so sorry, Will," he told me sweetly. "I'm sure I don't know what you mean. Can you elaborate?"

"But quietly," added Lysander, showing caution for the first time since I'd known him. "I'd rather no one else get any kind of thrill out of our conversation, okay?"

"Oh sure," I agreed flippantly, rolling my eyes. I was sobering up from the wine much too soon, the cold sobriety of Lysander's words, and what I was about to confess was chasing away the slight haze. "So I...kind of happened to think, out of the blue, that you'd maybe..." God, it wasn't that I was embarrassed for liking *sex* with them.

But this was something else.

Lysander moved his hand under the table to rest it on my thigh. "Out with it, kitten," he purred in my ear. "I'm not into giving punishments like Rhys is, but if you keep me waiting for the answer you promised, I'm sure I can think of something." His fingers splayed out against the skin covered only by my thin leggings, the pressure a promise that radiated heat into my thigh and higher. "What do you think about us doing to you when we caught you?"

"I...like to think maybe you would've picked me up and-and instead of letting me go, you'd take me inside and-" Hell, I couldn't say it out loud.

What kind of person would they think I was if I voiced *this* particular fantasy to them?

His grip tightened on my thigh.

"And you'd-you know. *Fuck me*."

"Right there? On the sofa?" Azriel asked. "In front of the windows?"

Oh, Azriel. Always looking for the exhibitionist option.

"No, I mean. I guess? Location isn't necessarily the point. But I just sometimes think about the four of you *doing whatever you wanted* with me. And it's not *murder* when I think about it." Unconsciously, I pressed my thighs together.

"And what do we do to you? Do we punish you for breaking in?" Lysander's voice was a soft whisper at my ear. "Or do we skip straight to the point where we're each claiming your body for our pleasure?"

I was going to die. His words made heat rise to my face and gather somewhere much lower.

I was *clearly* going to die of embarrassment.

For a moment, I barely noticed that his hand had left my knee and, instead, was rubbing against me lightly, now between my clenched thighs.

"That one," I breathed deep in reply, fighting to keep the arousal off my face.

Damn, I hoped I was succeeding.

"What then? Once we strip you naked and cuff your hands behind your back, so you're vulnerable and exposed, what do we do then?"

I was *definitely* not succeeding.

Not when he spoke like that.

"We're in public," I reminded him, nearly stumbling over my own words.

"Then tell me fast. What do we do to you, once you're *ours*?"

"Everything." I blurted the word out, unable to stop myself. "You-you each take turns. You don't ask-you *take,* and you make sure I love every minute of it. And you don't *stop* for-" I swallowed heavily. "For a long time, okay?"

Lysander pulled his hand away, and I found I *missed* the sensual contact instantly. I went back to clenching my thighs and pretended I wasn't aware of how wet I must be.

"Oh." Azriel looked thoughtful. "That's a lot better of an idea than what he would've done."

CHAPTER THIRTY-FOUR

LUNCH with the two boys and the call from the vet's office that October would be fine and I could pick him up in a few days made my birthday the best in my memory.

Which, admittedly, was probably a little sad. It wasn't like I'd gotten any presents, other than the promise of my stolen cat coming home with me and lunch.

But I didn't *need* gifts other than that. Except for money.

I would've gladly accepted *money* to keep myself going without having to do something dangerous like steal from the museum.

Curled up on the sofa, knees tucked under me, and with the television on for white noise, I hardly noticed the sounds that shouldn't have been there since I had been half asleep.

The hand on my ankle, even, didn't register past a small part of my brain that remembered I lived alone now.

Until the hand *tugged.*

My eyes snapped open, and I gasped, turning onto my back and lashing out at the person.

Only to realize I wasn't on my sofa at all. I *distinctly* remembered what I'd done to wind down. I'd changed into my comfy tank top and sleep shorts, and with my comforter over me, I'd planned to spend the night dreaming of whatever played on the tv while I drifted in and out of consciousness.

That way, with the noise and distraction, I wouldn't have to think of *other* things.

But here I was, blinking away the dredges of sleep and staring into the shadowed face of the hooded figure who had a hold of my leg in a firm, long-fingered grip.

"Let me go!" I gasped, kicking out at them with my other leg, only for that ankle to be caught as well.

The man looked up, showing me startling blue eyes and a macabre grin that showed white, sparkling teeth.

"*Lysander?!*" I yelped, mind spinning. Was I dreaming?

When I tried to sit up, hands grabbed my wrists, pinning them down over my head.

"Ah, ah!" Azriel's tone was disapproving as his face loomed into sight. "That's not how this goes, remember?"

Remember...*what*?

Then it hit me, and my stomach dropped.

Were they...*were they reenacting what we'd talked about during lunch*?

"Just so I know...we're following *my* kidnap plan, right?" I asked nervously, still kicking and wrestling to get free of Lysander's hands.

The blonde rolled his eyes and jerked his head, so his hood fell back. "No," he replied, voice mocking. "You just woke up before I could *stab you*."

"God, you'd better be joking."

"You should know that he's not going to stab you," Azriel chuckled, his eyes glittering. "We like you too much."

"*I* like you too much to stab you," Lysander reminded me, kneeling on the edge of what I realized was a bed.

But it wasn't the bed of the guest room I remembered. This one had soft, silky black sheets and a plush black comforter that had been shoved to the side. Over my head hung a dimly lit chandelier, the crystal reflecting just enough light to see their faces.

"Who's room is this?" I suspected Lysander's, but I hadn't thought his taste to be so luxurious.

"Rhys's." The impish amusement was impossible not to recognize in Azriel's voice. "Who is not home, by the way. Neither is Nyko."

"But they're going to be," Lysander added, kneeling between my knees so he could run his large hands up over my thighs. "And they're going to find you here, on Rhys's bed, and I doubt their control is that good."

"Not Nyko's," Azriel promised, dangling a pair of handcuffs in front of my face before clipping the cold metal over my wrists. I shivered at the feeling, all of my nerve endings suddenly on high alert.

Holy shit.

This was really happening.

In my current predicament, I couldn't decide what I felt. Excitement? Most certainly. Fear?

Yeah, abso-fucking-lutely certain.

But that just made things easier to focus on.

Azriel guided my hands up to the headboard, clipping them to another pair of handcuffs already there. When I tried to pull on my hands, they didn't go much of anywhere.

I was trapped—more than I had been before when Nyko had me in the hallway.

More than I had *ever* been with the pack.

"Rhys's control isn't *perfect*," Lysander added conversationally. "He's the only one of us that hasn't had you, right?"

"Maybe you should let him have her first," Azriel suggested. "Before we wreck her."

Lysander paused, his eyes distant as he appeared to consider the suggestion. "That would be the *nice* thing to do," he agreed, voice mild. "But..." He reached down, his fingers hooking in the hem of my *very* thin shorts. "I don't think anyone's ever accused me of being nice...do you?"

Before Azriel could answer, Lysander *jerked* my shorts down, over my knees and ankles so quickly that I hadn't even realized he'd ripped them until I saw the fabric hanging unnaturally from his fingers before he tossed them to the floor.

"I liked those!" I protested, my heart hammering in my throat.

"That's a shame," Lysander sighed. "Suppose you like this, too?" His hands on my thighs ran upward, tickling over my hip bones and creating a warm pressure on my sides as he rucked up the fabric of my tank top.

"It's kind of my favorite," I told him breathily.

"Oh." Lysander met my eyes, no concern at all in his features. "Well that's a real shame then, isn't it?" With brutal efficiency he tore the fabric, finally pulling the shredded material out from under me and tossing it somewhere too. "And you know, you don't have *any* clothes here," he added, eyes surveying every inch of my body that was bared to them.

I couldn't help it. I squirmed, testing my cuffs and drawing my knees up as much as I was able.

"So you really can't leave...can you?" Azriel finished, stretched out beside me and with his mouth pressed to my ear. "Not until we're done and take pity on you."

"Which won't be for a long, *long* time," Lysander went on. "There are *four* of us. Think you can last long enough for us to be satisfied with you?"

I wasn't sure if that was a real question, and with my insides tied up in knots, I doubted I could answer.

Not that either of them seemed to care. Azriel turned my face to his, drawing me into a sweet, lengthy kiss that started as almost chaste and had grown into something else entirely.

Something else that involved his teeth biting into my lip, his tongue tasting every inch of my mouth that he could find, and his hand that wasn't clasped in my hair to keep me *right* where he wanted me, cupping and massaging my breasts.

I gasped when his fingers found my nipple, twisting and teasing until I pulled at the cuffs to try to pull away for some relief.

Azriel only chuckled, took a breath, and switched to the other one with the same rough, teasing touches.

All while Lysander *watched*. I could feel him where he sat, hands rubbing over the fronts of my thighs as he watched Azriel touch me. Twice I glanced down at him, only to find his shining gaze intent on my reactions and the way I twisted at a particularly rough bite from Azriel.

Of course, being Lysander, it only took about a *minute* of watching before he grew tired of it. The touches on my thighs became less innocent. Seconds later, I felt his mouth on my skin, just under my navel, as he pressed a soft kiss there.

I jerked anyway as if I'd been branded, and his teeth scraped against my body, following his kisses that seemed to be going in a strange pattern over my hip bones.

By the time I felt his hot breath between my thighs, and he urged my thighs wider, I was ready to wrap my legs around his shoulders and pull him exactly where I wanted him.

Though, I doubted that would've made him go any faster.

Fingers trailed over my slit, circling my clit before spreading me open for him and causing a flicker of embarrassment to curl through my body.

"Sometimes I think it's something *questionable* that always has you so wet for me," the blonde chuckled conversationally, teasing my clit with his thumb.

I writhed, needing more but unable to voice my desires with Azriel's mouth on mine.

"Maybe it's not us working you up at all," he went on. "I kind of think you get off on *what we are*. Is that it? You can tell us, you know. Is it the killer in us that gets you going, Will?"

Azriel pulled back, grinning. "I think it might be the crazy," he growled before claiming my mouth again. "Don't worry, it's not an *insult*." He sank his teeth into my bottom lip until I shrieked, back arching off the bed.

If I'd expected the pain to be a turn *off*, I was sorely mistaken.

"Is it because you haven't learned to let go like us? You could, you know," he urged, as Lysander's rough kisses found the inside of my thighs and just over my clit. I shivered, unable to focus on both Azriel's words and Lysander's fucking *mouth*.

Especially, when he licked over my clit once, then again, the pressure light and teasing and *dreadful* when I wanted more.

A lot more.

"Maybe she doesn't know how," Lysander purred, taking only a momentary pause before focusing his attention on my clit again. However, this time his hand left my hip and two fingers slid into me, causing my hips to jerk in appreciation.

"Oh, I think you do," Azriel laughed, descending on my mouth *yet again* to keep me from speaking.

When Lysander pulled away, leaving me needing more and absolutely surprised, I tried to look down at him, only to be jerked back upward with a growl from my darker-haired male. The look in his eyes was a warning, and I let him guide me back into a kiss as Lysander moved between my knees.

Seconds later, I felt him, his length against my thigh,

causing shivers to trail up my spine like the touch of fingers as he gripped my thighs again.

"I had a plan, you know," he told me in a soft, husky tone. "I wanted you to come apart from my mouth and my fingers."

I most certainly had not, so clearly that plan had not worked.

"But it's your fault I stopped early," he went on, his cock brushing against me as he forced my thighs wider and urged me to wrap my legs around his waist.

My fault?

"He's right," Azriel continued, his hand moving so he could splay his fingers over my throat and press lightly. "Do you know how you look right now?"

"Of course she doesn't," laughed Lysander and roughly thrust into me without any more warning than that.

Free from Azriel's lips, I gasped, my back arching off of the bed at the thick, welcome intrusion of Lysander inside me.

"Holy *fuck*," I whispered, loving that it was just as intense as the first time he'd fucked me.

"You should let us keep you this time," Azriel purred in my ear, nipping at it. Still pressed to my side, he glanced down between us to see Lysander sitting, giving small, experimental thrusts.

"*Let* us?" Lysander grinned wolfishly. "We're past you *letting* us do anything to you. We'll do whatever we like." As he spoke, he began to move, sliding out only to roughly thrust back in.

"If he says so, then you're never leaving." Azriel wound a hand in my hair, moving to toy with my nipples once more. His mouth was on mine again, barely giving me a chance to breathe.

It was a *lot*. My mind could hardly keep up, and soon

enough, I was happy just to float on the feeling of Lysander's deep thrusts and Azriel's hands on me.

"You're getting complacent," Azriel growled against my jaw, his hand leaving my body and instead began stroking down, *down*...past my navel until he could press my thighs back to the bed on either side of Lysander, rendering me unable to move at all.

"Look at how much she *wants* you," he laughed darkly, throwing me a side-eyed, dark look. "If I uncuffed her, she'd jump up and be all over you. Even though we quite literally *broke into her apartment* and brought her here while she *slept*."

"Yeah," Lysander growled in agreement, fingers brushing over the skin below my navel. "This is what you've always wanted, isn't it? For us to chain you to our bed and keep you here?"

"You could've just asked to be our little fuck toy," the dark-haired male chuckled. "We would've let you. No need to go to so much trouble since you *clearly* love our cocks this much."

"And she hasn't even had yours or Rhys's," Lysander added, his thumb finding my clit.

"Wait-" I wasn't sure how long I'd last, not with how much they both already had me worked up and the way that everything seemed so much better when I couldn't even *move*.

If he played with my clit, I'd come apart. No way around it.

"*Wait*?" Lysander parroted. "Did you hear that?" The touch of cruelty in his voice should've scared me or *something*.

It should not have been an absolute turn-on.

"Why should we? What are you going to do when we don't *wait* or *slow down*?" Azriel's voice held its own kind of icy edge. "Are you just embarrassed because of how much you clearly *need* to be fucked like this?"

Lysander teased my clit, lightly at first, then harder, and with incessant touches that had me moving to try to give myself a bit of relief.

"Wait-" I tried again. "For like *two seconds*-"

"No," they both answered lightly. "Hurry up, Lys. I don't really care if she cums, but if I don't get her *soon,* I'm going to fight you for it."

Lysander bared his teeth at the jovial male, something territorial on his face for a brief moment. But Azriel's grin only widened.

"All right," he said finally and pushed Azriels's hands out of the way to grip my hips harder, fingers digging marks into my skin. "It won't take long," he promised, eyes finding mine again. "Not with how she's so *tight* for me. So fucking *perfect,* aren't you, Will?"

His movements increased in speed as he spoke, until all I could do was let him hold me as he fucked me with long, hard strokes.

Much too soon, he stiffened, sliding into me one more time and holding me to him as he came with a shudder inside me. "Oh, poor *thing,*" he panted, staring into my eyes with a savage grin. "Did you not come, too?"

"A *shame,*" Azriel agreed.

"Come on-*please*?" I tried unsuccessfully to pull my arms free of the cuffs, my legs still locked in Lysander's hold. "That's not *fair*-"

"Life's not *fair,*" Lysander broke in, moving away from me and getting to his feet a second later.

Azriel took his place a second later, his jeans unbuckled and cock in his hand. "Well, life's looking pretty fucking sweet for *us,* right now," he told me with a grin, and sank into me a second later.

Unlike Lysander, Azriel was slow. He drew back and thrust into me with a controlled, even motion as he watched my face. "You truly are such a pretty sight," he laughed. "Not even halfway done, and you look all messed up and ready to kill one of us yourself."

"I might," I snapped. "I really, *actually*-"

Lysander lunged, knees on the bed as he captured my lips in a savage, dominating kiss. I fought back, biting at his lip and earning a growl from him and, a second later, his hand around my throat pushing me down *hard* against the mattress while Azriel fucked me.

"Bite me again," he invited, pulling back with a bright gleam in his eyes. "I *dare* you to-"

I didn't wait for him to finish. Surging upward, I found his lower lip and bit down, sinking my teeth in enough that I knew it hurt.

Azriel made some kind of strangled snicker, though I couldn't see him past Lysander.

The hand around my throat tightened more than it ever had, on the edge of actual pain as he shoved me down against the bed.

"Oh, pretty girl," he growled. "You're tempting fate with me." He licked at his lips, eyes locked on mine as he leaned down for another kiss.

Or so I'd thought. Instead, his mouth fastened on the junction of my shoulder and my neck, his hand moving so he could clamp teeth down on my skin and bite down.

I yelped, surprised, as my hips arched into Azriel's as his fingers sank into my thighs and his thrusts became faster.

"If you're going to *bite,* you'd better make it count," Lysander snarled, teeth bared as he met my eyes. "If there's no mark, you didn't really mean it." His thumb rubbed over the place he'd bitten me, my skin oversensitive. "Do you need another demonstration?" He moved again, biting more onto my shoulder and taking the time to suck a mark into my skin before doing it again and again.

His bites lessened in intensity, somewhat, as he worked

his way down my chest until he could run his tongue over my nipple.

Was he going to *bite me* there?

He didn't...exactly. His teeth sank into the swell of my breast, and again I could feel him suck a mark into my pale skin.

"When I'm done with you, no one will have any doubt of what you did tonight," he promised.

I tried to answer, I opened my mouth with the intent to tell him off or tell him something witty, but I was too close to the edge for it. The next time he bit down, this time on my opposite shoulder and just outside of the area where I'd been cut, I couldn't muffle the choked cry, nor could I hold back as I came. My orgasm had hit me harder than I would've thought possible as Azriel groaned and followed me with one final, rough thrust that buried him deeper inside me.

I was sure I saw stars as I panted, half aware of Lysander's kisses on my jaw and how Azriel was drawing his own orgasm out as long as possible as my legs kept him pressed to me.

"That's nice and all," a new voice, Nyko's, drawled from the door. "But you told me we were going to use her, not treat her like she's *delicate*." He sneered the last word, and Lysander scoffed, sitting up.

"Well, I'm so sorry," the blonde replied, a grin on his face as he looked towards Nyko and Rhys, where they stood against the door frame. "Would you like to show us where we went wrong?"

My stomach twisted into anxious and expectant knots.

"Oh, I suppose," Rhys agreed, his eyes on me. "I just hope we don't break our new toy. It'd be such a *shame* to have to fix her if we're too rough with her."

CHAPTER THIRTY-FIVE

I WASN'T EXPECTING Azriel to laugh and roll to the side, gesturing towards me while Lysander snorted and pulled away.

Nor was I expecting Nykos to prowl to the head of the bed and uncuff my hands.

"I don't need handcuffs for you, do I, princess?" he breathed. "I don't need a knife, either, no matter how much you like it."

I shook my head slowly, feeling uncertainty for the first time.

Not that I was afraid of them...not exactly.

But while Lysander and Azriel were both becoming familiar enough that I could anticipate their actions, Nykos, and *definitely* Rhys, were still mysteries to me.

And mysteries that came in bloody, killer packages were rarely safe ones.

Tangling his fingers in my shoulder-length hair, Nykos pulled me to my knees and drew me into a kiss that was not nearly so sweet as Azriel's, but not quite as forceful as Lysander's either. No, his kiss was something completely different that drew me closer, causing me to relax against him and let him draw my hands down to the front of his jeans.

"Don't make me tell you twice," he warned when I hesitated.

Technically, he hadn't told me *anything*.

But I supposed that was irrelevant, and something he didn't want to necessarily hear. My fingers fumbled over the button of his jeans, and as he purred encouragements against my lips, I pulled out his cock from his jeans, running my fingers over the warm length of him in my hands.

Nykos moved, standing at the side of the bed and shifting me forward until I was on my hands and knees in front of him, my knees sinking into the soft mattress.

"Sorry," he said, eyes flicking upward and behind me. "I know this isn't really your *preference*. But I figured you wouldn't mind tonight."

"I don't mind." Rhys's voice was an aloof sigh somewhere behind me, and I felt the bed dip near my feet.

When I tried to turn and look, however, Nyko's grip on my hair tightened. "Now, who said you needed to look?" he asked, eyes glittering. "Come on, Will. I shouldn't have to ask, should I?" He urged my face towards him, very obvious in his intent, and I let him move me until my lips were just over the head of his cock.

Teasingly, I ran my tongue up the underside, trying to look up at him as I did, only for him to lock his hand in my hair once more, nails brushing my scalp.

Fine then. Focusing on what he clearly wanted, I got used to the feel of him in my hand and mouth, mind steering away from wherever Rhys might have been.

Which came back to shock me a moment later, when a knee pushed my thighs apart, and the pack leader settled between my thighs. "I don't *mind*," he repeated. "But I want you on my own, soon. I don't want you getting the wrong idea about me, Will," Rhys explained, knelt behind me on the bed with my hips in his bruising grip.

When I felt the head of his cock at my slit, I stiffened,

surprised, but Rhys didn't seem to care much. He slid into me, not giving me any sort of warning or time to get used to him inside me.

I gasped, mouth open just in time for Nyko to use the moment to slide his cock into my mouth, hand in my hair keeping me there as his hips rocked forward, the underside of his length brushing my tongue as my eyes watered.

"I don't think she has much of an idea of you at all," Nyko said mildly, pausing for a moment before urging me to take him deeper. "Come on, princess," he purred. "I know you can do better than that. Don't make me *convince* you."

Arousal twisted in my belly. I loved the note of danger in his voice—the almost threat.

There was something about being held between them, completely at their mercy, that had me already feeling the beginnings of interest in my body again. The feel of Rhys's cock in my oversensitive pussy should've been unpleasant. And it was, for a moment.

A very brief moment.

"Might as well just enjoy it," Rhys told me, running a hand down my spine.

"She enjoys it," Nyko said. "You can't see her like I can. This is what you wanted, isn't it? Sure, you like Lysander's cock and Azriel's teasing-"

Both men who now sat, watching, from the far side of the room made noises of indignation.

"But this is what you *want*. Right, Will?"

I didn't have the ability to agree or disagree.

"I'm the first one to take your mouth, aren't I?" Nyko went on as if we were having a conversation I could actually participate in. "The first of *us*, anyway. I like that. The first to discover how much you love playing with sharp things, and the first to take you like this." His hand loosened in my hair, until Rhys's thrusts picked up, driving me forward and causing me to take more of Nyko in my mouth.

He used the advantage, grip tightening once more as he continued to buck his hips lazily against me.

It was a *damn* good thing I didn't have much of a gag reflex.

And while I loved being at their mercy, I didn't want them to think this was all I could do. My hand at the base of his shaft moved, taking the scant inches of him that I couldn't get in my mouth and making sure *no* part of him felt abandoned.

He hissed at the sudden stimulation, tugging on my hair approvingly.

"Come on, princess," he encouraged, Rhys's movements slowing. "You can do better, can't you? The faster you get me off, the faster Rhys gets *you* off."

That sounded pretty damn great, actually. I hated that he'd slowed down and would much rather Rhys be throwing me into the bed.

But beggars couldn't be choosers.

At last, Nyko's grip in my hair stiffened, becoming painful enough that tears pricked my eyes as he held me to him. He started to pull away, probably trying to be polite and *not* cum in my mouth.

But I wasn't looking for polite.

Not in the least.

I reached out and grabbed onto his jeans, holding him to me and taking as much of him in my mouth as he came with a gasp, Rhys's murmur of absolute approval driving me to rock my hips back against him in appreciation.

Finally, Nyko pulled away, and I let him, wiping my mouth with the back of my hand while he watched me with something on his face I couldn't quite understand.

In a way, it reminded me too much of how Lysander looked at me when he got into one of his 'you're ours forever' moods.

I didn't hate it.

"Careful," he chuckled finally, moving to sit on the bed beside Rhys. "Or we really *will* have to keep you this time."

"Oh yeah?" I asked, surprising myself with the challenging words. "You know, that threat is starting to lose its edge."

I wasn't prepared for Rhys to pull out of me, leaving me empty and *hating* it.

And I *certainly* wasn't ready for the way he flipped me onto my back under him, the leader of the pack leaning forward on his hands until he could gaze down at my face where I lay under him, trapped.

"Don't test us," he breathed. "We don't take jokes well."

"Maybe it wasn't a joke."

What was I *saying*? Was the haze of great sex really so amazing that words like this came bubbling out of my mouth without getting my brain's approval?

Maybe my brain-to-mouth filter had just been fucked out of me?

"*Maybe* you should reconsider that statement." He nudged my hips upward until he could enter me once more, sliding into me smoothly.

I couldn't help the moan that left my hips, or the way my hips bucked as I silently begged for more.

"Do you know what you're even asking for?" He was moving again but much less relaxed and languid than before. This time he fucked me like he meant it, like he was trying to make a point.

If the point was to make me drown in his eyes and his movements, he was succeeding in spades.

Nyko leaned down, drawing Rhys into a sloppy, loud kiss as I watched. Enraptured, I wished I could reach up and twine my fingers in Rhys's black hair, or Nyko's, but that seemed rude. Especially without asking.

And I sure as hell was not about to *ask*.

In the end, I didn't need to. Nyko lunged down to press

his lips to mine, his mouth devouring mine and tasting of *Rhys*.

And then, as if summoned by my thoughts, the pack leader joined in as well, pushing Nyko's jaw to the side so he could slant his lips against mine.

Not that Nyko went far. His mouth on my neck, licking over the marks Lysander had left on my shoulder, and finally back up to my lips was intoxicating. He turned, joining in the kiss that I shared with Rhys until I wasn't sure who bit at my lower lip and who coaxed my tongue against theirs.

Nor could I tell whose hand was kneading and massaging my breast, gentleness absent from the actions.

Still, more of a mystery were the fingers that rubbed against my clit, driving me that much faster to my own climax.

"Wait," I panted, finally reaching up to twine my fingers in Rhys's silky hair. "Wait, I'm seriously-"

"We know," Nyko purred against my mouth.

"We never need you to tell us," Rhys chuckled. "Not when you're so *obvious*, little girl."

"You can cum for us, princess," invited Nyko. "You've been so good, after all. For *all* of us."

"But you haven't-" I directed the bitten-off statement to Rhys, who just grinned.

"I'm trying to wait for *you*," he growled, nipping at my lip. "So, how much longer are you going to make me do that?"

Well, when he put it that way...

"Do you need just a little more?" It had to be Nyko's fingers on my clit, and as he spoke, he rubbed against me more insistently, nearly short-circuiting my brain.

"Oh fuck-no that's-that's *way* too much-"

"No it's not," he disagreed, chasing my movements. Not that I could go far. "Come on, Will. Fall apart for us."

"While we're asking *nicely*," Rhys added wickedly.

Opening my mouth to retort, I found that I couldn't. Not when I was suddenly trying to suck in air as my brain whited out, riding the orgasm that I hadn't realized was *that* close.

Distantly, I heard Rhys say something, felt the change in his movements, and wrapped my legs around his waist when he shuddered and came.

At last, he pulled away to sit back on his knees, watching me with that interested yet aloof look.

"Oh, Will," he sighed finally as Nyko checked my wrists for marks from the handcuffs. "What *are* we going to do with you?"

Keep me, my treacherous brain wanted to say.

This time, at least, I clamped down on the words and only smirked up at him.

CHAPTER THIRTY-SIX

IF I, as a klepto, was terrible at stalking, then Detective Yates was even worse.

Sitting at the coffee shop across from *Grill Fiesta*, I was glad that I wore a hoodie and sunglasses, and happy that the day called for it.

The detective sat at a table outside the restaurant, peering around with obvious intent. He had to be looking for the pack, that was obvious.

But he wouldn't find them here today.

In fact, I was pretty sure I didn't want to be found here by him either. Not when he had questions about them that I certainly wouldn't answer.

Not to mention, I'd prefer if he didn't get offed by Uncle Liam, who so clearly would pull the trigger with only a moment's notice.

It was a bit sad, actually, that the detective didn't understand how close he was to a horrible fate and that all he had to do to avoid it was walk the other way and forget the pack existed at all.

I got to my feet, the wind blowing the loose locks of my auburn hair into a frenzy around my face.

And then, as if somehow sensing my presence, Yates looked right at me and immediately stood up as I did.

Fuck.

Backing away from the table, I started casually down the street, wanting nothing to do with the detective or his questions.

It was too bad he didn't feel the same way. Hurried foot-steps caught my attention, and I rolled my eyes and turned down a side street that would lead me back towards my apartment.

Maybe if I ignored him-

"Miss Carlysle!" His voice wasn't friendly, exactly. I stopped anyway, not wanting to be arrested for something he thought I might have done.

The detective stopped short, not at all out of breath from his sudden sprint in trying to catch up to me. "What are you doing here?" he asked quietly, glancing around. "You're looking for *them* too, aren't you?"

Two weeks ago, he would've been right.

Now, a week after my birthday and having spent a lot of the time since with the pack, I could say confidently that he was *wrong*.

Why did I need to spy for them or wait at their haunts when I could just call or show up at their house?

The knife that Nyko had slipped me as a 'late birthday present' weighed heavily in the pocket of my jeans, making me just a tad nervous.

What if the detective somehow saw it?

"I'm not looking for anyone, detective," I told him, taking off my sunglasses and looking at him with wide eyes. "Did you need something?"

"The same thing as before." I started to walk away, but he caught my arm and pulled me back. "Hey, don't walk away from me, Carlysle. I don't know why you seem to not give a shit about any of this, but you don't get it. These men are *bad*. They may have all of my peers at the station under their influence, but not me. Do you know what they *do*?"

"I don't even know *them,*" I lied. "So how would I know what they *do*?"

"They dismembered a man and threw him in the lake last year," Detective Yates said, beady eyes fixed on mine.

Was he testing me?

"Sounds awful," I replied, only half-meaning it.

"I've seen the pictures."

"I can imagine. I have cable."

He stared at me, finally shaking his head and turning away, disgusted. "One day, you're going to need my help getting out of a situation if you keep looking for them," he informed me.

Wrong as always, it seemed.

I'd never need his help because the pack wasn't a danger to me like they were to him.

"And I hope I can help you more than you've helped me, when that day comes." Without another word, he turned on his heel, stomping away down the sidewalk.

I watched, mildly irritated and worried for him.

Why didn't he understand this was incredibly unhealthy for him, and that he needed to find a new way to get a damn promotion?

Don't make it your problem, Will, I told myself, shuffling down the street. *Especially when that's one issue you can't solve.*

Nor would I want to. If he pissed off any of the boys, I had a feeling being dismembered was going to be the least of his issues.

I had bigger problems on hand, anyway–like figuring out why the mention of the awful things the pack had done barely phased me at all.

I should have cared.

I *definitely* should have cared more than a passing shrug and being able to put it from my mind.

Not if you're like them.

The thought nagged at me like a fly buzzing through my skull. The inkling had been there for a while, but my birthday had made that little thought grow louder and louder in my head, until a few times a day, I caught myself wondering what awful things I'd do, if pressed to.

Or even if *asked* to by the pack.

Caught up in a web of thoughts, I didn't notice when I passed the street to my apartment. Nor did I notice when a group of guys stopped talking to glance at me, one of them elbowing his friend and whispering in his ear with a jerk of his chin in my direction.

I did see, however, when I stopped at the end of the side street and turned back to find the man surprisingly close, his own hood drawn up over his head to somewhat obscure his features.

The man held my gaze, both of us wearing sunglasses and our hands in our pockets. Again the knife in my pocket seemed to grow heavy, but I reminded myself that I was just getting stupidly jumpy.

Not everyone in Chicago was a bad person waiting to strike.

Some people were just *people.*

I kept walking, retracing my steps enough to take me to an even *less* populated street and finally a back alley that I knew would take me pretty close to my apartment.

Which, admittedly, was not my best idea.

"Emily was my *aunt.*" The voice rang out behind me, surprising me into pausing and swiveling to look at the speaker.

The man from the edge of the street was there, sunglasses gone as he glared at me.

"Emily?" I tilted my head to the side. "I don't know anyone-"

"Did you give them the contract? No one was going to go after your *stupid* pack. They didn't need to know about it."

The pieces clicked finally.

He was talking about the paper I'd stolen from the lady at the restaurant.

Immediately I was on guard, taking a step back from him and wishing that one of the pack would loom out of the shadows to shoot him like Lysander had before.

"I don't know what you're-"

"But you aren't *pack*." His voice was soft. "So you're fair game, and maybe they'll be hurt enough to do something stupid. Something my boss can't overlook."

My heart hammered in my chest, constricting my breath. If he had a gun, I was dead.

Hell, if he had *any* weapon on him, I was dead.

"Why don't you just leave me alone, okay?" I whispered. "I really don't know what you're talking about."

"You don't?" The man bent down and picked up a thick piece of wood from the ground. To my dismay, a few nails stuck out of the end wickedly, giving it a danger that it didn't need.

I was so fucking dead.

The thought had my legs trembling, and I wondered how far I'd make it if I ran.

Not far enough, probably.

"You should've picked better friends," the man informed me, walking towards me and eating up the distance between us much too quickly.

What should I do?

What *could* I do?

"We're not friends!" I protested, hands up in surrender in front of me.

He snorted. "Lovers? Do you fuck all of them, or just that nasty blonde dude? He's a real piece of work, you know. I bet it'd make you *squirm* if you knew what he liked to do to people."

I had an inkling that it involved a bat and would not, in fact, make me squirm.

"Why don't you just take this up with them?" I demanded. "Yelling at me seems like a waste of time."

"Then consider it stress relief." He lifted the hand with the piece of wood, arcing back and swinging it forward.

I ducked, stumbling forward and swerving around him as he lashed out at me again.

Holy fuck.

I was going to die.

My phone wasn't the bat signal. Even if I could call one of the pack, the most I could do was probably let them listen to my death.

They wouldn't be here in time to save me.

My hands shook as I dodged again, stumbling this time and allowing the man to catch me on the side of the face with the wood.

Thankfully, not the side with the nails.

It hurt, the blow sending my head snapping to the side and nearly sending me to my knees.

"Hope it was worth it," the shorter man goaded, eyes bright with rage. "It will be for me. I'll see the looks on their faces when they find *you* all fucked up and long dead."

He lunged again, this time lifting both hands over his head and preparing to drive the wood down to bash me in the head.

But I was faster.

With the hand that had been hidden from him, I had slipped the blade out of my pocket and as he moved, so did I. The knife came up, flicking open in my hand, and I drove it upward into his chest.

Only...he didn't just fall over *dead*.

The man choked and stumbled backward, using the momentum to free himself from the blade.

I trembled, blood on my hand as adrenaline rushed

through my veins, and my wide eyes found his, where his sunglasses had long since clattered to the ground.

"Go away," I gasped, not wanting to do it again. "I don't want to-"

He dropped the piece of wood and charged, knocking me to the ground, and tried to pull the knife from my hand.

Desperation aided me more than him, however. I yelled and ripped my hand away from him, moving sideways and slashing a cut open in his jaw.

But he didn't stop.

Not then, nor when I stabbed him in the hand, the blade parting flesh as easily as butter and coming out the back of his palm. He *howled* and ripped himself free.

But he *didn't stop*.

Not until my switchblade was buried in the base of his throat, and I knelt on top of him, trembling as blood soaked my light grey hoodie and the knees of my leggings.

"You should've stopped," I breathed, eyes wide as I watched the light leave his. "You should've just...*left*."

I stared at him as he died and waited for the guilt and the pain and the remorse.

But it never came. Not even when I tried to summon it, looking for the feelings that had been there when I'd killed Donald.

I was in shock, clearly.

That was why I felt so...*fine*.

Still trembling, I pushed away from the man's body and dug around in my pocket for my phone. While I considered calling Lysander first, my thumb instead tapped on another name, leaving a bloody fingerprint behind.

"*What, Will?*" Nyko didn't sound particularly ready to put up with my bullshit. "*If you're looking for an invitation-*"

"I killed a man." That was not what I'd intended to say. Not at *all*.

But here we were.

Nyko was quiet, though the silence felt thoughtful, rather than him gearing up to be mad.

"*Where*?" he asked finally.

"I'm near my apartment. In the alley behind it. What should I-"

"*You should wait right there and hope no one notices. Are you alone?*"

I nodded, realized he couldn't see it, and added, "Yeah. This place is pretty deserted."

"*Good. I'll be there soon.*" He hung up before I could answer, leaving me in silence with only a dead body for company.

"I'm so fucked," I breathed, and set myself to watch both sides of the street for the inevitability of someone showing up *way* before Nyko to call the cops.

Somehow, that was not the case.

The sun was setting when headlights flickered at the end of the street, causing my stomach to twist and excuse to bubble to my lips as the black car pulled up beside me.

But only Nyko and Rhys got out, Rhys surveying my face while Nyko went to look at the body on the asphalt.

"Are you all right, Will?" Rhys inquired, reaching out to touch my shoulder.

I nodded jerkily, letting him turn my face to see the red scrapes and light bruises from the piece of wood. "I'm fine. He barely got me."

"So, all this blood...?"

"It's his. He wouldn't *stop*. I kept telling him to *stop*, but he just kept coming."

"Well, of course he did." Nyko used one shoe to turn the man's face towards Rhys. "Look at him. He's one of Andy's stupid boys."

I stared at the dead man's face and missed what Rhys said next.

"What do we do?" I asked, when both of them had finished their conversation about the *whys* of him attacking me.

I hadn't needed to contribute when they were spot on from the beginning with their guesses.

"We?" Rhys repeated delicately. "Nyko, stop that."

The black-haired knife-lover stopped, his gloved hands inches from the younger man's body.

"Stop...what?" he asked, confused.

"Cleaning up for her."

My heart jumped in my chest, and I whirled on him, suddenly terrified. "You can't just leave me here!" I protested. "Or-or leave *him*! The cops are going to show up-he came after me because of *you!*" Fear made me bold, and I stepped closer to him, my accusing finger close to his face.

Rhys, who was barely four inches taller than me, didn't move one bit. Not a flinch, a backstep, or even a sigh.

He watched me until at last, he raised a brow. "Are you done?"

"I don't know! That depends on if you're going to leave me-"

Gently, but firmly, Rhys reached out and pressed his hand over my mouth, surprising me into silence. "I did not say we were leaving you," he pointed out. "I merely told Nyko not to clean up after you. Would you like to know why?"

He didn't move his hand, relegating me to only nodding.

"Because you are not a *child*. Every member of my pack cleans up their own messes."

But I'm not pack, I wanted to remind him. *I'm just me.*

Just *Will*.

"Oh." Nyko straightened and removed his gloves,

handing them to me. "I thought you were going to be *cruel* for a moment, Rhys."

The pack leader shot him a surprised glance. "I didn't expect you to start cleaning up for her like that," he admitted.

I took the gloves and stared at them, then looked between the two men. "I don't know what to do," I told them quietly, suddenly feeling very tired.

"No one does when they start out. So they either get caught, or they have someone to teach them. You're rather lucky. You have us to teach you, and you're in our territory, which is a little more forgiving."

"Forgiving for *you*," I reminded him. "But not me."

They traded a look. Nyko grinned, looking utterly amused, and shrugged. "I hope you don't like that hoodie," he told me. "You're going to have to burn it."

"And the leggings," Rhys added.

Pulling the gloves over my hands, I fought not to act like a coward or a child. I'd *killed a man*. But they were here acting like it wasn't that big of a deal whatsoever. Like this happened every day, and they weren't phased at all.

"Doesn't it bother you?" I asked finally, looking at the dead man's body.

"Does it bother *you*?" Nyko asked, coming forward to stand beside me. "You look a lot less upset than last time."

"I..." He'd touched on my fears and what bothered me the most.

"Does it?" Rhys asked from my other side.

"I'm afraid of getting caught," I said at last, wringing my hands in front of me.

That was good enough, right?

They traded a look that was not lost to me. Nyko shrugged. Rhys shook his head ever so slightly.

"You used my knife, didn't you?" Nyko asked, kneeling beside the man and examining the slice across his face. "I have to admit, I gave it to you because I thought your reaction to it was adorable. But this is..."

"Horrible?" I filled in as he got to his feet and shifted. "Shitty? Unlucky-" He moved again and I looked at him, startled, to see the dark-eyed look he gave me was full of lust.

Oh.

Well then.

"Keep it in your pants," Rhys sighed. "And don't encourage her. She has to clean this up before we go anywhere, got it?"

"I don't have to throw it in a river or something, do I?" I demanded, my voice brittle. "Or dunk it in acid?"

Both of them scoffed.

"No, princess," Nyko promised. "You don't have to go that far. You just need to make sure no one can connect you to the scene. At least not blatantly. And we'll drop the body off on our way home."

"At the guy who makes cement shoes?"

"At the morgue," Rhys was clearly trying not to laugh, and he shook his head. "Cement shoes? You watch way too many movies, Will. Now stop trying to put this off." He gestured at the body. "Pick him up and put him in the trunk."

Do I have to? I wanted to whine the words but instead clenched my teeth together, hating every moment of this. Slowly I gathered the man up, hating how *slack* he felt against me.

"Drag him," Nyko suggested. "I doubt you'll be able to carry dead weight."

As he spoke, the dead man's head lolled against my shoulder, and I shuddered.

"This is awful," I muttered, taking the suggestion and *dragging* the man by his arms down the length of the car to where the trunk was-helpfully-already popped.

And lined with a tarp.

"It's like you do this often," I hissed, maneuvering the body into the trunk.

An arm flopped out, prompting me to glance at the man's face in surprise.

Was he still alive?

The man didn't move. If the arm had been a weird spontaneous movement, hopefully it was done.

I hated it even more now.

After bundling him into the trunk, I looked around the car to the two men, my eyes still wide. "Can I close it now?" I asked, my tone dry.

Rhys shook his head, hands in the pockets of his leather jacket. "Come back up here and look around," he ordered. "Did you leave anything? Anything that the police can use to make life hard for you?"

I looked around, eyes wide, and was ready to say *no* before my gaze fell on the long piece of wood.

"Oh. Right." I stepped forward and picked it up, hefting it in my gloved hand. "This. It's what he hit me with. But why didn't he have a weapon? The last guy had a knife, and Lysander has a gun all the time, doesn't he?"

"Because Andy's boys aren't so bright. *And* he doesn't trust them to have weapons," Nyko explained. "Toss that in the trunk as well."

"That seems detrimental." I took the piece of wood to the back and let it fall on the guy's dead body.

"Now you can close it," Rhys added helpfully.

I did so.

"Do I have to drive it to the morgue?" I asked, trying to sound nonchalant.

"No. But only because I don't want you driving my car," Rhys informed me sweetly. He beckoned me closer with one finger and I went, surprised when he reached out to run fingers through my sweaty auburn hair. "You aren't lying to me, are you?" he asked, taking off my sunglasses and pocketing them. "Are you hurt anywhere? You can tell me. I won't be mad, but I need to know in order to make sure you're safe."

He spoke as if...

As if I really *was* pack.

My heart thundered in my chest, sending the wrong idea to my brain.

"I'm fine," I whispered once more. "It's okay. I'll just go home and...burn these, I guess."

"*Or,*" Nyko suggested in his quiet voice, exchanging a look with Rhys. "Why don't we just take her home with us? I can send Lys to her apartment and tell him to get her some clothes."

"He doesn't have a key," I pointed out dryly.

Nyko rolled his eyes pointedly in my direction. "He doesn't need one," he reminded me.

"Yeah, okay, but-"

"All right," agreed Rhys, like I didn't have a say in the matter.

But even if I did, would I really have said no?

"I could just go get them?" I argued once more. "I'm not a fragile turtledove. My apartment is *right there.*"

Smiling, Rhys cupped my jaws in his hands and drew me close. "Oh, my little turtledove," he sighed, face close to mine. "I don't give a damn that you aren't hurt. You, my darling, are covered in blood." He looked down at my clothes, then back up at me. "So you are going to get in the back of my very expensive car and try not to get all of that blood on my seats. And then, when we're home, we shall burn your clothes, and *you* can have the privilege of using my shower. Am I clear, darling girl?"

It was unfair of him to do that. My stomach curled in delight whenever he spoke in this tone, and I had already stepped closer to him, drawn in by the way he purred almost against my lips.

"All right," I agreed finally, looking down and back towards the trunk. "I'll do what you think is best."

"Keep doing that," Rhys advised. "And I promise to make your life very interesting and unforgettable while you're with us." Gently he pushed me into the back of his lovely sedan and closed the door with a sense of finality.

I sighed and curled up on the seat, waiting for the remorse and guilt to set in now that I'd calmed down. *It'll come,* I promised myself, not for the first time. *You're not a killer, Will. You'll feel bad about this sooner rather than later.*

CHAPTER THIRTY-SEVEN

WITH MY HAIR damp and dressed in a loose t-shirt and pajama shorts from my apartment, I stepped out of the shower expecting to find Lysander or Azriel looming around the corner of the hallway.

But only darkness, and the distant sound of the television, met my ears.

Was everyone gone?

I'd been here alone before, and gotten myself unchained, but now I felt a bit unsure about it.

Annoyed, even, if I let myself go that far.

Not only had I cleaned up a body, accompanied Rhys and Nyko to the morgue, and then actually helped them drag it out of the car and *into* said morgue, I'd had to burn my clothes when I got here to get rid of any evidence.

It sucked.

Now I wasn't even sure when I was going home.

Not that I was a prisoner this time.

Sighing, I rubbed my bare arms and made my way towards the sound of the television, half wishing that I wore something more than the thin shorts and t-shirt that Lysander had grabbed out of my apartment for me.

Sure, I had a hoodie and jeans in a bag as well, but I didn't want to go around all night in *jeans*.

Exiting the hallway into the upstairs living room, I wasn't particularly surprised to find that the lights were off, and the only illumination came from the large flatscreen itself. The sound was quieter than I would've preferred, and I definitely didn't enjoy watching this kind of true crime.

I'd rather stick to my cheesy, scripted reality shows instead of watching someone re-enact a crime unless it was one of the rather dramatic ones.

"Where are the dogs?" I asked, seeing the shadowed shape of Rhys on the sofa, his phone illuminating his face and washing it in pale silver light.

"With Azriel," he replied. "He and Lysander took them out with them."

I wondered what *out with them* meant. Were Frank and Angie the newest members of the pack in more ways than just the at-home pets?

"They aren't letting them eat anyone," Rhys informed me, seeing the look on my face and snorting. "I doubt they even would. A chihuahua could take them down."

Biting back the smile at his words, I started to move but stopped.

He wasn't *like* Lys and Az and, to an extent, even Nyko.

I wasn't so sure he'd welcome me if I came skipping over to sit on the couch with him.

"When can I go home?" I asked instead, the words leaving my mouth before I could think about them.

Nice going, Will, I chastised mentally. *Now he thinks you don't want to be here.*

"Do you want to go home?" He looked back at his phone.

"Well. No. Not…really. But I didn't know if this was the same as last time."

"Is there a chain around your wrist, or any other part of you?"

"No."

"Then I would think we can infer that you are free to come or go at your leisure. Though I would also think you'd want to spend the rest of the night here instead of going home."

"Why's that?"

Rhys turned to look at me, gaze inscrutable. "Because I have the time, energy, and interest to play with you tonight."

Oh.

Oh.

That obviously meant what he was implying, didn't it?

Even though I wasn't sure what, exactly, *play* meant to him. With Azriel, things really were a game with spectators unwillingly involved. With Lysander, it was all about aggression and *claiming*. Nyko was the master of games that involved sharp objects that caused my heart to flutter in my throat and my knees to go weak.

But my only experience with Rhys was a birthday orgy.

I had a feeling that him in that setting and all of his attention *just* on me were going to be two very different things.

Not that I had any intention of shutting him down, of course. I was more than interested in seeing where this led, even if my stomach twisted in knots with the nerves I hadn't quite expected to feel at the prospect of well…*him.*

"Are you going to stand there and stare at me all night like a deer in headlights?" He asked flippantly, locking his phone and tipping his head back on the sofa cushion to stare at me levelly.

"No. Totally not going to do that." Not now since he'd brought it to my attention, anyway. Briskly I walked around the sofa, wondering what he wanted from me.

Did he just want to watch television and make fun of the reenacting?

I'd kind of be down for that, honestly.

"Floor," Rhys sighed patiently.

I stared at him, my brain not computing the words.

"Excuse me?"

"Get on your knees." Still with disinterest in his voice, Rhys only flicked his gaze up to mine before looking pointedly at the floor in front of him.

Oh.

Well then.

"That's not quite what I was expecting," I admitted, linking my hands behind my back and wondering if I was making a huge mistake. The others enjoyed it when I pushed them.

Would Rhys?

He sighed loudly, eyes narrowing ever so slightly. "I didn't ask what you were expecting."

"Doesn't seem very overly sexy with me on my knees and you, clothed, on the sofa."

I certainly felt *bold* tonight, that was for sure. But perhaps it was because of what had happened.

Maybe I just wanted to push *myself,* even just a little bit. If I was going to be around them I couldn't be meek and shy all the time.

I'd rather them know me for a person, rather than a doll they could play with however they wanted. Though I had to admit, that was a pretty damn good thought to have.

I'd have to file it away for later use in a fantasy that may-or-may-not be shared with the group.

"I'm not going to ask again," Rhys informed me, patience still overflowing in his words.

"Are you angry?" I had to ask. It certainly would *not* be sexy if he were mad with me, and I didn't want to push him that far.

The look he gave me was one of amusement and arrogance. "Do I seem angry to you, sweet girl?"

Well, I hadn't been expecting *that* to come out of his mouth, and I found myself wanting to drop to my knees on the spot if he continued saying things like that.

Stay strong, Will.

I met his gaze. "Why do you want me on the floor?"

"I already told you."

Had he? I scanned my brain, shifting my bare feet on the rug as I thought. He'd said we'd play, but that was incredibly vague. I was sure I hadn't missed it somewhere.

"Last chance," he hummed, still looking mild about the whole situation. "I'll even count to three. Don't let me get there, Will."

My stomach twisted deliciously at that. *What would happen when he got to three?* Would he kick me out?

"One."

Was this a test? Did he maybe *want* me not to do what he asked?

"Two."

I was confused. And I was thinking myself into circles instead of deciding on an action to take.

Floor? Or no floor?

"Three."

He was up and moving before he was done speaking, precise in his motions as he reached around to grasp my wet hair roughly.

My stomach flipped a few times, and I opened my mouth to gasp as he jerked my face around to his.

"I was kind of hoping you wouldn't listen to me," he admitted. "I suppose that's unfair of me, huh?"

Before I could answer, he dragged me down to the sofa, forcing me over his lap with one of my thighs trapped between his, the other thrown over his lap to keep me in a somewhat uncomfortable position with my face pressed to the sofa cushion.

Maybe I'd fucked up after all.

"I know how much the others like the *fight* when they play," he told me, one hand over my lower back to keep me in place while the other stroked up my thigh. "And it's cute, when it comes from you. Especially when you think you're going to get your way."

I shivered when his fingers skimmed over my pajama shorts, and on the second pass up my thighs, he brought my shorts up with his fingers. It was easy for him. They fit incredibly loosely and barely covered my ass as it was.

It was easy for him to move them out of the way so that his warm palm could press against my upper thigh.

He was not going to do what I was thinking.

Was he?

"Rhys..." I struggled lightly against his hold, but the older man held me down.

"Since I could've given you more warning and you don't know me that well, I'm going to take pity on you, all right?" He rubbed his hands over my warm skin slowly, comfortingly.

I wasn't very comforted.

"So you're going to let me up?" Did I even want him to?

"Is that what you want me to do?"

When I didn't answer, he chuckled. "I didn't think so." Without another word, he lifted his hand off of my thigh.

I barely had time to register the loss before his palm came down, stinging, on my ass.

I yelped, surprised at the sharp, sudden pain and writhed in his lap, unintentionally grinding against his thigh that held mine apart.

"Oh calm down. It wasn't even that hard. Nine more, if you're quiet, darling." His palm came down again, this time on the other cheek, and I was anything *but* quiet. Twice more he spanked me, the searing pain becoming a spreading warmth that moved from my ass to my thighs and straight between my legs.

"Will..." His voice held a warning tone. "I told you to be quiet, didn't I?"

I nodded, my face pressed into the cushion so he couldn't

see my expression. I couldn't help trembling, though, and my hands had found holds in the sofa cushion to grip.

"Don't make me start over." He hit me again, and I bit my lip this time, trying so hard not to make a sound.

Rhys paused after three more swats, hand coming to rest against my skin that felt like fire under his touch. "This doesn't seem to be much of a punishment for you, huh?" His words were teasing, as was his tone.

"I'm really sure it is," I told him in a voice that trembled slightly.

"Are you?" His hand moved, fingers stroking down my thigh, then making their way inward as he came back up.

Until, instead of going back to my ass, his fingers pushed away my shorts in order to rub teasingly against my slit.

"If I'd known you'd like being punished so much, I would've done something about it days ago," he told me in a husky, soft voice as his fingers teased at my opening, never truly entering me.

I couldn't help the way my hips arched against his touch, nor the way I secretly wanted him to finish the ten he'd promised.

Maybe he wasn't so wrong in his accusation of me really, *really* liking his idea of punishment. After all, it hadn't taken much of anything to get me *this* far.

"Maybe when we're done," he murmured, pulling his fingers away. I tried not to tense, knowing what he was about to do even before the last two hits to my skin made me bury my face further into the sofa and try to keep my body still on his lap.

I was pretty sure I failed at being quiet *and* being still, but he didn't say anything about it.

Instead, Rhys pulled me up so I was sitting on his lap, gasping when he ran his palm over my ass.

"Want to listen to me now, little girl?" He asked conversationally, eyeing me as I nodded once.

"Then thank me."

"For *what*?" I couldn't help the way my words escaped from between my lips in a breathy rush.

"For giving you what you deserved."

I took a moment to glare at him balefully, wondering if he was serious.

He raised a brow, no sign of a joke on his handsome, angular face.

"Thank you," I muttered at last, shifting on his lap.

"For?"

"For..." Did I really have to say it? Humiliation burned in my chest at the idea. "For giving me what I deserved." Some part of me felt like a misbehaving child, while the other drank up his purr of approval that he gave at the words.

"On the floor," he ordered again. This time I slid to my knees between his thighs without hesitation, eyes up and watching as he unbuttoned the front of his jeans and beckoned me with one finger.

Yet again, I didn't need words to figure out what he wanted. I rose up to the fullest height that I could, drawing his semi-hard length into my hand and leaning forward to run my tongue over the tip.

He sighed, one hand coming out to tangle in my loose, damp hair. "Take your time," he advised. "I'm not in a rush, and I quite like the sight of you there."

Take my time? That was cruel. I didn't want to take my time when I'd much rather him be touching me, or fucking me, instead of just having my mouth and hands on him.

Would he even notice if I casually rushed? Just to get him to want to do more than this?

I tested my theory, bringing his tip into my mouth and swirling my tongue over the head before releasing him so I could lick up the underside of his shaft.

Rhys sighed, his hand in my hair tightening. "I know you

liked it, but I should think you wouldn't want another punishment so *quickly,*" he told me. "I'm sure I can think of something far *less* fun than spanking you."

"Like what?" I asked, my eyes on his as I took him in my mouth again.

"Like a lot of things. I could tie you to my bed and tease you, not letting you cum all night. Sounds fun now, but I promise in a few hours you'd be *very* unhappy with your choices." When I moved to take more of him between my lips, he used his grip on my hair to draw me back, just a little. "Will," he said again, disapprovingly.

I rolled my eyes but slowed my pace, taking my time to work him up.

If I'd thought he'd ignore me or let me go to my own devices, I was wrong.

Rhys's hand never left my hair, he never looked away, and almost always he murmured his approval or *dis*approval, in some cases.

It was certainly intense to have his attention on me like this especially when I wanted so much more from him.

I wondered if he was going to have me get him off, then just leave me to my own devices.

Was he that mean?

Suddenly he jerked me up, more gently than I would've expected, to push me down onto the sofa once more. This time, however, I was on my back, my knees spread wide around his body as he knelt between them.

"Sharing you is fun, and all," he sighed, reaching up and pushing my loose t-shirt off easily. "I get the appeal. But I like you a little better like this, I think. When that look is all for me. So. Let's think about this." He smoothed his hands over my hips, palms going up along my ribs until he could cup my breasts in his hands. "There are a lot of things I want to do to you, Will. Most of them require things from my room and a gag, but not all of them."

I didn't reply. I watched as he massaged my breasts, shivering when his thumbs brushed over my nipples.

"I don't think you need anything on at all, do you?" He asked, pulling back enough that I could shimmy out of my shorts and send them to the floor somewhere near the sofa.

"Good girl." His voice had that delicious husky tone again, and when he said the words, I felt a rush of heat go straight between my thighs. My breath caught in my throat, drawing Rhys's gaze from my body to my face.

"Does my good girl have a bit of a praise kink?" he murmured. "You're such a *brat* when you want to be. I admit I'm a little surprised."

Yeah, he wasn't the only one.

When I didn't respond right away, his fingers on my nipple pinched harder, turning from pleasure to sharp pain.

I gasped, back arching off the sofa and hands going to grip his wrist.

Not that I had any intention of pulling him away.

"I asked you a question," Rhys said slowly. "Don't make me ask again."

"I guess I do." He moved, only to give the same rough treatment to my other breast. "What–"

"That's not an answer. Give me a real one."

"Okay! Okay, yes-I definitely like it when you say some of the things you've said."

"Like what?"

"I like it when you call me a good girl." I could feel the blush spreading over my face at my own words.

"Do you?" His grin was wider than I'd ever seen it, and all of his usual casual dismissal was gone. He moved his hands, running his fingers over my breasts much more gently. "Do you just like the words, or is it because you want to *actually* be good for me?"

"I want to actually *be* your good girl." I couldn't believe the words were out of my mouth, but here I was. I threw an arm over my eyes and was unsurprised when Rhys gripped my wrist and pulled it down.

"Don't you dare hide from me, sweet girl. I want to see your face." He pushed my thighs wider around him, hands brushing my inner thighs as he forced me to stay open and vulnerable for him. "Not that I can't see it, but I want to hear you ask for my cock."

My lips felt numb as I formed the words, haltingly doing as he'd asked. "I could really, *really* get behind you fucking me right now," I whispered.

"That's pretty vague." He didn't move, even when I squirmed under his grip.

"Please fuck me, Rhys."

"How?"

"However you want."

I'd thought the words would be too vague for him. But his eyes darkened, and seconds later, I felt his length brush against my slit, eliciting a quick gasp from me.

"What a good girl." He smiled as he spoke, thrusting into me.

Without his fingers opening me up, I felt every inch of him, and my body tensed at the delicious burn.

He didn't move, not at first, choosing instead to watch my face as I went through a few reactions that ended in pleasure.

"I love that you're so tight for me." His hands left my thighs, one of them finding my clit as he rubbed lazy circles over it. He began to fuck me a moment later, his thrusts slow and languid as he drew almost all the way out before sliding back in with a controlled pace.

"Please go faster," I begged, needing more than this teasing motion.

His mouth curved into a smirk. "I thought you said I could fuck you however I wanted."

Fuck.

I looked up at him, eyes wide. “Well-yeah. But I just thought-” I gasped at a particularly well-aimed thrust that had me momentarily speechless.

"You thought what?” He did it again, sliding over that same spot inside me with agonizing slowness. “That I’d be rough like the others? That I’d pin you against the wall and take you hard and fast?”

I couldn’t answer. Not when he kept on with that *perfect* aim, and his thumb drew lazy circles around my clit that were teasing me towards the edge.

“I don’t really need to though, do I? You come apart for me just the same, Will. Are you getting close for me, darling girl?”

I nodded, not quite trusting my own voice. When I moved to wrap my legs around his hips, his hands were instantly there, pushing my thighs back down to the sofa and *keeping* them there.

“If I have to hold you like this, I can’t play with your clit,” he reminded me. “I want you just like this. Arms above your head. Can you do that for me?”

I’d much rather be wrapped around him like a spider monkey.

Still I managed, throwing my hands over my head and gripping the sofa like I wanted to grip *him*.

One of his hands left my hip, going again to rub my clit with the same slowness as he had before.

“Tell me how close you are,” he ordered, eyes on mine.

“I’m-” I gasped, hating that he’d taken that moment to rub over that sweet spot again. “Really close, Rhys.”

“Don’t cum, understand?”

“But I-”

“Don’t cum, Will. Not until I tell you that you can.” His movements picked up, his own mouth falling open as he began fucking me in earnest.

But that made it harder to keep myself under control.

Anytime I tried to move under him, the hand on my hip kept me in place, not letting me move enough to get what I wanted.

And *God* I wanted *more*. He was such a tease, even though he was undoubtedly pushing me mercilessly towards my own end.

"Don't do it, Will," he reminded me, still sounding just as in control as he had been this whole time.

I hated him a little for it—just a little.

"Please, *please*," I found myself begging, voice breathless.

He smiled, eyes on mine. "Please, *what?*"

"Please, I just want-"

"Not like that."

I hissed in frustration. "Rhys please-" He'd sped up to the point that my body was singing for it, and his finger on my clit was enough to push me over.

But I didn't let myself. Though I felt as tight as a bowstring and could feel my thighs trembling under him, I forced myself not to let go.

"Please, Rhys, please let me cum."

Those must have been the magic words. He leaned forward and down, capturing my mouth in a kiss. "Cum for me, baby girl," he growled against my lips, putting just enough extra pressure in his touch that, even if he hadn't said that, I would've been cumming anyways.

I did, feeling his movements change and finally feeling him sink into me one last time before he came as well.

Panting, I managed to wrap one leg around his hips, and when he didn't protest, I tangled my fingers in his hair.

He still didn't protest and kissed me again approvingly. "What a good girl for me," he breathed, tugging at my lower lip with his teeth. "Now, come with me to my room so we can do it all again."

Oh God, I hoped he was serious.

CHAPTER THIRTY-EIGHT

"WAKE UP, WILL."

Rhys's voice was firm, and the hand on my shoulder was just the same.

I didn't want to wake up. Not when I ached in all the best ways possible and wanted to stay curled up against Rhys for the rest of the day.

But I did anyway, drawing myself to the surface of sleep and opening my eyes, expecting to see Rhys looking grumpy or something similar.

I didn't expect his face to be full of worry. "Get dressed," he murmured, brushing his lips against my cheek. "There's a problem."

A problem?

I murmured my agreement and stood, glad that my clothes were so close and ready for me to jerk on the black jeans and red t-shirt under a lightweight, black zip-up hoodie.

Already dressed himself, Rhys was out the door before I could even reach down to slip on my sneakers.

What could be such a big deal that even *Rhys* seemed concerned?

For a moment I paused, wondering if someone had

found the man's body from the night before and connected it to me.

Was I going to jail?

At last, I followed Rhys out of the room, tugging my sleeves down over my hands and looping the fabric over my thumbs.

Nykos sat on one sofa in the living room with his legs tucked under him, the dogs on either side of him, while Azriel paced.

I did a double-take, seeing Azriel's face in the better light when he turned towards me.

He was *hurt*.

"Holy shit, Az," I breathed, going to him and cupping his face in my hands.

I froze.

His eyes were cold, the humor gone from them, leaving his dark brown gaze empty.

Not empty, I realized a second later, my stomach twisting.

He was *angry*.

Furious, with a look on his face that promised something terrible for the target of that hatred.

"I'm fine, Will," he told me softly, reaching up to grip my wrists in his hands. "I don't need you to make a big deal over this."

"You're hurt," I breathed, seeing a cleaned cut that sliced the top of his shirt and skimmed over his shoulder. Another slash mark parted the skin of his cheek deeply, and his nose looked more swollen than not, blood still crusting the skin underneath it.

"I'm fine." He met my eyes again. "But Lysander isn't."

My knees nearly buckled. "Is he *dead*?" I wasn't sure I could handle that.

"No," Rhys said. "They won't kill him. They want him to

bring in *all* of us." Rhys walked past, hands shoved in his pockets.

"*They*?"

The door downstairs crashed open, prompting the men of the pack to glance at each other in confusion as footsteps clattered up the steps.

"Boys!" Liam appeared at the top of the stairs, not bothering to even pay attention to the dogs by their feet, hackles raised. "We have a problem."

"We *know*," Nyko snapped. "Lysander's been taken."

"*What*?" Liam's face fell, the surprise mixing with something almost like fear.

I stood back, watching, and wondered what in the world could make Liam himself afraid.

"Isn't that what you were coming to tell us?" Azriel's words were slow. "Andy's boys got the drop on us and dragged Lysander off to their boss?"

Before Azriel had finished, Liam was shaking his head. "No," he said. "No, that's..." He closed his eyes hard. "The police are on their way," he said after a moment, looking up to meet each of our gazes.

"The police?" parroted Azriel. "What the *fuck* do you mean by that?"

The man beside me vibrated rage that should've frightened me. It was terrifying, in its way.

But I didn't move.

"They're coming for *you*." He looked at Rhys. "They're going to arrest you. That *goddamned detective* found some judge with a death wish to get the warrant."

He trailed off as the tickle of sirens found my ears.

"Shit," I breathed, going to the window and pushing back the heavy burgundy curtains.

Sure enough, three cop cars were slowing down at the end of the street, coming towards the pack's mansion in single file. "Rhys-"

"Well, you can't let them *arrest* you!" Azriel snapped. "No fucking way. We need you, Rhys. You've got to think of how we're going to get Lysander out of this shit."

Rhys flicked his hand dismissively, though I saw the frustrated set of his shoulders under his t-shirt. "They can't hold me for that long," he said slowly. "A few hours, at the most."

Looking outside again, I found that cops had poured out of the cars, a van driving up behind them that had released armed officers of its own.

"They're coming," I whispered, the curtain trembling in my hand that shook. "I can see them. They're in the driveway." We only had another few minutes or so, by my count. If that.

"You need to hide," Liam said suddenly, catching my eyes. "They don't know that you're here or that you're a part of this. We could use that to our advantage later."

I hesitated, looking at Rhys again as he leaned back against the couch with a posture that *screamed* irritation. When he saw me staring at him, he smiled crookedly. "Don't worry about me, Will," he promised. "Just hold your shit together until I can come back and get Lysander out of whatever crap he's in."

At last, I nodded and left, going to a small closet off of the main living room and ducking inside. In theory, the cops wouldn't search that hard, especially since Rhys was *right* out in the open.

I was right. I watched as the police officers swarmed in, their guns raised and focused on all four men.

Stupidly, I wanted to do something. My blood roared in my ears, that stupid part of my brain begging me to do something *other* than stand in the closet and watch Rhys get thrown to his knees and cuffed by one of the officers.

"I thought you'd be more of a problem." The confident tone of Detective Yates made my nose curl in disgust as my eyes tracked his swagger from my position in the closet.

Don't do it, Will, I told myself. *You'll just get shot.* Already my body trembled, unsure of whether *fight* or *flight* sounded better.

Flight. It would have to be, when I wasn't sure how I'd ever fight anyone in this kind of situation.

"Detective Yates, I presume?" Rhys asked in his best, purring lilt. Even as he was dragged to his feet, the most the pack leader showed for the situation was a bit of *disdain,* if not outright boredom. "If you wanted to discuss something with my pack, you did not need to bring so many officers."

"*Oh*?" the detective spat. "As I said, I thought this would be a problem. I know what the four of you are." He looked around the room, his eyes falling on Liam, who didn't look away. "Or rather...the *three* of you. Did something happen to Lysander Ashford?"

Azriel, always the worst at hiding his feelings, shifted on his feet.

"It has, hasn't it?" Yates' voice was soft. "I could help with that, you know. I'm sure a jail cell for him would be preferable to whatever he's going through right now. Tell you what. I'll make a deal with you four. If you'd like to save your *friend*-"

"No." Rhys' voice was mild, the word directed just at Azriel.

And I saw why.

In his hand, the dark-haired male held a switchblade behind his back.

But Detective Yates, in his arrogance, assumed Rhys was talking to him. I watched from the slit in the door as he turned away from the danger, giving Azriel his back.

Rhys's eyes flashed. He shook his head again, and Azriel's hand relaxed on the blade, though he still vibrated with rage.

How could the detective not *see* that?

It was obvious, to me at least, that Yates was walking a very thin line.

Azriel would kill him, even if he died trying.

"*No*?" Yates looked at him, smirking in his victory. "You could do with a bit of humility, *Rhys*. I could save your friend."

"I'm sure you could if you were so inclined. But I am not inclined to take the help." He moved to walk towards the stairs, causing the police officer that held his hands to stumble after him. "Come on, then," he sighed, impressing me with his confidence and aloofness. "You're taking me to jail, yes? Some damp, decrepit cell? A *dungeon,* perhaps? Well, I do not have all day, and I expect my lawyer will be waiting for me."

Yates rolled his eyes and looked at the other men, eyes narrowing. "This is it for all of you," he said softly. "I'll take him, and none of you will see him on your side of the bars again, that I promise. Once he goes, the rest of you will be soon after." A wry, unamused smile stretched his lips wide.

He left, followed by the man who dragged Rhys none too gently behind him, even though the pack leader had made it obvious he'd walk on his own.

The others stood still, and after I was sure the police were gone, I left the closet and went to stand beside Azriel once more, wringing my hands in front of me.

Liam sighed and pinched the bridge of his nose, tipping his head back with his eyes closed. "What a *fucking* mess," he grumbled, not looking up.

"So...what are we going to do?" I asked, folding my arms over my chest.

All of them turned to look at me, looks of varying surprise on their faces that made me incredibly uncomfortable.

"*We*?" repeated Nyko.

"Yes," I sneered. "As in the royal *We*."

"We need to get to Lysander," Azriel growled. "Yates won't do *shit* to Rhys. He can't. Lock him in a cell? Sure, I guess. But that's nothing compared to what Lysander's going through right now."

I hated each and every word he spoke. I hated that I could *imagine* a myriad of awful things happening to my favorite blonde.

But more than that, the feeling of rage that settled in my bones confused me. I hadn't been serious about the *we*, or so I'd thought until it came out of my mouth and anger simmered just over my skin as if by touching Azriel I'd drawn some of his fear and fury into my own body.

In that moment, I knew, without a doubt, that I would do *anything* to save Lysander and Rhys and bring them back here, where they belonged.

And that alone absolutely terrified me down to my very bones.

If I was so willing to imagine doing *anything* for them, when they were *what* they were, and I had barely known them a month, what in the world did that make *me?*

CHAPTER THIRTY-NINE

THE TWO REMAINING members moved quickly, in a whirlwind emotion as both of them unearthed guns from hiding places, and Azriel put the dogs in a room just for them.

I stood with Liam, confused, and watched them go. "What are we going to do?" I asked.

"We?" Azriel looked at me, eyes bright. "No offense, Will. I get that you want to help. But I don't think you *can*."

"Why not?" I asked, voice sharp.

"Because we're going to go do what we're good at," Nyko replied coldly, shoving a gun in the waistband of his jeans. "And you're not exactly a stone-cold killer like us." At any other time, I would've snorted at the fact he was being incredibly dramatic for no reason.

Now I just watched him, my heart pounding in my chest.

Perhaps he was right, and I couldn't do anything to help in this situation.

But…

Lysander's face flashed in my mind, which then decided to conjure up the idea of him lying prone on some cold floor, a pool of blood around him.

What if he really died?

Sure, the four of them operated in *death* on what seemed like a weekly basis and had no qualms about it. I understood, rationally, that if anyone had a shit load of karma waiting to dump them into an early grave, it was definitely the pack.

But that didn't matter right now.

"I can do *something*," I pointed out. "What about Rhys?"

"*I'm* going to get Rhys," Liam informed me. He looked at me, surveying my face, and sighed. "You can come with me if you want."

It sounded more like a pity tag-along,

But I didn't have anything *else* to do.

"Do you still have the knife I gave you?" Nyko asked curiously. "Not that I think they'll let you in with it."

"I…" I thought back to it and remembered Rhys plucking it out of my hand when we'd gotten back to the house. He'd told me he'd clean it and give it back but hadn't done so. "No. Rhys said he was going to clean it last night."

Reaching into a drawer, Nyko held up a shiny switchblade, much like the ones he and Azriel carried. "Don't lose it," he ordered, stepping forward and shoving it in the pocket of my black jeans. "I like that one."

"Sorry," I told him with a crooked half-smile that I knew didn't make it to my eyes. "Next time I'll bring my own from home."

"I'll buy you six. You look like someone who loses things," Nyko told me blithely, reaching out to grip my shoulder. "Don't do anything stupid, okay? I'd really hate to bring Lysander back, only for him to kill *me* for letting you leave the house."

"I'll be fine," I told him. "I'm just tagging along."

Part of me wanted to ask for a gun, just in case.

A bigger part of me was relatively sure that I'd never have the guts to fire on anyone. I wasn't a *killer*, like that.

Then again…

Closing my eyes, I couldn't help but see the face of the man I'd killed outside of my apartment and Donald Deerling's face just after.

But they had been *accidents*. They'd attacked me first. I never would've killed them otherwise.

"You guys will be careful, right?" I asked quietly, my heart fluttering at the thought of never seeing *any* of the pack again.

Both dark-haired males looked up at me with that same cold look I'd seen back in Scheffield.

When I'd first realized *what* they were.

That seemed like such a long time ago, and the person I was now couldn't even begin to fathom what had led me from being scared shitless of them to being terrified they might die.

"We'll be fine," Azriel told me. "This isn't exactly new for us, Willow." He rested a hand on my head affectionately, ruffling my hair.

I scoffed and knocked his hand to the side, hovering and unsure of what to say.

"If you're coming with me, let's go," Liam barked, turning and making his way back down the stairs.

"Yeah-okay." I ripped myself from my thought and followed, hand sliding on the mahogany banister easily as I followed him out of the front door that had been left ajar by the cops and to the long driveway beside the large house.

This wasn't the first time I'd wondered at how the pack had secured so much space in the wealthiest area of Chicago, and I also couldn't help but question how they'd gotten this kind of massive house in the first place.

Had they killed for it too?

Did it even *matter?*

Liam's dark red sedan, a BMW with all the shine of the brand new car it was, sat unobtrusively just off the driveway, the drivers' side tires sinking into the damp ground at the side of the pavement.

At his gesture, I got in on the passenger side, wondering just how long he'd had this car that had that brand-new smell and spotless, black leather seats.

"How are you going to get Rhys out of jail?" I asked quietly as he threw the car into reverse and peeled out of the driveway.

"Pure grit and determination," Liam said at first. "And my good looks. Maybe a bit of *money*."

It sounded to me like he didn't know. That, or he just didn't feel like telling me. Either way, his words weren't exactly comforting, and I shifted in my seat with a sigh. "You think they'll really be okay?"

Liam was quiet. The only sound was the drumming of his fingers on the steering wheel. "I think that they would've been a lot better off with Rhys. He would've kept them from doing something stupid or not stopping to *think*. But..." he trailed off, his eyes distant, then shook his head to refocus. "I also think counting them out here would be a mistake. They aren't amateurs, Will."

Of course not.

We rode in silence until at last, Liam pulled up to the front of the police station I'd been so cordially invited to only a few days before.

"Wait here," Liam snapped when I started to move.

"*What*?" I turned to look at his retreating form as he got out.

"If something happens, I can't protect you *and* get Rhys out," he explained mockingly, sticking his head back in the car and grabbing his sunglasses from the visor. "So *wait here,* and I'll bring Rhys out with me. Probably."

Why had I even come?

He didn't wait for me to answer. The man slammed the car door and jogged into the building, not bothering to wait for any sign or even slow his pace as he *slammed* the glass doors back on their hinges.

I wanted to help. That was my plan, and it had been all along. *To help.*

Somehow.

But instead…I waited.

My foot tapped against the floorboard, and my heart pounded as I half expected to hear the sounds of a gunfight or watch the building explode.

Liam knew what he was doing.

Glancing at the clock, I found that I'd been waiting for almost an hour.

This was ridiculous, in my opinion.

While I had no idea how long it took to get someone out of jail in an illegal fashion, I had also been under the impression that people were terrified of Liam.

Couldn't he just waltz inside, look terrifying, and get Rhys out that way?

Knowing he'd be pissed if he could see me, I opened the door of the sedan to stand in the parking lot, looking around at the sky that was darkening in preparation for another storm. A breeze kicked up around me, tossing litter this way and that in the parking lot and causing my auburn hair to whip around my face.

Why hadn't I put it up?

Inhaling, I smelled the rain that the sky promised and figured it couldn't have been that far off.

How much longer was this going to take?

Every bone in my body vibrated with tension, and my limbs seemed to hum with frustration at being out here instead of seeing what was going on inside.

Surely there had to be something I could do.

With that thought, I headed to the glass doors, my heart hammering as my insides twisted nervously. Would I be helping, by going inside to figure out if we could get Rhys out faster?

Or would I just be in the way?

A flurry of movement caught my attention, and I turned to see more clearly what was going on, confused at the sudden whirlwind of movement.

To my left, beside the parking lot, two buildings came close together to form an alley that appeared to be one way, and with barely enough room for the black truck halfway down to squeeze through.

My eyes scanned the alley until the door to the building that was the police station slammed open once more, and Rhys was shoved unceremoniously through.

Liam had succeeded after all, it appeared. Though now I wondered who-

The person that appeared behind Rhys was not Liam.

It was Yates.

Sucking in a breath, I tiptoed to the mouth of the alley, flattening myself against the wall that formed the edge of the parking lot and looking down the small space.

"Not *this time,*" Yates was snarling as he shoved Rhys up against the truck. Upon closer inspection, the 'truck' looked much more like a prisoner transport—the kind I'd seen in the movies.

What was he *doing*?

He slammed Rhys against the truck again, though the pack leader only grunted and looked at him with narrowed, uninterested eyes.

Thankfully, neither of them saw me.

"You think your *friend* can just get you out of any situation, huh?" Yates laughed darkly. Even from my spot a good twenty feet away, I could hear the tremble of fear in his voice. "Well, that won't work anywhere else. Once you're out of Chicago, you're fair game."

Rhys tipped his head to the side, studying the man. "Are

you going to steal me away yourself?" He asked finally. "Seems a bit dangerous for one man."

"*Yes,*" Yates spat. "Since none of the other officers here have the balls to do the jobs they were hired for. I have a judge waiting who will lock you up, and I can *assure* you that the rest of your pack will be on the way, just in time to see you walked into death row with chains dragging from your wrists and ankles."

His words painted a picture that made my blood run cold.

Death row?

Though I supposed, that was the inevitable punishment for someone like Rhys, if they got caught.

But he wasn't in prison yet.

Yates opened the door to the back of the truck and yanked Rhys's cuffed hands out behind him, trapping them to the bar that ran along the floor. "You just wait right here for me," he laughed, his voice low and shaky. "I'll be right back." With that he left, going back into the door he'd come out of and closing it quietly behind him.

This was the only chance I was going to get to free Rhys.

"Holy shit," I breathed, darting around the wall and into the alley as the door closed.

Rhys's chin jerked up, the black-haired male's eyes widening in surprise. "Will," he greeted, unable to hide the shock in his voice. "What are you doing here?"

"Oh, you know, hanging out," I told him conversationally, sliding to a stop in front of him and digging into my pocket for my trusty lock picking kit that always managed to end up on my person, even if I didn't quite remember grabbing it.

At this point, they were a necessary part of my identity at all times.

"You have a lot of practice picking handcuff locks?" Rhys

went on as I leaned into the truck, my side brushing his and my thigh pressed against his own.

"Yeah, actually. Got really good at it not that long ago."

Not that long ago, they'd *kidnapped* me with the intention of not letting me go.

At one point, they'd even considered killing me.

So why in the world was I here, trying hard to break Rhys out of prison and also hoping to find a way to save Lysander?

"Will." I felt him stiffen against me, and his hands clenched.

"I've almost-" I heard the sound of the door open.

"Run."

"*No.*"

"Will, I said-"

"I don't have to listen to you!" I hissed the words more loudly than I intended, just as I heard the *click* of something close to my hair.

"Stop what you're doing." Yates' cold voice was unmistakable, and all of the fear that I'd tried to push away came rushing back to me.

Fuck.

I needed to be faster.

I stopped, going stock still and cramming my eyes shut. My jaws clenched together as I tried to think of a way out of this, but all I could consider was how this had gone *wrong.*

"Back up. Hands in the air." I hesitated at the detective's words, trying to buy myself time for a miracle.

"Do what he says," Rhys murmured, turning to press his nose against my hair.

"But-"

"It's okay, Will. You tried." I didn't need to turn to recognize the resignation in his body and his voice.

Shoulders dropping in defeat, I lifted my hands in the air and stepped back, the lock picks still in my hand.

Yates, eyes cold and incredibly unfriendly, reached out and grabbed them. He pocketed them himself, shaking his head in disbelief. "I knew there was something off with you," he told me. "Even from the beginning. I just thought maybe they had you, too. But you actually *like* them. You *want* him to be free."

I didn't answer. My eyes were on Rhys's face, though his own expression was inscrutable.

"You should be thanking me." He gestured for me to take another step back, and I did. "I'm doing you a favor, *Will*." He turned away from me, giving me his back as he moved to unhook the cuffs that trapped Rhys in the back of the truck. "I'm getting you out of this before you become like them."

Before I became like them?

The words echoed in my head, and suddenly the knife in my pocket felt very heavy against my body.

Hadn't I worried about the same thing for so long now? Even back in Scheffield I'd worried that there was something wrong with me. That I was changing, somehow.

And now, here was Yates, echoing my own questions back to me.

But said out loud, I realized something very, very wrong with his statement.

I'd become too much like them already for him to draw me back now.

His mistake was thinking I was just a victim. His *mistake* was not looking for the blade I had in my pocket.

I wouldn't let him make it again.

With his back to me, he didn't even *see* when I reached into my pocket with trembling fingers and pulled the switch-blade free. He didn't see my hesitation. Nor the way I stared at the blade for a millisecond too long, while he struggled with the cuffs in his excitement and his haste.

He would have shot me if he had.

Rhys saw. I looked up and found his eyes on me, for the

first time looking unsure and not offering me an easy answer.

He could've told me to do it, and I would've.

And then, later, I could've blamed it on him and gone back to my way of thinking.

But without his orders and with the cop's back to me, I knew that if I did this, it would be *my* choice.

It would be *my* fault.

And I wouldn't be able to back up from what I was about to do.

As if in slow motion, I stepped forward, the blade in my right hand as I lifted it up. Would it slip? I couldn't help but worry as the knife plunged downward, grasped so tightly in my clammy fingers.

What if I messed up?

The blade parted flesh, sinking deep into the space between the detective's neck and shoulder. He yelled in surprise and pain, his hand with the gun moving around so he could shoot me.

But Rhys, now not cuffed to the van, moved faster. He knocked the gun from the detective's hands and sent it skidding, leaving him weaponless.

He was *harmless* now, with his eyes wide and mouth gaping as he faced me. His movement had ripped the switchblade free, and he reached up with one trembling hand to press it over the stab wound.

"What have you *done*?" Yates hissed, sounding more disbelieving than anything else. "You're not like them-"

I stepped forward, hand moving again, and plunged the blade into the center of his chest. This time, when I pulled it free, blood followed it in an arc that spattered over my t-shirt.

My hand came down a third time, and thunder roared in my ears as I stabbed him one more time, blood pooling around my fingers and dripping to the ground and my shoes.

"I am, though," I whispered, realizing that my hand trembled the same as my voice. "Don't you see. I think-I think I was always like them." My eyes moved to Rhys's as he stared back. "Just a little. And-and maybe all it took was *them* to show me what I am."

"They're monsters," Yates told me, blood staining his white dress shirt and the skin above it. His hands were drenched in crimson, and more of it sprayed to hit my face like heavy, warm rain when I ripped the blade free again.

He fell to his knees between Rhys and me, eyes never leaving mine.

"Then maybe I am too if this is what that means," I murmured and tried not to let my hands shake any harder than they already did.

CHAPTER FORTY

RHYS WATCHED ME, not speaking and quite obviously-not moving much with his hands still behind his back.

"You killed him," he said at last, eyes raking over me.

"I…" I blinked and rubbed the back of my hand over my face, only succeeding in smearing blood over my skin.

I should have felt terrible.

I should at least have felt *something*. Guilt, shame, embarrassment-hell, even disgust at having *killed a man*.

But all I felt was utter relief.

"Are you okay?" I asked, hand still clasped tight around the blade in my hand.

"I'm fine. And I don't mean to hurry you along, but…" He walked towards me, showing me his hands that were still cuffed.

"Right. Yeah, I got it." I flicked the switchblade closed and shoved it into my pocket, happy for the first time that I wore mostly black. Today, especially in my black jeans and hoodie, the blood was mostly invisible.

Except on my black and white sneakers, of course.

Bending down to Yates' body, I helped myself to my lock picks and fished around in his pockets until I found the small handcuff key that I'd expected to get. This was easier than trying to unlock the cuffs myself, and within another few seconds, Rhys's wrists were free and he stood still, massaging them as he stared down at Yates.

I sighed heavily and knelt, looping my arms under his shoulders and hefting the big man up.

"What are you doing?" Rhys asked mildly, watching me struggle with my burden.

"Dancing," I snapped, dragging Yates closer to the truck.

"You aren't going to leave him there?"

"I thought I'd throw him in the truck, actually. *Someone* taught me how to clean up unless you've forgotten." I hated how shaky my voice was and how my heart still fluttered with nerves.

At last, Rhys cracked a weary smile. "I thought you might've forgotten, is all." He bent down and picked up the detective's legs, helping me in tossing the body in the truck.

With that done, I slammed the truck's doors, cutting off my view of Yates' body. "Someone's going to find him," I sighed, reaching up to run bloody fingers through my hair. "I'm so fucked."

"No, you aren't." The dark-haired male pulled me away from the truck, casually walking back towards Liam's car. "This is Chicago, and this is *pack* business. You'll be fine."

How could he say that when I wasn't pack as well?

The glass doors exploded outward, Liam exiting with a look full of threats and promise. "I *promise* you that-" he paused, his eyes flicking from me to Rhys. "You didn't stay in the car," he said in an accusatory tone.

"I'm not very good at following directions," I agreed, opening the back passenger door.

Rhys slid in beside me, surprising me when he didn't take the front seat instead, and Liam slammed the driver's door shut and had the engine going a moment later.

"I thought you were long gone," Liam said, jerking the car out of the parking lot and joining the flow of traffic.

"They stalled me so that *Yates* could get you out. I was going to say I'd make him regret it, but..." His eyes found mine in the mirror. "I take it that it's a bit late for that."

I didn't answer.

"Luckily, Lysander did a good day's work when he turned his eye on Will," Rhys chuckled in agreement, though the sound lacked any real humor. "Have you heard from Nyk and Az?"

Lysander. The mention of his name made my clammy hands clench into fists, and with a jolt, I realized my fingers were wrapped around Rhys's.

When in the *world* had I done that?

But he didn't seem to mind.

"I've heard from them. I was going to head their way when I couldn't find you. Figured you'd kill me if I didn't help them," Liam explained. "Some of Andy's boys have Lysander in a warehouse down by the pier."

That sounded way too much like a movie with an unpleasant ending for my taste.

The two of them spoke, talking about people and things I wasn't sure I understood as we drove, and thankfully left my mind to race and replay what had just happened on repeat.

Until the car came to a stop and the engine was cut off, prompting Rhys to open his door.

Liam did the same as I got out of the back seat, and the older man looked from me to Rhys. "She really should stay," he said quietly but firmly. "She's not like *us*."

"She's not?" Rhys's brows rose as if Liam had said something surprising. "Are you sure we're seeing the same Will?"

I looked down at myself, covered in blood, and sure there was more of it on my face.

"She's covered in blood," Liam pointed out. "*And* she doesn't have a gun."

"So give her your spare."

My stomach flip-flopped at that.

"She won't-"

"Give me your spare," I said quietly, one hand out as I found and held Liam's gaze.

I could wonder who this woman who'd entered my body and possessed me to act like this was.

For now, I wanted so badly to help Lysander that my teeth ached.

Snorting, the older man shook his head but reached into the car, opening the console to pull out a smaller handgun. "Don't shoot anyone on our side, please," he requested, handing it over.

I nodded and tucked it into my waistband with shaking hands.

A knife was one thing.

But a *gun*?

Holy *fuck*.

Rhys moved around the red car, his footsteps making little noise on the pavement as his hand came up to wrap around my shoulders and pull me closer to him. "If you don't think you want to do this, tell me," he said quietly. "I will not judge you for it. You can wait here, and we will get my boys out alive."

He was giving me an out.

I could take it. I *should* take it.

Instead, I found myself shaking my head, feeling like I might throw up. "No," I said. "I'll help you."

"Walk and talk, kids." Liam had already set off at a quick trot, and I was happy to see that we were in a not well-lit, nor well-populated part of town. While I'd tried to scrub the blood from my face and hands in the car as we'd driven, I wasn't sure how well I'd succeeded.

I didn't need anyone seeing me and calling the cops because I was covered in *blood*.

To that end, I took off my hoodie, tossing it back into the

car before we left it and leaving me in a t-shirt light enough that I shivered in the winds that were picking up in front of the encroaching storm.

Thankfully the walk wasn't nearly as long as the drive. I felt almost detached as we went, hating that I couldn't just get *over* what had happened.

But it wasn't because I felt bad, or guilty, or anything like that.

Those feelings had still yet to surface. No, the lack of remorse bothered me and had me questioning all of the things I thought I was sure of, regarding myself at least.

Maybe stealing had been the gateway drug all along, and now I was bouncing along on my merry way to becoming just like the pack.

We heard the warehouse before we saw it. Gunshots rang through the side street, prompting Liam and Rhys to break into a run a *second* ahead of me.

"Stay out here!" Liam yelled, looking back at me. "Don't *argue* with me, Rhys! Unless you want her getting shot."

Rhys nodded his head in agreement. "Do what he says," he ordered, and both of them vanished.

But now, after what I'd done before, I had no intention of doing as they'd said. Sure, my steps had slowed, and I'd considered it for about half a second, but when they disappeared into the open door I ran around the side of the building, finding a side door and *yanking*.

Of course it was locked, but that wasn't an issue for me.

My lock picks were out in the blink of an eye, the kit back in my pocket as I pulled the pieces I'd need into my hands and set to work unlocking the heavy side door of the warehouse. I inhaled as I worked, the smell of old metal and rain harsh and poignant in my nose.

I would have to practice more, I decided, as the door swung open a few seconds after I'd expected it to, having taken me that much extra time to give the lock the last jiggle that it had needed.

My tools went back into my pocket, though I didn't bother to put them away as I ran inside…and stopped.

What was I doing?

Without the drive of adrenaline fueling me, I felt frozen.

I had no idea what to do here! Without Rhys to tell me what to do, I was just floundering.

All I'd managed to do was unlock a damn *door.*

Someone screamed, a man cried out, and in front of me, another door slammed open to admit two men running towards me, blood on their faces and looking particularly terrified.

Though I was sure that whatever they were afraid of would have had me dead before I could blink.

Still, I managed to get the gun out, holding it up as the two of them slid to a stop in front of me.

"Who the hell-that door was *locked,*" one of them spat, his eyes blazing.

The other elbowed him. "Andy, let's *go*. If you thought shit was bad with Nykos and Azriel, it's about to get a lot worse with *them* here."

I had a very good idea that they meant Rhys and Liam.

"Andy?" I tilted my head to the side, remembering the name. "You're the one who took Lysander."

They looked at each other, then back at me.

"You're with them?" *Andy* asked, his eyes narrowing. "Who the hell are you, anyway?"

I shrugged one shoulder. "A girl with a gun and a shaky trigger finger. So maybe you back up a bit, okay?"

The man beside him wavered, then broke. He ran down a side hallway, out of sight within seconds.

I let him. If I could only stop one of the men from leaving the warehouse, it was going to be this one who'd caused so much trouble for my pack already today.

"You won't shoot me." The sounds of the gunfight behind him echoed in my ears so loudly that I barely heard him. "You don't have the look of someone who'd kill another person."

Oh, how wrong he was. Especially after tonight. I shrugged one shoulder. "Try me."

He didn't move.

"Why in the world do you want to protect them?" He went on, sweat rolling down his tan forehead. In the half-light of the small room, I could tell that Andy had dark hair and eyes, and to my eyes looked a bit rodent-like, with a small nose and thin stature.

Even his voice was high and nasally.

A whine, if I'd ever heard one.

"Do you know what they *are*? They killed my cousins without provocation. David and Donald did absolutely nothing to them, but Rhys and his *pack* went out of their way to go to Scheffield to kill them. None of *us* would have done that."

He didn't know who I was.

But then again, how would he?

"You knew them? The Deerling brothers?" I clarified. When he nodded, I went on. "They killed my roommate. Did you know that? They kidnapped her and murdered her in cold blood, for no reason other than because she was *their type*."

A month of anger and frustration bubbled up, unleashed from the box I'd put it in as I stared him down. "Did you know they killed people for the fun of it?"

"We all have problems, little girl." He sighed, eyes going this way and that while he looked for a way out. "And we all go sooner or later."

"*Excuse me*?" My voice was cold and empty, which matched the way I felt when I looked at this sorry excuse for a man in front of me. "She'd never done *anything* to anyone.

She wanted to be a nurse. She wanted–" I broke off with the realization that this man didn't *deserve* to think of Ashley at all.

"Did you know they were going to Scheffield to kill someone?" I asked at last.

Andy sighed, his shoulders dropping, and he looked up at me with hands raised in surrender. When he did, his smile was rueful and apologetic. "You think I could've *stopped* them?" He laughed humorlessly. "When they were the family's favorites? Not a chance. No way in-"

My finger tightened on the trigger as my hand moved downward, aiming not for his face but for his thigh instead.

Thankfully I hit, though I was surprised at the loudness of the gunshot, and the gun seemed to vibrate in my hand after it was fired. Ringing filled my ears, informing me unkindly of the dangers of firing a gun in a small room.

Gradually the ringing faded, replaced instead by the cries of the man on the floor in front of me as he held his hands to his thigh and tried to stop the bleeding there.

I wouldn't kill him. Not when I was still unsure if Lysander was okay.

"Get up," I told him, voice like ice.

He looked up, eyes wide. "You shot me-"

"And I'll shoot your other leg if you don't get up."

As I stared him down, he did so, staggering to his feet.

"Where's the pack?"

"Don't do this. They'll *kill* me," Andy's voice had raised again, sounding desperate.

They'll kill me, he'd said.

Somehow I couldn't find it in me to care.

"So will I. And I'll drag it out." I wasn't sure I could do that, and even the suggestion had my heart twisting in my chest. "So let's go."

I walked behind him as he staggered, cursing me with

every step until he'd led me down the hallway and into a larger, open room.

Inside, the boys appeared to be cleaning up. Lysander leaned on Azriel, looking the worse for wear with a myriad of injuries that I couldn't see clearly.

Had they tortured him?

The others were walking around the room, looking at the bodies that lay on the ground with distaste and finishing off those that weren't completely dead with a blade or gun.

I flinched as Rhys's gun went off, and when I looked back at him, I found his eyes on mine.

But it was Azriel that spoke.

"*Well, well, well,*" the dark-haired male laughed excitedly, prowling closer and circling Andy. "Just look at what our newest puppy brought home. Do you know who this is, Will?"

"Andy, right?" I asked, voice flat. Azriel noticed and moved to stand behind me.

"What's wrong?" He looked over at me, worry creasing his features. "Are you hurt?"

I shook my head. "No, it's-" For the first time, I felt tears burn my eyes, begging to fall.

I wouldn't let them.

I couldn't let them.

"He *knew,*" I snarled, jaw tight with tension. "He *knew* about what David and Donald were doing in Scheffield. He could've stopped them, but he thinks it's *funny.*"

Andy threw me a look of utter confusion. "What's the big *deal*?" He asked, voice still a high-pitched whine. "You guys get it, right? We can't go around being bleeding hearts! They did what we all do."

"What we all do? *We* don't do any of *this,* Andy," Rhys reminded him. "We do not kidnap, nor do we kill people for *fun* when they have nothing to do with us. *We* do not cross state lines for the pleasure of murder and sadism." He walked forwards slowly, a gun in his hand that he didn't raise.

"Do you want to kill him, Will?" Nyko asked mildly, coming to stand on my other side and draping an arm around my shoulders. Lysander moved as well, quiet in his approach until he could rest his head on my shoulder.

Rhys, standing next to Andy, looked up at me with a question in his eyes. "It's your choice. You have every right, and there won't be any consequences for it. Especially after today."

He was giving me permission.

I didn't really *need* it, I supposed, with a gun in my hand and one dead body already getting cold a few miles away.

I could kill him for what he was and what he'd done.

Andy turned on me again. "You won't kill me." He sounded relatively sure. "You're not *like them.* You're not a murderer, and you aren't a criminal. *Will,* was it?" He looked between Rhys and me. "If you ask them to, they'll let me go. You don't have to do this."

"You're right," I whispered, leaning back into the embrace of my boys. "I don't have to."

Andy's face fell open in relief. His eyes widened, and he blinked. "I-"

The gunshot washed over me, my hand raised and pointed straight at him. This time I watched, unable to blink or look away as I shot the man who was indirectly responsible for Ashley's death, and felt only a tickle of satisfaction as he fell, gasping, to writhe in a pool of his own blood.

"But I wanted to," I finished, the gun unsteady in my hand. "And it felt pretty damn good."

Lysander murmured his approval into my neck as Azriel's snickers reached my ears. Nyko, ever quiet, tightened his grip in approval as a smirk curved Rhys's full lips.

"You really are terrible at following directions," he told

me, walking over and running bloody fingers through my hair. "We'll have to talk about that when we get home."

"Can I sleep first?" Lysander asked quietly, voice slurred from pain just a little. "Because I'd love to see that, but god *damn* it, I need a nap."

Laughing, Azriel dragged his friend off of me and towards the car, leaving the rest of us to follow. Rhys went next, keeping both boys in his sight as Liam fell in beside him and Nyko brought up the rear with me.

"I'm glad you followed us here like an idiot," the usually-stoic male said with a grin. "Think of how bored we'd be if you hadn't."

Before I could answer, my phone vibrated in my pocket. Nyko took the gun so I could dig my phone out, and I snorted when I saw the message on the screen.

Are you coming home soon? Not shockingly, it was from my mother.

I opened my phone and quickly responded, then shoved it back into my pocket with the intent to ignore it for a while.

"What did you say?" Nykos inquired, having seen the message but not my response.

"I told her I'd be gone for a while, and to stop asking me to come home," I told him. "After all, I rented out my new Airbnb for two months, and there's a *lot* of Chicago I haven't seen yet."

"Agreed," Nyko nodded solemnly. "You should make Lysander and Rhys drag you around all the tourist spots after this. God knows you've earned it."

CHAPTER FORTY-ONE

THE DETECTIVE WAS NERVOUS.

But I couldn't really blame him.

Across the vast mahogany table, Yates' replacement shifted on the comfortable seat, notepad on the rich wood in front of him but no pen in sight. As if he wanted the appearance of taking notes but had no plans of actually doing it.

In the long run, that was much better for him.

Even if most of the pack wasn't around at the moment, that meant very little when he was in *our* territory.

"I just need to ask a few last questions." Beads of sweat rolled down his pale forehead, the journey made so much longer by a badly receding hairline.

The one-eyed, orange and white cat I'd dubbed October hopped up onto the table, shaky on legs that were still too spindly.

Not that I expected that to last. While I was feeding October the best cat food available, I also knew for a fact that the boys loved to slip my cat people-food whenever they could.

Even Rhys. Which surprised me a little. Though the cat had only been here two weeks, the same amount of time since I'd given up my Airbnb apartment and moved into the pack's huge house, October had made himself quite at home.

The dogs loved him, revered him, and most likely feared him. And the homely tomcat had definitely won the hearts of my lovers with no problem whatsoever.

"Ask," I invited with a shrug, reaching one hand up for October to nuzzle against aggressively in his quest for affection.

The male detective blinked, flinching as if snapping out of his unpleasant thoughts. "Okay. Well." He looked down at the blank notepad. "We're closing the case on Detective Yates' murder," he said slowly, looking around as if he expected one of the pack to leap out of the kitchen or the hall closet.

I had a feeling that Rhys was nearby, listening, but he had every right to.

Even though all of us already knew most of this from Liam.

"Oh?" I asked blithely, not necessarily needing an explanation as I scratched October's head. "You found his killer?"

Of course they had. It was me.

Killing Yates had changed something in me.

Or maybe...not so much.

I had come to the conclusion that I'd always been this dark-hearted, cold thing that cared only about her boys and her animals. I just hadn't met them yet.

Maybe my mom had been right, a little, all those times she'd told me I was heading down *the wrong path*.

Wrong for her, anyway.

I was right where I belonged.

"Andrew Whitely's gang killed him, with one of his higher-ups being directly responsible." The detective sounded like he was reading from a script. "Now Whitely is missing, with most of his men seemingly on the run with them as well."

I blinked, still feeling the rush of uncertain thoughts that went through me every time I thought about killing Yates and Andy.

What if they changed their minds? Sure, I was technically a part of this *pack* now and all.

But still…

"Okay," I replied, trying to look nonchalant. "It's a shame he died. He seemed like a good guy."

The detective glanced up at me almost sharply. Was I trying too hard for the sympathy I barely felt?

"He didn't have any family here," the man went on. "His sister is coming to take care of his final wishes. And his burial."

A closed casket one, I figured, unless they sewed up those stab wounds with more efficiency than I expected.

"Is there anything else?" I'd thought it would be easy to hold my head high and act as calm, cool and collected as any of my boys, but that was proving to be more difficult than I'd expected.

He shook his head and stood, then hesitated. "There was…an inquiry," he admitted, the words sounding hesitant and cautious. "From a small town in northern Michigan. They asked us for some information about you, and about connecting you to a string of burglaries there."

Holy *shit*. Seriously? After all of this, I was going to have to deal with *that* now?

Maybe I wasn't getting away so scot-free after all.

"But we told them that we couldn't help them," he went on quickly. "I assume that was acceptable to you, Miss Carlysle?"

Miss Carlysle? It sounded strange from his lips, the way he was literally *asking* for my approval of it.

"I…" I trailed off, uncertain and somewhat confused about his words.

Of course I didn't want to go to jail.

But it felt too easy for things to go away just like that, because of what I was now.

Because of what I'd done.

At the end of the day, I was still just me, still just *Will*.

Wasn't I?

"That's fine." I was grateful for Rhys's smooth voice, hand waving dismissively at the detective as he approached from the kitchen with a steaming mug in his hand. "Handle it the same way in the future, if you would, Detective? It's unfortunate that the Scheffield cops want to blame things on her just for leaving, but small towns are what they are, I suppose."

The detective seemed to deflate, the anxiety falling out of his shoulders. He shared an almost companionable-if nervous-chuckle with Rhys and nodded his head. "Yessir. I know how those small-town cops are. Like dogs with bones they can't give up, all of 'em. Well, don't worry. I'll make sure to keep setting them straight." He looked between us as if waiting for some kind of approval.

Rhys gave it. "If that's all…?" he asked, brows raising by increments. "I hate to rush you out, but this is the first time I've had a break in the past week since the incident."

Incident. That's what he called it.

I supposed that was an accurate description of what had happened.

Or bloodbath would've worked, in my humble opinion.

"Oh-of course. I'm so sorry. I was being thoughtless." Given a chance to run, the detective took it. Nearly forgetting the notepad, Rhys had to remind him of it as the detective moved towards the door in a tornado of motion, eyes so fixed on his target that he barely slowed when the door opened to reveal Nyko and Lysander both coming in.

They moved to the sides, happy to give the detective his space, though Lysander did so with a particularly predatory smile that caused the older man to go white under his ruddy complexion.

"So..." I kept my voice quiet as I scratched October's ears. "People from back home know what I did."

"They may suspect," Rhys shrugged. "And I may even suggest you not pay Scheffield a social visit for the next few years. Otherwise, I might have to send Lysander and Az there in advance to..." He blinked and turned to side-eye me with a deceptively friendly grin. "Pave the way for you."

He meant to kill someone. Or several someones.

"What did he want?" Lysander inquired, walking into the dining room and leaning down to rest his hands on my shoulders. Affectionately he kissed the top of my head, his fingers digging lightly into my shoulders comfortingly.

"Is this where you give me a back massage?" I asked, slumping forward theatrically. "I deserve it, you know. After-"

"All the trouble you went to in order to save me?" His blue eyes sparkled with amusement, but I hated seeing the still-healing cuts and bruises on his face. "Yeah, so you've said. *Every* time you want something, even a sandwich. How long will you be holding this over me, exactly?"

"Oh, if I were her, I'd be milking it for at least a year," Nyko said, sitting down at the table at my left elbow.

"A decade," Azriel amended, coming down the stairs with the dogs at his heels and dragging a chair over to sit down close enough to me that his arm nudged mine.

"However long you want. Don't let him rush you," Rhys agreed. "He owes you his *life*."

"She owes me hers!" Lysander argued, trying and failing to look serious.

"Yeah, but it's different." Nyko reached out and picked up October to cradle the orange and white cat against his chest.

"Totally different," I laughed, the sound turning into a

yelp as Lysander yanked me to my feet so that he could switch places and sit down on the dining room chair.

Before I could protest, the big, violent blonde pulled me down onto his lap, arms around my waist.

"Fine." He sniffed, still trying to play the victim even as he adjusted his grip around my waist to keep me balanced on his thighs. "But *only* until I'm the one dragging you out of your own mess that you've created."

"So that means you're all really okay with me sticking around, then?" I'd hoped, of course. And with how readily they'd allowed me to move in-or rather, demanded it, I hoped I was something more than temporary.

"Oh, Will," sighed Nyko. "Always so *careful*. It's adorable."

"I don't think you can get rid of us," Azriel agreed. When I looked at him, he glared up at Rhys pointedly. "*Well*?"

The dark-haired, solemn-faced man rolled his eyes with near-audible irritation at Azriel's urging. "I was waiting for the rest of you to stop fawning," he informed them.

"Waiting to do what?" I stared at him, confused, and readjusted myself on Lysander's lap so I could look at him better. "Are you giving me a key? Since you haven't yet? It can be symbolic and all, but I could really use a key so I don't have to keep stealing Nyko's."

The blade-lover froze, turning to look at me with suspicion on his face and mouth open, ready to speak.

"*Wait,*" Rhys growled. "Threaten her after. I want to go back to bed within the next *two hours*." He looked between both of us sternly until we both ducked our heads, pretending to be sheepish.

I succeeded at it better than Nyko did.

"Will, you can stay here with us as long as you want," Rhys explained slowly. "As far as I'm concerned, you're a part of this family now."

Family.

The word felt strange in my brain. I'd never referred to them as such. Not even in my own head. They'd always been like a pack of violent, terrifying wolves to me.

But *family*....that meant something different.

Especially if they were saying I was part of it as well.

"Really-" I looked up, ready to continue, only to see Rhys pull a small box from his pocket. "Oh my god, you're proposing." My voice went flat. "Rhys, darling, I'm pretty sure polygamy is outlawed in this state."

He met my eyes, remaining quiet, until I fell silently and pressed my lips together to fight the urge to grin nervously.

Behind Rhys, Azriel wasn't even trying to hide the silent laughter that shook his shoulders at my *hilarious* joke.

"We aren't getting married," he sighed. "I don't even know which of us you'd marry. *And I wasn't asking for suggestions*." He looked between Lysander and Azriel, who'd both started to speak. "This isn't a proposal."

"It kind of is," Nyko amended. "Just give it to her already, Rhys."

Rhys rolled his eyes and opened the small box.

To my surprise, it wasn't a key.

It *was*, however, a ring.

A black stone set in gold, with a snake wrapped around the band and ending beside the black stone.

The same ring that all of them wore.

"Holy *shit*," I breathed. "You're really giving me one?"

Rhys tilted his head slyly. "Are you saying you don't want it?"

"No! Of *course* I want it. I..." I reached out, hand hovering over the box. "But I mean-are you sure?"

Lysander growled in my ear, loudly enough for the others to hear, "Of course we're sure, gorgeous girl. I told you a long time ago, didn't I? That you were ours and nothing was ever going to change that?"

"Well, yeah, but I thought you meant-"

"It goes for all of us," Azriel cut in. "The invitation isn't just from Lys or Rhys. It's from *all* of us, Will."

Still, I hesitated.

It was more than just an invitation to be in a relationship, or be friends, or share a house with them.

All of those things were easy for me to say yes to.

It was the rest of it that I forced myself to think about. The part that made them what they were.

If I stayed with them, I'd be accepting that I was *like* them.

My hand closed over the ring. I pulled it from its box and gazed at the multifaceted black stone.

Gazing at the ring in my hand, moving it between my fingers in the light, I saw multicolored fires spark in its depths, drawing my eye to more color than I'd thought had been there before.

"Oh, I *suppose,*" I sighed, sliding the ring onto my left ring finger.

It fit perfectly.

Like it was meant to be there.

"But seriously, Rhys," I looked at him, trying my best to ignore the grins on *my* pack's faces. "I could really, *really* use a key before Nyko finds where I hid his."

"I thought you could pick locks," the pack leader reminded me.

Before I could answer, Lysander stood, towing me up with him.

"Sure, sure," he agreed. "Get her a key, Rhys. Or let her keep Nyko's and get him another. But I'm going to need her for a while." He bodily picked me up, eliciting a yelp from me when my feet left the ground.

"For what?" I couldn't help but ask, a smile curving my lips wide.

"For *everything,*" my killer growled. "But specifically

right now? To fuck you while you wear nothing but that ring and remind you how fucking *perfect* you are for us."

"Is group participation allowed?" teased Azriel, standing up from the table and stretching.

"Oh, I think it's *encouraged,*" Lysander promised in his most tantalizingly wicked purr.

And well, when he talked like that, who was I to argue with his perfectly fine suggestion?

EPILOGUE

"YOUR MOTHER KEEPS CALLING." Lysander's voice was languid and loose, and when he glanced over at my phone with narrowed eyes, I wondered how much he actually gave a damn about my *mother* calling.

Well, enough to say something, obviously.

I rolled my eyes as noticeably and as over-dramatically as I could, making sure he saw it as I stopped rocking my hips against his.

This really was the absolute worst time for his shit. And I didn't want to talk about *my mom* with Lysander's cock inside me and me *riding* him.

But the shit-eating grin on his face and the way he couldn't keep the glitter from his eyes proved that he knew exactly what he was doing. Because of *course* he did. Lysander and the other boys always knew exactly what they were doing. It was a skill I wanted to learn.

My ring glittered in the light that streamed in his window. The ring that they'd given me only two weeks prior.

Honestly, it seemed like I'd have a long time to figure out how they managed to be so effortlessly confident.

With a sigh, Lysander laid his head on his arm, looking

up at me from under long, thick lashes. "You stopped," he informed me, a sweet grin on his handsome face that was only made more attractive by the scar.

I kind of loved the scar. I ran my tongue along it weekly by now, and when I'd asked him what it was from, he'd only chuckled and told me curiosity killed the cat.

But that didn't mean I didn't *want* to know.

"Yeah, I fucking stopped," I agreed aggressively. "You brought up my *mother*." Lightly I slapped his bare chest, finding that it *was* a bit hard to just sit here when I was so close to my own release and riding him was one of my absolute favorite activities.

His grin deepened. "I didn't say you could stop," Lys reminded me.

"No, but you might as well have. Mentioning her gives me *chills-*" I broke off with a surprised squeal as Lysander flipped us over, his hand tangling harshly in my hair and *yanking* my head back.

"Then I'll keep you warm for as long as I need to," he purred, taking over in the way he knew best. His body rocked against mine, causing my thighs to press open wider as he sank deeper into my body. His length was always just a bit of a stretch, and it always started off as feeling like just a little too much.

But that was perfect for me. And it summed up everything about Lysander perfectly. He really was just a little too much. Especially on a good day.

"Moan for me, pretty, pretty girl," Lys breathed against my cheek, grazing his teeth along my skin. But of course, by the time he found my throat, Lysander did more than *graze.*

His teeth sank into my skin, causing my moan to become more of a yelp and my hands to twist into the sheets under me. I writhed against him, knowing how much he loved to hold me down even when I'd like to pin him under me and return his favor with marks and bites of my own.

I'd have to find a sneakier way to do so, however. Lysander was *brutally* strong, and pinned me under him easily as he took his time with taking *me* apart.

But, true to his own nature, Lysander was impatient. He wasn't like Rhys, who could slow-fuck me for an *hour* while watching some true crime documentary, or Nyko who would much rather draw knives along my skin and watch me come apart from that. He was closer to Azriel's nature, as they both wanted everything *when* they wanted it.

He quickly set a savage pace, pressing me to the sheets with his mouth at my throat. I didn't try to stay quiet; instead letting him hear how much I loved everything he was doing, and my promises that I'd get him back for the bruise that he was currently sucking into my skin.

Suddenly he moved, gripping my throat with one hand while he sank into me and held himself there, forehead pressing against mine and his other hand finding my clit. "Cum for me," he purred. "I want to feel you cum around my cock."

He was good at that by now, too. His fingers had me tipping over the edge, and then plummeting into my own release right along with him.

Though, Lysander cried out louder than anyone I'd ever known before when he came. It filled my ears, and a second later my mouth when he kissed me and fucked me through both of our orgasms.

Finally he sat back onto his heels, and I clambered out from under him to sit up on the side of his bed.

Sure enough, my mother had called three times and texted twice. I let out a long, low *huff* as Lysander sat behind me, wrapping his arms around my shoulders and kissing the mark he'd made on my neck.

"What does she want this time?" he hummed against my ear, his breath tickling my skin.

"Hopefully to disown me," I mumbled, opening her texts and reading them twice over before stopping to think.

You should come home soon. You've missed quite a bit. And Ashley's mother was asking about you.

I expected you home for your birthday. All of your stuff is back in your room here for when you grow up and come back.

For all that I was *free* from my overbearing mother and didn't answer to her morally *or* financially, it was hard to finally hit that block button and really be done with her. The Child-Will that lived in my heart still held some aspirations and belief that Mom would come around and see that I was a real, live person with autonomy and decision making skills. One whose worth did not rely on her college degree, or lack thereof, and who could make her own way.

Though, I'd realized for a few years now that it was a stupid dream. My mother was *never* going to change.

"You *could* visit. You didn't pack much when you came to Chicago, did you?" Lysander had, of course, read the message over my shoulder.

I looked at him with wide, incredulous eyes. "Are you ill? Did that last orgasm fry your brain, Lys?"

"As if he had much of one to begin with," Azriel called, passing in front of the open doorway with both German Shepherds at his heels.

"Hey–get back here for a sec, Az," Lys called, ignoring the 'compliment' from his best friend. "What do you think?"

Azriel poked his head back in the door, dark eyes looking us over in our various states of undress. I wore nothing except my t-shirt, while Lysander simply wore *nothing*.

Which was, of course, my favorite attire for him. Azriel too. And Nyko. And *definitely* Rhys.

"What do you want?" he asked as he stepped inside and closed the door behind him, preventing the dogs from coming in. That was probably for the best. Especially until we cleaned up.

"Will's mom wants her to visit."

Azriel glanced at Lysander, one brow raised, and I was struck with a fit of giggles at how similar he looked like Nyko when he glowered like that. "Will's mom *always* wants her to visit. But it's never really a visit she's after, is it?"

"Yeah, she definitely wants me to move back," I agreed, showing Az the messages. "There's no *visiting* on her mind with these. I guess she's going with guilt today, too."

"Oh yeah, she's taking the brutal approach today, huh?" He made a face, then passed my phone back to me. "So what do you want, Lys?"

"I think she should go visit," Lysander said slowly, his blue eyes lazy. "With us. Because your car is *shit*, Will."

"Sell it," Azriel added, not for the first time. "It is pretty awful."

"And buy *what* exactly? I know it's Chicago and I don't need to drive most of the time, but–"

"Take his car," Lysander interrupted.

"Take *Rhys'* car," Azriel corrected.

Both of us stared at him, as if we couldn't believe what we'd heard.

"What?" I asked, easily distracted by that awful suggestion.

Az's grin hitched wider on his lips and he reached up to run his fingers through his dark hair. "Yeah, okay. It's a selfish suggestion. I just like watching him pin you down and punish you until you say you're sorry. Call it a kink."

"One time," I reminded him. "*One time*. And it was not my fault that–"

"*Anyway…*" Lysander cast us both a quick look from narrowed eyes. "I'm serious, Will. Your mother probably isn't going to believe shit if you don't say it to her face. Besides, we'll go with you. We can pick up some shit you left there, if you want."

"Or buy you new shit," Azriel pointed out. "If you'd rather do that."

I looked at Lysander, appraising his expression as I mulled over the words in my head. Finally I narrowed my eyes, and accused, "You were so *against* me talking to her on my birthday. Remember that?" He tried to look away innocently, his eyes widening, but I wasn't going to believe it. I tucked strands of light brown hair behind my ear, and went on. "So what's with the change?"

"I just..." he trailed off, then sighed. "Okay, *okay*. You caught me. I want you to go because I want to see her face when we walk in. She definitely doesn't seem like she'd be *okay* with us. That's pretty clear whenever I answer the phone for you."

Another of his hobbies that I probably should've discouraged by now. But it was fun to hear my mom's squawk of displeasure and surprise.

I couldn't help myself from enjoying the little joys in life, such as that.

"I would ask if you *really* think it would make a difference," I sighed, still running my hands through my hair. I got to my feet, hunting for my leggings as I spoke. "But you don't. You're just doing this because you think it would be fun."

Then I needed a second opinion.

"We'll go with you, if you want to go," Azriel said, getting to his feet as well and running his fingers up my spine as I bent down to pull on my black, spandex leggings. They were my favorite pair, and made my ass look pretty amazing, if I were going to have an opinion on the matter.

Which I did, obviously. It was *my* ass after all. No matter how much the boys loved it.

"I'm going to ask Rhys and Nyko." It wasn't that they were the more responsible boys of the Pack. Certainly not.

Okay, they kind of were. That had become *abundantly* clear in the weeks I'd been living with them.

"Don't let them talk you out of it," Lysander said, going towards his bathroom, probably to wash up. He threw a grin my way, his unruly blonde curls in his face. "Their ideas aren't always great. Or their restraint, I should say."

"Uh huh." Azriel followed me out of the room, and when I opened the door I found that Frank and Angie were down the hall, both of them vying for whatever dry food was left in their bowl.

I turned the other way, expecting to see Nyk and Rhys hanging out in the upstairs living room, watching the new documentary that both of them were *obsessed* over.

But the room was empty.

Behind me, Azriel made a whistling noise. When I turned to glance his way, I found him making non-subtle motions towards the shorter hallway that led to their rooms. Or, what was really Rhys's room that both of them shared quite a bit and Nyko's room that didn't see as much use.

But who could blame Nyko for not liking to sleep alone, when he had the option of Rhys' king sized luxury bed?

Or mine, lately. I'd woken up two nights ago to Nyko in my bed, already hard against my back and murmuring softly in my ear as his nails pricked my skin and he fingered me open for him.

We hadn't gotten a lot of sleep.

I followed Az's motions, and at the end of the hallway found that their door was mostly closed.

Which did not stop the sounds that spilled out from inside. Not by a long shot.

Rhys was murmuring something, but Nyko was the one most definitely panting and *begging* the older man to keep going.

I stopped where I was, riveted by the sound, but I didn't have the guts to actually push the door open.

So I supposed it was a damn good thing Azriel was there. He reached around me to push the door open wide, sending it creaking back on its hinges and showing both of us the scene of Rhys' bedroom.

It was the first time I'd ever actually caught the two of them fucking. At least without me involved. My stomach tightened, causing my body to take interest even though I'd just been so thoroughly fucked by Lysander.

Nyko didn't look up from the bed. He was on his stomach, chest pressed to the mattress with Rhys' hand on the back of his neck to pin him there. Rhys' other hand was on Nyk's hip, keeping them up so he could fuck him slowly, and very thoroughly.

Rhys' eyes wandered up to us when the door swung open, but he didn't stop his movements. If anything, when Nyk started to move, his hand around his partner's neck tightened and he pinned him tighter against the bed. A smile crept along Rhys' features. "Just because we have an audience doesn't mean you get to look *up*, Nyk."

He was met by a soft whine that I was sure I'd never heard from the knife-loving sadist under him.

"I'm really sorry that we're, umm, here. We could go?" I offered; glaring daggers at Azriel who was still grinning like he was enjoying the show.

I was too, but it felt weird to admit it with such an eager expression.

"Why?" Rhys' tone was full of dry humor. "You're the reason we're here, anyway. You *scream* when Lysander fucks you. Did you know?" Nyko moved again, but Rhys pressed a kiss to his spine, his hips stilling for a moment. When he sat back up, I saw that sweat glittered on his chest, and he grinned at me like all of this really *was* a show.

Of course I knew that I was rather…loud. But there wasn't much I could do to help it. Especially when all four men seemed to enjoy it quite aggressively.

"It got Nyko all excited as well. But you weren't around to play with, so...." he trailed off with a shrug of his lean shoulders. "I guess you can see where I'm going with that. He really is *so* pretty when I'm fucking him like this, isn't he?"

"He's always pretty," I said lightly, my eyes on the pretty picture they made.

"Hear that?"

Nyko said something into the sheets under him that I couldn't hear. But I figured it was either a quip about me, or agreement to Rhys. Both were equally as likely in this situation.

"He's prettier when he's cumming." Without warning, Rhys *jerked* Nyko upright, pulling the slighter man against his chest. His arms wrapped tightly around Nyko's, and I looked into his flush face, surprised to see that he was looking at Rhys the same way I felt when I looked at him.

Like I was probably in love, and I wanted him inside me *all the time.*

Rhys held Nyko still, his hips moving faster now that I could actually see Nyk's face. Which, thanks to Rhys' hand under his jaw, was pointed up so that I could very easily watch.

His mouth fell open, soft moans and cries leaving him while Rhys whispered in his ear something too low for me to hear. His mouth moved, teeth nipping and biting down Nyko's neck and shoulder, until finally he bit down like he meant it.

And by the look of it, Nyk was going to have just as dark of a mark on his throat as I did.

Absently I rubbed the spot that Lys had paid so much attention to, and leaned against the doorframe as Nyko let out a loud sound somewhere between a moan and keen, and came. His body stiffened, then rested back against Rhys' form as Rhys came as well, fucking him through it and finally gently lying Nyk back down on the bed.

After a few moments, and with a long and aggrieved sigh, Nyk flipped over so he could stare balefully up at me. "Did you want something, Princess?" he asked lightly, as Rhys crawled over him to kiss his neck again.

Yeah to be a part of *that* sandwich.

"Lys thinks she should go visit her *mother,*" Az explained. "I said we needed a second opinion. He just wants to rile your mother up, after all. We all know that. But do you think it's worth it? To get Will's stuff and flip off her mom to her face?"

Both Nyko and Rhys looked up at me. "Do *you* think it's worth it, Will?" Nyko asked forwardly.

I frowned. "I…think so? Maybe. If you guys come with me. I don't know. She gets under my skin really easily."

Nyko opened his mouth, but Rhys pressed his palm against it with a grin. "Murder is off the table, lovely," he informed him in a purr. Nyko rolled his eyes.

"What's the worst that could happen? We won't let her *keep you,* Will," Nyko pointed out, once he'd removed Rhys' offending hand. "Not when you're *ours.*"

I loved it when they said that. I was *theirs.*

And this pack was *mine.* I wouldn't let anyone, or my mother, come between me and them.

The thought made me feel a little better. A little lighter, even. "Okay." I stood straighter, no longer leaning on the doorframe. "If you guys will go? I'll tell her that I'm done. That she has no right to keep thinking I'm going to move back in, and to sell my stuff I don't want."

"I won't let Lysander stab her," added Rhys helpfully. "When do you want to go?"

Azriel grabbed my hand, tugging me back the way we'd come.

"Umm whenever? Next weekend?" I asked, knowing

that my schedule was wide open. It wasn't like I was a cool, impressive criminal like *they* were, after all.

"We'll talk about it," Nyko called, and finally I turned to look at Azriel as I nearly stumbled after him.

"What are you doing?" I demanded, letting him march me back down the hall.

"Finding Lysander." When he looked at me, his eyes were bright with arousal. "Those two are so hot when they fuck. We're going to play a little, uh, show and tell with Lysander. He can watch as I *show* him just what they were doing. You know. On you."

I snorted, but found I *really* didn't have an issue with that. "Where's the 'tell' part, then?"

Azriel's grin was wicked. "It's there when he *tells* you you're a good girl who should be using her *mouth* on him."

"I still can't believe we flew first class," I admitted, standing next to Rhys while we waited for Lys and Az to bring the car around. "I kind of thought we'd drive."

Rhys shook his head, reaching out a second later to throw an arm over my shoulders and drag me closer. "I'm *never* driving all the way to your hometown again."

"Lysander makes it miserable," Nyko piped in from my other side. "He makes any drive miserable."

He didn't mean that, I figured. Or if he did it was more of a joke than anything. Probably. For all of his comments about the blonde, Nyko did like him. Otherwise they wouldn't be pack, obviously.

But more than that, I'd seen how they looked at each other over bloodied remains, their eyes shining bright, like two wolves about to rip into a kill. Their bond might not be over sex or anything of that variety. But it was there, all the same.

"First class was nice," I added, seeing the rental car stuck behind a truck. I'd never been to the Cherry Capital Airport in Traverse City before, but Mom had picked people up from the closest airport we had to Scheffield.

"I can't believe you didn't take Az up on his offer to join the mile high club," Nyko commented slyly. "Airplane bathroom sex too adventurous for you, Will?"

I rolled my eyes, unable to believe that *he* was the one to propose that something was too *adventurous* for me. When I met his gaze, I saw that he was smiling ruefully.

"Yeah. If by 'too adventurous' you mean 'too cramped?'" The black SUV Lys had rented pulled up in front of us, near enough to the sidewalk that I could see Azriel sitting in the front, looking triumphant in his sunglasses.

"One moment," Rhys said politely, and yanked the passenger door open. *"Back,"* he ordered, jamming his thumb towards the back seat.

"Possession is nine tenths of the law," Azriel pointed out sweetly, flashing his very white teeth in a grin.

"We don't follow the laws." Rhys reaffirmed, unmoving, until finally Azriel gave up with a heavy huff and crawled into the back seat. "*Thank* you, Azriel," Rhys told him, and got in the passenger seat beside Lysander, who had watched the whole thing with half a grin, and obviously no intention of moving out of his driver's seat.

That was fine with me. It wasn't like *I* wanted to drive, after all. I opened the back door and slid in, only for Nyko to crawl in beside me.

"It's a good thing we're only about twenty minutes from Scheffield," I mumbled, wondering how one got *passenger seat* privileges. That seemed nice, and Rhys would never be hurting for elbow room like I was.

"Why, Will?" Azriel slung an arm over my shoulders and pulled me to him. Somehow I'd thought that he'd get *less* touchy as I spent more time with him, being that I wasn't about to leave or disappear. But in fact, it was the exact opposite. Which, really, was okay too.

"Because elbow room is a myth here," I replied, unable to stop my quick smile.

The drive wasn't terrible, no matter that I was half in Azriel's lap for the whole thing and Nyko sighed to my right like a Victorian lady who was upset at not having room to *lounge* appropriately in her solarium. The sixth time he did so, he looked over and caught both Azriel and me staring at him, just to look away and do it again.

I couldn't help my snort, and Azriel chuckled under his breath.

When the car pulled up in front of my mother's house, I let out a sigh to rival Nyko's and slid out after Azriel, my eyes on the door warily as if it might *bite* me.

She didn't know I was coming.

But it was better that way.

Maybe she wouldn't be home? That was always a possibility. If she wasn't, I could just jimmy the lock open, get a few of my things that I was sure she'd shoved away in boxes, and be out of here for the rest of my life.

She probably *wasn't* home, actually. As I walked towards the door and considered the time, I figured that was a very good probability. Mom did stuff. She went out, she schmoozed, and she worked at the governor's office. She didn't have time to wait around at her house for me, especially when she didn't know I was here.

I was in the clear.

Rhys prowled up to stand beside me, beating the slow raise of my hand to the door and with a quick movement rapped on it three times.

It set my teeth on edge.

"You have to at least *look* like you mean it," he told me airily, turning to glance down at me. "Because right now you look like you want to run."

I did want to run. Right back to the airport, back to Chicago, and back to my bed.

"She's not here," I said, trying to sound *confident*. "It's the middle of the day. Mom's....somewhere else-"

The door was suddenly pulled open in front of me, showing me the woman I wanted to see least in the entire freaking world.

My mother.

She looked at me with her lips parted, confusion clear on her face. Her eyes then flicked to Rhys, then back to me, to where I was sure I looked like a mess after the plane trip, the drive, and my own frazzled nerves.

Wonderful. Good job Will. I couldn't help saying to myself silently. *Way to make an impression.*

"You didn't call." My mother never had time for hellos.

"I didn't," I agreed, crossing my arms lightly as I looked up at her.

"Where are your things? Is he helping you move back in?" She shot Rhys an appraising, unimpressed look, but he just smiled sweetly at her.

"I'm not *moving* back in," I told her, trying to keep my voice level. "Like we discussed. A lot." *Over and over* I'd told her I wasn't coming home, but here we were, with her insisting that I was. Uncomfortably I shifted in place, moving my weight from one foot to the other.

God, I didn't want to be here.

"Then what are you doing here?" The confusion was still very audible in her voice, as if to her there really was no other option. Either I was moving back, or I simply was not here.

"I'm coming to pick up a few things that I couldn't take with me when I left," I said, hoping that I wasn't about to lose my nerve with her. What *was* it about my mother that so easily reduced me to not wanting to talk, and feeling like a little kid that was in trouble for something?

Why could I never talk to her the same way I spoke to so many other people, even though she'd treated me quite a bit worse than most people in my life?

Her mouth twisted into a frown, and her eyes narrowed slightly. "Is this your *boyfriend*, then, Willow?" Because of course, she had never in my life relented to calling me *Will*, like I preferred. The word *boyfriend* sounded dirty on her tongue, and the look she leveled at Rhys was anything but friendly.

"One of them," he answered, before I could. "And I'm here to help her get whatever she'd like to take back with her."

"*One* of them?" my mother repeated, like she'd suddenly become hard of hearing. "There are *more*?" The question was directed at me, not Rhys.

"Yep," I sighed, fighting to stay firm. She did not own me, nor could she influence any of my choices anymore. I was an adult who lived in another damned *state* at this point.

The only thing she could do was disapprove. Loudly.

Trying to remind myself of that, I smiled. Or attempted to. It was hard to smile in the face of my mother's disdain. "We've been having communication troubles over the phone, I guess?" The trouble being that she did not want to listen to me or accept my choices. "So I thought we could talk. I came here to-"

"To tell me that you're *pregnant*? Is that why you've moved out?" She glared once more at Rhys, hate in her eyes, as if he were the source of all her problems.

At least until Lysander wandered around to the porch, coming into view and giving her a new target for her ire. "Who are you?" she demanded, hand tightening on the door.

"That's boyfriend number two," I said, not wanting to

stand here and let her judge my life choices all day. "Mom, are you letting us in, or not?"

She wavered. I saw it on her face as she looked from one man to the other. And I couldn't help but wonder what *she* saw on *their* faces.

Whatever it was, it convinced her to open the door wider, a breath leaving her mouth between tight-pressed lips that made her sound like a steaming kettle.

"Anything you want us to grab?" Lys asked, walking in behind me to look at the well-decorated living room.

"Where's my stuff, Mom?" I asked, following her down the hall and to the kitchen. She jerked her chin towards the staircase, which I hoped was an indication that it was in the attic.

"Up there, turn left," I told Lys, who had suddenly gained an Azriel. The latter walked beside the blonde, humming under his breath as he looked around the house as well. "Just umm. I want my lucky cats. There should be five of them, they're porcelain-"

"I threw them out," My mother informed me, cutting me off before I could finish.

I froze, and turned to look at her as my heart sank in my chest. "You threw them out? Even though you thought I was moving back *home*?"

The lucky cats hadn't fit in my car, and had seemed, to me, like they wouldn't survive the trip. I'd secretly hoped, since knowing Mom had brought all my stuff back here, to get them back.

But she'd *thrown them out*?

"Why?" I demanded, standing in the kitchen across from her, balanced on the balls of my feet.

My mother shrugged and sat at the table, hand going to the coffee mug that sat, steaming, on a coaster. "You didn't take them with you, so they must not have been that important."

She was wrong.

My heart twisted and writhed in my chest, and if nothing else, I knew at least that my feelings towards my mother were never going to change.

And I didn't need anything from here at all. I'd brought the things from my dad, like my stuffed hawk, with me to Chicago. I'd brought the little elephant statue Ashley had gotten me for my birthday.

I'd just have to get new lucky cat figurines to replace what she'd thrown away.

"Fine," I murmured. "Fine, Mom. I had really hoped you wouldn't do this to me...but *fine*."

If she wanted to play this game, then I was done.

"I'm not moving back in. *Ever*. I don't want to be here. With Dad and Ashley gone, there's nothing for me in this town anyway."

She flinched at the words, and I wondered if that had been going too far.

"If there's nothing for you here, then it's all your own doing," she pointed out icily. "I tried to get you involved. I did everything I could to get you through college and into something meaningful. But instead you'd rather fuck around with shelter dogs and barely make enough to pay rent."

I'd made rent in other ways. Like stealing. But she didn't need to know that.

"Sure, Mom," I agreed. "Whatever you say. You did *so much*. I thought, maybe, that if I came here to talk to you, that you'd at least try to see my side of things. That we could salvage some kind of relationship and you'd *respect* the decisions I've made-"

My mother's laugh sounded humorless. She shook her head and got to her feet, leaning instead on the counter that held the dishwasher and microwave. "The decisions you make are *childish*. Just what are you doing in Chicago to make money, hmm? Last time I checked, you didn't have a real resume, or job skills." When she saw the hurt in my face, her own softened. "Honey, I'm just trying to be honest with you. I don't want things to come crashing down when you realize you don't have anything-"

"As *entertaining* as it is to stand out in the hallway and listen to you insult Will..." Nyko strolled into the room, walking past Rhys to stand beside me. "No, I lied. It's not. You're her mother, right? Weird that you treat her like the orphan you keep locked in the cupboard."

Rhys snorted behind him.

Before my mother could ask, threaten, or say whatever was on the tip of her tongue, Nyko went on, "I'm so, *so* sorry that you can't seem to find any of Will's good qualities. There are many, I assure you. Though I'm not going to sit here and list them, since it occurs to me that you'd find a way not to hear them. But she's an *adult*. And she can make whatever decision she wants."

Nyko turned to me, a half-smile curling his lip. "C'mon, Will." It was out of character for *him* to stick up for me, and I couldn't help but stare at him, slightly-open mouthed, in surprise. "We're leaving. *You're* leaving. You don't need anything from this shithole." He gripped my hand hard, tugging me towards the door.

But I resisted.

"Wait." I faced my mother again, watching her expression on a face that looked so dissimilar from mine that it was sometimes a shock to remember that she had given birth to me.

I really had gotten everything from my father.

"Stop calling me," I told her flatly, my hand tightening in Nyk's. "Especially if it's to tell me to move home. I thought I'd come here to talk and, like I said, maybe work through some of our differences. But you don't want that. So I'm not going to keep wasting my time on you." My voice was soft, but I knew she could hear me all the same.

"Then go," she gestured dismissively, her voice loud in the small kitchen. "Go on, Will. You think you're doing so much better? *Go.*" It was meant as an insult. Especially with the way she looked between the men in the room with me.

But it wasn't an insult.

Because I *was* doing so much better.

I grinned at her, the look full of not-so-nice joy. "I'm gone," I promised. "Have a good life, Mother."

Nyko pulled me out the front door, dragging me to the car even though I could see Rhys still in the kitchen, his lips moving as he said something to my mother that I couldn't hear.

"I'll *personally* buy you every lucky cat in the world as long as we never have to come here again," Nyk informed me, pushing me against the car. "This place is *shit,* Will. I don't see how you grew up here." Without giving me a chance to reply, Nyk kissed me hard, his mouth lingering and tongue flicking against mine.

The passenger door opened beside us, and I glanced sideways to see Rhys getting in, all business-like once more.

"What did you say to her?" I asked, nearly breathless from his kiss, and leaned in before he could close the door.

Light hazel eyes met mine, wide in surprise as if I'd asked something he wasn't expecting. "Me?" he asked, placing a hand to his chest in mock-innocence.

I frowned. "Yeah, *you.*"

"Oh, I just told her that we'd take good care of you. And that if she kept calling you just to upset you, then she'd be getting a *very* unfriendly response from…not you," he said, his blithe smile slow to curl over his lips.

"You can't murder my mother, Rhys."

Lysander scoffed from behind me, walking around to get into his side of the car. "Why not? She doesn't seem worthy of being *missed.*"

I didn't have a great answer for that, and slid into the car beside Azriel again.

"We could," Azriel added, throwing an arm over my shoulders while Nyko got situated to my right. "I mean, she's just kind of an oxygen suck at this point, you know? Doesn't seem like she does anyone any good."

While I couldn't deny that statement, I still grimaced. "Because she's my *mom*. It would feel weird," I said, poking him in the side. "So don't."

"Fine, *fine*." He looked momentarily put out, before straightening again. "We're not getting back on a plane yet, right Rhys? Can we go visit that guy that you've been moaning about who lives somewhere up here?"

"He lives back in Traverse City," Rhys corrected. "And he isn't even that much of an issue anymore. *You're* just blood-thirsty."

Azriel thought about that, and then nodded thoughtfully. "Well, okay. I mean I guess I am *a little*. But Will would like it."

"She would?" I asked, my brows raised.

"Absolutely," Lysander agreed whole-heartedly. "Especially the part where we kill him, and you steal all his shit."

That probably should've sounded bad. Wrong, even.

But if some guy in Traverse City, Michigan had pissed off any member of my pack enough that they wanted to be paid back in blood, then they probably had it coming.

"I'm only stealing from him if he has good shit," I said at last, leaning into Nyk's shoulder. He didn't mind, and his huff was only for show as his hand found my thigh. "I'm a thief, not a hoarder."

"You're a bit like a magpie," Nyko pointed out from beside me. "Always looking for something shiny."

"Yeah," I agreed, grinning sweetly. "And I guess that makes you guys the shiniest things I could find." It was such a stupid thing to say that it even produced a chuckle from Rhys.

"Then we go home," the leader of our little pack said firmly. "No more detours."

Home, he'd said. And for the first time I was thrilled at the idea, not subdued at the fact that home was with my mother, or an okay apartment with Ashley that we could barely even afford.

Home was with my boys in Chicago.

Where it would be for the rest of my life.

ACKNOWLEDGEMENTS

Thank you to everyone who helped me put Playing With Knives together. *And* all of my readers who love Will and her boys enough to make me so excited to revisit them for the epilogue. You guys are all amazing, and I'm glad I'm not the only one who loves the bad guys too much.

An extra thanks to you, Gretchen. It's a wonder you haven't disowned me yet for all of the weird ideas I call to talk to you about. It's too late now. You're stuck with me forever.

As always, thank you Mom. It's a miracle you've continued to claim me for a whole 29 years now. You are a saint. It's also too late to return me. You're stuck with me and these books I release that all mention you in the acknowledgements.

ABOUT THE AUTHOR

AJ merlin is an author, crazy bird lady, and rampant horror movie enthusiast. Born and raised in the midwest United States, AJ is lucky to be right in the middle of people who support her and a menagerie of animals to keep her somewhat sane.

Connect with her on facebook or instagram to see updates, giveaways, and be bombarded with dog, cat, and pigeon pictures.

Made in the USA
Las Vegas, NV
20 September 2024